"Readers who enjoyed Lori Benton's wonderful novel *Mountain Laurel* will be thrilled to read more about Seona and Ian's frontier adventures and remarkable love story. Lori has a unique gift to bring a historical era and setting to life and then weave those story elements together in a way that captures your heart and soul. Overcoming past hurts and forging strong family ties are two important themes in this captivating story. Well-written and highly recommended!"

CARRIE TURANSKY, award-winning author of *No Ocean Too Wide* and *No Journey Too Far*

"With every book Lori Benton writes, I'm reminded again of why she's one of my very favorite authors. Her characters are refreshingly layered and wonderfully complex—to the point that I find myself thinking about them long after the end. Through a rich tapestry of detailed history, she weaves a story that's as thought-provoking as it is emotional and romantic. With vivid writing and an intriguing plot, this story of redemption and second chances will stay with me for a long time."

MELISSA TAGG, Christy Award–winning author of *Now and Then and Always*

"Lori Benton masterfully weaves fine strands from her haunting debut novel, *Burning Sky*, into *Shiloh*, the gripping conclusion of the Kindred duology that began with *Mountain Laurel.* The result is a powerful saga that reaches from the bitter aftermath of the American Revolution into the very beginnings of slavery's agonizing unraveling."

J. M. HOCHSTETLER, author of the American Patriot series and coauthor of the Northkill Amish series

"*Mountain Laurel* is the sort of book where you really hope there will be a sequel because you want to spend more time with the characters. It's a fascinating story, rich in emotion and a sense of the time and cultures in which it takes place."

DIANA GABALDON, *New York Times* bestselling author of the Outlander series

"Lori Benton's epic family saga *Mountain Laurel* thoroughly immersed me in plantation life in the 1790s and in the moral dilemmas created by the evil of slavery. Her lush, descriptive writing made every scene vivid and real. This engrossing tale of love and sorrow and redemption kept me turning pages!"

LYNN AUSTIN, Christy Award–winning author of *If I Were You* and *Chasing Shadows*

"Love forbidden, sacrificed, redeemed. *Mountain Laurel* casts long shadows of kinship through generations of a society that breeds slaves and secrets. . . . Exquisitely penned, with all the beauty of a highland song, Lori Benton throws wide the door of a culture born in Scotland and wedded to the American South in years before that region dreamt of abolition. Stunning portrait of a past made real."

CATHY GOHLKE, Christy Award–winning author of *The Medallion* and *Night Bird Calling*

"Lori Benton is an extraordinary storyteller. . . . Every page delivers a unique, satisfying, and enriching read, where faith and family exposes and nurtures the journey of the human heart. I loved *Mountain Laurel*!"

JANE KIRKPATRICK, *New York Times* bestselling author of *Something Worth Doing*

"Poignant. Impeccably researched. Tender and romantic but with a powerful message of clinging to faith over fear, *Mountain Laurel* is Lori Benton at her finest. . . . This is a stellar series debut!"

KRISTY CAMBRON, bestselling author of *The Butterfly and the Violin* and *The Lost Castle*

"Vivid and complex, Lori Benton's newest offering is penned within the backdrop of yet another stunning setting that touches the senses. In the truest threads of Lori's fiction, *Mountain Laurel* is an intricately woven tale of love and heartache, wrapped up in a sweeping family saga."

JOANNE BISCHOF, Christy Award–winning author of *Sons ofBlackbird Mountain*

"With a masterful pen, Lori Benton creates a poignant story that will have readers flipping pages late into the night. . . . I finished *Mountain Laurel* with both a sigh of satisfaction and a longing of expectation for what comes next for these characters. I highly recommend this novel!"

HEIDI CHIAVAROLI, Carol Award–winning author of *Freedom's Ring* and *The Orchard House*

"Lori Benton's *Mountain Laurel* is a compelling masterpiece, a stunning dance of romance, sacrifice, yearning, betrayal, and redemption. Benton weaves an exquisite tale that delves into the world of slavery while unearthing the treasure of what it truly means to be free. Seona and Ian's story continues to captivate me long after the pages have closed."

TARA JOHNSON, author of *All Through the Night* and *Where Dandelions Bloom*

Shiloh

Shiloh

A KINDRED NOVEL

LORI BENTON

Tyndale House Publishers
Carol Stream, Illinois

Visit Tyndale online at tyndale.com.

Visit Lori Benton's website at loribenton.com.

Shiloh

Designed by Libby Dykstra

Edited by Sarah Mason Rische

Published in association with the literary agency of Books & Such Literary Management, 52 Mission Circle, Suite 122, PMB 170, Santa Rosa, CA 95409.

Scripture quotations are taken from the *Holy Bible*, King James Version.

For information about special discounts for bulk purchases, please contact Tyndale House Publishers at csresponse@tyndale.com, or call 1-855-277-9400.

Library of Congress Cataloging-in-Publication Data

A catalog record for this book is available from the Library of Congress.

ISBN 978-1-4964-4436-3 (HC)
ISBN 978-1-4964-4437-0 (SC)

Printed in the United States of America

27 26 25 24 23 22 21
7 6 5 4 3 2 1

For Nancy and Gary Jensen—

you have so often cheered me on

Cast of Characters

NORTH CAROLINA

Ian Cameron, planter, owner of Mountain Laurel; *Judith*, his wife; *Miranda (Mandy)*, their daughter

Malcolm, Mountain Laurel's oldest slave; *Naomi*, his daughter; *Ally*, his grandson

John Reynold, friend and neighbor to the Camerons; *Cecily*, his wife; *Robin*, their son

Charlie Spencer, friend and neighbor to the Camerons

Lucinda Cameron, Judith's mother, Ian's widowed aunt, now living at Chesterfield Plantation

Rosalyn Pryce, Ian's sister-by-law; *Gideon Pryce*, her husband and master of Chesterfield

Esther, former slave at Mountain Laurel, now living at Chesterfield; *Maisy* and *Jubal*, her parents

BOSTON, MASSACHUSETTS

Seona Cameron, freewoman; *Gabriel*, her son with Ian Cameron

Lily Cameron, sempstress, midwife, freewoman, Seona's mother

Robert Cameron, bookbinder, Ian's father; *Margaret*, Ian's mother

Catriona Cameron, Ian's sister

Ned Cameron, Ian's brother; *Penny*, Ned's wife; *Robbie* and *Eddie*, their sons

Morgan Shelby, New York City merchant
Thomas Ross, Ian's boyhood friend

SHILOH, NEW YORK

Neil MacGregor, Shiloh's physician, Ian's neighbor on Black Kettle Creek; *Willa MacGregor*, his wife; *Jamie* and *Liam*, their sons
Matthew MacGregor (called Owl by the *Kanien'kehá:ka*), adopted son of Neil and Willa MacGregor
Maggie MacGregor (called Pine Bird by the *Kanien'kehá:ka*), adopted daughter of Neil and Willa MacGregor
Joseph Tames-His-Horse, *Kanien'kehá:ka* warrior, Wolf Clan brother of Willa MacGregor
Colonel Elias Waring, magistrate, former militia colonel; *Goodenough*, his common-law wife; *Lemuel Waring*, their son
Anni Keppler, Elias Waring's daughter; *Charles Keppler*, her husband, Shiloh's miller
Francis Waring, Elias Waring's son, Anni's younger brother
Jack Keagan, owner of Shiloh's tavern and trade store
Hector Lacey, squatter and recluse

COOPERSTOWN, NEW YORK

William Cooper, judge, congressman, land speculator, founder of Cooperstown; *Mrs. Cooper*, his wife; *James*, his youngest son
Moss Kent, lawyer, William Cooper's assistant
Aram Crane, frontier troublemaker with a history of violence
Mr. Hansen, storekeeper

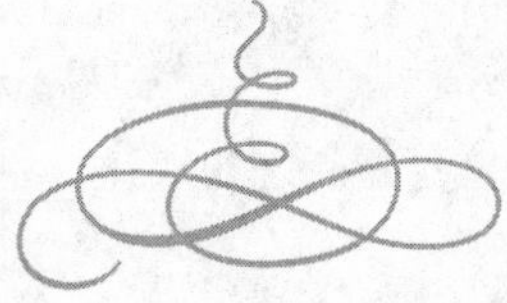

Is it fitting for a body to miss a place she once walked in fear? A place that broke her heart and bruised her soul? Still I dream at night of Mountain Laurel.

By day I walk this new world with its smelly cobbled streets teeming with people brusque and busy. With its tolling bells and ropewalks and ships lining wharves that poke into salt-tanged waters like the spokes of the wagon wheels that brought us here. Boston swirls around me like the sea wind, too fast to catch before it shifts again. Face after strange face. Ship after taller ship. Season after passing season. I have learned to trade the coins Mama earns for things we once made ourselves. I know the best time to bargain for fish and fruit, tea and coffee, notions and thread, and I know their fair worth. No one obliges me to go or stay, though there's plenty needing done and me and Mama do our share. Some things did not change with freedom—like who I am inside where no one sees. That girl with the bruised soul who learned to say, "Yes, sir," and "No, ma'am," to white folk smart-quick. That girl who walks now in a waking dream, calling herself free. But she's not.

The house that shelters us, the room we sleep in—the very bed—all of it was Ian's. I see him in the faces smiling with his smile. None more so than the son we share.

There is no forgetting. No letting go of who I was. Who I am still? There is only this place in between where I wait, harbored but unanchored, like one of those tall ships with its moorings frayed, set adrift.

What it is will anchor me, I cannot say.

PART I

Winter 1795–Summer 1796
North Carolina and Massachusetts

1

CARRAWAY MOUNTAINS, NORTH CAROLINA

December 1795

The crevice in the earth, widened by pick and shovel, permitted a man of average size to hunker comfortably within.

Ian Cameron, taller than average and broad through the shoulders, felt his coat sleeves brush the sides of the tunnel dug into the creek's steep bank. The creek itself, near its spring-fed source, was narrow enough a man could bestride it. That small distance placed the vein of gold the digging contained on his neighbor John Reynold's land. Not on Mountain Laurel, Ian's farm.

John and another neighbor, Charlie Spencer, crouched outside the tunnel, hats dusted with the snow feathering down from laden clouds, as Ian ran a hand over its clammy roof, fingers exploring the stone embedded some three feet back from the entrance. Charlie's pick had exposed all but one edge of the roughly rectangular mass. No telling how deep the fourth edge went into the bank. A foot or more and it might pose no threat. Inches would be another matter.

Thought of being buried alive sent Ian crab-walking out into the frigid gray.

"Was I right?" Charlie's breath clouded before his whiskered face. "That rock set to drop and bring half the ridge down after it?"

"Ye're right to leave off digging." Ian dipped muddy hands in the ice-rimmed creek, then stood, chafing reddened fingers.

"Can it be shored? Or should we cease the business altogether?" Worry made John Reynold's voice more crisply English than usual. Nose red-tipped, he cast a dubious glance at the raw cutting in the earth. "I'll not put Charlie in harm's way for *gold*," he added with such disregard for the substance Ian laughed.

"No doubt that's why the Almighty saw fit to put it on your land, John. Ye're the only man in the Carraways who'd cover that vein and put it out of mind if one of us half urged ye to it."

Wry humor lit John's brown eyes. "I won't say it's more trouble than it's worth, but it does present its complications."

The gold had been discovered on the Reynolds' land by Mountain Laurel's overseer—a secret taken to his death the previous autumn. Not until Charlie Spencer stumbled upon the abandoned mine had Ian learned of its existence.

After choosing to keep the gold a secret between the three of them—and his wife, Cecily—John had faced a quandary. How was he to make use of the ore without arousing speculation as to its source?

Between the ongoing work of farming, John had made two trips east over the past year, to Wilmington and New Bern—long-established coastal towns—to exchange the gold for coin, which was more discreetly spendable for the modest improvements to his farm he wished to make. And to portion out wages for Charlie, who swiped off his drooping hat to knock away snow, then snugged it back over his balding head.

"Ain't more'n a thread in spots, that vein, but looks to keep going. No telling how far, apart from digging."

"I'm not sure the stone would fall even without support," Ian said. "But I'd feel better about your chipping away up here if ye let me do a bit of framing first."

Charlie nodded, fondling the ear of one of his hounds come nosing up along the creek, paws muddying the snow that sugared the ground.

"Right then," John said. "I've some pine down to the barn . . ." He caught Ian's brief frown. "I don't intend taking anything needed in your shop."

"It's not that." Ian fetched his neighbor a half smile, tempered by the reminder of his reduced circumstances since last year's fire claimed his uncle Hugh Cameron's life and home and marked the desertion of all but one of his uncle's field hands. "Pine's too soft. I've some hickory curing. Give it a few weeks, be sure the green's gone out of it, then I'll get to work up here."

John grasped his shoulder in thanks, then turned to the smaller man scratching the dog's ear. "You hear, Charlie? No digging 'til we have that stone supported."

A grin showed Charlie's snaggled eyeteeth. "Won't say I'm not gratified by the share ye've staked me, but truth to tell I'm most tickled at keeping the secret from folk got no business poking their noses in it."

Ian knew who Charlie meant: Lucinda Cameron, his uncle's widow—and Ian's mother-by-law. Ian suspected she had been the instigator of his uncle's erstwhile overseer's hunt for gold on the ridge. The man hadn't lived long enough to confirm its existence to Lucinda, and since the night of the house fire she had removed herself to nearby Chesterfield Plantation, her eldest daughter's home. Still, the woman cast a formidable shadow.

Ian replaced the brush-screen used to conceal the digging. What traces their boots had left, the snow would cover. Through it now came a distant baying: another of Charlie's hounds. Ian knew the sound of a dog with a critter treed. So did the hound at their knees. With a joyous yelp, it raced off to join the hunt.

Charlie hoisted pick and shovel. "Let me know when I'm to get back to it. Meantime, me and the dogs are going hunting."

Ian declined John's offer of a chat by his hearth, appealing though the invitation was. Instead they parted and followed their own paths back down the steep ridge, Ian keeping to the creek that dashed through a landscape obscured by slanting snow: shadowed pine and dark-leafed laurel, outcrops of lichen-speckled stone, the skeletal shapes of oak and hickory.

The going was slick in spots. Ian had only half his mind on where he placed his boots. The other wandered a more treacherous path, ahead to where the creek led: home, eventually, where Judith, his wife, and Naomi, their cook, were likely at work in the warmth of the kitchen, spared by last year's fire. Between him and that snug refuge was the hollow, bowered in white-limbed birches, with the creek plunging in its glassy fall. And the memories, waiting to ensnare.

He hadn't set foot there since Seona, his uncle's former slave, left to live with Ian's parents in Boston, taking with her their son, Gabriel, conceived in that hollow when he and Seona had been handfasted, his headstrong attempt to claim his heart's desire—*her* heart—and give her what she deserved—freedom. Or the promise of it, since the Scots custom of handfasting wasn't recognized in North Carolina.

Even that tenuous plan for a future together had been ruined through Lucinda Cameron's manipulations. She had convinced Ian that Seona had run for freedom without him, leaving him devastated yet unable to abandon the rest of Mountain Laurel's slaves to Lucinda's harsh care. And so he had stayed, become his uncle's heir. And he had married Judith, his uncle's youngest stepdaughter, to assure his determination didn't waver—months before learning Seona hadn't spurned him, hadn't run, but was sold into drudgery farther south, pregnant with his child. Too late to do anything about it except bring her back to Mountain Laurel, shelter her, and try to keep his distance.

He had failed at the latter, to Judith's heartache, before he surrendered his will to the Almighty. Even then it had been a constant battle, day by excruciating day, until the house fire and the revelation that Hugh Cameron had already freed both Seona and her mother, Lily, months before his death.

With Seona, Gabriel, and Lily removed to Boston, Ian had set himself to love his wife as Scripture bade and banish memories of Seona to the far edges of his heart. All these months he had stayed away from that birch hollow with its spilling fall of memories, yet here he was, tempted as if no time at all had passed.

He ought to have accepted John's invitation. Had his friend seen into his soul, back at the digging, and recognized the disquiet burrowing there?

It was the silence undoing him. He had had one letter from his sister, saying Seona, Gabriel, and Lily had reached Boston safely and been given shelter in the Cameron home on Beachum Lane. He had written back, enclosing what he could by way of provision for their keeping.

A year ago.

No further news was promised. He had asked for none. Yet the longer the silence stretched, the harder it grew not to wonder. Did Seona find life with his family agreeable? Or had she and Lily found a place for themselves and Gabriel? Were they flourishing? Surviving?

He *would* go to the birch hollow. Not to linger, he told himself, grasping at a stony outcrop to descend the creek's bank. Merely to pass through and—

His boot came down on a moss-slick stone and shot from under him. Next he knew, he lay sprawled among jumbled rocks, scraped and bruised, snow landing cold on his upturned face.

He sat up, yelping as pain shot through his knee, twisted in the fall. With the help of those bruising stones, he pushed himself to his feet, hands scraped, coat and breeches stained by mud and moss. He hobbled to where his hat had fallen, shook it free of snow, shoved it back on his head.

He would never make it down the steep drop into the hollow now.

While snow sifted down and the creek chattered on, oblivious to his small drama, relief swept him. On its heels came a wash of shame. He closed his eyes against the throb of his wrenched knee, the aching of his heart.

"Right then," he said. "I'll go home by the straighter way."

In the whitewashed kitchen house, Judith was slicing carrots. Knife arrested at the gust of cold Ian ushered in when he entered, she took in the sight of him, expression caught between amusement and dismay. "What on earth does John Reynold have you doing, Ian? Digging a privy?"

He had washed the mud from his face and hands at the well but knew his foolishness had created more labor for his wife. Even with Naomi doing most of the kitchen work and a share of the laundering, Judith was worn to exhaustion most days with the endless tasks of keeping their household clean, dry, and ordered.

"Took a wee tumble on my way home," he said, hoping to stave off curiosity. Neither Judith nor Naomi knew of the gold—or the birch hollow.

The half-truth burned on his face.

Naomi stood before the massive brick hearth to shield its flames from gusting air. His daughter, Miranda Grace—whom they called Mandy—rode her broad hip. "Mister Ian, come all in or go back out. You letting in cold."

Judith peered past him. "It's snowing? I've wash on the line."

Ian shut the door but knew as soon as he turned, Judith had noted his limp. She put down the knife and rounded the worktable, skirts swishing. "Ian, you're hurt. Sit by the fire and let me see."

"Knee's bruised, is all. Sorry about the coat."

"I'll take it. I need to get the wash off the line before it's soaked again."

"I've work in the stable. Best let the mud dry, brush it off there."

Judith searched his face, then with a smile that prettied her plain features, wrapped herself in a woolen shawl. "I'll take Mandy, Naomi, so you can make some headway with supper."

"Your mama gonna let you ride the toting basket, baby girl. You like that, don't you?" Naomi skimmed a fingertip under Mandy's chin, eliciting a giggle as she handed over the child.

It was early days yet, but it seemed Mandy hadn't taken much from Ian in looks. Not the eyes, brown like Judith's instead of his blue. Nor the hair. Mandy sported a cap of wisps darker than his wheat-gold shade, though now and then in sunlight he had caught a hint of russet in the brown. Like his sister's.

Mandy's head was covered now in a knit cap pulled snug to plump cheeks, to one of which Judith pressed a kiss. "Isn't your daddy a sight? You'd think he was five, not five-and-twenty."

She tucked a fold of shawl around their daughter and went out through the herb shed at the back of the kitchen. Over her shoulder Mandy grinned at Ian until the door closed between.

"Supper ain't for a spell," Naomi said. "Want something to tide you afore you go down to Ally at the stable?"

Since the house burned just over a year past—the day of Mandy's birth—the kitchen had become the heart of Mountain Laurel. They all ate there, he and Judith and Mandy; Naomi, her grown son, Ally, and her aged father, Malcolm. Yet Ian never thought of this space with its ropes of onions and peppers, its perpetual smell of smoke and herbs and grease, its gleaming copper and oiled cast iron, as anything but Naomi's kingdom, where she presided in her calico crown.

He told her he could wait for supper. "Is Malcolm with Ally?"

"Last I knew." Naomi took over chopping the carrots. Potatoes lay in a heap next to the cutting board. It looked to be a vegetable stew. They were low on meat save for the hams and sausages put up in the smokehouse, meant to last until next autumn. He needed to take a leaf out of Charlie Spencer's book, bring in some venison. Or a turkey.

"I'll head on down. I need to work with Juturna," he added, speaking of the two-year-old filly born days after he arrived at Mountain Laurel to take up his uncle's offer of becoming his heir.

"You gonna work that filly in this snow?"

"This little skiff's no proper *snow*. Ye've clearly never seen the likes of Boston in winter."

Naomi dropped the carrots into a steaming kettle. "Reckon not. Ain't been more'n five miles off this farm in my lifetime."

Her words sent a stab through Ian—guilt of another kind. He had never grown easy with his uncle's owning of slaves. That he now owned this woman, and her kin, was a fact he couldn't reconcile. "Would ye like to?"

Naomi turned from the hearth, eyebrows vanished beneath her head wrapping. "Not if that mean leaving my menfolk behind. Who'd tend them—Miss Judith and Mandy, too—did I go traipsing off to wherever?"

"There's that." He tried to smile but was blindsided with longing.

For his kin in Boston. For Gabriel. *Seona* . . . He jerked his head, dispelling such thoughts for what seemed the hundredth time that day.

Naomi hadn't shifted the kettle over the flames. "You ain't had but the one letter from your sister."

"No" was all he said.

Naomi turned to swing the kettle-crane but got the last word in, loud enough Ian heard it at the door. "It gonna help things, us pretending they never drew breath here?"

Behind its fence pales the kitchen garden lay in repose. The trellised walkway that ran beside it led to a looming emptiness where the house once stood.

Mountain Laurel was a shadow of the plantation it had been the day Ian and his boyhood friend, Thomas Ross, first rode into the stableyard. Ian and Judith were living now in the old overseer's cabin, out by the tobacco barns. He had expanded the cabin to two rooms, while Naomi and her family had their cabins nearby in what had been the slave quarter, all but the soundest two dismantled.

Besides a full smokehouse, they had garden produce and corn put by to see them and the stock through the winter, but the fire and the flight of his uncle's field hands—with Thomas leading them to freedom—had reduced them to subsistence farming.

Last year's tobacco harvest had amounted to less than half of what the tired land once yielded, and he had only Ally to help in the fields come spring. Malcolm never shirked his work in the garden, but he was beset with rheumatism. Judith needed Naomi in the kitchen and yard. The last thing Ian wanted was to acquire more slaves. He would rather free those he had inherited, but his responsibility toward them wouldn't end with manumission granted by the North Carolina Assembly. Freed slaves were required to leave the state else be subject again to enslavement. With Seona, Gabriel, and Lily to help support, he was stretched thin already.

Chasing worries and gathering snow wouldn't accomplish any of the tasks demanding his attention. Shaking off both, Ian rounded the kitchen and caught sight of Judith taking down the wash as snow blanketed the yard. Nestled in the toting basket, Mandy played in the mound of garments piling up around her.

Judith's shoulders bowed as she worked. She had always been thin, left fragile from a childhood bout with yellow fever, yet in the gray of afternoon, obscured by snowfall, she appeared exhausted.

She looked up as he neared, brushing at a snowflake that landed on her nose. He moved her hand away from a petticoat as she reached for it. "I'll finish this. Take Mandy down to the cabin where it's warm."

She gave way, bending to scoop their daughter from the basket, not quite stifling a groan as she straightened. "There's mending I can see to."

"Never mind the mending. Rest yourself 'til supper."

He glimpsed her relief before she covered it with a smile. "All right, Ian."

He woke in the dark, disturbed by a sound, thinking it only moments since he had drifted to sleep. Or had he overslept and left Ally to tend the stock alone? Hard to tell, these long nights.

The sound came again. He pushed up on an elbow. His wife knelt beside the bed, retching into the chamber pot. Moonlight slanted through the room's window. The clouds had cleared. The cold air smelled of sick.

He waited while Judith washed at the basin, then came silently back to their bed. Across the chilled sheets he reached for her, sick himself with knowing. Softly, so he wouldn't wake Mandy in her cradle, he asked, "How far along are ye?"

"I didn't mean to wake you." Judith's voice was small in the winter dark.

"How far?"

"Three months."

That would make it . . . June. If she carried this one to term. The lingering effects of childhood illness weren't all that had taxed Judith's strength. She had been carrying again two months after Mandy's birth but lost the babe in late spring. Mourning the tiny girl they named Elizabeth, he had dug another grave on the ridge beside his resting kin.

The bedtick rustled. Judith turned toward him. "Are you pleased?"

A tightness gripped his throat. He found her brow in the dark and kissed it, nose pressed against her ruffled nightcap. "Of course. Try and sleep a bit longer."

Ignoring his own advice, he lay thinking. Perhaps he ought to head out to his cabinetmaking shop, whatever the hour. Work awaited him there as well. Beside him Judith's breathing deepened. He thought her asleep until her whisper rose in the dark.

"It will be all right. I'm not afraid."

Which of them she sought to comfort, he couldn't have said.

2

BOSTON, MASSACHUSETTS
March 1796

As she stepped into the book-lined shop, Seona Cameron reveled in knowing she could tell one shelved volume from another just by opening their covers. She had been reading words on a page for a sixmonth now. Rarely did she need help sounding out a new one, though plenty kept coming at her.

Opening book covers was a thing Seona's companion had been doing since they passed under the wrought iron sign proclaiming *Cameron & Son, Binders & Sellers of Fine Books.* From across the shop Catriona Cameron waved a slender volume. "Da's got in Freneau's new collection! Wouldn't you think he'd have mentioned it over breakfast?"

Catriona's raised voice drew a frown from a cloaked woman waiting at the counter spanning the shop's front, dividing the bookselling business from the binding. Seona feigned interest in a copy of Mr. Franklin's *Almanack* displayed near the window, hoping Catriona would bring the book over—away from the woman at the counter. Never mind she could read, had even tried adapting her speech to better blend with the people of that northern city, it still came as second nature to deflect attention. To go unseen.

To hide yourself away, her mama had noted.

I'm out of the house, Mama, running errands for you, she thought back in imaginary argument, shifting the basket of purchases made earlier as Catriona approached, riffling the book's crisp pages. Their fresh-inked scent mingled with the shop smells of leather and dye and binding glue.

"Listen," Catriona said. "This is from a poem called 'The Indian Student'—

"From Susquehanna's utmost springs
Where savage tribes pursue their game,
His blanket tied with yellow strings,
A shepherd of the forest came.
Not long before, a wandering priest
Express'd his wish, with visage sad—
'Ah, why (he cry'd) in Satan's waste,
Ah, why detain so fine a lad?'"

Listening to her read, Seona minded her surprise at first hearing Catriona speak with none of her parents' marked Scots lilt. Born in Boston, Ian's younger sister had never set foot in Scotland, unlike the rest of the family.

Now Seona cut in, *"Satan's waste?"*

Beneath a trim jacket, Catriona's shoulder bobbed in a shrug. "All that wilderness to the westward, I suppose, waiting to be conquered and set to order."

The rise of voices made Seona aware of Catriona's father at the counter, attending his customer. Her heart gave that little trip of recognition it did whenever Robert Cameron smiled, with the corners of his mouth turning up just so. *Ian's smile.*

Catriona nudged her. "Listen—

"'In Yanky land there stands a town
Where learning may be purchas'd low—
Exchange his blanket for a gown,
And let the lad to college go.'

"Hmm," she murmured, skimming the next verses. "The Indian lad goes to Harvard decked in skins and feathers and impresses everyone with his fine mind. But he isn't happy. He misses the forest. . . . Do you think they're as Freneau paints them, the western Indians? They cannot all still be wild men in feathers. Does Lily truly know nothing about your people? The Cherokees?"

Your people. Faces rose in Seona's mind. Not the bronzed faces of Cherokee Indians. Darker faces with broader features. "Mama never knew her mama, much less her daddy. He was the Cherokee, far as we know."

In the eighteen months they had shared a roof, Catriona had wheedled many such details out of Seona, until she doubted anyone in Boston, saving her mama, knew more about her past, which wasn't something she meant to discuss in the middle of Mister Robert's shop. No matter what she and Gabriel looked like, there were plenty who would view them askance were the truth of her past widely known.

The woman at the counter left with her book purchase, casting them a raised brow Catriona was too absorbed to notice.

"A shame Lily doesn't know."

Seona was seeking to change the subject when Robert Cameron beat her to it, coming from behind the counter to join them. "Ye've found Freneau then, *mo nighean*?"

Seona's heart warmed to the cadence of his Highland speech, though it brought an ache of missing others who spoke the same. Malcolm. Master Hugh. *Ian . . .*

"Yes, Da," Catriona said. "No thanks to you!"

"Who d'ye think made sure the man's wee book was in Shelby's last shipment from New York?" Mister Robert's crinkling blue eyes ruined his attempt at sternness. He rubbed a hand behind his neck, where hair like Catriona's, russet brown, was clubbed. "Off home wi' ye now. I'm sure Lily's waiting on something in Seona's basket."

"Lily works too hard. I waged an absolute *campaign* prying Seona from their sewing to try out our new muslins on such a fine spring day."

"Spring?" Seona peered through window glass at clouds scudding above smoking chimneys. From the moment they stepped outside, she had regretted being talked into wearing their new spring attire instead of waiting another fortnight for the season to arrive. The gowns were made of fine muslin, fitted in back, loose to the ankles in front, gathered by drawstrings at the neck and high waistline, sashed with colorful bands. Seona had suggested they wear their cloaks.

"And ruin the effect?" Catriona had argued. Instead they wore short jackets with fitted sleeves—called *spencers*—leaving their legs beneath the thin gowns and their shifts to prickle in gooseflesh with the slightest puff of breeze, dispelling the joy of being outside not bundled in woolens.

That was Catriona, always rushing ahead, her eagerness as catching as the ague.

Seona pretended to shiver, though a grated fire warmed the shop. "In Carolina we'd call this the dead of winter."

Chuckling at her remark, Mister Robert returned to the rear of the shop, from which other male voices arose, one in unbridled laughter. Not Mister Robert's. Surely not his firstborn's. Seona hadn't heard Ned Cameron laugh since Christmastide.

Catriona was back to her poem. "Listen to its end, Seona.

"'*Where Nature's ancient forest grow,*
And mingled laurel never fades,
My heart is fix'd;—and I must go
To die among my native shades.'
He spoke, and to the western springs,
(His gown discharg'd, his money spent)
His blanket tied with yellow strings,
The shepherd of the forest went.
Returning to the rural reign
The Indians welcom'd him with joy;
The council took him home again,
And bless'd the copper-coloured boy."

Catriona sighed. "I wish I could see them, these Indians on the frontier—buy a horse and head west, like Ian did years ago. 'And bless'd the copper-coloured boy,'" she quoted as two men emerged from the shop's rear portion.

Ned Cameron, a younger version of his daddy in looks, moved as if an ox yoke spanned his shoulders. He met Seona's gaze with blue eyes older than his eight-and-twenty years. Grief-shadowed eyes. He and Penny, his wife, had lost both their little boys to a fever that swept through the city in midwinter. While Seona thanked the Almighty for sparing Gabriel, it pained her to see Ned putting one foot afore the other, doing what he must to carry on.

In stark contrast to Ned, the second man moved with a jaunty step as he passed through the counter's opening. A well-dressed and prosperous man, Morgan Shelby was of an age with Ned, though not as tall and darker of hair, which he wore cropped and brushed toward his temples in the new fashion some men were adopting.

Catriona curtsied, favoring the man with a smile. "I didn't expect you in Boston along with your shipment of books, Mr. Shelby. Did your winter sojourn to the southern ports prosper?"

Morgan Shelby doffed his tall-crowned hat in a sweeping bow. "I confess I've quite forgotten what I did this winter past, so astonished am I at overhearing you profess a yearning interest in *le bon sauvage*."

Catriona's eyes sparkled. "I'm sure I had no intention of astonishing."

"Yet I must know, does this interest in Indians have to do with the two lovely creatures who have taken up residence in your home?" Mr. Shelby spared Seona a sweeping look that ended in an appreciative nod—and a bubble of panic in Seona's throat.

Flirtation, that sort of talk was called. Catriona clearly relished it, but such attention left Seona off-footed, like speaking to a person wearing a mask.

As Catriona made a clever remark that answered Mr. Shelby's question without really answering it at all, Seona's gaze sought Ned, leaning against the counter, watching them. The faint line between his brows, permanently etched there now, deepened.

"May I?" Morgan Shelby took the book from Catriona's hands. He studied the verses she had found fascinating, dark brows dancing over hazel eyes. "The fellow makes them sound untamable. Or is that the allure? Miss Cameron, you shock me."

Catriona raised her chin. "Tease as you will, Mr. Shelby. I shall not recant my liking for Freneau's verses nor their subject. Whatever my reasons."

Mr. Shelby closed the book, returning it to Catriona. Seona looked down in time to see the tips of their fingers brush, then up to see pink spotting Catriona's cheeks.

Mr. Shelby radiated approval. "That's the spirit. I'm of the opinion one's likings, of verse or anything else, oughtn't to be swayed by a breeze as trifling as a gentleman's repartee."

Ned pushed off the counter and joined them, his attention on Seona and her basket. "Purchases for Lily?"

She nodded. "Mama's waiting on these pewter buttons to finish a pair of breeches. I should get them home."

The first time Lily altered a gown for Margaret Cameron, Ian's mother, the quality of her work had drawn attention at Old North Church, where they attended meeting of a Sunday. Lily now had more bespoke work from Miss Margaret's friends than she could keep pace with. Seona helped with the piecing and hemming so Lily could give attention to the detailing for which she had gained a steady custom.

Ned straightened, drawing away. "I've work to finish, Shelby, but I'd appreciate your escorting Seona and Catriona home. Ye're welcome to take supper with the family. I'll be along with Da."

Catriona bounced on her toes. "Please do, Mr. Shelby!"

Seona hid a frown at her enthusiasm. If grief had made Ned heavy as one of Boston's ships riding low at anchor, it had made his sister a rudderless vessel in full sail, at the mercy of whatever wind blew. But who was she to judge? A body grieved how they grieved, and there was handsome Morgan Shelby, smiling in his fine clothes, saying it would be his pleasure to escort two lovely young misses through Boston's North End and to share their table.

"Catriona." Ned's voice stopped them on the threshold. "Freneau writes of subjects besides the heathen on our frontier. Try reading 'To Sir Toby.'"

Clutching her book of verse, Catriona turned back to her brother. "What's that one about?"

"Slaves," Ned said, glancing at Seona. "And the men who own them."

Ned Cameron's words bit sharper than the chill wind that cut through Seona's gown as she and Catriona, each on an arm of Morgan Shelby, traversed the busy North End toward the Camerons' home on Beachum Lane.

Ian had warned her his reputation in Boston was tainted. In letters to his father, which Seona had carried north, he had finally told the truth about the incident that for years had strained relations with his kin. He had taken the blame for the improper advances of the wife of the cabinetmaker who held his indenture. The unhinged woman, desperate for the baby her marriage hadn't produced, had tried to seduce Ian. Failing that, she had attacked him in a rage. Ian had given his word not to shame his master by telling the truth, never thinking the woman herself would spread it about, twisting the tale until Ian was made the villain, she the victim.

Learning the truth might have changed Robert Cameron's opinion of his youngest son, but Ned had found something else to hold against Ian: Seona and Gabriel and those Ian had held enslaved since Master Hugh's death. Never mind it was Robert Cameron who had urged Ian to go to North Carolina and become his half brother's heir in the first place.

Family was like the sea hemming that port town, full of hidden currents and undertows. Even on the calm days—or so Seona had been warned. She hadn't drummed up courage to more than stick a toe in the surf last summer, when it had been warm enough to countenance the notion.

Summertime was hard to conjure here at the end of her second Boston winter. Despite the chilly breeze, gangs of youngsters played on the streets, some up to mischief. Others ran errands for whomever held their indentures. Men traveled afoot, bound for taverns or warehouses, women for the shops. Cart and carriage wheels rattled over cobblestones. A bell pealed from one of the many steeples piercing the sky.

Catriona had taught her to find her way through Boston's winding streets. At first the city's bustle, especially in the crowded markets or the wharves where porters unloaded cargo from tall-masted ships and clerks argued over ledgers, had overwhelmed her senses. And that wasn't even mentioning Boston's stink. Between marshy mudflats, rotting fish, and hogs rooting in alleys, streets as ripe as Mountain Laurel's privy had turned her stomach those first weeks. She had learned to watch her step on the narrow lanes.

As they turned the corner onto Beachum Lane and were met by a gusting breeze, Catriona peered past Mr. Shelby, laughing through chattering teeth. "Fine, Seona. You may say *I told you so*. I'm utterly frozen!"

"But 'tis the soul amenable to taking risks," Mr. Shelby said before Seona could reply, amusement warming his mannered voice, "not the one who shrinks from them, that is bound in the end to prosper."

Aglow with Mr. Shelby's praise, Catriona exclaimed on the teasing bursts of sunshine and would spring never truly arrive? Seona wondered if she knew how smitten she behaved. Mr. Shelby drank it up, seeming nigh as smitten in return.

That puzzled Seona. After their first business deal, a shipment of marbling dye offered at a lower price than the Camerons had ever paid, proved satisfactory, Morgan Shelby had struck up a friendship with Ned Cameron. Judging by the cut of his coat and what Seona knew of him—a graduate of the College of New Jersey, son of a New York merchant who had made his fortune during the war, with business dealings now in every major seaboard city—Morgan Shelby seemed above the station of a bookbinder's daughter.

All men are created equal. These Bostonians claimed to think so. At least the white ones. Was she still thinking like a slave, doubting Mr. Shelby's attentions because he had more wealth than the Camerons? Still they seemed of different worlds.

Like Ian and me. Only now Ian lives in mine. I live in his. With a son to raise and no husband to shelter us.

"Mama . . . Mama, loo-tis!"

Mama, look at this. Flaxen curls flopping, Gabriel came trotting along the crushed-shell path behind the brick-and-timber house on Beachum Lane, clutching what he found. Seona had watched him hunker over whatever it was, knowing by and by he would come with small fingers opening, offering up his treasure: a crumpled feather, remnant of the redbird pair that nested in the apple tree overhanging the fence from the next garden over. As sunlight broke through clouds overhead, she knelt to admire it.

"So pretty, baby." She pulled him close, snug in his woolens, and twirled the feather under his chin.

Gabriel giggled, then squirmed, spying something new of interest. A striped cat had appeared as if by magic atop the fence pales, having leapt up from the other side.

Seona let him go, straightening to search the boughs in case the cat was on the hunt. Sure enough—a flash of scarlet. The redbirds had survived another winter.

Spying Gabriel, the cat leapt back down from whence it came.

Sun, birds, her boy at play—all conspired to make it feel like spring had come after all. It was almost warm enough to set up to paint, now she was cloaked proper. She knew better. An hour's time could bring rain. Even snow. Northern spring was the worst tease.

"Are ye wishing ye were painting?"

Seona turned. Ned Cameron, topped with a round-crowned hat, stood at the corner of the house where an alley gave access to the shed that housed Mister Robert's saddle horse and the laying hens. "I didn't hear you come up."

"Unca Ned!" Gabriel came at an unsteady gallop, stumbling as he reached his uncle. Before he could fall, Ned swooped him off his feet, a long-practiced maneuver that made an ache twist in Seona's chest.

Ned's hat had fallen forward to perch on the bridge of his nose, covering his eyes. "Where did that wee nephew of mine get to?" When Gabriel pushed the hat brim up, his uncle smiled. "There ye are!"

"Wobbie! Eddie!"

Ned's smile tightened as Gabriel bounced in his arms. "No, lad. Just me."

Lower lip pouted, Gabriel pressed his brow to his uncle's shoulder. Seona moved to retrieve him. "He doesn't understand."

Ned shifted away. "I ken that. It's all right."

Gabriel seemed content, so Seona let him be. "Is Miss Penny come for the evening?"

Ned avoided her gaze. "What have ye been about today, wee mannie?" he asked Gabriel, who babbled a stream of words even Seona only half understood. "Oh, aye?" his uncle asked when her boy paused. "Had a busy time of it, I gather."

Gabriel fell to fingering the buttons on his uncle's coat. At last Ned caught Seona's eye. "Penny's to home. She bade me go without her."

Though Ned and Penelope Cameron lived but a few streets over, Seona hadn't laid eyes on Ned's wife since the January day they saw the boys buried, up on Copp's Hill. While Ned managed to go through the motions of living with the loss of his sons, Penny had succumbed to a lasting melancholy and would not leave their house or receive visitors.

In the apple tree, the redbirds trilled. Harsher came the keening of gulls, wheeling over rooftops. The sun went behind a cloud, taking with it its warmth.

"You meant Ian, didn't you?" Seona blurted. "What you said about that poem in Catriona's book. The one about slaves."

"I did."

Ned had never made secret what he thought of his younger brother, but Seona rarely knew what to say in the face of his disdain. She had papers telling the world she and her mama were free, but speaking up boldly to a man like Ned Cameron wasn't something they could tell her how to do. Her heart thumped simply asking, "Why?"

Ned's eyes hardened. "Tell me, Seona. Did he do what he did to ye against your will?"

Shock gave way to anger, loosening her tongue. "Don't you know your brother at all?"

"Well enough, I daresay."

Gabriel looked up from the coat buttons, then put his hands to either side of his uncle's mouth and patted, as if to mold it back into the smile that had greeted him.

Ned's mouth trembled. He slid Gabriel to his feet and straightened. "I spoke too bluntly. It's only . . . to have done what he did, then married one of Uncle's stepdaughters and sent his *son* away. I cannot fathom it. Or excuse it."

Pity stabbed through Seona's anger. Still, Ned couldn't know how it had been with her and Ian, and poor Miss Judith caught in the middle of it all. "It wasn't what you're thinking. Ian never—"

Behind Ned's back the scullery door opened. Seona's mama stepped out onto the paving stones, where they boiled laundry on fine days. "Seona," Lily called. "Mister Robert asked to speak to ye afore supper. Evening, Ned."

Seeming relieved at the interruption, Ned took Gabriel, clutching at his knees, into his arms again. "Lily . . . good eve."

Mystified by the summons, Seona stepped past them.

Lily searched her face as she drew near. "He's in his study."

Living so close with Scottish folk had deepened her mama's faint lilt, but something else made Seona hesitate. Below sleek black hair pinned under a cap, Lily's features were composed, yet something troubled her dark eyes.

"What's wrong, Mama?"

Instead of answering, Lily strode into the yard. "It's time this boy was tidied for supper." She reached for her grandson. "Come here, baby."

"Ganny!" Gabriel leaned out to be taken. Ned gave him over.

Seona lingered on the threshold, uncertain, until Lily reached past her for the scullery door. "Go on. Mister Robert's waiting on ye."

"Come in, Seona." Robert Cameron rose from feeding the fire sheltered by a blue-painted mantel. "Dinna shut the door. This willna take long."

Seona took the seat he indicated, a finely wrought upholstered chair, match to the one behind his writing table. Clasping her hands in her lap as Ian's daddy took his seat, she heard laughter from the parlor, where Ned must have joined his sister and Mr. Shelby. "Yes, sir?"

Mister Robert smiled, deepening the lines beside his eyes. "Ye and Lily—and Gabriel—may I presume ye've found Boston to your liking?"

They had had nowhere else but Boston to go, set loose from slavery. Seona knew they were fortunate there had been any place at all outside North Carolina. Ian's parents were her kin too, if distant. She had grown fond of them. She felt toward Catriona like she might a younger sister. They had a roof over their heads. Food in their bellies. What was Mister Robert thinking, searching her face with his gaze, asking her such a question?

"You and Miss Margaret have been every sort of kind. Mama and I are thankful for everything you've done for us."

"Which I've never doubted," Ian's daddy replied, warmth in his words. "Ye're a part of our family, Seona. That willna change no matter your answer to what I'm about to propose." He shifted in the chair, clearing his throat. "In point of fact . . . Margaret and I wish to make the connection between us more secure."

"Secure?" Seona echoed. The only way she knew for that to happen was impossible now. Ian had married Judith Bell, and that was that.

But Mister Robert was nodding. "We wish to claim ye, to make ye ours—ye and our grandson. By adoption."

Seona felt the chair holding her up, heard the crackle of the fire, saw the paneled walls surrounding her reflecting back its glow, yet that one word—*claim*—had sent her mind spinning. She shook her head, wrestling down her shock. "You want to adopt us? What about Ian? Gabriel is *his* son. And what would *I* become . . . my own baby's sister?"

Mister Robert's voice gentled, as if he had expected the proposition to rattle her. "I've written to Ian of the matter. I havena sent the letter, mind. I wanted first to ken your wishes. Aye, legally ye'd be Gabriel's sister but we would consider ye his mother first. Or if ye'd rather, we could adopt just Gabriel—and nothing about your relationship with him need change if we did. Whatever ye decide, ye and Lily are welcome under our roof for as long as ye wish. But as to Gabriel . . . one day he'll need to make his way in the world, as a man must. I'd see him given every advantage in my power to provide. As my legal son."

Astonishing how relief and fear could tangle. Seona had grown up without a father to claim her, had thought Gabriel's fate would be the same. Now here was a man willing not only to shelter them but to become that covering they lacked.

Ian's parents had never cast shame upon her or Gabriel for his being born out of wedlock, but Mister Robert was right. There was a wide world beyond the haven of Beachum Lane. A world Gabriel would need to contend with. To have a man like Robert Cameron giving him a name and place—maybe even a trade—was no small thing.

"I would, of course, entitle him to a portion of my estate," Mister Robert added as if she needed the enticement. "Upon my death."

Seona cast an appraising glance over the man, sitting straight in his tradesman's coat, robust of health despite the silver twined in his hair. He was of similar coloring as Hugh Cameron had been, but she saw none of the sickliness that had marked his older half brother in his last years of life.

"Does Mama know about this?"

"Margaret spoke to Lily while ye were at the shops with Catriona. She's of a mind to leave the decision to ye—and to Ian."

Seona wrenched her gaze to the fire as a log shifted, spraying sparks across the bricks. She should write to Ian. Oughtn't she to be the one to discuss this with him?

"Can I think about it?" she asked.

"Of course," Robert Cameron said. "There's no rush. But we think it for the best, Margaret and I . . . given how things stand."

Given that Ian was married to Judith, raising up their little girl. Maybe more children besides, by now.

Seona did her best to shut out that thought, to think about what was, not what couldn't be. To shove aside all feelings but the ones that had to do with here, now, and what was best for Gabriel.

Going on those feelings alone, what Ian's daddy had proposed seemed an answer to her prayers.

3

MOUNTAIN LAUREL, NORTH CAROLINA
April 1796

For the third night since the letter came, Ian dreamt of Seona, waking in the dark to lie immobile, afraid his tossing had disturbed Judith. Hearing nothing but even breathing, he eased out of bed, wincing at every rustle.

In the cabin's front room he stripped off his sweaty shirt, doused it in the water bucket by the door, then used it to cool his heated flesh. Naked in the dark, he stirred the banked hearth, laid on wood, then spread the wrung shirt before it. As the fire took hold, he sat, head bowed, trembling at the visceral memory of the forbidden. "For mercy's sake," he whispered. "Free me of this."

Behind him a floorboard creaked.

"Ian?" Judith knelt behind him, the roundness of her belly pressed against his back as her hands cupped his shoulders. "You said her name."

His breath released in a shudder of resignation. "Judith . . . I'm sorry."

"I know." She turned her face into the curve of his neck. He felt her tears on his skin. "The letter . . . was it from her?"

He started. "From Da. I wanted to tell ye. I just . . ." He hadn't wanted to hurt her. "There's a drawing too. Of Gabriel. In my satchel."

"I'll get them. Here, you're chilled."

Her shawl fell across his shoulders, warm from her body. While he clutched it, staring into the flames, Judith's feet padded across floorboards. Paper crinkled. She settled in one of the chairs he had made after the house fire, the letter held close in the dim light. He reached for more wood, added it to the flames, piece by piece, while Judith read the words in his father's hand, emblazoned on his soul.

It happened just after Epiphany. Forgive my delay in relating the News. Frankly, I have not had the Heart to do so. Ned soldiers on but Penny will receive no one, so deep is her melancholy. Gabriel cannot be made to understand why his Cousins no longer visit . . .

As if that wasn't bruising enough, his father had delivered a second blow: *Your mother and I wish to make known to you the Proposal we have made to Seona, to formally adopt both her and Gabriel . . .*

"Ian?"

He looked aside, knowing by the shape of the paper Judith now held that it was the sketch of his son, tucked in with his father's letter: rounded face surrounded by curls he thought must still be fair, long lashes downswept in a state of near slumber. A portrait formed of simple lines, conveying a mother's loving scrutiny of her offspring. Beneath it, in careful letters, the briefest note had been penned, thrilling him to see, breaking his heart with its unspoken distress: *What do you want me to do?*

For the past three days he had carried the portrait through the tobacco's seeding, at every chance taking it from the satchel slung at his side to scrutinize the image as Seona had done their living boy.

Boy he was now. No longer the tiny bairn Ian last cradled to his chest. A little boy on his feet with words to say—mostly of his own devising, his father had related. A boy in whose face Ian caught an echo of his blood and bone. A boy who didn't know him.

"Judith," he tried, knowing how this reminder of his divided heart must wound.

"He's beautiful, Ian. How you must ache for him."

Judith laid aside the portrait and rose. He felt the brush of her shift as she knelt, took him in her arms, stroked his hair like a hurting child.

He lowered his head to rest against her belly. She was past six months along now.

"A boy this time, I think," she said. "Perhaps . . . perhaps he will bring comfort."

"Aye. Or *she* will."

Judith had carried this one longer than the last. She was rounder with this babe, fuller, having put on weight once the sickness passed.

"Do you want to talk about the letter, what your daddy is proposing?" she asked, endearingly brave.

She deserved to know his mind, but he couldn't speak. Not with that dream still haunting his thoughts. "We'll talk in the morning, aye?"

"All right." Her fingers smoothed his hair before she rose. "Come back to bed?"

"Soon."

When he heard the rustle of the tick, he rose and shook out his wet shirt, draped it over the chair back, then went out to empty the water bucket into the garden. With Judith's shawl kilted around his waist, he trudged through starlit dark to the well near the old house site and refilled the bucket. Resting it on the well's edge, he listened to the furtive night stirrings in the nearby wood—hooting owls, the snort of a deer, a nighthawk's cry. A breeze raised gooseflesh on his chest.

He could see the advantages of his da giving Gabriel the security of a formal connection, but what did Seona think of it? And Lily? Seona was her daughter. Gabriel her grandson. What counsel had she given?

Ian wrenched the heavy bucket from the stones and started back to the cabin, barefoot in the cool dark. Ned and Penny's loss mingled with thoughts of relinquishing a father's rights to Gabriel, grief washing over him like waves crashing and receding. Seona's question tumbled like flotsam in their pull.

What do you want me to do?

He ached to look into her eyes, to tell her, "I want ye to say *no*. A thousand times—no."

Or that had been his answer. He questioned it now. If his da adopted Gabriel *and* Seona, Ian would cease to be the man who must concern himself most intimately with their well-being. The man who said aye and nay. That duty—and privilege—would be Robert Cameron's. Was it for the best? Was it the deliverance for which he had prayed? It felt like penance.

Whatever it was, he had sown its seeds. Dare he flinch from the crop springing from them?

"Not my will," he whispered on the cabin doorstep. "But please . . ."

At a loss for how to pray, he set the bucket in its place and shut the door on what remained of the night.

24 April 1796

To Robert Cameron
Beachum Lane, Boston

Dear Da—

Your News of Ned and Penny's loss is grievous. Indeed I find myself thinking much of my Brother, praying earnestly for his Comfort and that of you all. I am so sorry, Da, but thankful Gabriel was spared.

Speaking of my Son, I have bided my Soul in Patience these four Days since receiving your Letter, torn between the haste my Heart bade me reply and the need to deliberate most carefully upon such a weighty Matter as the lifelong Disposition of my Firstborn. There is much I could say to your desire to adopt Gabriel, cases to be made for and against. Instead I put to you the Question which must be answered before another word is exchanged. Is this what Seona wants? Can you say to me in Truth there has been put upon her no degree of Pressure, no constraint of Obligation? Unless I can rest assured this is Seona's choice, I cannot seal it with my Agreement.

She may, if willing, write to me herself and let me know her mind, as I see Catriona has proven a commendable Tutor in the Art of Penmanship. I will expect to hear from her, or you on her behalf, concerning this Matter soon. Until then I remain your devoted Son &c.

Ian Cameron
Mountain Laurel
Randolph Co., North Carolina

May 1796

The tobacco seedlings rested snug in their mounds. The sweet corn was sown. Ian had taken the afternoon to climb with John Reynold to the creek bank Charlie Spencer had resumed digging after Ian constructed a support beneath that worrisome stone. It was his first chance to check the structure for any weakening that might endanger Charlie in his periodic mining.

The frame proved sound. Since Charlie wasn't present, he and John concealed the dig with a brush-screen and started back down the ridge in companionable silence. Cutting down the final wooded slope, Ian noticed his neighbor's frown.

"Something on your mind, John?"

"Always." John fetched him a half smile. "Just now I was thinking of Gabriel. Is there any news?"

Under the boughs of an oak in fresh leaf they paused. Ian put a hand to the tree's trunk, its bark rough against his palm, and told John of his parents' plan. "It's but three weeks since I wrote, and it's heavy on my mind. Though for Judith's sake I've kept it there."

"She knows of it?"

"She's praying for me," Ian said with no small wonder. "For all concerned."

"A remarkable woman, your wife."

Ian looked away down the wooded aisles of the ridge, at the great boles of oaks and hickory and chestnut, the slender locust and birch. "I know."

"What do you mean to do?"

Ian met his neighbor's quiet gaze. "I need to know Seona's mind. She'll have to convince me this is what she wants before I consent."

"You would give up a father's claim on Gabriel?"

"What if I'm meant to? What if this needs to happen, willing or no?"

"Were I faced with such a choice over Robin, I don't know whether . . ." John's words trailed off at a sound that had both men lifting their heads in the direction of the Reynold homestead: a child's wailing.

"That *is* Robin." John plunged off through the trees, Ian on his heels. Before they reached the path, a booming voice mingled with the wails.

"Mister Ian! Where you be?"

They burst through a laurel thicket to find Ally, Naomi's tall, strapping son, standing where the trail branched off to the Reynolds' homestead. Dwarfed in his massive arms was John's two-year-old son, Robin, red-faced and furious.

John was first to reach them. "Ally! What's amiss?" Robin reached for his father, who hoisted him into his embrace.

Sweating freely as if from running hard, Ally shouted over Robin's crying. "Mister John, Mister Ian . . . it real bad."

John's face went chalky. "Cecily?"

Ally wagged his head. "She gone to help. Left me with Robin to mind and find you iffen I could."

He swung toward Ian, who felt his whole being suspended, as if time itself had skipped a beat. His lips shaped a name. *Judith.*

"Yes, sir. Fell to paining in the washhouse. She having that baby."

He was frozen, blood gone cold. "John."

"Go," John told him. "We'll come behind."

Ian gripped John's arm, mouth too dry for speech. Then he was pelting down the path, staggering as his shocked limbs sought to devour the distance home. The babe was meant to come in June. Another month. Had Judith got the timing wrong?

Ian raced into the clearing where the house once stood, cutting behind the kitchen, making for the cabin where they would have taken Judith. He heard no cries above the pounding of his boots, his ragged breath. No sound at all.

With a stitch in his side like a knife jab, he ran straight into the cabin through the open door. Mandy stood in the front room, tiny and barefoot in her shift, curls mussed, fist jammed in her mouth.

He nearly collided with Naomi coming out of the bedroom, arms full of rags so blood-soaked there was no knowing what their color had been. He halted, gasping.

Naomi pushed past him and tossed the rags out the door. "Go in, Mister Ian. Baby's come."

Even as she spoke, he heard a newborn's mewling. He went in.

The room looked like a slaughterhouse. Blood soaked the tick, the sheets, and the arms of Cecily Reynold, hovering over Judith in the bed, pressing what must have been the last clean wad of cloth they owned between her legs. The wet-copper scent of blood was thick enough to taste. Judith's eyes were closed, her face ghastly white, but she lived, else Cecily would not be trying so frantically to stem the bleeding. Swallowing back the urge to gag, Ian started for the bed.

Naomi caught him, strong hand on his unresisting arm. "Can't stop it," she whispered, voice throaty with grief. "But you got here in time."

She left him standing and hurried to a table pushed to the side where she bent over the bairn.

Ian went to his wife, barely acknowledging Cecily as he knelt and took Judith's hand in his. She turned her bloodless face toward him as her eyelids blinked open. Even her lips were drained of color. "Ian . . . a son."

He smoothed her damp hair back, then glanced at Cecily, who looked up, tears coursing down her cheeks, dark eyes asking the terrible question.

Numb with shock, he nodded.

Cecily slumped in defeat. Staggering a little, she pushed off the bed and went to join Naomi, doing something with the bairn still making his fretful sounds.

"Is he well?" Judith asked, eyes darting as if searching for the babe.

"Can ye not hear him?" Her fingers were limp, cold against his lips as he kissed them. A stone lodged at the back of his throat. So many things he wanted to say, should have said a thousand times before. "I'm sorry for the pain I've caused ye. So *sorry*."

Judith's brow tightened as she asked again, "He's well?"

The bairn had fallen silent. "He's bonny," Ian said, though he had yet to see their son. "Thank ye for him, Judith. And for Mandy."

"Miranda . . ." Her breath sighed out of her, and she closed her eyes, a faint smile curving her lips. "Grace. It *is* enough . . ."

He leaned closer. "Mandy, do ye mean? D'ye want her now?"

He searched her face, desperate to know what she needed. She had said, *It is enough*, but it wasn't. He had never given her enough.

"Judith?"

Her eyelids fluttered. Her chest rose. "Call him *Ian*."

"I will," he said. "Judith, I love ye. D'ye hear me? I love . . ."

Her breath went out on a long exhalation that seemed born at the roots of her, leaving her parted lips agape. She didn't draw another.

He was breathless too, the air driven from him as if by a blow. Then he laid his head across his wife's still breast as a keening arose in the room. The sound of an animal bewildered and in pain. Too robust for a newborn's. He wondered who made it, until he clamped his lips tight. There was silence for a time before a hand touched his shoulder.

"Ian?"

He lifted his head. One look at Cecily's trembling lips told him he had another farewell to make. "Bring him to me."

Cecily brought his son, cleaned and wrapped in a wee quilt Judith had pieced, to where he knelt beside the ruined bed, and laid the bairn in his arms. There was no time for unwrapping him, for counting fingers or toes, perfect as he might have been—save he had come a little too soon to thrive.

"Water," he said, never taking his gaze from the tiny features that bore striking resemblance to Mandy's at her birth. "Hurry."

A stir of bodies moving, the splash of water pouring, then Naomi set a cup beside him. He was vaguely aware of John in the room now, holding Robin, an arm around a weeping Cecily, of Malcolm and Ally hovering in the doorway, Mandy whimpering, Naomi scooping her up, humming a sound like the drone of distant bees. Then all stood silent. Witnessing.

His son was silent too. Ian burrowed his fingers past quilted folds to the sunken little chest, felt a fluttery heartbeat. He wasn't too late to do this last thing for Judith. Dipping fingers in the water, he sprinkled droplets across his son's scrunched brow.

When he spoke, his voice was steady. "I baptize ye, Ian Hugh Cameron, in the name of the Father, Son, and Holy Ghost. The Almighty bless and keep ye, my wee son. And your mother with ye."

A choked chorus of *amen*s filled the room, but Ian had replaced his fingertips against the struggling little heart and did not raise his eyes from his namesake's face until the beat beneath his touch fell still. He kissed the anointed brow, then laid the bairn beside his mother.

They buried them so, where Ian's kin rested on the ridge overlooking Mountain Laurel. Judith's mother would have taken their remains into her keeping and seen them buried at Chesterfield, but Ian wouldn't hear of it.

The day of the burial was the first he had seen Lucinda Cameron since Mandy's first birthday, when the woman had descended upon them like a crow bearing baubles, with nothing but disdain for the state into which her youngest daughter had sunk—living in the cabin once relegated to Mountain Laurel's overseer, with no domestic help save Naomi. The only thing the woman approved was Mandy, but the gleam in her eyes as she dandled his daughter on her lap had not pleased Ian. Mandy was her only living grandchild, the union between Rosalyn and Gideon Pryce, Chesterfield's master, having thus far borne no fruit.

Anticipating conflict from the Chesterfield contingent, Ian set Charlie Spencer as guard over his daughter. While Lucinda was permitted to visit with Mandy, Charlie wasn't to let the pair out of his sight.

Ian lingered at the gravesite with Malcolm after the others began the long walk down the ridge, then descended the trail with the old man, aiding his way. Catching Charlie's raised voice as they reached the cabins, Ian sprinted ahead.

"No, ma'am! I ain't lettin' go this child. I got my orders, which don't include you taking her off her daddy's land."

Ian came panting up the track past the stable. Gideon Pryce had departed, taking his mother and sister in one of their two coaches. The liveried driver perched atop the remaining coach—Jubal, Mountain Laurel's former stableman—appeared to take no notice of the attempted abduction playing out below. Charlie held on to Mandy, frocked in a gown Judith had sewn, while Lucinda attempted to pry the child from his arms. Mandy screamed in fear of their raised voices, their clasping fingers. Ally and Naomi hovered nearby, the latter looking furious enough to attack her former mistress should she prevail in the tug-of-war.

"Unhand my granddaughter," Lucinda demanded. "I have every right to her."

"That ye do not!" Ian thundered over his daughter's crying, shouldering Lucinda back from Charlie and taking Mandy into his embrace.

Overwrought and bewildered, Mandy sobbed into his shoulder. "Mama . . . Mama!"

Lucinda stepped back, grief and fury pinching her features. "The child needs a mother. And a decent providing. Judith's sister shall raise her—at Chesterfield," she added, casting a look of loathing at what was left of Mountain Laurel.

Rosalyn's pale face peered from the coach's window. Earlier, Ian had been startled at the change in her when she had alighted from the coach. Though still golden-haired and lush of figure, the gloss had worn off her beauty in the two years since she wed Gideon Pryce, leaving a more brittle version. She had not spoken during the burial, though more than once he had caught her chilling stare.

Rosalyn said nothing now. Her blue eyes burned with jealous longing as they fastened on Mandy.

"*My* daughter," Ian said with emphasis, "stays with me. And I'll ask ye civilly—the once—to get into your coach and go home. Both of ye."

To his surprise Lucinda did so, sweeping her black skirts into the conveyance before Jubal could climb down to assist. She made no threats. No promises to wrest Mandy from him by other means. "For today" was all she said.

Far from reassured, Ian closed the coach's door and gave Jubal a nod. An instant before the man snapped the lines and urged the horses forward, Rosalyn leaned nearer the coach's window, her voice cold and clear.

"You never deserved her, *Cousin*."

"Aye," Ian whispered against his daughter's head as the coach wheels rattled on the drive. "In that we are agreed."

10 May 1796

To Ian Cameron
Mountain Laurel

Your Mama says it is fine for me to write. No one here will read this but me, and I will seal it and post it my own self. Give my regards to Miss Judith if you will ~~and tell her~~.

Gabriel is walking good. Talking too. Mister Robert says he will not take my Baby from me. He will take us both into his Family if I want, or just Gabriel. ~~I wish the choice was~~ No one is making me do anything. Is that what you wanted to hear?

It is a Wonder I can speak to you from so far distant. I admire the sight of words put down by my hand. That is all I have to say.

Seona

"It's dated two days after Judith died," Ian said, staring at the well-creased letter in John's hand, his own lying restless on the Reynolds' table. John passed the letter to Cecily, seated beside him, who held it to a nearby candle's light to better read.

Ian clenched his hands, going over in his mind all Seona had not said, the things she had begun only to scratch out—not well enough to disguise the words beneath. What had she wanted Judith to know?

He glanced aside to where Mandy played on a rug with Robin, a pile of whittled farm animals between them. No word had come from Chesterfield in the fortnight since the ugly confrontation with Lucinda and Rosalyn. Still the threat of interference lay like a shadow across his mind.

His son in Boston. His daughter here. He ached to protect them both. Provide for both. *Raise* both—a prospect too raw to risk examination.

Cecily set the letter on the table and reached for his fisted hand, covering it with her own. "It is good to see these words from Seona—such a bright soul to have learned so well, as she did the *français* I once taught her. But, Ian, does she truly not know what it is she wants? Or does she hesitate to own to it?"

For two days, since the letter's arrival, Ian had wondered the same, trying to read between those few lines. *Is that what you wanted to hear?*

He wanted to know her heart on the matter.

"Did I do wrong, sending her and Gabriel north? I wonder if it only made it harder. Now she's being forced to make decisions for herself she'd no way to prepare for."

"What other way could she learn?" John countered. "Besides, you had little choice. They couldn't stay in North Carolina."

"Don't forget Lily is with her," Cecily said. "I think it would take a great deal to frighten Lily into seeing Seona do anything against her will. I cannot imagine your parents would do such a thing as to pressure them so. Can you?"

"No," Ian admitted, but there was only one way he could learn these things to his satisfaction, and it wasn't from eight hundred miles away with weeks or months between letters that obscured more than they revealed. "But I think I must return to Boston. As soon as I can manage it."

John's brows rose. "To see this situation sorted?"

Ian's glance flicked to Cecily, whose open dismay showed her quicker grasp of the truth. "Not a visit, John. I think it best to divest myself of Mountain Laurel and return north. To stay."

The depth of disappointment on their faces was, in its way, a comfort.

John cleared his throat. "I cannot say the notion hasn't crossed my mind, but, Ian, let me counsel you not to do anything hastily. Judith's passing has changed things but—"

"John," Ian interrupted. "I've no intention of shrugging Judith off like an ill-fitted coat . . ." He put a hand across his lips, ears ringing with the silence at the table. They hadn't seen him grieving, not since they witnessed his son's baptism, then watched the bairn follow his mother out of this life into the next. They hadn't seen a tear since. Only one other had.

When everyone else had left them at Judith's grave, Ian had knelt, Malcolm beside him. They had wept together and talked of Judith, of the bond she and Mountain Laurel's oldest slave had formed in those trying weeks before Gabriel's birth. It had been Malcolm as well who guided Ian to a place of surrender to the Almighty, a yielding of his willful heart. Only with Malcolm had he shared the depth of his grief or the guilt he struggled to release.

"I'm not ready to think beyond doing what's best for my children," he said now. "If I remain here, I risk losing both. Rosalyn Pryce will raise Mandy over my dead body, but I can hardly suffer the notion of Gabriel calling another man *father* any better now that . . ."

Cecily wiped away a tear. "Now that there may be another way?"

Ian nodded.

John looked at him across the table, head tilted as though listening. After a moment, he reached to grasp Ian's wrist. "We are going to miss you. All of you. Terribly."

"Ye're not rid of me yet," Ian said, needing to lighten the moment. "I'm going to need your help."

"What help, my friend? I'll do what I can."

"My uncle's land was precious to him. Too much so. Still, I'll not see it entrusted to just anyone. In fact, I'll not sell it at all unless it be to ye and Cecily."

4

He should have waited until after their dinner to broach the topic that had them letting Naomi's good ham soup cool in their bowls. *Cool* being a relative term in the kitchen at midday, even with the door propped wide to let in breeze and sunlight. Naomi had paused in feeding Mandy, spoon suspended, when Ian cleared his throat and asked, "What would ye three think of no longer being enslaved to me? Or to any man," he clarified.

While dumbfounded surprise marked his mother's and grandfather's faces, Ally sputtered, "M-mister Ian . . . you aiming to sell us to a *woman*? You don't mean Miss Lucinda! No, sir. I would not like that. She one mean white lady."

"Ally!" Naomi batted his meaty arm. "That ain't what Mister Ian means." She eyed Ian, suddenly wary. "Is it?"

"It is not," Ian said.

Gazing at the spoon still hovering inches from her face, Mandy smacked her lips. With a trembling hand, Naomi popped it into her mouth. "We'd take our freedom, Mister Ian, if that's what you offering. But then . . . where we to go?"

"Go?" Ally blurted. "But them *horses*. This their home—and mine."

"Mister Ian," Malcolm cut in with considered calm, "might ye share what it is exactly ye have in mind to do wi' us?"

"Aye," Ian said, relieved for the chance. "Though I'm not yet certain what *I* mean to do—with myself, I mean—once Mandy and I get there. But I won't hold ye in slavery any longer."

To his consternation, tears welled in Naomi's eyes. "Get there? You taking this baby away?" She put a hand on Mandy's head, as if expecting him to sweep his daughter out of the kitchen and make off for parts unknown.

"Aye. To Boston." Ian set down his spoon and tried to say it plain. "I'm asking whether ye three want to go with us. Ye'd be free in the north. Free to stay with me, and welcome, or to go your way."

Understanding banished Naomi's dismay but left her feathers ruffled. "Why couldn't you say so to start with?" She popped another spoonful of soup into Mandy's mouth, catching dribbles with its edge. "Ain't kind to go scaring a body like that."

Ian's face warmed. "I've said it poorly but . . . what d'ye think?"

"Boston?" Ally looked from one face at the table to another. "Where that at?"

"'Tis where Seona and Lily went," his grandfather reminded him. "A long way from here."

"A world away," Ian agreed. "But I hope ye'll come."

"Ye dinna want us here, tending the place for ye?" Malcolm asked.

"It won't be mine to tend. I'm selling Mountain Laurel to John Reynold."

"Mister John gonna own this land?" Naomi said after another stunned silence.

"We've agreed upon it." His uncle's solicitor would arrive on the morrow to facilitate the arrangement. "Here's the thing about ye three, though. I'd see ye manumitted before leaving the state, but there's reason for me to go as soon as may be."

"Miss Lucinda," Naomi muttered.

"Aye. And reason for reaching Boston quick as I can manage." He told them of his da's offer to adopt Seona and Gabriel, of Seona's uncertainty. "I want ye to have free papers, but the time it'll take to arrange them concerns me. Weeks. Maybe months."

Naomi and Malcolm shared a look. When she gave a nod, he said,

"That's all right, Mister Ian. Take us north wi' ye, call us free. It'll be enough."

It is enough. Judith's dying words pierced him afresh. He denied them again with the force of conviction. He hadn't done enough for these three either. But it was all he had at present. The promise of freedom and whatever support and protection he could lend.

"Amen, Daddy." Naomi leaned over to give Mandy's head a kiss. "Like it say in the Bible, Mister Ian. Where you go, we go. Keep doing like we do."

Ian caught Malcolm's gaze, sensing a transaction had taken place, one as binding as what would happen on the morrow. Only by the sale of the ground they had plowed with their sweat, sowed with their tears, reaped without possibility of gain, could he hope to give them something more lasting.

"Right then," he said, trying not to sound as choked as he felt. "We'll go together. Though if ye change your minds down the road, I'll help ye toward the path of your choosing, as well as I'm able. On that I give ye my word. And . . ." He swallowed, knowing the appalling inadequacy of what he meant next to say. "I want to thank ye—each of ye—for your service to my kin. It was never your choosing but . . ."

"Mister Ian," Naomi said gravely. "There been hard times in this place, plenty hard and mean. We bear the marks on body and soul. But ain't none of us chafing under the yoke you lay."

When Ian could speak, he said, "I don't mean to lay any yoke upon ye. Ever again."

"But you need us," Naomi said. "You and Mandy."

As if to underscore her statement, his daughter made an urgent gurgle. Naomi spooned more soup down her.

"'Tis the Almighty casts our lots," Malcolm added. "I learned that long ago from the man first preached Jesus to me, back when Naomi here was a wee lassie learning to cook. I never expected the day to dawn I'd be a free man on this earth, to come and go as I pleased, but long ere ye lived to walk it, Mister Ian, I was set free in my spirit. I've told ye as much. No' that I'm ungrateful for what ye're doing," he added. "My life is all but spent, but Naomi and Ally, they've a heap o' living yet to do."

Ian reached to lay his hand over the old man's, rested on the table. "I know."

"Well, *I* don't know any such thing," Naomi said, eyes gone moist with tears. "Daddy, you'll outlive us all."

Ally had followed the conversation, a beat behind the rest. "So we going to Boston, we gonna be free, but . . . what about them horses? They going too?"

"Ruaidh and Juturna for certain," Ian said. "Perhaps her dam. And we'll be needing a team with draft blood to pull a wagon."

Ally half leapt from his bench at that news. Naomi told him to sit and finish his dinner. The talk turned to travel, the long road north, finally to Lily, Seona, and Gabriel.

"We gonna see them again!" Ally exclaimed.

"Ye glad about that?" Ian asked, though the answer was plain.

"Yes, sir. I miss their faces. Prettiest faces I ever see."

"Huh," Naomi said in feigned offense, even as she and Malcolm chuckled.

Ian laughed with them, sharing their anticipation, though a pang shot through him, double-edged. Hope cut as deep as sorrow, it seemed. Joy as deep as regret.

With the air on the ridge warm and clinging, alive with flitting birds, Ian stood on the small parcel of Mountain Laurel containing his resting kin. All was settled, everything drafted, fair-copied, signed, and witnessed. Ian, John, and Charlie had climbed the ridge to bid more than a few farewells. And to speak of the future.

"For now, I'll get the lot of us to Boston," Ian had said as they ascended the trail his uncle's slaves had worn to the clearing by the burying ground, where they had prayed and sung to the God of their hope. "Then see what follows. Not much as plans go, but I cannot know what I'll find there."

Would his and Mandy's arrival make matters better or worse? None could say. But John, whose opinion he valued, had agreed it was best

Ian return to his father's house and learn for himself what Seona and Lily desired.

They had trudged along in silence after that, Charlie's hounds loping ahead, noses to the ground, until they reached the plot of headstones. Ian had first stumbled upon the place before making the fateful choice to marry Judith, thinking Seona lost. The graves had been neglected then, the forest threatening to subsume the stones in its mossy embrace. He had cleared away debris, driving back the wild.

"We'll keep it tended," John assured him. "And give you a moment now." He shot a glance at Charlie, who chirruped to his milling dogs and shouldered his ever-present rifle. They waited in the deeper shade of the surrounding wood while Ian went among the graves, sweating from the climb. He pulled sticky linen from his chest as he surveyed the collection of markers.

The oldest belonged to Mountain Laurel's original settler, who, in disdain for the English, precipitators of his exile and that of countless sons of Scotland, had spoken only the *Gàidhlig* and caused his slaves to learn it too. Not quite as old were the headstones of his uncle's first wife, Miranda Cameron—for whom Mandy was named—and their son, Aidan, Seona's father, dead before her birth.

"I'll see them safe," he promised the kin he had never met. "They'll want for nothing in my power to provide. Rest knowing it, if ye can hear my words."

And, Uncle . . . , he continued in silence, gaze moving to one of the newer stones. Hugh Cameron, his father's elder half brother, a man misshapen by his choices in life, broken by his loves torn away too soon. A wife and bairn dead in childbirth. Their surviving son taken by violence at eighteen; the ripples of that long-ago tragedy had ever widened, crippling hearts and minds in the silence of their secrets. *Forgive me my sins, Uncle, as I have forgiven ye yours.*

He looked last at the newest stone, as unassuming as the woman whose name was carved thereupon. *Judith Ann Bell Cameron—beloved wife and mother.* Below it, *Ian Hugh Cameron—son.* He crouched to trace the letters. "Judith. Rest ye well with my lad. And his sister," he added, touching Elizabeth's tiny marker, snug next to Judith's. Then he stood. "I'll see ye again. All of ye."

Wiping his eyes with a shirtsleeve, Ian turned from the graves, picking his way to his friends waiting in the wood's deeper shade.

"Ye're set to continue digging, Charlie?" he asked briskly to drive away the concern furrowing the man's scruff-bearded face.

Charlie Spencer grinned, showing a gap where he had lately lost a tooth. His hand dropped to fondle the ears of his nearest dog. "Aiming to. And keeping things mum. Too much a lark to think of stopping either."

"Speaking of . . ." From his coat John withdrew a leather pouch. "The earnest we agreed upon. Small nuggets, shavings, and flakes. I'll send more as I'm able."

Ian took the proffered pouch, curled his fingers around the soft leather, hefted its weight. "Never entrust an amount this large to the post, aye? A little at a time will do." The gold he held rendered him able to keep the promise just made to his kin—once he found the means to convert it into coin, best left until they reached Boston if what tender he had lasted. "I'll write ye, give ye a reliable address. My da's will do for now."

"Take care on the journey," John said.

"Sounds a fair piece of travel," Charlie chimed in. "Some folk on the roads not to be trusted. I've met a few."

"Aye, well," Ian said, moved by their concern, "I've made the trek a time or two before, and somehow I doubt anyone will think to try Ally."

"Long as he keeps his mouth shut," Charlie agreed. While of imposing stature and intimidating strength, Naomi's son was as gentle as a kitten, as simple as the child he had been when a mule kicked him in the head.

"Listen, both of ye." Ian put a hand to each man's shoulder, gripping hard. "I couldn't have asked for better neighbors. And friends. I know ye both prayed long for me. Ye'll have my prayers, if not my presence, always."

"And you ours," John said, taking him in a thumping embrace.

"God will make the way for you, Ian. He's gone before you, preparing that path. Be ready to be surprised by His goodness."

"I'll hope for it," Ian said, unable quite to hold his friend's gaze.

"Expect it," John said.

Charlie Spencer bobbed his head, then called his ranging dogs, gave a final salute, and tromped off along the ridge, rifle shouldered. Ian watched him go; then wordlessly he and John Reynold turned from the Cameron graves and went down the ridge together a final time.

5

BOSTON
June 1796

It was sultry for early June. Even with the window propped to catch a breeze off the water, Seona sweated over the hem she stitched in the tiny gown meant for someone's newborn. In his corner bed, her own baby napped, overwarm for comfort to judge by his thrashings. Pausing to blot her brow with a kerchief, she gazed down at the street below, still surprised to find herself a world away from tobacco fields, cabins, and corn.

"You mind how cool it was on the ridge of a night, Mama, when we'd go up for the singing?" She heard her old way of talking nudging up through the polish put on her speech since coming to Boston, as if the memories had conjured the ghost of the girl she had been.

Lily raised her head from the meticulous stitching she was adding to a bodice. "And I mind that stifling kitchen of a day. It's plenty hotter there than here. Ye forgotten?"

"I ain't . . . *haven't* forgotten." Speaking of the singing minded Seona of the night Ian had followed Mountain Laurel's slaves up that ridge. The night he gave himself, heart and will, to the Almighty.

"I know ye haven't, girl-baby."

Whatever else had changed, one thing remained the same: whether in a sweltering kitchen in Carolina or a stuffy room in Boston, her mama hardly ever broke a sweat. Seona turned from the window, taking in the sleekness of her mama's upswept hair, a few white strands among the black. "Think we should go see Penny?"

"Penny?" Lily's brow flickered at the change of subject.

Gabriel sat up in his bed, fair hair plastered to his head. "Eddie and Wobbie?" He screwed a fist against sleepy eyes and let out a fretful whine.

"No, baby." Seona put down the sewing and went to scoop him up, never mind it was so warm their skin stuck where they touched. She walked him to the pitcher on the washstand and poured a cup full of tepid water. "Thirsty?"

Gabriel sipped it, looking cranky and unrested.

"It's been months," Seona said, returning to the subject of Penny. Not even Catriona, clever at ferreting out who thought what about whichever, had seen Ned's grieving wife. Penny was still shut up in her home, refusing to see anyone save Ned and the hired woman who came to clean a day or two each week. "Maybe if you and I knocked on her door, she'd see us. We're the only ones haven't tried."

Gabriel's head fell against her neck and nestled there, damp and warm. She wanted to lay him down, see would he nap longer. He fussed when she tried, so she held him and paced the room.

"We could go," her mama said.

"To see this boy's auntie?" Seona asked, forbearing to speak Penny's name again. Until today it had been weeks since Gabriel asked for his cousins, but he hadn't forgotten them.

Lily held her gaze. "I mean *go*. Take our leave of the Camerons."

Seona halted in the middle of the room, Gabriel heavy in her arms. "What about all this adoption talk? You saying you don't want that?"

"I'm saying I have enough clientele now. If we both work at it, we could set up for ourselves. Not in a house like this but somewhere decent. It's another path we might follow, is all."

Panic coiled in Seona's chest at thought of leaving the Camerons, stepping out from under their covering. Further fraying the threads binding her to Ian. Had she the freedom to up and make such a break?

Ian was Gabriel's father. He had a say in matters. Hadn't she written to tell him so?

"No, Mama. I don't want that. Not yet anyway."

"What do ye want?"

"Joy in this family, like it was before . . ." Her head ached from the heat. "You notice how Ned's coming round less? How quiet Miss Margaret's been? I don't even know half the time anymore where Catriona's got to."

Her mama glanced up from her work. "Calling on a friend this afternoon, I thought."

"That's what she said." Catriona had been gone considerable longer than such a visit ought to take. Though it wasn't the first time Seona had made that observation, she shook her head, refusing to be sidetracked. "Nothing's going to bring the boys back, but maybe talking to their mama will help matters. I don't know."

Lily sat a moment more, gazing out the window, then put aside her sewing. "Reckon it won't hurt to try."

Mainly on account of his crankiness, Seona took Gabriel along, though she worried whether his presence would be comfort or cruelty to Penny—and hers to him.

Gabriel perked up at the North End's sights and sounds, but when they knocked the door clapper of Ned's narrow, white-painted home, neither he nor Penny answered, but the woman who kept their house, dustrag in hand. When Lily asked for Mrs. Cameron, the woman waved her rag and exclaimed, "Law to me! Miss Penny's not to home."

Seona wondered if she meant what Boston folk sometimes did by those words—that Penny was home but unwilling to be sociable.

"You're the boarders, aye?" the woman asked, eyes fastening on Gabriel, riding Seona's hip. "Living with Mr. Ned's kin?"

"Yes, ma'am," Seona said. "Might you tell Penny we came to call?"

"I cannot do that."

"What?" Seona said, taken aback by the woman's blunt reply. "Why not?"

Below her frilled cap, the woman's brow furrowed. "How is it ye don't know? Gone a fortnight now is Miss Penny. Back to her parents in Deerfield. I've no notion when she means to return," she added when they asked. "That's a question for Mr. Ned, I'm sure."

At the last street to cross before they reached Beachum Lane, they were stopped by a harried, sweaty boy attempting to drive a flock of noisy geese along the cobblestones toward somewhere they didn't seem inclined to go. Not of a mind to risk threading a path through darting beaks, Seona and Lily stepped back to wait. Seona shifted Gabriel to the other hip. "Best we tell the family about Penny?" she asked over the honking and the boy's shouts. "Or might they already know?"

Lily cast her a look. "Robert and Margaret may, but if Catriona knew . . . wouldn't ye? How long has she ever kept a secret?"

Seona caught her mama's smile, tempered by this new knowledge of Ned Cameron's pain, as the boy, hair as flaxen as Gabriel's, got his wayward geese on past and shot her a triumphant grin that made her think of Ian . . . who had lost a son to a distance so great it might well be forever.

Was Ian as distraught as Ned and Penny had been all these months? Would the last thing he wanted be his daddy adopting Gabriel?

"Come on, girl-baby," Lily called, already crossing the street.

By habit now, Seona cast another look along the busy lane to be sure nothing else was bearing down. Off through the shifting bodies pausing at vendors' stalls or ducking in and out of shop doors, she glimpsed a girl crossing at the next intersection over, arm in arm with a male companion. The girl turned her face up, features catching the sunlight, to laugh at something said by the man to whose arm she clung. The well-dressed man doffed his hat to someone in passing, revealing dark hair brushed toward his temples. It was that New York merchant, Morgan Shelby. With Catriona.

Someone bumped Seona's shoulder and she sidestepped. Before she got another look down the street, the couple had walked on, swallowed by the shifting crowd. Seona hurried to catch her mama up, asking, "Who was it Catriona visited today?"

"I never caught the name," Lily said. "Didn't ye?"

"I forgot." Seona smiled as if it made no matter. Hoping it didn't. Hoping Catriona hadn't been keeping secrets after all.

"Pudding, Mama?" Gabriel asked as they entered the house.

"I'll take him," Lily said, reaching for her grandson. "I hear Miss Margaret in the kitchen. I best go have a talk."

Gabriel and his grandmothers were in the keeping room when Seona joined them. A glance at Margaret Cameron's face, wreathed in dismay, answered two questions. She hadn't known about Penny leaving Boston. She did now.

"Ye'd think I'd have heard of it from *some*one afore now," Ian's mama was saying as Seona entered the heavily beamed room. She had long since realized she judged every Cameron face by Ian's, in all their moods searching their features for his likeness. Of his siblings, Ian was the only one who had come away with his mama's blonde curls, though Miss Margaret's were streaked with white.

"Penny shut herself up for months." Lily had Gabriel on her lap, spooning bites of corn pudding into his mouth. "Not just from us. Everyone."

"Ach, my poor dears . . ." Miss Margaret let her words trail off, glancing at Seona with pained eyes, then fondly at Gabriel. "Did I ever tell ye Ned was as fair as this wee laddie when he was a bairn? But his hair darkened to his da's shade by time he was nine. Only Catriona was born with the russet fuzz."

"Wussit fuss," Gabriel said before Lily popped another spoonful of pudding into his mouth, deftly catching a spill.

Margaret Cameron looked from her grandson to Seona and sighed. "Ye ken we're awaitin' Ian's word on the matter Robert put to ye? No one means ye to do anythin' agin' your will—or Ian's. But I do wonder—"

"If it's high time we heard from that brother of mine?" Catriona asked, coming in from the back of the house, through the scullery. She untied her light spencer and shrugged out of it, then looked around the silent room. "What's wrong? Have we word from Ian at last?"

"No," her mother replied. "'Tis Penny—awa' to Deerfield a fortnight past and Ned's kept us in the dark aboot it. Or did ye ken?"

"Penny's gone?" Catriona went still, faint color rising in her cheeks. "How did you find out?"

"Her housemaid told us today," Seona replied.

Catriona's blush was fading. "Why did Ned keep it from us?"

"I dinna ken." Margaret Cameron rose, unpinning the apron covering her gown. "But I'll be hearin' the why of it today. That *gowkit* firstborn o' mine will put his feet under my table this evenin' if I've anythin' to say aboot it. And I do!"

"I'm sure he will, Mam," Catriona said as she went out, the smile she blazed bordering on unfitting, given the news of Penny.

Seona slipped out after her, leaving her mama minding Gabriel and Margaret Cameron donning a hat to leave for Mister Robert's shop. She found Catriona in her room, spencer tossed across the bed's coverlet.

Ian's sister turned from the window, where she stood. "I knew about Penny going back to Deerfield. I didn't want Mam to know I knew."

Seona frowned. "Knew for how long?"

Catriona crossed the room and shut the door. "All of an hour—at most. Don't look at me so. I haven't been keeping secrets."

"Haven't you?"

Catriona sat at her dressing table to unpin her cap. "Whatever could you mean?"

Seona perched on the end of Catriona's bed and folded the discarded spencer. "I saw you out today."

A fumbled pin was the only indication she had startled Catriona, who shook her hair down to coil around her shoulders. "I didn't see you," she said into the looking glass mounted above the table, then reached for a brush to attack her curls.

"I hadn't heard Mr. Shelby was in Boston again," Seona said. "How long have you known about that?"

Catriona's brushing stopped. "A quarter hour longer than I've known about Penny." She set the brush down and faced Seona. "Mr.

Shelby managed to get the news from Ned today and presumed we all knew. He and I met on my way home—quite by chance. He mentioned Penny's being gone and, once he saw I was distraught at the news, suggested we take a cup of tea at the Red Lion, seeing as we were practically on the doorstep."

"I see." Seona had never been inside that particular tavern but knew it for a decent sort of place. "Still, you maybe oughtn't to have gone with him alone."

Catriona's cheeks flamed. "Mr. Shelby was all kindness, never for a moment inappropriate."

Had it been appropriate for the man to suggest such a thing in the first place? Ought he to have seen Catriona straight home instead?

As if she read the thought, Catriona said, "After our tea, Mr. Shelby escorted me home as any gentleman would. But as we made our way, we came up with a plan." Hope surged into Catriona's face. "Mam doesn't have to ask Ned to supper. Mr. Shelby's arranging it as a particular kindness to me—to us all. He's talking to Da now and to Ned. By the end of their conversation—he assured me—both he and that brother of mine will be under our roof for supper. Ned can hardly refuse if Mr. Shelby is invited again—and *I* invited him. He can hardly refuse to explain about Penny, now we all know of it. So you've no need for concern," she finished. "For I see you are concerned."

"I was," Seona admitted.

Catriona returned to her hairdressing. Seona watched her coil the long strands high again, set them with pins, then pull loose a few artful curls to spill down her neck. Her gown's capped sleeves bared her graceful arms. It was more skin than Seona would ever be comfortable showing. She had insisted on sleeves to the elbows on any new gowns, despite Catriona urging her to try a more current fashion.

Ian's sister glanced at her in the glass. "I don't think you like Mr. Shelby."

"Never mind what I like. It's you . . ."

"What about me?" Catriona asked when she hesitated.

"Promise you won't get mad if I ask?"

Catriona faced her. "I won't. What is it?"

"Is this the first you've kept company with Mr. Shelby, since the day we met him in the shop?"

"He's only just back in Boston—yesterday, he said. Our meeting was by Providence."

"You called it chance."

"Well, I hope it proves more than that."

Seona bit back a sigh. Catriona was the nearest to a sister she had ever had, aside from little Esther, at Mountain Laurel. Though Seona was the elder by a few years, Ian's sister had been her teacher in many ways since coming to Boston, always with a notion to lead them into something new, especially since her nephews' deaths. But never anything truly reckless. Was she being reckless now?

A knock at the door had Catriona jumping up from her dressing table. It was Lily, Gabriel squirming in her arms. "I need to finish up that bodice afore supper and this little man still wants nothing to do with napping."

Gabriel leaned out from Lily's embrace so precariously Seona hurried to rescue him. "Come on, baby. Let's go see what the redbirds are doing."

"Save time to dress for supper," Catriona called after her. "I've faith it will all work out as planned."

6

PENNSYLVANIA

At the first rumble of thunder, Ian nudged Ruaidh nearer the wagon to be heard above the drumming downpour. "We'd best get out of this!"

Perched on the driver's bench, Ally nodded, funneling rain off his hat onto an oiled lap cloth. Despite a similar cape draping Ian neck to knee, rain had wicked its way inside even his shirt. Naomi, Mandy, and Malcolm were drier in the wagon with its canvas covering, but the horses were taking the brunt of the late-spring thunderstorm.

The rain had commenced innocently enough when they had stopped to eat a cold dinner. Within an hour a steady drizzle had settled in. In two it was sheeting down, the day darkened to twilight.

Big hands clenched around swollen traces, Ally squinted at the road. "Trees too thick to get the wagon under!"

Lightning highlighted the stretch ahead, densely wooded on either side, the road itself disintegrating into a quagmire, threatening to stick fast a wheel or turn a hoof and break a leg. Having traveled that road, Ian minded an inn thereabouts. He told Ally so. "Will ye be all right if I ride ahead, see can I find it?"

Ally waved him on. As Ian heeled the roan into a trot, he granted that, despite the present situation, they had had better grace for their journey than he could have hoped for.

In the new-minted village of Asheborough, a few miles from Mountain Laurel, he had acquired a wagon and a four-horse team to pull it. Along with some hard coin, he had traded nearly all the household goods he owned, lumber from the shop, and one of his uncle's last two broodmares. The other, Juturna's docile dam, was hitched to the wagon's tailgate with her filly.

Into the wagon had gone his joiner's tools and the cookery Naomi couldn't—or wouldn't—part with. Two trunks held their clothing. Sundry casks contained provisions. There was bedding and a canvas shelter; Ian had meant to camp along the road when possible rather than spend for bed and board. Blessed with dry weather, the plan proved sound through the Valley of Virginia. They spent an extra day in Philadelphia, where, having need of provisions and nothing to trade, Ian found a banker willing to exchange a small amount of gold flakes for coin, few questions asked. Fewer answered.

At Philadelphia they had left the wagon road and were now on the old King's Highway, which would take them through New Jersey, New York, and on to Boston. Ian thought they were near a village he had ridden through three years past. He minded an inn, mostly for its name, which had struck him as fanciful then. But what had it been?

The wind whipped sidewise, drenching his face. After a mile of road curving through forest unbroken by farm, field, or sign to mark the hoped-for inn—the Blue Goose? Blue Door? Blue *something*—ahead on the verge he spied a humpy shape, indistinguishable through the rain. Smaller shapes moved around it.

His first impression threw him back to his fur-trapping days in the wilds of Canada, before his sojourn to Mountain Laurel. The scene ahead looked for all the world like a great bull moose brought down by a pack of wolves, busily tearing at the carcass. A few yards nearer and the shape resolved into what it was, a small coach overturned. Three men moved about, releasing its team, getting them off the road.

Ian approached with caution, seeing, as he dismounted, one of the horses down in the miring mud. He shouted to the men as he walked Ruaidh to the wood's edge, where one, likely the driver, had hitched the team minus one.

The man bellowed a greeting and they joined the others next to the downed horse. Plainly there was no helping it. As Ian had feared for his own, it had taken a misstep, broken a foreleg. The passengers drew back as the driver produced a pistol from some dry corner of his person and did what had to be done for the creature.

Even muffled by the storm, the shot left Ian's ears ringing.

The driver, tall and broad-chested under a voluminous cape, handed the spent pistol to one of the others, then turned to Ian and in a hearty baritone boomed, "Yesterday I dined in state with President Washington! Today finds me ankle-deep in mud, soaked to the hide, putting down my best carriage horse. Providence keeping me humble!" Reaching out a beefy hand, he continued, "But your kindness in stopping is appreciated, sir! As we can do no more for my poor horse than roll her carcass off the road, might you be willing to aid us in righting my coach—if the deed can be accomplished?"

Ian shook the man's hand, as wet as his own, hastily reassessing. His horse. His coach. The *president*'s table? The other two collected the baggage fallen in the crash, moving muddied trunks aside.

"I've a wagon coming!" Ian shouted over grumbling thunder. "And a driver of considerable strength. He'll lend it if we four cannot prevail. Is there damage?"

"Not presently ascertainable." The burly owner looked past Ian. "That your man coming now?"

It was. Ian waved Ally to halt the wagon and climb down. Naomi's face appeared briefly in the canvas opening behind the bench. Then Ally was there, looming over even the coach's owner, shaking his head sorrowfully at the dead horse in the road.

"We need to right this coach!" Ian shouted.

Ally turned from the unfortunate horse. "Tell me what to do, Mister Ian."

With the brute strength of five they had the coach tilted up, then over onto its wheels, creaking and rocking, with a drenching that made little difference in anyone's state. Ian checked the coach over but found it serviceable, if battered. As he rounded the conveyance, he caught the burly owner straightening from examining the undercarriage with an air of one acquainted with its mechanics. Still he turned to the man Ian had finally identified as the driver.

"What say you, Eldredge?"

"It's but two miles, Judge, to that inn ye're aiming for. Reckon did we take it easy, we'll make it. But we'll only be hitching two horses."

"That'll be the Blue Moon?" Ian asked, recollecting the name at last.

"The same," said coach's owner—a judge, if Ian had heard aright. "Do you make for it yourself?"

"We do. And if ye'd care to make a full team, I've a spare horse ye can hitch for the distance. She's pulled a wagon and is biddable even in this *stramash*. Should ye like to try her?"

The man's blunt features beamed. "I would—and thank you kindly. May I know your name, sir?"

"Ian Cameron," Ian said as rain slapped him in the face. "Lately of Carolina."

"Returning north to settle?"

"God willing. And you, sir?"

"Judge William Cooper, returning to Otsego County, New York, where I am well settled indeed. But let us make for the Blue Moon, where you, your man, and anyone else in that wagon shall bide the night at my expense."

"That's generous but—"

"The least I can do!" Cooper clapped a hand wetly to Ian's shoulder. "Though not all."

"What mean ye, sir?"

The driver and the second passenger were leading the horses back onto the road.

"Let us get out of this," William Cooper said, "sufficiently dried—and watered of a different sort. Then I shall make it plain."

By the time coach and wagon reached the Blue Moon, the storm had nearly abated. Ian drove the wagon beneath a shelter running the length of the inn's stable. With the horses boxed, Ally saw to their feeding while Ian checked on the wagon's passengers. Naomi knelt at the open tailgate. "Provisions we got in Philadelphia be fine," she reported. "Everything but some bedding that wicked up rain. I'll spread it to dry if you help Daddy out."

Ian did so, half-lifting the old man to the ground. Naomi handed down Malcolm's cane. Ian pulled Mandy off the wagon and hooked her to his hip, where she squirmed against his damp coat. "Wet, Papa!"

"Aye," he said, grinning. "I need changing. How about ye?"

Mandy shook her curls. "No, no!"

"I saw to it whilst you was putting up the horses," Naomi called from the wagon's depths. Possessions sorted to her satisfaction, she clambered down. With the rain subsided to a sprinkle, Ian hung his cape in the wagon to dry and escorted his party across the muddy yard, handing Mandy over to Naomi to give Malcolm an arm when the old man's knees proved stiff.

"Too long sitting idle. I'll be a spoilt auld man, Mister Ian, afore ever we reach Boston."

"If ye never lift a hand to work again, ye've earned it."

"I'm no' through living yet. Ye'll have another garden to tend, by and by."

God willing, he would, Ian thought. But where? He supposed that depended on Seona. He hadn't written of his return, fearing such news might frighten her into doing something rash. He had only asked she do nothing until she heard from him on the matter of their son. She would hear, soon as he stood before her to speak his mind. A thought to set his heart racing.

The inn sat level with the yard, nothing but a stoop to mount. A foyer greeted them with a stair to the rooms above, a parlor to the left. To the right a taproom emitted a sharp tang of spirits and pipe smoke, the buzz of conversation, and a hail: "Be out to you folks directly. I've just had word of your coming."

Moments later the innkeeper, a bespectacled man of middle years and stature, emerged to greet them, smelling much like his establishment. "Mr. Cameron? The congressman had a room set aside for you, although . . ." He eyed Malcolm leaning on his cane. "Mayhap I should be putting you on the ground floor instead of abovestairs?"

"We'd appreciate that," Ian replied, then frowned. "The *congressman*, did ye say?"

"Congressman Cooper." With a scratch at a grizzled sideburn, the innkeeper regarded him. "Met him on the road, coach overturned?"

"His driver called him Judge."

"So he is. Judge, congressman, and more besides." The innkeeper looked them over. "Is this all your party? Will one room suffice?"

"It will," Ian assured. "I've another man I'm guessing will be sleeping in your stable, if it's agreeable?" Ally would want to stay with the horses. Ian had imagined the rest would share floor space somewhere. Judge, congressman, whatever else he lay claim to being, William Cooper was generous beyond all bounds.

The innkeeper took the situation in stride. "He may stay in the stable loft. I'll see he's victualed."

A plump woman of an age with the innkeeper had appeared in time to hear their last exchange. Pausing with hands on ample hips, she assessed them, gaze settling on Naomi and Malcolm. "Oughtn't they to sleep in the barn with the other? We're not running a boardinghouse for slaves."

She firmed her lips as if expecting argument.

Ian gave it. "Firstly, madam, this man and woman aren't slaves. Second, Naomi minds my daughter. If she's to sleep in the hay, so must my child—as will I. Ye may tell the congressman so."

"Slaves or no," the woman said, "they're still—"

"We could certainly all move on," came the hearty voice of William Cooper, who stepped from the taproom, "if we're causing inconvenience. There are other inns along this road."

"No." The innkeeper raised a conciliatory hand. "We've the room free—empty, I mean. Let me show you, Mr. Cameron." The man shot the woman a quelling glance.

Faced with the prospect of losing the congressman's business, she relented. Partially. "They ain't supping at my table," she said over her shoulder, making for the depths of the house. "There I draw the line."

William Cooper eyed the innkeeper, as did Ian, wondering who had the final say.

The man cleared his throat. "My sister is the law in her kitchen. As for the rest, they're welcome to sup in your room if they wish."

Ian looked to Naomi and Malcolm. "What d'ye say?"

"Fine by me," Naomi said, arms snug around his daughter. "Daddy's wore out. This girl gonna sleep soon, too. We'll take supper in the room."

"All right." Ian nodded to the innkeeper. "Let's see it then."

At William Cooper's invitation, Ian sought his supper in the inn's taproom. Seated with his driver and fellow coach passenger, Cooper poured Ian a cupful of the inn's hard cider and dove headlong into a proper introduction. Born not far from that very inn, the man had begun as a wheelwright by trade, then progressed to a merchant. "After the war I took an interest in lands to the west, which is proving a lucrative investment." Now deep into a political career, Cooper had founded a village at the foot of Otsego Lake, christened it Cooperstown, and become a promoter of settlement on the New York frontier. And the man was not above five and forty years, if Ian was any judge.

"But you, Mr. Cameron," Cooper continued, changing tack between helpings of the hearty Cheshire pie served for supper. "I catch a hint of Scotland in your speech. Born across the water, were you?"

"I was," Ian confirmed, glancing aside as the coach driver produced a pipe, knocked its dottle onto the boards, then swept it to the floor. "But I barely remember Scotland. My father sailed for Boston when I was a bairn. He set up for a bookbinder, then sent for us—me, Mam, my older brother—just in time for the British to blockade the city, us within, him without, fighting with the militia."

"A blockade ending with the British expelled from that port," Cooper said. "Did your father survive the war?"

"Still binding books in the North End."

Cooper's eyes sparkled with enthusiasm—and the cider he had

downed. "I've recently acquired a bookbinder for Cooperstown. Have you the art and mystery yourself then?"

"No." Ian inhaled a lungful of the driver's pipe smoke, pungent but sweet; the scent reminded him of Uncle Hugh. "That's my brother. I was apprenticed to a cabinetmaker, a trade I've pursued since. On and off."

"What have you ventured in the *off*?" Cooper asked, quick to pounce on the detail. "Did you farm in Carolina—I believe that's where you're from? North or South?"

Ian took a swallow of cider before answering. The man's probing might be rooted in curiosity naturally felt for any chance-met fellow traveler. Or not. "Until recently I owned a tobacco plantation in the North Carolina Piedmont—Randolph County. I farmed it long enough to know I'd do so again."

Cooper quirked a brow. "Surely not tobacco this far north?"

"No," Ian agreed. "Corn. Wheat. Cattle maybe."

"All of which grow with abundance upon the rich soils and grazing of western New York," Cooper assured him, "while the forests would give your cabinetmaker's heart joy. Particularly the maples, from which sugar is derived—an enterprise I'd hoped by now to see better prosper. Alas, the product competes poorly against the refined sugars of the Indies."

"It's good sugar, made right," Ian said. "I've seen the process."

"Have you?" Cooper's eyes, which drooped at their corners, now went nearly round with surprise. "When and where?"

"A few years back, in Canada. I've an uncle settled among the Chippewa. I trapped furs with him before I went to Carolina. His wife has a sugar bush, as they call it."

"Indeed!" Cooper slapped the boards with delight. The thump rattled cutlery, drawing glances from diners at the table's other end, though not, Ian noted, his driver and the other passenger, doubtless accustomed to the man's exuberance. "Now there's a thing I hadn't expected to look at you. Cabinetmaker, planter, *and* frontiersman. One might wonder what you'll be up to ten years hence."

"One might," Ian agreed with a dry laugh.

Though disposed to like the congressman from New York, he sensed Cooper's queries had been driving the conversation to an intended point, but some question about their journey arose between the driver and passenger, demanding Cooper's attention, leaving Ian to down the dregs in his cup and make a surreptitious exit, heading to the stable to check on Ally and the horses.

Outside, clouds hung low in the twilit sky. The stable welcomed him with the muggy warmth and scent of horseflesh. Ally rose from a bench where he had polished off his supper.

"I liked them apples baked with pork, Mister Ian. What you call it?"

"Cheshire pie. And if ye think that was good, wait until ye taste Mam's beefsteak pie. All's well then?"

"Got a blanket in the loft yonder." Ally canted his head toward the ladder. "Everybody brushed. Fed. Feet tended. No harm taken from the day."

"Good." Ian gripped Ally's arm. "Thank ye for your help today, with that carriage. We'll move on in the morning. I'll be out early to lend a hand."

He found a girl at work in the kitchen and returned Ally's plate, then slipped away unremarked by anyone lingering in the taproom. It was from the parlor across the foyer his name issued.

"Mr. Cameron?" William Cooper filled the doorway, tumbler in hand. "Share a dram before turning in?"

Manners won out over Ian's desire for bed. They weren't long settled in the rustic parlor before Cooper came to the point. "Back in that downpour I said I'd more to offer than a night's shelter. Having made your better acquaintance, I feel the more compelled to keep my word."

Ian sipped his whisky. "Ye've my curiosity piqued."

"As I mentioned," Cooper went on, "I've dabbled in frontier land speculation. Now I find myself in possession of vast tracts of New York land, north and south of the Mohawk River. A wilderness, empty and untrodden. My primary aim of late has been the matching of suitable men to the task of taming it."

Such land was in truth neither empty nor untrodden. Or had not long been. Ian had once visited Grand River, where the displaced

Mohawks had settled in Upper Canada, but the New York river valley that bore their name had been their homeland and that of the other Iroquois tribes. In the wake of their forced departure, or confinement to reserves, the face of the land was inexorably changing. Emptied, aye, but fast filling again with a different breed of men.

"I suppose the one must follow the other," he allowed.

Cooper looked pleased. "If but the half of what you say of yourself is true, you're a young man of gumption, willing to venture to better yourself and your dependents. I'd like to see you do so in New York. My home county of Otsego naturally commands my heart, and you're welcome there if a situation can be found to suit. If not, I've lands available north of the Mohawk River, as I said."

Cooper let that dangle, a baited line.

Ian rested his half-empty tumbler on his knee, surprised by the offer but seeing it for the thing the congressman had been angling toward since supper. It was good bait, but Ian wasn't ready to bite. He opened his mouth to say so, but Cooper, the skillful fisherman, gave another tug.

"I'd offer you a sizable tract, fit for farming or grazing, at *half* the price of the land around Cooperstown—if you're willing to claim the acreage near one of the villages I'm establishing in Herkimer County, in the Adirondack foothills. There would be opportunity to ply your cabinetmaking craft as well."

Ian's heart leapt at the offer, despite the barrier of unknowns preventing his grasping it. He took a breath, let it out in a long exhale.

"What say you?" Cooper prompted, certain he had set the hook.

He nearly had. "I'm intrigued by the offer, sir. And very much tempted to give ye an aye this minute. But there are matters in Boston which require my attention before I decide where I mean to settle." He would make no rash decisions. Not this time. "I'm a father, ye see."

If the man was disappointed, he concealed it. "Being a father several times over myself, I understand. I didn't immediately remove my own family to the frontier, though they're settled now in Cooperstown. Does a wife await you in Boston?"

The answer to that was more complicated than Ian could possibly explain. "My wife died back in Carolina, birthing our son, whom I buried with her."

Cooper heaved himself to his feet and reached for the decanter. "You've my sincerest sympathies for your loss, Mr. Cameron. I see now why you've chosen to uproot yourself again."

He refilled his glass. Ian proffered his. "Hold on to it for a moment," Cooper said before Ian could take a swallow. The congressman crossed to a writing table provided for the inn's guests, took up a quill, uncorked an inkpot, and scratched several lines across a half sheet of foolscap.

Ian stood as Cooper held out the page. He took it and skimmed it—poorly written, badly spelled, blazingly clear: *Up to Six hundrud & fortey Ackers of pryme Farmland . . . a Town Lot in which to set up a Joyner's Shoppe . . . exact Locayshun and Terms of Payement to be determun'd . . .*

"'Upon the down payment of a shilling,'" Ian finished reading aloud, raising his stunned gaze to Cooper. "D'ye mean that, sir?"

"Heartily I do," Cooper said.

Ian read it again, noting the offer was dated but unsigned.

"The innkeeper may witness our signatures, ere we retire," Cooper said.

Ian was momentarily lost for how to refuse such generosity—or whether he should. In that brief space John Reynold's words came to him. *God will make the way for you, Ian. He's gone before you, preparing that path. Be ready to be surprised by His goodness.*

"I'm mindful my small service to ye today is in no wise equal to its reward, and I wish I could give ye an answer now. I simply cannot." He made, reluctantly, to return the agreement, but Cooper raised a hand.

"I'll sign it, regardless. Keep it in your possession to remind you your options for a future aren't limited to Boston. If ever the time is right, come to Cooperstown. Present the note to me at the Manor House—or to my agent, Kent, should I be attending Congress. The offer stands—for as long as I have land to sell. Now, let us drink to it."

They raised their glasses, Ian with a heart pierced by wonder, the sense of possibilities opening wide. Yet doubt remained to worry at its edges. If New York was the path prepared for him, how would Seona and Gabriel figure into it?

7

BOSTON
July 1796

Catriona and Morgan Shelby, cozy as two peas, sat on a bench outside a bookseller's shop—*not* her daddy's. A book lay open on Catriona's lap. Mr. Shelby put a finger on the page, leaned in, said something that brought forth laughter. From behind the fruit vendor's stall, where she had stopped to purchase peaches for Miss Margaret, Seona stared, disbelieving her eyes.

Twice since the evening Ned joined the family at table, accompanied by Mr. Shelby, Seona had asked Ian's sister whether the man was still in Boston. Twice Catriona said she hadn't the faintest idea.

The pair had carried on a lively conversation with the elder Camerons through that supper. Seona had eaten in silence, aware of small feet thumping abovestairs, where Lily supped in peace, watching Gabriel. Ned's strain had been evident. Seona doubted his presence at table, or his acknowledgment of what everyone knew, had changed anything. Penny had fled her grief, her home, her husband. Ned was still miserable. Soon as manners allowed, Seona had retreated to the scullery before going up to put Gabriel to bed.

Ned caught her as she started up the stairs.

"Bide a moment, Seona?" Poised on the landing midway, she looked down at Ian's brother, looking up at her, hands clenched at his sides as he nodded toward the dining room, where the others' voices could be heard. "It was ye, I take it, brought this about? Ye went to my house today?"

His bitter tone made her flinch. He clearly knew nothing of Catriona and Mr. Shelby's scheming. Maybe she should have given them away, but just then all she saw was an unhappy white man, accusing her. All she felt was unreasoning fear.

"Mama and I were worried. We're all worried."

"Penny will be back." A wall candle's flickering light caught what his eyes couldn't hide. Doubt. Despair.

"Will she?"

Ned's eyes narrowed. "I didn't drive her away. Not like Ian did ye."

The mention of Ian caught her off guard. *Drive* her away? She swallowed and said, "I won't speak of Ian. Not if all you mean to do is run him down."

Ned came closer. The toe of his shoe bumped the bottom step, making her jump. "Tell me at least if ye've word from him. Da wrote him months ago. Does he not even care about his son?"

"He cares," Seona said in reflex, like warding off a raised hand. "And no, I haven't. Now . . . I'll bid you good night."

Morgan Shelby called to Ned. He answered, saying no more to her, but she felt his gaze as she ascended the stairs.

Later, with Gabriel asleep and her mama gone down to help put the kitchen to bed, she extinguished her candle and, in her shift, sat by the open window of their upstairs room enjoying the cooling twilight. Fear had leached away, leaving her to realize it was grief—mostly—that had prompted Ned's bitter words. *Does he not even care about his son?*

Though Ian's brother was the last person she would admit it to, of late that very question had nudged its way into her thoughts. There might be any number of reasons why they hadn't heard from Ian. Letters got delayed. Went astray. *God forbid something's happened to prevent his writing at all . . .*

Sounds of Ned and Mr. Shelby leaving the house by the back garden, talking low, broke that train of thought. Her window overlooked the alley between the houses, so she caught some of their conversation when their voices rose.

"Supping together is one thing, but I'll not trust ye again."

"Come, Ned. If you would only see reason . . ."

Seona shook her head, thinking it was Morgan Shelby's turn to fall under the lash of Ned's tongue, for meddling in his affairs, but though their voices had sunk, she caught a few more of Ned's words that made her think they spoke not of Penny, but something else—*overpromised . . . under-delivered . . . the cost . . .*

"You've not told him yet?" Mr. Shelby cut in, relief sharp in his voice.

"Ye wouldn't have sat at his table tonight had I done so! But I must."

"All right, Ned. Just grant me a little more time . . ."

They had moved off, their footsteps on the crushed-shell path drowning their talk. That was the last Seona had seen or heard of Morgan Shelby until now, out buying the peaches Miss Margaret had forgotten to mention to Catriona when she sent her daughter out to the butcher's. An errand that had flown from Catriona's mind?

Seona debated what to do. Step from behind the stall, march up to Ian's sister, tell her she was needed at home? Pretend she'd seen nothing?

Before she could make up her mind, Morgan Shelby stood, reaching for the book, offering Catriona his other hand. She took it to rise, then let him tuck hers under his arm. Seona's heart thumped, thinking she was about to be spied, but the pair strolled the other way.

Tempted to trail them, Seona forced herself to purchase the peaches, then made a beeline for the house on Beachum Lane.

Pink-cheeked and glowing, Catriona swept into her room, spied Seona seated on the bench at the bed's foot, and whipped a book—the one she had been reading with Morgan Shelby—behind her back. "Seona! Have you been waiting on me?"

Seona gripped a handful of petticoat, bracing herself. "I have."

Catriona crossed to the dressing table and slid the book beneath a crumpled fichu, then sat to unpin her hat. "I said I'd be visiting some while."

"The butcher, you mean?"

"What?" Catriona frowned at her reflection. "Oh . . . right. Mam sent me to pick up a leg of lamb. I didn't forget. Silly me, I wasn't visiting today. I'm just distracted."

Brushing at the wrinkles in her petticoat, Seona stood. "I know. I saw you. Outside that bookseller's shop."

Beneath her hat's wide brim, Catriona's expression was guarded. Several replies slid across her eyes as she removed the hat before she said, "Seona, I . . . I wasn't entirely truthful with you."

"Today, you mean? Or those other times you said you hadn't seen Mr. Shelby?"

Catriona lunged off her seat and shut the room's door, then swung to face Seona. "I never said I hadn't *seen* Mr. Shelby. I said I didn't know whether he'd returned to New York. He doesn't inform me of all his doings, so it was true . . . when you asked."

Ignoring this skating on the knife-edge of honesty, Seona asked, "This isn't the first you've met?"

Catriona crossed to the bench, gripped Seona's hand, and urged her to sit again. "I'll tell you, but you *must* keep it between us. Today was the third time. But he's not courting me," she added when Seona frowned. "We're *friends*."

"Friends who meet in secret with no . . ." The word she wanted escaped her. "With no one looking on?"

"No chaperone?" Catriona released her hand to gesture toward the window. "Only the entire North End—including you, apparently. Don't make more of this than is needful."

"I don't know what's needful, but you ought to tell Miss Margaret about it. Or your daddy."

"It's not that simple." Catriona rose to pace the room, reminding Seona piercingly of Ian, who did the same when agitated. "Ned and Mr. Shelby had a falling-out. Over business—paper, marbling ink, something. Ned got impatient with a delay in the supply and cut ties with Mr. Shelby. Won't even *speak* to him now. Mr. Shelby has put considerable capital into expanding his family's business into Boston. Ned and Da aren't the only ones at risk."

The impassioned concern for the man troubled Seona, but at least the half-heard argument below her window weeks ago made sense now.

"Mr. Shelby's father worked hard after the war to build their family's fortune," Catriona was saying. "Now he's ill. Mr. Shelby says this sort of disruption will prove injurious to the business and, he fears, to his father's fragile health. If only Ned could have shown a bit of grace. But then you know about that, don't you?"

"What do you mean?" Seona asked.

"I heard my brother, that night he came to supper—pressing you about Ian." Tears gathered in Catriona's eyes. "He gets a notion in his stubborn head and won't let it go. Not his resentment of Ian. Not this situation with Mr. Shelby. Even Penny! He probably did drive her away, whatever he says!"

She clapped a hand over her mouth as a sob burst forth.

This is grief talking. And no wonder. Her nephews' deaths. Ned's distancing. Penny's abandonment. Seona knew how grief could pile on grief and muddle a mind. Or a heart. She stood, snatched a handkerchief from the dressing table, and drew Ian's sister back to the bench.

Catriona wiped her nose, sniffling. "Oh, Seona, why must things change? I miss Ian and Penny, the *boys*. Even stubborn Ned. And Mr. Shelby has been so . . ."

"So what?" Seona asked warily.

"Attentive," Catriona admitted. "He's charming—and so well-read. He seems to find me of interest."

"You are. But the man needs to have a talk with Mister Robert if he wants to spend his charm on you. Doesn't he?" While still uncertain of the social rules among these northern folk, Seona knew she had hit this nail square when Catriona colored pink.

"I doubt I'll see him again," she said as her gaze slid away. "Not if Ned's pigheadedness runs true to form."

Ned's pigheadedness did run true to form. So did Catriona's, but nearly a fortnight passed before Seona had an inkling of what had, despite her cautioning, been going on. The truth came to light on a day when a summer rain set in after Ian's sister left the house. Seona had meant to accompany her on an errand and a call on a friend until she saw Lily had more bespoke work than was manageable. She stayed to help with the sewing.

The upstairs room was stuffy and warm. Rain plinked against the window glass, dimming the light. They lit a beeswax candle apiece to better see their stitches, still a luxury Seona appreciated. Around midday Margaret Cameron came upstairs, asking if Seona knew where Catriona had meant to go besides running her errand to a confectioner's shop.

"She meant to call on a friend," Seona said, schooling her face not to show the suspicion that leapt instantly to mind.

Miss Margaret glanced at the rain-streaked window. "Which friend?"

Lily looked up from her work. Gabriel ceased his play with a set of painted blocks strewn across the rug and grinned at his grandmother in the doorway.

"She didn't say," Seona replied. "Likely she's waiting on the rain to let up."

Miss Margaret left them to their work. The plinking of rain filled the room again. After a bit Lily asked, "Have ye a better guess where Catriona's at than ye let on?"

Gabriel abandoned his blocks to grip Seona's skirt, whining like he used to when he wanted feeding. At just turned two, he had no more need of it but sometimes still suckled for comfort. Seona unpinned her bodice, settled her son warm and heavy in her lap, then looked across the room at her mama seated at the window, a half-embroidered petticoat draping her lap. "She may not be with a friend. A girlfriend, I mean."

"Morgan Shelby?"

It was easy to forget how much her mama noticed. "I hope not." She recounted the conversation overheard the night Ned and Mr.

Shelby came to dinner and what Catriona told her since, about the business trouble.

Gabriel had fallen asleep in her arms. She laid him in his little bed. Repinning her bodice, she murmured, "I always wonder was it the last time he'll want that."

She turned to see Lily's gaze softened. "Ye grew up fast, girl-baby. So will he."

"Too fast." Seona looked at her sleeping boy, limbs sprawled, pale curls falling over his brow. She longed to see the boy he would make—and the man—even as she pined for the infant she once cradled in her arms. She studied his face, adoring every soft curve of bone and flesh. Hers. Ian's.

Would she *never* hear word from the man?

The rain was letting up, the light growing brighter. They blew out the candles, thrifty by habit, and smiled at each other for doing it.

"You give any thought to the three of us finding a place?" Lily asked.

Before Seona could answer, they heard Catriona enter the house. "Watch him for a spell?" she asked with a glance at Gabriel. "I'll come back and help. But first . . ."

Lily nodded. "Aye. Go on."

It was worse than she had feared.

"Seona, I told you—I'm merely attempting to mend things between him and Ned," Catriona protested in a half whisper when Seona found her in the scullery, scrubbing carrots for a stew, and asked straight-out if she had sheltered somewhere with Mr. Shelby during the rain. "He tried again yesterday. Ned refused to see him."

Seona kept her voice low, aware of Miss Margaret clanging pots in the kitchen, just through the pantry. "How many times have *you* seen him?"

"Twice more. Maybe three times."

Maybe nothing. "What is it you do together?"

Catriona's face flamed. "Nothing like what you're thinking."

"What am I thinking?"

"That I fancy myself in love with Morgan Shelby." Catriona set the carrots on a board and reached for a drying cloth. "That I've done something I . . . oughtn't to have done."

"Have you?"

"*Keep your voice down.* And you're one to ask with the evidence of what *you* did napping right upstairs."

Blood stung Seona's cheeks. She opened her mouth but found nothing to say to the accusation. The scullery was stone-floored, windowless, but the yard door stood open, emitting a watery light. By it Seona watched Catriona's face drain of its blush.

"Aside from my brother," she went on, voice shaking, "what experience have you of men to make you so suspicious of Mr. Shelby?"

Like a collie fetching in stray sheep, Catriona's question gathered in the vague suspicions Seona had harbored about Morgan Shelby and produced an answer: *Gideon Pryce.*

"He reminds me of a man I knew in Carolina, who took what he wanted from whomever he willed—tried to take it from me." Seona turned heel and left the scullery, heading for her *evidence*, asleep in his cradle bed.

Never had Catriona thrown in her face what happened between her and Ian at Mountain Laurel. Never had she condemned.

Lily took one look at her and didn't probe, but after a few moments Seona put aside her stitching and made for the door, unable to leave things so with Catriona.

She wasn't in her room.

Seona stood inside the door, thinking Ian's sister surely had fallen in love with Morgan Shelby. At least infatuation. But was that wrong? Despite the man reminding her of Gideon Pryce, the situation couldn't be as it was between herself and the master of Chesterfield Plantation—a mouse to his stalking cat. Catriona was no man's slave.

She lingered, admiring the table desk Ian had made, using the morning glory designs he'd asked her help with after discovering her secret love of setting down the likeness of things. She minded those days in his shop, the work they had done on this desk and others, before those contrary tides of heart and duty—and the meanness of some—yanked them hither and yon, eventually sweeping them apart.

Nothing had been simple then. Was it simpler now?

Maybe her mama was right. They should break free of the Camerons, no matter they had heard no final word from Ian.

"Seona?"

Startled, Seona turned toward the door to see Ian's sister, tears streaming, rushing at her with arms outstretched.

"I'm sorry!" Catriona threw slender arms around her shoulders, curls pressed to Seona's cheek. "I don't know what came over me to say such horrible things. Please, please, forgive me."

Seona held her, patting her back. "It's all right."

"There's no excuse for what I said," Catriona replied, sniffling. "But thank you." They parted, smiling weakly at each other. Catriona searched her gaze. "Will you tell me what happened with that man you mentioned?"

"Gideon Pryce," Seona said and wished she hadn't. It seemed to conjure the man and the fear he had caused. Still she told how the master of the neighboring plantation had stalked her every chance he got. "Once Ian came, he saw right off what Mr. Pryce wanted. He stood between us and warned him off—calling me his uncle's property."

"*Ian* called you that?"

"It was a thing Mr. Pryce would understand—maybe respect. Later Ian told me if he ever laid a finger on me again, he'd skin Mr. Pryce like he'd do a wolf."

Catriona plunked down on the edge of her bed, brows vaulted high. "That sounds more like my brother." She bit her lip, looking at Seona. "Was this before you and he . . . ?"

Seona touched the morning glory vines carved across the desk's drawer, knowing what was asked though the query hung unfinished. "It was."

Catriona reached for her hand. "Please don't be angry at my asking this. You know I love my brother—but how was Ian different from that horrible Mr. Pryce?"

The wood beneath Seona's fingertips felt as smooth as the day

Ian finished the piece. "I reckon friendship doesn't know anything of slave and free, which is how it started with Ian. He was kind to me. More than kind. He saw me. Not just his uncle's slave, but *me*. After a while . . . I saw him back."

"That's how I feel about—" Catriona broke off as Seona pulled out the desk drawer and, minding well its secret, sprang the latch to the hidden compartment within. Catriona released her hand and stood. "You knew!"

"Ian showed me."

The whole upstairs was warm and stuffy. Back in the scullery, with the door open, the air had been rain-washed, like Seona wished her heart could be. She ought to tell Catriona to let Mr. Shelby alone. To let whatever had soured between him and Ned work itself out.

Before she could open her mouth, Catriona opened the lid of the desk, revealing her painting supplies.

"There's a breeze in the garden," she said as outside the window clouds parted and sunlight broke through. "Let's do some painting, if Lily can spare you."

With her mama keeping an eye on Gabriel while he napped, Seona and Catriona set up their easels at the garden's edge, a table set between to hold their paints and brushes. Catriona favored the flowering borders of Miss Margaret's vegetable garden as a subject, but Seona was drawn to the herb garden, expanded since she and her mama joined the household. Lily missed the fragrant shed off the kitchen at Mountain Laurel where she once prepared her powders, salves, and draughts. Seona thought about her mama's idea of leaving Beachum Lane and wondered if she longed to be mistress of her own domain again. Of more than just an herb shed.

The thought tugged her concentration from the stalks of milk thistle, its purple-pink flowers just past full bloom, that she was capturing on the heavy paper clipped to the slanted easel. Brush suspended over the washpot, she thought about her mama, sixteen when she bore Seona. Aidan Cameron, Seona's father, had died before her birth. They had planned to run away, find a place to be together. Be a family. All those years since, had her mama been longing for a husband, a home?

From the open scullery door, Gabriel burst into the sunshine, done with napping, and raced down the walkway to the gardens, Lily a step behind. Seona plunked her brush into the waterpot in time to scoop him up.

"Have a good nap, baby?" She pressed her face to his damp curls, loving his smell, his solid, wiggling weight.

No more than a few feet away, Catriona glanced over, emerging from her painting trance—one of the few times she was ever disengaged—to notice Gabriel, squirming to get down again. "Where did you come from?"

"Go on with your painting," Lily said. "I'll mind Mister Mischief a bit longer."

"Thank you, Mama." With the chatter of their voices a background, Seona took up her brush and grew absorbed in painting the milk thistle, concentrating on capturing the pointed, white-veined leaves, until an outcry shattered her focus.

"Where did *ye* come from?" Lily's sharp echo of Catriona's question had Seona whirling, searching for her boy.

Gabriel was safe in his granny's arms, the two crouched on the walkway, until he broke free to gallop toward the side of the house.

Seona put down her brush and took half a dozen steps before spotting the man who had entered the back garden from the street. With a cornered hat obscuring his face, he bent to intercept Gabriel, sweeping her boy up with the ease of one who knew his way around small children. At first she thought it was Ned, despite the unfamiliar coat and hat. Then he raised his face and sunlight caught his features, the wheat-gold tail of his hair spilling around his collar.

Seona stopped in her tracks.

"Ian!" Catriona all but sent her easel tumbling in her haste to cross the yard to her brother, who shifted Gabriel to one arm and with the other gathered his sister into an embrace.

"Cat," he said, smiling down at her. "Look at ye . . . all grown up."

"And done with *Cat*," she said, laughing. "It's Catriona now."

"Is it then? And, Lily, it's good to see ye." Ian turned his gaze to Seona's mama, who stood as frozen as Seona.

"Mister Ian," Lily said, voice faint with surprise. "Good to see ye too."

The last word had risen in a question. The same that beat with Seona's blood. How was Ian standing there, when all this while she had pictured him at Mountain Laurel? Far, far away.

Ian. He was holding Gabriel with Catriona beaming at him, and all Seona could do was fight to keep her knees stiff enough to hold her up. Then his gaze fastened on her, and everything shifted.

Feeling like the scattered pieces of her world had snapped back into place, Seona started toward him.

8

By the time they sat to a table extended to accommodate twice the number Margaret Cameron had expected for dinner, Seona knew the pieces of her world, old and new, in truth no longer fit as they had. They never could. Miss Judith was dead. Mountain Laurel was sold to the Reynolds. Ian had returned north to stay.

"To make a new life."

That last he announced to Mister Robert, home to his dinner—careful not to look at Seona as he said it. Still she felt the tension flowing toward her as if he had boldly stared.

With so many gathered, each with something to say, Seona found it easy to hold her thoughts inside. As if she knew what to think about seeing Ian again, hearing that voice so surprisingly deep, the rumble of his laughter.

Her heart raced to look at him, skipped a beat when he caught her at it, only to have her gaze drawn back again. And again.

Over the moon to see others long missed, she let Naomi dandle Gabriel on her knee before dinner. Grinned at Ally grinning back at her. Cried as she hugged Malcolm, whose accent was so like Ian's parents' that, under the joy and shock of it all, it felt like two halves of a family come together after years apart.

The gathering of threads on a loom.

Though Naomi was relieved to be inside the house on Beachum

Lane, every corner of which her curious gaze roved, being waited on by Catriona and Miss Margaret had rendered Mountain Laurel's former cook mute. The ways of these Boston Camerons took some getting used to, like Ian's had done when he first came to them. A lifetime ago, that felt.

Mandy clung to her daddy, shy with so many new faces trying to coax a smile. She was growing into a pretty child, with features maybe more like Ian's but her mama's tea-brown eyes, hair somewhere between Judith's mousy brown and the richer shade Mister Robert and Catriona shared. Ian answered questions about the journey north while persuading Mandy to eat, casting looks across the table at Seona and Gabriel, taken onto her lap to keep his wiggling self still enough to feed.

Ian with his daughter. She with their son. Sundered by a laden table and a tide of voices lapping over them, talking about the land sale, the surprise of it all, how good it was to have Ian home and everyone with him welcome. No one asked the questions cutting deepest across Seona's heart. How had Miss Judith died? What did Ian mean to do about Gabriel? What did he want from her?

Lily leaned close above Gabriel's bobbing head and asked, "All right, girl-baby?"

Seona scarcely knew.

"Reckon this changes things," her mama added under her breath as Ian glanced across the pickle bowl. A look Seona felt to her toes.

Since the lean days of the war, the Camerons had become a family of comfortable means, but they had always been rich in their library. With relief Ian shut the door of his da's study and, among the calfskin spines recalled from his youth, grasped a moment in which to regather mind and heart. Both had frayed when he rounded the house, spotted Seona and Catriona painting at the garden's edge, then was himself spied by his son.

Weeks on the road to brace himself hadn't prepared him for the avalanche of emotion seeing Gabriel again had triggered, nor the sight of Seona coming toward him, green eyes stunned wide, bright in the sunlight breaking through clouds.

What was she experiencing behind that shuttered face—a skill in which his uncle's slaves had been well practiced?

"I should have written," he chastised himself as his da crossed the room. A hand rested warm on his shoulder.

"Aye, ye might have," Robert Cameron agreed without recrimination. "But ye're here now. Meaning to stay, I gather?" Seating himself in the high-backed chair behind his writing table, he motioned Ian to another.

"Not here. This house, I mean." For now he had hired adjoining rooms at the Chestnut Inn and stabling for the horses. "I'd never ask ye to accommodate us all."

"Tight fit or no, ye're welcome. There's always the attic."

Ian thought his da had something else on his mind. No mention had been made of the request to adopt Seona and Gabriel. Ian supposed it the subject his da meant to broach, but when Robert Cameron spoke again, it concerned a different matter.

"When I arrived home to that *kebby-lebby* in the keeping room, everyone talking at ye at once, ye let it be brushed aside without much comment, your news of Judith."

They hadn't known his wife, even secondhand. He hadn't written of her kind heart, her steadfast faith, her boundless patience. "I'd intended to tell ye more of it—of her. Just not then."

His da nodded. "Was it childbirth?"

"Aye. I buried a son with her." Ian fixed his gaze on a painted seascape hung above the mantel and breathed in the room's familiar smells: book leather, his da's pipe tobacco, the stale ashes of the last fire laid, yet to be swept. He had always liked that room. "She wanted him named for me. He lived barely longer than she."

He paused, memory of those final moments with Judith still prone to choke off speech. Sympathy and sorrow softened Robert Cameron's features. "'Tis the hardest thing I've ever kent, watching my sons grieve."

Reminder of his brother's loss weighed. Ned had left the shop and gone his way at the dinner hour, unaware of Ian's return. A message had been sent. Ned hadn't been home to receive it when the neighbor lad who bore it clapped the knocker.

"Have ye decided what ye mean to do, now ye've come back . . . to Boston?"

Had his da been about to say *home,* then thought better of it? Of his siblings, Ian was the rootless one, calling one place, then another *home* but somehow never quite meaning it.

"I've promised Malcolm and his family a place with me for as long as they need. Lifelong, do they wish it. Not just for the sake of what's owed them."

He waited for his da's reaction. It came in an approving nod. "When I pressed ye to go south to Hugh, I confess I did so with one grave misgiving—that the life there would change ye."

Ian forced a smile. "I thought my changing was what ye wanted."

Though he smiled in return, Robert Cameron shook his head. "I meant in a way that would've been regrettable."

Ian knew what was meant: the corruption of soul the practice of slave owning wrought in a man. He had seen it in his uncle. And others. "But I have changed, Da."

"Aye, ye have. But not in the way I'd feared. I'd thought perhaps it was only Seona and Gabriel—and Lily—ye desired freed when first they came to us. Now I see that's no' the way of it."

"Aye, Malcolm and his family are free now. I'll hold no soul in bondage again. Even so, I might have become like Uncle Hugh in the end, if not for Malcolm. Between him and John Reynold, my neighbor, I'd slim chance of escaping without my knee, and heart, bowed to the Almighty at last."

"One day I suspect ye'll ken how glad I am to hear that." His da cleared his throat, studying him. "Did ye come awa' a farmer as well?"

William Cooper had asked a similar question. Ian wondered should he tell his father of the congressman's offer. He drew breath to do so—then shut his lips on the words, feeling it too soon. "I liked it well enough but mean to take my time deciding my course."

"Ye've settled meantime at the Chestnut? That'll prove no small expense, depending on how long ye stay. I ken ye sold my brother's land—your land—but will ye no' be needing those funds to resettle—if ye were paid in a form that might be used to buy land or shop?"

They were come to a subject needful of address. Robert Cameron could be trusted to keep a confidence, even from his mam, should Ian ask it. He did so.

His da's countenance altered through stages of surprise as Ian spoke of the gold discovered on John's land, the payments forthcoming which could, in Boston, be exchanged for coin.

"I may set up for cabinetmaking again. But not here. Or Cambridge."

"No," Robert Cameron agreed, memory of Ian's unfortunate history with that guild no more than a shifting in his eyes. "But not too far afield?"

"A day's ride at most. I don't wish to be separated from Gabriel again, if I can help it."

His da leaned back in his chair, bottom lip caught between teeth still strong and straight. "Which answers my next question."

"Da." Ian shifted forward. "I cannot let another man raise my son. Not even—"

He had meant to add *ye*, but a knock, heavy and insistent, had him straightening and turning toward the door.

The knock proved preemptory. The door pushed open and Ian's brother came uninvited into the room. As tall as Ian, but thicker through the chest now than their father, Ned Cameron stood unmoving for a heartbeat, then shut the door on the hum of voices from the crowded house.

Their father stood. So did Ian. Ned refused to meet his gaze.

"Ned," Robert Cameron said. "We'd hoped ye'd join us sooner. I sent a lad round to the house to fetch ye."

"I dined at the Red Lion, then found the shop deserted. Catriona fetched me. So here I am—and here I find *you*," Ned added, acknowledging Ian at last. "What are ye doing back in Boston?"

Mister Robert's study door wasn't thick enough to drown Ned's words. Not for someone hovering on the stairs a few steps away.

Soon as dinner was done, Seona had left Gabriel in Lily's keeping and vanished into the scullery. By the time she emerged, Ian had gone to ground with his daddy in the study. Hearing the little ones upstairs playing, knowing her mama would be with them, she had left Naomi, Malcolm, and Ally with Miss Margaret and planted herself on the stairs, hoping everyone would stay put for a bit. She wanted to know what Ian and his daddy were saying behind that door.

The talk proved too hushed to catch, until Ned arrived. Seona shrank into the landing's shadow as he barged into the study, shutting the door again.

"What are ye doing back in Boston? Did ye abandon your wife to come chasing after Seona?"

Every word out of Ned's mouth came clear, but she had to strain to hear Ian's reply: "I've abandoned no one, Ned."

"Ye've dragged Judith along with ye?" Ned's voice held no restraint. "What does she think of ye pursuing your bastard's mother eight hundred miles north?"

Mister Robert intervened. "Ned! I'll no' be having that language in my home. And ye dinna ken anything about it."

"I know enough, Da. Seona was Uncle Hugh's slave. She'd no choice in what happened—I don't care what she says now. My brother does as he wills, gets her with child, then banishes the inconvenient pair as if they were *nothing*. Ye'll not suffer a misspoken word from me, but ye'll have *him* under your roof?"

"Gabriel is everything to me," Ian retorted. "He's my *son*."

"Da's been more of a father to Gabriel than ye ever were! For that matter, so have I. At least he kens who I am."

"Hold your *wheesht*, Ned," Mister Robert said. "Ian didna abandon his wife or drag her across the country. He buried her."

"He . . . what?"

"Judith is dead." Ian's words were so muffled Seona caught only a few that followed. ". . . the hour our son . . . months ago . . ."

"So ye've another son?"

"He's called Ian. He's with his mother. As is our wee daughter."

"I thought your daughter lived?"

"Mandy, aye. Not our second-born, Elizabeth. So believe me when I say I *do* understand the grief—"

"Ye don't!" Ned interrupted. "Ye didn't ken those bairns ye buried. Not like I knew Robbie . . . Eddie—" Ned's voice caught on his sons' names. A second later the study door flew open. Ned passed the foot of the stairs, clapping on his hat, making for the door to the street, features racked with bitterness and pain. He didn't see Seona, perched on the landing.

Ned was through the door and gone, shutting it ungently behind him, before anyone in the study spoke again.

"Ian. There's no excuse for what your brother said . . ."

"He's grieving," came Ian's heavy reply. "I know that."

Seona didn't move a muscle on the stair where she sat, hand over her mouth. A fist around her heart. Ned wasn't the only one grieving. Two babies dead. *Ian. Elizabeth.*

"There's more." Mister Robert explained about the business doings with Morgan Shelby that had soured, for which Ned blamed himself. "And if that wasn't enough, Penny's gone awa' to Deerfield."

"Gone? Is she coming back?"

"We dinna ken. Ned only comes to the shop because I've agreed to stop asking."

Seona missed what Ian said to that, then heard his weighty sigh and knew he must be near the door now. "All right, Da. But I think for now I'll shift my tribe back over to the Chestnut. We all need rest."

Ian had barely finished speaking before he emerged from the study, making for the stairs. Seona shot to her feet as he mounted the first step. He looked up, features catching light from the landing window.

Had his eyes always been so blue? Like a jaybird's wing, she recalled thinking them. Or a smoky autumn sky.

"Seona." It was the first he had said her name since appearing in the back garden. "How long have ye . . . ?"

"Long enough," she said, turning to mount the stairs.

He reached the landing fast. "What did Ned mean—*I don't care what she says now*? Those were his words. What did ye tell him about . . . us?"

Seona shook her head as if she didn't understand the question. A peal of giggles from above saved her answering.

Ian stepped back, gazing at her with eyes bruised by grief and weariness. "Sounds like they're in my old room, the bairns."

"It's our room now. Mine and Mama's. Gabriel's."

She headed for it. His nearness on the stairs had set her trembling. She was relieved to find Lily and Catriona with the children, for one thing was clear enough. She wasn't ready to be alone with Gabriel's daddy or to answer his questions, whatever they might be.

Which meant her own must wait.

9

August 1796

Ian was gone on his red roan, Ally with him. "Spying out the land, he said," Catriona told Seona as they headed for the Chestnut Inn. "Looking for a place to set up shop."

The knot in Seona's belly, lodged there since Ian's appearance in the garden five days ago, unraveled at the news. She wouldn't be seeing him again in the time it took to cross Boston's North End. A brief reprieve.

Looking for a place to set up shop. One like he had at Mountain Laurel? Ian hadn't shared his plans with her—not that he'd had a chance to do so. She had made sure of that, keeping company with Catriona, her mama, or Naomi and Miss Margaret whenever Ian was at the house.

There would be no adoption. She had known it that moment in the back garden when Ian scooped up their son, by the joy and relief that seized his features. It was, she realized as they reached the inn, a weight off her mind.

Others had taken its place.

They had come to bring Malcolm and Naomi to the house before the day got too hot. Already the city's smells lay thick on the muggy air—roasting coffee and rotting fish uppermost—while along the wharves the rising sun poked rays through the masts of moored ships like it had done through the woods of Mountain Laurel. Overhead, gulls floated white against a pink-and-peach sky, their cries high and plaintive.

They found Malcolm at the inn's stable, sitting near the box occupied by Juturna, with whom Catriona had fallen in love at first sight. Ian's filly put her brown nose over the slats to greet his sister, who cooed, "There's my beautiful girl."

"Morning, Malcolm," Seona said as the old man rose with the help of his cane. "Ready to head over to the house?"

"Naomi's sorting through some quiltin' pieces she means to take along."

"I'll see if she and Mandy need help," Catriona said but continued stroking Juturna's nose as if unable to pull away.

Malcolm smiled. "Has Mister Ian told ye this filly was born just after he and Thomas came to Mountain Laurel?"

"He didn't," Catriona said.

Thomas Ross had lived with the Boston Camerons until he was apprenticed to a cooper, though he had still called their house his home and visited often, Seona had been told. But none of them had seen Thomas even once since he hightailed it south to chase down Ian, headed to Mountain Laurel, four years back. Thomas had gone to Mountain Laurel pretending to be a slave for the purpose of leading true slaves to freedom, if he could. Seona hoped he had.

"I suppose you've had no word of Thomas?" she asked.

"No' since he ran off wi' the field hands."

The same day Hugh Cameron, Seona's grandfather, met his end as the big house burned around him.

"I'll let Naomi know we're here," Catriona finally said.

Seona watched her cross the stable-yard, then turned to find Malcolm watching her. Bereft of Catriona's attentions, Juturna thrust her nose between them. Seona obliged the horse with petting.

"You mind me, sweet girl?" She glanced at Malcolm. "He break her to the saddle on the way?"

"Aye. He did." No need to ask who she meant. "Didna tell anyone about our coming, did he?"

Seona found it easier to look into the long-lashed eye of Ian's horse than into Malcolm's. "Not even his daddy."

Silence. The smell of horseflesh and stalls in need of mucking. The sounds of stamps and whickers. The voices of stable lads.

"'Twas much prayed over," Malcolm said.

Comfort poured through the cracks around her heart. "What all did you pray over?"

"Everyone we journeyed toward. Everyone left behind."

"Esther," she said, picking just one of many faces missed. "You ever see her after we left?"

"She came along to Miss Judith's burying. She's gettin' taller, our Esther."

Did Lucinda Cameron have Esther serving as a house girl? Likely, if she had brought her along to serve. That was too close to Gideon Pryce for comfort. Especially Esther's.

Seona blinked away tears. "I'm so glad you're here. And free."

It struck her afresh that it was Judith's death had set him free. She wanted to ask if Ian had loved Judith but was of two minds about the answer. It wasn't as if she wanted to step right into Judith's place like she never existed.

The place she took from me.

Seona clicked her tongue at such a thought. Judith Bell had never taken anything from anyone in her life. She was offered a gift unlooked for and knew no reason to refuse it. What followed had been her fault least of all.

If only it hadn't been offered.

"I'm still praying," Malcolm said as voices drew near across the yard.

Wiping hastily at her eyes, Seona turned to greet Catriona, with Mandy in her arms, and Naomi, who had the quilt she had started on the journey bundled around its pieces. She, Miss Margaret, and Lily meant to stitch on it that morning. Atop that were balanced two jars of apple butter brought from Mountain Laurel's kitchen.

"Aiming to give these to Miss Margaret. Best get on through this rabbit warren though." Naomi nodded toward the street, noisy with the shouts of children and the honking, lowing, and squealing of stock being driven to market or to graze the Common. "Good you come fetch us. I'd still never find my way."

The bells of one of Boston's churches tolled, announcing the opening of markets. Seona grinned at Naomi, whose hands were too full to clap over her ears as she did the first few times she heard the city's pealing bells.

"You'll learn, by and by," she said, wondering if Naomi and the others would stay long enough for that.

Catriona had gravitated to Juturna, letting Mandy pat her soft muzzle. "I could stay right here until Ian gets back. Do you think he'd let me ride her?"

"He done made you that desk Seona and Lily brought north, Miss Catriona," Naomi said. "Reckon he'd let you ride that horse, did you ask."

Seona offered Malcolm her arm. He was frailer than she minded, more stooped, but he looked about them keen-eyed at the sights, wrinkling his nose at the smells. For folk accustomed to fields and fresh air, Boston took some acclimating. It still felt odd, being walled off by homes and shops and harbors lined with ships, caught in a tide of bodies—white, black, red, and every shade between.

Seona had heard a saying since coming to Boston. *Fish out of water.* That was what they were, she and her mama. Naomi, Malcolm, and Ally, too.

Did Ian feel it?

With the November presidential election months away, the town of Braintree, home of Vice President John Adams, hummed with talk of government more insistently than the heavy air buzzed with cicada call. Since President Washington had declined to serve a third term, party politics was figuring strong in the campaign, with the Federalist Adams standing against Thomas Jefferson, the Democratic-Republican from Virginia.

"Folk sure worked up about it all, but I can't tell if they happy or riled," Ally said as they left a baker's shop with the bread they meant to put with a cheese and some apples for their dinner, to eat while they made the twelve-mile journey back to Boston. Hopefully before the cloud bank building to the west dropped its promised rain along the coastline.

"Some are one, some the other," Ian said as he secured the provisions in a saddlebag, tossing Ally an apple. He felt removed from the proceedings practically, if not in interest; he wasn't a landowner, thus could have no vote in Massachusetts.

Perhaps that was soon to change.

Ally unhitched Cupid, his favorite of the sturdy half-draft bays that had pulled the wagon north, which they had saddled for him to ride along with Ian in what was proving a tedious search for a shop suitable for cabinetmaking, situated within twenty miles of Boston. Having found a prospect in Braintree, currently a tailor's shop, Ian had spent hours with the elderly proprietor, touring the structure and talking, inescapably, of politics.

"Safe to say most here support their local son, Adams," Ian added. "But not all do." Not the tailor, a staunch Republican in favor of that party's stand on less federal interference with state's rights.

With a glance at Ally's blank expression, Ian wondered should he use the ride back to Boston to explain the concept of political parties. Thoughts of Gabriel and Seona and what he ought to do for them—and the rest—proved too consuming as he unhitched Ruaidh and mounted.

Was there a single decision that might do right by everyone? How could he come to it if he didn't know Seona's mind? How could *she* know what she wanted when he hadn't been back in Boston a week, most of that time spent roaming nearby townships to see what prospects they offered?

The Braintree property would take little effort to convert into a cabinetmaking shop. The payments the owner was willing to accept would allow Ian to invest in lathes, benches, tools, and supplies he no longer possessed. Braintree was near enough to Boston he could visit Gabriel often. There were rooms above the shop for him and Mandy, a cottage in back where Malcolm, Ally, and Naomi could be comfortable. Ally could find work. Naomi could look after Mandy and, if she wished, take in washing, sewing, extra baking. Malcolm could tend a garden in the yard.

Ally was silent as they reached Braintree's outskirts. A cart rattled by on the road. Once it passed, he said, "I thought Gen'ral Washington be president 'til he died. Like kings do."

"We fought a war to be free of kings. Now we're doing things different. A man doesn't have to go on being president if he doesn't wish it, once his term's expired."

"Doing things different," Ally mused.

Another silence lengthened as they rode. Ally finished his apple. Riders and wagons and one fine carriage passed them by. Thunderclouds built high. The air hung heavy, salted with the pervading smell of the sea.

Ian was starting to doubt they would make Boston before the storm broke when Ally asked, "Like *we* doing things different now?"

"Aye. Ye're no more a slave, for one."

"Well then. What I supposed to be? What I meant to be doing?"

Ian glanced sidelong at the big man, floppy hat pushed high on his gleaming forehead. "What d'ye want to do?"

Ally's brows soared. "Reckon I'll go on taking care of the horses. Maybe sweep that shop, iffen you take it?"

"Or ye could learn a bit of cabinetmaking."

Ally scratched his nose. "I ain't too handy with hammer and nails, Mister Ian. And them bitty wooden joints you make?" He raised one broad, thick-fingered hand. "I don't know."

"Can ye think of anything else ye'd like to do?"

"Guess we won't be planting nothing, 'cept my granddaddy growing a garden. He don't need my help with that past driving stakes or putting up a fence." Ally shook his head. "Aside from working a field, all I know is tending critters."

"Maybe ye could find a paying job in town to suit ye," Ian suggested. "Inns have stables . . ."

The next pause lasted nigh a mile before Ally asked, "Mister Ian, what do *you* want to do?"

"About that shop?" He didn't know. He felt no strong leading for or against a shop. Of one thing alone he was certain: he wanted to raise his children together but shied from the full picture that notion sought to birth—one that tightened his chest with a sense of longing and guilt too tangled to sort.

He guided Ruaidh to the verge, letting a massive, blue-painted Conestoga pass with a clanking and creaking and the shouted encouragement of its mounted driver. Ian looked back as it rattled on. From the rear of its canvas awning a girl and boy looked back at him through the dust in its wake.

The sight made Ian think of his bairns together, but he didn't picture them playing in the streets of Boston. Or Braintree. He saw them in the woods and fields of an untamed land.

He slowed the roan, letting Ally draw abreast. "What do ye think I should do?"

Ally chewed his lip, pondering the question. "I'd say . . . marry up with Seona so them babies got a mama *and* a daddy. That seem good."

Ian changed the subject. "Who was your daddy, Ally? If ye don't mind my asking."

"Him? He was off some other farm. Mama say he was big in the bones, like me. Best I mind, he got sold away when I was a baby. Mama would know."

Ian felt ashamed he had never thought to ask, sorry for the man who never knew his son, whom Ian had come to value in ways having nothing to do with the buying and selling of human beings.

"Reckon you'll do right in the end, Mister Ian," Ally added with a confidence Ian wished he shared.

"I'm praying on it. And about that shop we saw. About everything."

"About that man with the dead horse?"

"Man with a . . . ? Judge Cooper, ye mean?"

The mention was startling, coming on the heels of his thoughts of untamed land. Frontier New York land, he supposed it had been, tucked into the back of his mind all the while. William Cooper and his offer hadn't figured into Ian's prayers since. Yet carving out a place for Gabriel and Mandy, a home with no memories of slavery or grief attached—a fresh start in every way—held an appeal suddenly greater than when the offer was made.

Seona wasn't ready to have her life uprooted again. But waiting in limbo while his funds drained away wasn't an option either. What if he went west now, got himself established? Would Seona, given time, agree to follow? Could he endure another separation from Gabriel, even with that goal in mind?

From the west thunder rumbled. He turned to eye Ally, riding beside him.

"What made ye think of Cooper? All this talk of politics? Or the rain about to catch us again on the road?"

Ally glanced toward the darkly piling clouds. "Neither, Mister Ian."

"What then?"

"I minded how you looked when you first told us about the land that man offered you."

Ian breathed a laugh. "How did I look?"

Ally's gaze flicked over his face. "Like a light was shining inside you, bright behind your eyes. Ain't no light shining, Mister Ian, when you talk about a shop."

10

They almost beat the rain. After a mile of racing sprinkles, a downpour overtook them at the Neck, the narrow spit of land linking Boston to the mainland. While Ally stabled the horses at the Chestnut, Ian dodged rain showers through the North End. Even in such weather, Boston felt bursting at the seams with humanity. As a boy he hadn't minded the press and bustle, but now he missed the sight of open fields, of wooded hillsides threaded with the trails of deer and bear.

Pausing to shake off his oiled cape on the threshold, he called first at his da's shop and learned a parcel had arrived for him, marked from North Carolina. "Catriona stopped in before the rain and mentioned it," Robert Cameron said, wiping his hands on a piece of sacking as he met Ian at the counter.

Surprised John had already sent payment, he asked, "How much do I owe ye?"

His da waved away the postage. "How fared ye in Braintree?"

Ian described the shop, which his da said sounded the perfect fit. "It does," Ian agreed. "Yet I don't know that it is."

"What's *perfect* to do with it?" Ned asked, emerging from the back. "Who of us can be so choosy?"

Ian had spoken to his brother since Ned stormed from the house the day of his arrival—as no doubt had their da—but the tension between them had yet to pass. He kept his calm and said, "I've more futures to consider than mine and Mandy's."

Ned's face darkened. "D'ye mean to drag Seona along to wherever ye strike out for next? Or does she get a choice this time?"

"Your brother means to do right by Seona and Gabriel," Robert Cameron told his eldest. "And by your uncle's former slaves. Why should—?"

The bell jangled as a half-drenched customer entered. Outside, the rain was abating. Ian put a hand to his da's arm. "I'll go. See ye at supper."

With a dismissive scowl, Ned went back to whatever work he had left. Ian turned to go, nodding to the customer who had entered, but his da stopped him, saying softly, "Ned had a letter today too. From Penny. I dinna ken what it says."

Clearly nothing to comfort his brother's heart.

The parcel from John Reynold lay on the table in the keeping room, in a patch of feeble window light. Seona had contrived one reason and another to pause and ponder it since Catriona put it there for when Ian returned from his rambles.

John and Cecily Reynold's firstborn was the only baby she had ever midwifed without her mama by. She and Ian had found Cecily in her cabin, too far along in childbed to run for Lily. Ian had stayed to help, letting Seona boss him with nary a complaint, never balking at a task however menial or discomfiting. That was the day she knew she felt something different for him than she had for any other man. Something terrifyingly deep.

"There you are," Catriona said behind her. "Thinking about North Carolina? The Reynolds? Or my brother?"

Breaking off her thoughts quick as snapping beans, Seona put her back to the parcel. "All three, I reckon."

"At least Ian's in there somewhere." Catriona took her by both hands, fixing her with a smile that glowed in the keeping room's gloom. Catriona was looking smart. Her gown was high-waisted, its amber sash a compliment to the red-brown curls arranged in bunches on either side of her head.

"No man's perfect, you know. I hope you can forgive Ian his trespasses and love him again. How I'd joy in calling you my sister in truth. Who knows? We could have a double wedding!"

Seona's mouth fell open. "It's not about forgiving," she managed. "Ian's not ready to be thinking of marrying again. And what do you mean by—?"

She had meant to say *double wedding*, but Catriona dropped her hands, trying to look sober and failing. "Oh, he's thinking about it—or wants to be. I see how he looks at you."

"He just buried his *wife*."

"But not his heart. And he loved *you* first. Don't you still love him?"

"Stop this talk," Seona all but hissed. Miss Margaret and Naomi were in the kitchen swapping recipes. Malcolm was likely within earshot.

Catriona's tone turned pleading. "Don't you see? You and Gabriel, Ian and Mandy, you make a family. Or you could. One might argue *should*."

"Catriona . . ."

"It's meant to *be*, Seona. Why can't anyone but me see that?" Catriona tried to say more but burst into tears.

Abovestairs so did Gabriel. Seconds later Mandy's wail rose in harmony. Seona felt their pull but hesitated, troubled by Catriona's odd swing of mood. "What's got you so upset?"

Catriona brushed away her tears. "Nothing. I'm tired. I think I'll lie down until supper."

"You're sure?"

At another screech from abovestairs, Catriona winced. "You best go."

She found the children on the rug, gowned in their loose frocks with bare legs splayed, painted blocks spilled around them. Gabriel was red-faced and angry. Mandy bereft. Both little mouths were wide, going full bore. Lily crouched before them, holding a block. The red one, Gabriel's favorite.

"Mama? What did he do?"

"They were playing nice," Lily said, clearly bewildered. "I was getting a bit of sewing done. Then Mandy snatched up the red block right as Gabriel reached for it. I thought he'd raise a fuss, so I took it from her. That's when his screeching started. *Here*, baby."

Lily gave the block to her crying grandson. Tears still tracking his cheeks, Gabriel thrust it at Mandy, who ceased her crying and took it. Peace was restored. Both women stared.

"He *wanted* her to have it," Seona said, stating the obvious.

"But he's jealous of that block," Lily said.

"To say the least." It could be hard to pry it from his clutching fingers of late, even long enough to feed him. "You don't think he remembers . . . ?"

Lily rose to return to her sewing. "He couldn't. They were babies."

"They act like they've never been parted."

Gabriel, three months older than his half sister, was always on the move, often rough in his play. All boy. But as Seona settled on the floor with the children, she realized he had been different since Mandy arrived. Willing to play more gently. Giving her his favorite block. Mandy was all smiles now, though Seona sensed she wouldn't fuss if Gabriel took back his red block. She had cried because he cried. A thing her mama might have done.

Tears stung Seona's eyes for the girl who had been her playmate until Miss Lucinda put a stop to it. *Can you see this, Judith? Our babies look like they're becoming friends.*

Only to be parted again? Though she hadn't heard him say it, Seona sensed Ian wasn't happy being back in Boston, aside from seeing Gabriel. Much of that had to do with Ned. And with her?

"Ye cannot avoid talking to their daddy forever, girl-baby," her mama said, glancing up from her stitching. "Talking about a thing won't set it in stone. But the man's got a decision to make and a heap of futures resting on it. He needs to know what ye're thinking. What ye want."

"I know," Seona said. "But, Mama, I *don't* know. I'd just about got my mind wrapped around you, me, and Gabriel striking off on our own. Then he shows up."

Lily's needle paused. "It's not just us now. Unless that's still what ye want and what Ian wants."

Seona watched the children stacking blocks on the floor, building something only they could name. *What Ian wants.* Exactly what she feared finding out.

Ian came in before supper. Passing by the keeping room, Seona saw him slip into his coat something small that had come inside the parcel from John Reynold. Ned didn't join them, though Seona heard Mister Robert saying he had asked him to. At supper she heard all the news from Carolina. Charlie Spencer was living in the old overseer cabin now. Mr. Allen, a neighbor who lost his wife in childbirth, had married again. They were planting cotton over at Chesterfield. No more tobacco. Then Miss Margaret asked to know about a shop in a place called Braintree, one Ian was thinking of buying.

Seona listened to his answer with a keen ear, pretending to be absorbed in watching Naomi spoon bread pudding into Mandy's mouth, or Lily feeding Gabriel, or Catriona picking at her food and eating precious little of it. She felt Ian's glance as he spoke but did not meet his gaze. He didn't sound like a man who had found what he was looking for.

"Ally?" Miss Margaret asked when Ian finished his account. "What did ye think of Braintree?"

Spoon paused midway to his mouth, Ally said, "Folk there worked up about who gonna be president next. Mister Ian thought it made me mind the man with the dead horse, him that asked Mister Ian to come live with him."

Around the table silence fell. To judge by their blank expressions, Seona wasn't the only one trying to make sense of that last bit.

"A man wi' a dead horse?" Miss Margaret asked.

"Ye didna mention that at the shop," Mister Robert said.

Ian was looking a mite cornered, as if he hadn't meant to broach the subject. "It wasn't a thing that happened today, but back on the road, just past Philadelphia."

Even Catriona perked up as Ian told the tale of being caught out during a worse thunderstorm than the one just passed, coming across a carriage overturned in the mud, owned by one William Cooper.

"I've heard the name," his da said. "A congressman, aye?"

"County judge and land seller too," Ian said. "Ally and I helped right his carriage, and I loaned him a horse to replace the one he'd lost, just for a mile or two. In thanks, he procured our accommodation for the night. I thought that an end to it, until he made me an offer of land near one of the frontier villages he's wanting settled."

"Frontier villages?" Catriona asked. "Where?"

"New York. North and south of the Mohawk River. He's named one for himself. Cooperstown."

Consternation gripped his sister's face. "You aren't going to accept the offer?"

"I've not dismissed the option."

"What of Gabriel?" his mother asked. "And . . . ?" Casting Seona a look, she bit back whatever else she meant to say.

"You cannot remove to New York," Catriona blurted. "You mustn't leave us, Ian. Not again!"

"Daughter," Mister Robert said. "Ian will do as he thinks best for all who concern him. Ye dinna top that list, aye?"

Without asking leave, Catriona pushed back her chair and hurried from the keeping room. They heard her footsteps on the stairs.

"What's got into my wee miss of late?" Miss Margaret asked. "Can anyone tell me that?"

Only Ally bothered answering. "Don't know, Miss Margaret."

Soon as Ian's mother started clearing the table, Seona got up to help, then stayed in the scullery to start the washing up—a chore she and Catriona usually shared—with the door to the yard open at her back for light. The rain had stopped.

Ian found her there, as she had half expected he would. He leaned against the doorframe, hands at his sides.

"Can we talk?"

When she nodded, he entered the scullery and took up a rag, started drying what she rinsed.

"Where's Mandy?" she asked.

"With her brother in your room. Naomi's with them."

She listened for Miss Margaret or her mama beyond the scullery but didn't hear them.

Ian set a plate atop the stack on a bench nearby. "Aside from those moments on the stairs, this is the first we've been alone since I came back. Have ye been avoiding me?"

He must know she had been. What he really meant to ask was *why*. She dipped her hands into the bucket for another plate. "I wasn't ready to talk, you showing up, no warning."

"I should have written."

"Mm-hm." She handed him the scrubbed plate. "So . . . all that New York talk. You aiming to settle there instead of Braintree?"

"Maybe." He held the dripping plate, blue eyes searching hers. "I meant to tell ye of Cooper's offer, talk it over with ye."

From out on the lane came the lowing of a cow being brought in from the Common. The air held aromas of other suppers in nearby homes. Of smoke, sea salt, tar, and a dozen other smells.

"When?"

"Now?" Amusement tilted his mouth. Seona couldn't help smiling in return. Nor the flipping of her belly as she remembered kissing that mouth. "I haven't decided," he went on. "New York's an option, as I said."

"It sounds good."

A light leapt to his gaze. "Does it?"

"If farming's what you want to do." She plunged her hands back into the bucket, coming up with a pewter cup.

He put down the plate. "Seona."

She let the cup slide back into the water and turned to meet his gaze, thinking how he looked older, more careworn, but even more handsome than she minded . . . so good that something in her wanted to rush toward him like a giddy stream, forgetting it wasn't like before. Her heart leapt about with a painful eagerness, just imagining. She caught an answering warmth in his gaze, flashing briefly before caution checked it like a wall rising. That stream rushing out of her surged against it, nowhere to go.

"I hardly know what to say to ye," he said. "What to think. What to . . ."

Feel? she wanted to ask but dared not.

"I'm trying to do what's best." He took her by the shoulders, hands warm through her summer muslin. "For ye and Gabriel—Lily too—and Mandy, Malcolm, Naomi, Ally. But I need to know what it is *ye* want."

A scuff of boots stopping short in the stone-paved door-yard was all the warning they got that Ned Cameron had shown up at last.

"Seona. Are ye all right?"

Ian stepped back from her, fixing his brother with a look both startled and annoyed. "We're talking, is all, Ned."

"Ye'd your hands on her," Ned countered. "What right have ye to touch her? By what right are ye here at all? As if ye deserved her—or Gabriel."

"Leave my son out of this," Ian said.

"The son ye sent away?"

"Ye know why I had to do that."

"Aye," Ned agreed. "It's one disgrace after another with ye. First ye make a botch of your indenture, then who knows what ye got up to out west before ye were dragged back half-dead. Then Da gives ye another chance to make something of yourself and what do ye do with it? Ye go off to North Carolina, flaunt yourself among Uncle Hugh's slaves, and bring his house down—literally—atop him!"

Ian flinched. Seona felt her belly cramp at the sickening thread of truth woven through the accusations—made the more gut-churning for the villainous role in which Ned cast Ian, as though he had intended to wrong everyone his life touched.

"Why couldn't ye stay away, Ian? Leave us all in peace to get on with things?"

The brothers were nose to nose now, of a height though Ned outweighed Ian by two stone. Ian didn't shrink from his brother as he said,

"Peace, Ned? That's what ye had going here, with Penny away to her parents? Maybe ye should get your own house in order before judging mine."

The rage in Ned's eyes had Seona whirling for the kitchen, her only thought fetching Mister Robert to put a stop to this. But Ian's daddy was already hurrying through the keeping room toward the conflict in the scullery—not only raised voices but now the scuffle of blows: a grunt, a crash, water spilling over stone.

"I hear them," Mister Robert said, rushing past.

Seona saw Catriona and Miss Margaret coming too before she followed Ian's father, who leapt over tumbled plates and cutlery and rushed out through the scullery door, where Ned and Ian grappled in the muddy yard. With his hat fallen to the ground, Ned got a fistful of Ian's shirt in one hand and with the other struck him in the face.

"Edward!" Mister Robert thundered. When he would have lunged for Ned, Ian, who had staggered but not fallen, caught his father by the arm.

"No, Da. Let it go. It's all right."

"All right?" Ned backed away, hair come half-untailed to straggle on his shoulders. "Seems it always is for him—landing on his feet like a cat. Back in your good graces after all he's done, whereas I've been here all this while working with ye, year after year, and losing no matter what I do. My sons. My wife. My home—" His voice broke as his face contorted.

"Oh, Ned." Margaret Cameron pushed past Seona, out into the yard. "Ye've no' lost Penny, surely. She needs time to mend her heart, is all. But your home? What d'ye mean by that?"

Ned wagged his head, desperation in his eyes. "Ye don't ken, Mam—Da's kept it from ye, how bad things are. It was more than just supplies lost, that whole Shelby debacle. I invested in one of his trade schemes and it failed. It's my own fault for trusting the man. All I can think to do is sell my home—the home I've tried to coax my wife back to for months. Maybe better I do. Go live with her in Deerfield, if she'll have me. Maybe it's the only way to get her back."

"Ned," Ian began, but his brother's forbidding glare silenced him.

Mister Robert moved next. He took his eldest son in his arms and held him, stiff and resisting at first. Then Ned appeared to melt. A sob broke from him as he shook. When Mister Robert started speaking, his voice was low, but Seona heard his words: Ned needn't leave Boston; he and Penny were welcome to live at Beachum Lane; the house would be his one day, the business besides; didn't he know that?

"What's left of it," Ned muttered, stepping back from his father's embrace. "I'm sorry, Da. I'll go."

He swept his hat off the ground and left without another word, gone around the side of the house leading to the street.

There was silence as Ian stood rubbing his jaw. Miss Margaret went to Mister Robert and cried on his shoulder. Seona hadn't heard a peep out of Catriona, even with this talk of Mr. Shelby. She looked, but Catriona was gone into the house. Ian's parents followed, murmuring of their troubles.

Seona went as far as the scullery, stared at the mess on the stones, then started picking up plates and cups. Pewter. Nothing broken.

"Let me help," Ian said, beside her again. "I'm sorry for this."

"Easier to clean up plates than words." Or memories. She faced him, wanting to turn his chin to the fading light, be sure he was all right. "I'm sorry he hit you."

Behind clouds the sun had set. Twilight pooled in the scullery. Across the yard one of Miss Margaret's chickens made a scuffle in the henhouse, then settled.

She couldn't read Ian's gaze.

"I've still all my teeth—and most of my wits," he said, trying to make light, but Seona's heart felt heavy as the wash bucket that together they hefted off the flagstones and set to rights.

11

Malcolm had gone out after breakfast next morning to do the weeding for Ian's mam. Just now he was having a standing rest, gripping the hoe's handle, face shaded by the battered straw hat he had worn for years. Spying him from the scullery, Ian paused to gather his thoughts. He had left Seona on that spot last night, frustrated by his inability to say what he needed to. Alone in the study with his da he'd had less difficulty.

By candlelight they had spoken of Morgan Shelby, who had convinced Ned not merely to purchase their bookbinding supplies from him but to invest in a massive purchase of paper, board, marbling dye, and more, which Shelby would distribute, providing their needs for years to come. Not so much as a spool of linen thread had materialized despite continued excuses for delays. Shelby had at last confessed the deal had fallen through and, their capital lost, fled back to New York. His da was hesitant to throw more funds after the man by hiring a lawyer to file suit.

"Your brother made a deal wi' a man he didna ken as well as he thought, but we'll recover," his da insisted. "Ned's taking it harder than he might, had it no' come on the heels of everything else this year has dealt him."

"Including me showing my face again," Ian said.

"No, Ian. This is your home, too. Dinna let Ned drive ye awa'."

"It's not just Ned."

"*Seona* wants ye gone?"

Ian found his surprise heartening. "Honestly, I don't know. She doesn't trust me enough to speak her mind." Not that he blamed her. He had handled their reunion with as much finesse as he had handled anything to do with Seona from the day he collided with her in the upstairs passage of Hugh Cameron's house and mistook her for one of his cousins. "I want Gabriel to know he's my son, that I love him. But I won't take him from Seona. I promised never to do so."

It would be both in his life or neither. And Mandy needed a mother . . .

Thought of Judith, but three months gone, pierced him through.

His da sensed it. "If ye need time to grieve, they've a roof over their heads and a welcome in our hearts. That willna change, whatever ye decide to do now."

"Thank ye, Da," he said.

They sat in silence while Robert Cameron lit his pipe, filling the room with the sweet pungency of tobacco cured at Mountain Laurel. A scent soon to pass into their family's history. Once the pipe was drawing well, his da asked, "It's to be New York then?"

He told his da of Ally's observation on the road from Braintree. "He's right. I've no longing for a life in town. Not that I wouldn't take that path if no other remained. But Judge Cooper made me an offer the like of which I'll not hear again."

"New York isna quite as far as Carolina." His da sighed, smoke curling up with the breath. "Tell me more of it."

He produced Cooper's note, implicit in it the promise of a future. A hope.

"Leaving aside Seona and Gabriel for the moment, there's Malcolm, Naomi, and Ally. Before we left Mountain Laurel, they were content to remain with me. Now though . . . if Boston's where they'd rather stay, I'll provide for their keep as I can. Ally's a fine hand with the horses and knows his business in a field. Naomi . . . well, ye've sampled her cooking. And Malcolm will likely work a garden 'til he drops, no matter what I say. They can look after themselves, given time, but would ye be willing to help them settle, if I was to leave sooner rather than later?"

Even by candlelight Ian saw the lines in his da's face, the silver dulling his hair, the steadiness in his blue eyes. "I'd do as much for any soul who served my brother in bondage. That's a debt that canna be repaid."

They had left it there and gone to their beds, where Ian had tossed in prayer until finally a hard-won resolution allowed him peace enough to sleep.

With that resolution propelling him now, he strode into the sunlight of a warming August morning, down the garden path to the old man still finding a way to serve his family, though the compulsion, Ian hoped, was removed.

"Malcolm? May I speak with ye a moment?" Too late he saw the old man's lips moving. "Sorry. I didn't mean to interrupt your prayers."

Malcolm's eyes opened as his face wreathed itself in deeper lines. "'Twas ye I was praying for."

"Then I hope *wisdom* came into it. I've been thinking about a thing I said to my brother. I told him to get his house in order, but I need to take my own words to heart. So I'd speak to ye now as the man of *your* house."

That raised a brow. "Ye've my ear, Mister Ian. Go on."

"If I was to leave and settle elsewhere, would ye go with me or stay?"

Malcolm blinked. "Stay?"

"In Boston. I haven't a place here anymore, but ye don't have to roam the earth with me forever. Not if ye feel this is your place now." He laughed, but there was little heart in it. "Da will help ye settle."

Malcolm nudged the straw hat higher on his brow. "What o' that shop ye and Ally looked o'er yesterday?"

Ian shook his head. "Ally as much as said it wasn't for me. He was right."

"And ye think that judge's offer may be?"

"There's one more conversation I need to have to be sure. But which would ye choose, between Boston and New York?"

Finding it mattered deeply but unwilling to sway the man, Ian held his peace and waited for Malcolm's answer.

He was still aglow with satisfaction when Catriona, gowned for an outing in town, intercepted him in the keeping room. "Seona's gone to deliver finished work for Lily, but you and she need to talk, Ian. Without chance of Ned, the children, or anyone else interrupting—and don't argue with me."

"I've no intention of it," he said. "I tried last night to talk with her but . . . Ned showed up. After that, I guess we were both too rattled."

"Proving my point." Catriona glanced sympathetically at his bruised jaw. "We mustn't have that again."

"Tell me something I don't know."

She brightened. "All right. *I* have a plan."

"Do ye?"

Disregarding his wary tone, she asked, "Would you be willing to climb Copp's Hill and bide there for a bit, once Seona gets back?"

"Up at the burying ground? Why?"

Catriona grasped his arm. "Leave the details to me. Just be there—somewhere not *too* conspicuous. In fact, keep yourself out of sight. Come out and approach us once we've arrived and got settled."

"Settled?"

She ignored his ignoring of her admonition. "Can you do that?"

He wasn't certain he should. "Will Seona approve this plan?"

She squeezed his arm. "Trust me, Ian. This will be good. For you both."

"All right," he reluctantly consented. Despite her satisfied smile at having gotten her way, his sister's eyes were puffy, underscored by shadows. "Are ye all right, Catriona? Ye've not seemed yourself these past days."

Her laugh was ready, if thin. "You haven't seen me often enough these past *years* to know what seeming myself should look like. Now I need to prepare things. I'll see you on the hill."

She made for the kitchen; presumably food was involved in the scheme. Leaving his sister to her machinations, Ian climbed the stairs and knocked on the door of Seona's room. He had been wrong about one thing. There were *two* conversations he needed to have before he could make a final decision about leaving.

As striking a figure as she made, it was surprisingly easy to overlook Lily—for the way she put Seona's and Gabriel's needs ahead of herself, diligently going about her work, unassailably self-contained, letting others make the decisions that altered the course of her life.

Alone with Lily and the children in their upstairs room, Ian sat with Mandy cuddled in his arms, ostensibly watching Gabriel at play on the rug with a wooden horse. His attention was as much on Lily, seated on the floor in a muslin gown, braided hair wound about her head like an ebony crown. Smooth-skinned and slender, the lines about her eyes still showed only when she laughed at Gabriel's play.

"Are ye caught up on your work just now?" he asked with a glance around the tidy room usually piled with sewing projects in various stages of completion.

The window was open to catch the morning breeze before the day heated. A buzzing fly had wandered in along with the salted air and the noise of the North End going about its business. Lily waved the fly aside and said, "For a minute. Seona's like to come back with enough work to keep me busy for a fortnight."

Gabriel stopped banging his wee horse against the rug and looked up at him—or at Mandy, grown drowsy in his arms. Ian dropped his face to the warm crown of her head and waggled his brows at his son.

Gabriel grinned, which cheered him. His son wouldn't long hold the memories of these fleeting days, should he leave again. That knowledge was a blade through his ribs. Mandy's small, limp body moved with his sigh. "Are they getting along, these two?"

"Like they've never been apart." Lily met his gaze. "I haven't said it, but I'm sorry. About Miss Judith and the babies."

Mandy woke with a jerking of soft limbs, then squirmed to get down. Gabriel abandoned his horse, and the two darted to the little painted chest where his toys were stored. Out came the patchwork bag that held his blocks, the contents spilling onto the rug.

"It was hard," Ian said at last. "I'm contemplating doing another hard thing, only I first need to know what it is ye want of me." He shook his head. "No. Leave me out of it for the moment. What do *ye* want, Lily? For yourself. For—"

Before he could complete the question, the door opened and the one he was about to name walked into the room.

"Mama, I've brought more work but . . ." Seeing him, Seona halted, then crossed the room and deposited a bundle of sewing on his old bed. "Catriona's insisting on climbing Copp's Hill for a . . ." With a glance at Gabriel, who tore his attention from Mandy long enough to squeal at her arrival, she mouthed the word *picnic*. "Just us two," she hurried to add. "Can you watch these babies a while longer?"

Lily said she would, then, after Seona slipped out again with no more than a sliding glance at Ian, eyed him straight on. "Ye and my girl-baby need to decide what it is the two of ye intend," she said as he stood to take his leave, ready to play his part in his sister's scheme. "That's when I'll ken what I'm to do."

Catriona had been so mood-stricken since Robbie and Eddie's passing, Seona wondered what possessed her to want to picnic on Copp's Hill. She didn't go near her nephews' graves but cut a path through the headstones of Boston's earliest settlers, some of which bore scars of bullets fired during the battles that raged over the city twenty years ago, when Ian was a boy fresh from Scotland.

Catriona halted before a weathered stone and read its words aloud. "'Captain Thomas Lake, aged sixty-one years . . . perfidiously slain by the Indians at Kennibeck, August the fourteenth, 1676.'" She heaved a sigh. "Remember that poem by Freneau, the one about the Indian boy? That day seems ages ago."

Seona cut her a glance, noting the pucker between her brows.

Movement down the walkway banished Catriona's frown quick as it had come. "Look. A couple left that bench. Let's claim it."

The seat overlooked the wharves below the hill's northwest slope, jutting out into the Charles River. There Catriona unpacked the basket brought from Miss Margaret's kitchen. Festivities were sometimes held on the broad crest of Copp's Hill, but it was quiet today, folk visiting graves or the fine homes built up the southeast side. Back the way they had come, the spire of Old North poked high.

"I suppose we can eat," Catriona said once all was arranged.

"This was a nice thought," Seona said, reaching for a stuffed egg. She liked how Miss Margaret made them, with vinegar and dill spicing the yolk.

Catriona popped a sugared biscuit into her mouth, casting a look round. There was nothing new to see save a pair of seagulls perched on the nearest headstone, eying their spread.

"Shoo!" The gulls ignored Catriona, whose gaze shifted past Seona again, this time lighting with recognition. Seona bit into the egg as a throat cleared behind her.

"Nice day for a picnic, ladies."

She nearly choked as she turned to see Ian, hat in hand, not even pretending to be surprised at finding them. She shot a look at his sister, whose astonishment was blatantly feigned.

"Ian! Why, of all the unexpected . . ." Catriona held her gaze for a suspended moment before the pretense crumbled. "Seona—don't be angry. I had to. You and Ian need to talk, away from listening ears."

Seona's heart was banging. The day felt suddenly stifling despite the breeze. She swallowed, holding the half-eaten egg in fingers that trembled. "I thought you wanted a picnic with me."

"It doesn't matter what I want. It's all about to change again!"

Seona stood but Catriona was quicker. "I'll see you both at home." She turned away and started walking. Fast.

"Catriona?" Seona called.

Ian's sister quickened her pace, headed for the path back down the hill.

Clearly discomfited by the turnabout, Seona assented to his sitting with her on the bench, Catriona's abandoned picnic spread between them. She finished the egg she had been eating but didn't touch another bite.

"Had I possessed a bit more courage," he said, "my sister wouldn't have needed to resort to this. Don't be upset with her."

Seona's mouth flattened. "I 'spect I'll get over it."

Her gown was finer than any he had seen her wear, pale-green muslin, high-waisted and sashed, with gathers in the elbow-length sleeves. Her fine straw hat, under which her hair was pinned, sported a matching green ribbon. The breeze off the water stirred stray curls around her face as she looked out over the river, showing him her slender neck and the hairs at its nape that made a little whorl, dark against her skin. She was as beautiful as he remembered, but today there was an elegance about her that stole the words he had prepared on the climb.

Sensing the weight of his scrutiny, she looked at him, stunning him with the clarity of her eyes—creek-water eyes, with bits of amber centered in the green—as on that day they collided in the passage of his uncle's house. Here he was again, jarring her world just as she was finding her footing in it.

"Does it hurt?" she asked. "Where Ned hit you?"

Ian fingered his tender jaw. "It's fine," he lied. "I don't want to talk about Ned now, though. I want to talk about the future. I need your help deciding, Seona."

Wariness sharpened her gaze. "My help? How?"

He imagined taking her by the shoulders, imploring . . . *by telling me what ye want of me, woman*. Instead he asked, "Could ye listen while I natter on for a bit? Maybe speaking things aloud will clear the fog."

"I'll listen."

She sounded relieved that was all he asked. Maybe this was the way. Tell her as much as he could of his own heart, hope she might reciprocate. If he could find those elusive words.

"I'm struggling with this choice," he began, "because it's not just my path I'm choosing. I know I must choose, but soon as I do, I sacrifice the man Gabriel might have become—or the woman Mandy might—had I chosen differently. And which would have been the better path for *them*? How can I know?"

Seona was staring now. "You got the weight of this world on your shoulders and you're imagining the weight of other worlds, too? Ones that won't ever be?"

Heat crept into his cheeks. "I guess I am. Am I ridiculous?"

"No." She dropped her gaze to her hands, knotted on her lap. "It surprised me hearing you say it, is all. I've thought on it too. What my choices mean for Gabriel. And Mama."

That recalled the conversation with her mother. "Is Lily happy in Boston?"

"She talks of us finding our own place here. She's doing well with the sewing. I could help more. We could take up midwifing again, too."

His gut plummeted.

"But Mama will stay with me and Gabriel, no matter what," Seona added.

No matter what. Was she leaving room then—for him to have a say?

"Malcolm and his kin mean to cast their lot with me," Ian said. "He told me so just this morning. So we can add them to that list of souls my choices now will forever impact."

Seona pulled her lower lip through her teeth. "Think you'll choose New York?"

"Maybe."

"Maybe?"

"Aye, well. Probably."

She sat gazing over the river below, pain gathering in her features. "You letting Ned drive you away?"

The question surprised him. "I hope that's not what I'm doing," he said, wanting her to understand the bent of his thinking. "Can I tell ye about New York?"

When she nodded assent, he told her everything he knew of William Cooper's offer of frontier land ready for settlement. "I'd have put little credit in it, only the man set it to paper, signed it, made the offer binding. And I will say being back in Boston has made me know I'd rather be on my own land farming, working with the cabinetmaking on the side. Rather than the other way around."

"Like it was at Mountain Laurel?"

"Aye. But it's more than just the offer of land I find appealing. It's the notion of a fresh start in a place that holds no memories. Not ours, anyway. A place new to us all."

A frown pressed her brows. "Us all?"

He realized how it had sounded, as if he presumed she was coming with them to New York. For one reckless moment, he was tempted to ask her, but he had been there all of a week, barely time for her to adjust to the fact of Judith's passing, much less to decide the course of her and Gabriel's future.

"Any who'll come with me," he replied at last and didn't know himself a wise man or a coward for stating it so.

"What about Gabriel?"

The question left him short of breath. "I promised ye I'd never take Gabriel from ye, and I won't."

"But you want him."

"He's my son, Seona. I'll always long for him, to be a father to him. But if this," he said with a gesture that took in all of Boston spread below them, "is where ye want to be, Gabriel stays with ye."

Seeming agitated by his answer rather than reassured, Seona stood and started stowing the untouched food.

"Seona, are ye all right?"

Seona's fingers trembled as she repacked the basket. She dropped a biscuit. It broke, scattering crumbs over trampled grass at their feet.

"Never mind it," Ian said when she bent to gather the pieces. "The gulls will thank ye. But ye didn't answer my question."

"I'm fine," she said, which was as true as when he said it about his bruised jaw. How could she tell him she wanted to leave Boston with him *and* wanted him to go and leave her and Gabriel behind, let them get on with this life they were finally settling into? How could she make him understand such a thing when she didn't understand it her own self?

What he hadn't said held her tongue. He hadn't said he longed for *her*. But saying so would be a slap in the face to Miss Judith's memory, no matter what he was feeling. They had shied from that subject, putting Gabriel between them, though she was as torn about her baby as she was about her own heart. She wanted him to know his daddy, who had just renewed his promise not to take him from her.

But there was only one way *she* wanted to be with Ian—without the ghost of Judith Cameron hovering between them.

"Let me carry the basket." He reached for it as he stood. "If ye don't mind my walking back to the house with ye?"

"I don't mind."

The silence as they started down the path prickled with questions unspoken, until Ian asked that last she expected: "Would ye show me where Robbie and Eddie lie?"

"No one's taken you there?"

"No." There was much to read in his eyes. Sadness, hope, worry. Tiredness, too.

Looking away to hide a rush of compassion, she took the lead.

Ned and Penny's sons shared a small stone set in the shadow of a weathered stone cross. In contrast, the boys' names and dates were cleanly inscribed. Ian stood before it in silence, then said, "My grief at being parted from Gabriel is nothing compared to Ned's."

His grief. Seona felt her heart squeeze. "Being parted from a child is always hard. But this thing with Penny leaving . . . I hope there'll be a mending between those two."

"As do I." Ian met her gaze. "Give me a moment with them?"

He removed his hat. Setting it atop the basket beside him on the ground, he knelt in the grass before his nephews' stone and bowed his head. Seona was reaching to stroke his hair before she caught herself and snatched her hand back. Hoping he hadn't noticed, she moved to a nearby headstone and, word by painstaking word, made out what a woman called Mary, or her loved ones, had seen fit to inscribe below her name.

Time, what an empty vapour t'is,
And days, how swift they fly:
Our life is ever on the Wing,
And Death is ever nigh.
The Moment when our Lives begin,
We all begin to die.

She promptly moved to a grave for another Mary and her husband, William. "'They were lovely and pleasant in their lives,'" she read. "'And in their deaths they were not dive . . . div . . .'"

"'Not divided.'"

Ian had spoken so near she felt the warmth of his breath on her neck. Startled, she drew away to look at him. "I didn't hear you come over. Was I disturbing you?"

"I was finished." He paused, then added with a tilt of his mouth, "I think it fine ye've learned to read so well."

A woman dressed in mourning black passed on the path. Seona watched her briefly, then asked a question that had pressed on her for a week. "Maybe you've some word of Esther, over at Chesterfield?"

"Not aside from seeing her at Judith's burying. Rosalyn and Lucinda had designs on taking Mandy from me. I left North Carolina as quiet as I could manage, and as quick. What of Thomas? Have ye heard from him?"

She shook her head. "Not a word."

He gazed at her, brows troubled. She turned down the path. In only a step or two, Ian's voice made her pause again.

"Look at this one, Seona." He pointed to another headstone, one belonging to a third Mary.

Stop here my friends and cast an eye,
As you are now, so once was I;
As I am now, so you must be,
Prepare for death and follow me.

When she frowned at the morbid warning, he guided her back a step on the path. Another message had been scrawled in chalk along the monument's edge.

"Read that," he said.

Seona canted her head to make out the words. "'To follow you I'm not content . . . unless I know which way you went.'"

She clapped a hand over her mouth, but the giggle bursting forth couldn't be stifled. Neither could Ian's laughter. They mingled on the warm air, turning the heads of those within hearing.

Seona didn't care. It felt good to laugh with him. Good but fragile. *Unless I know which way you went.* "When will you leave?"

Mirth fled Ian's gaze, which held hers now in sober acknowledgment of another parting, as wrenching as the last. "Before the week is out."

So soon. Maybe he was thinking that too, for he kept talking, words tumbling from his lips.

"It's too late to get a crop in the ground this season but time enough to raise a cabin, a shed for the animals. I can purchase what we need for the winter. Most of our things are still packed. It won't take long to gather the rest and be away."

A knot lodged in her belly, pressing up hard against her heart. "To where, exactly?"

"Cooperstown, to begin with, south of the Mohawk River. I'll find Judge Cooper, or his agent, present myself and his note. Then we'll see." He swallowed. "I'll write Da, let him know where we're bound once it's settled. But, Seona . . . may I write to ye as well?"

It felt like a rope tossed across a widening sea, a line to bind them. "You can," she said, grasping it.

A light sprang into his eyes. "Will ye write me back?"

She pressed her lips tight but was so pleased he could ask it, assuming her ability to grant his request, that her grin would not be contained. Freeing it, she said, "I will."

PART II

Summer 1796–Spring 1797
New York and Massachusetts

12

COOPERSTOWN, NEW YORK
August 1796

Ian sat in Judge William Cooper's study, shown there by Cooper's wife, provided tea and a copy of a newspaper, while the family's maid dashed out into the village that bore their name to find the judge and fetch him home. Mrs. Cooper had made some domestic excuse for leaving Ian to the paper's company. He didn't mind. The wait afforded a needful transition between seeing himself and his charges to Cooperstown and the next challenge: securing a home in which to settle them.

They had come thus far in reasonably good health, barring a mild ague that made its rounds beginning with Mandy, and with little to hinder their progress beyond the exigencies of weather. Crossing the Hudson had unnerved Naomi, down with the ague and never keen on ferries at the best of times, but all had debarked safely in Albany. From thence they had traveled overland to the fast-flowing Mohawk River and the town of Schenectady, where the wagon required a wheel's repair. While a local wheelwright completed the task, Naomi had recovered her health, Malcolm took sick, and Ian replenished a few stores, including fresh willow bark from a local apothecary.

Repairs made, and with Malcolm resting in the wagon's bed, they had continued westward along the river, past farms dating back to when the territory was Dutch-controlled. At a settlement called Canajoharie, they had left the river, veering southwesterly to cross more hills, sparsely settled by comparison. The road climbed through thick forests of hardwoods, passed the village of Cherry Valley, then lurched southward, crossing numerous small streams until, a fortnight and more after leaving Boston—with Ally shaking off that troublesome ague—they had skirted the base of a commanding ridge to find themselves at the foot of a blue-green gem of a lake, Otsego.

The village of Cooperstown spread along the lake's southern shore, tidy in its layout, its gridded lanes seeming to defy every natural barrier. Many plots stood empty, save for rotting stumps, awaiting industrious hands to erect some future edifice. Others were occupied by tradesmen's shops, homes, and taverns. Ian had settled his party at one of the latter. The horses had been stabled. Ally minded the wagon. Malcolm, Naomi, and Mandy rested in a hired room while Ian found his way to Judge Cooper's Manor House—a two-storied structure buttressed by single-storied wings, dominating a main street—and into the man's study, appointed with a glass-fronted, finialed desk of polished cherrywood that reminded Ian piercingly of his uncle's, lined with books, all lost in the fire at Mountain Laurel.

Afternoon sunlight from a pair of fine glass windows bathed the copy of the *Otsego Herald* open on his lap. He barely skimmed its pages. Relief at having come this far vied with the knowledge of all he had still to accomplish before snow fell.

Setting the paper on the chair beside his hat, he crossed to a table pushed against the wall, its surface cluttered with maps. One showed the gridded streets of Cooperstown, the lake, and surrounding natural features. He noted the high ridge they had passed, grandly labeled *Mount Vision*, but hadn't time to focus on the village itself before somewhere in the house a door slammed. Approaching boots thumped along a passage.

Seconds later the study door opened and Judge William Cooper strode within. Blunt features amiably set, he fixed his gaze upon Ian, who made the man a bow and said, "Ian Cameron, your servant, sir."

Recognition wasn't instant but full when it came. "Cameron? Ah, on the road from Philadelphia! My carriage overturned. You and your man offered aid—and the loan of a horse besides."

As tall and barrel-chested as Ian recalled, dressed in a finely tailored coat, brown hair in side-curls, the man strode forward with an outstretched hand. Ian met it with his own. "And ye made me a most generous offer in turn. I've come to avail myself of it, and your good grace." From his coat he produced the note signed weeks ago in the parlor of the Blue Moon.

Cooper nodded, accepting it. "So I did—so I did." He glanced over the note and, seeming satisfied, said, "You've come round to seeing the benefits of settling here, I take it? *Good* news. Very good news, indeed."

"Aye, sir." But lest the man assume he had chosen Cooperstown itself, a notion by no means resolved upon, Ian added, "At least, I've decided the frontier is where I belong."

"Frontier?" Cooper's brows soared as he chuckled. "Had you seen what I did upon my first visit to Otsego's shore, you'd not call Cooperstown the frontier now. But come," he said, drawing Ian away from the maps to the finialed desk, which bore a decanter and glasses. "First a toast to your safe arrival from . . . Boston, was it?"

Ignoring the tea his wife had provided, Judge Cooper poured them both a whisky. While they sipped, Cooper told of his first sighting of the tract of land that would become his township, from the top of the ridge christened Mount Vision on his map. "I was alone, three hundred miles from home, without bread, meat, or food of any kind. I caught trout in the brook and roasted them on the ashes. My horse fed on the grass that grew by the water's edge. I laid me down under the stars to sleep in my coat, nothing but the melancholy wilderness surrounding me . . ."

Ian gave courteous attention as Cooper recounted his initial exploration of the country, detailing how his heart had been charmed by its bounties, his mind enlivened with plans for future settlement. At last, whisky downed, the judge said, "Speaking of settlement, shall we get to it then, have a look at the map?"

"Now, sir?" Ian asked, setting down his glass. He had thought of merely making an appointment for the following day. "Aye, I'd like that, if my arrival doesn't pull ye from some other business."

"It does," Cooper said dismissively. "Don't let it trouble. I make it my aim to call regularly upon those to whom I've leased or sold town plots—and the nearer farms—to keep myself informed of their circumstances, discuss their political leanings, hear their complaints. The better to represent them in Congress, of course."

"Of course," Ian agreed but was thinking had he not already decided himself better suited to farming than town life, this admission of paternalistic hovering on Cooper's part would have convinced him of it.

Oblivious of the conviction, Cooper steered him to the map of his much-lauded town, talking the while of various land concerns as Ian, for politeness' sake, made a show of perusing the village site the man seemed determined to grow by persuasion, enticement, or sheer will. What grew instead was Ian's enlightenment: Judge Cooper was a man mired in legal and financial complications arising from the numerous patents and deeds, payments and defaults, boundary contentions, sales, repossessions, and repurchases due to the steady stream of settlers pouring in, eager for land, of which Ian and his wagonful were but a few leaves borne upon the tide.

When finally he stated his decision to focus his energies on farming rather than cabinetmaking, Cooper appeared crestfallen. The man, Ian was made to understand, believed one ought to be either tradesman or farmer, for to attempt both would necessitate neglect of one or the other. "Always at the most inopportune season for those depending upon him."

"Be that as it may," Ian maintained, "I should prefer to secure for myself acreage enough to raise both crops and cattle. I'll not abandon my trade, but it's not to be the main source of my livelihood. What of those lands ye spoke of north of the Mohawk River? Herkimer County, was it?"

Give William Cooper his due: the man didn't long drag his heels in following Ian's lead but recovered what seemed his natural enthusiasm to please. He unrolled the map of the requested patent, situated in the foothills of the Adirondack wilderness, which stretched north to

Canada—as far removed from the man's daily meddling as Ian could place himself and still partake of his offer.

With another half-hour's cartographic study, he narrowed his interest to two plots, a mere three hundred acres each. He was about to make his choice when a solitary tract on the map's edge caught his eye. It was situated up along West Canada Creek, which flowed into the Mohawk River at a spot marked *German Flatts*. The acreage, larger than the others he was considering, lay some miles east of a village called Shiloh, along one of the West Canada's feeder creeks. The southern reaches of the Adirondacks edged the tract to the northeast, to the south, the creek, Black Kettle. A small and nameless lake bordered it to the west. Its features promised good bottomland for cultivating, hillsides for grazing, even a spring near to a beech grove. A neighboring farm, west of the lake, was marked *MacGregor*.

"What of this tract?" Ian asked, cutting Cooper off midsentence as he extolled the villages he was attempting to settle north of the Mohawk. "Shiloh . . . is that one of your settlements?"

"Shiloh? No. That was settled before we won our independence." Cooper frowned, a finger tapping his blunt chin. "If memory serves, I acquired that acreage some years back from its previous owner. I haven't set eyes on it myself but doubt me the man ever farmed it. But look you." He slid another map across the lonely tract along Black Kettle Creek. "Would you not rather consider a parcel lying close to one of my Herkimer villages? There's more than one would suit . . ."

Ian half listened, turning the name *Shiloh* over in his mind. Call it fancy or fanciful, but he was as taken with the name as with the details of the acreage waiting to be claimed. While Cooper spoke, Ian silently prayed—made the very name *Shiloh* a prayer—and waited, feeling a growing certainty he had found the place. He wished there were time to journey there and back before he secured it, but that not being the case . . .

After swift calculation of his funds, including gold received from John Reynold before departing Boston, not yet converted to coin, he waited for Cooper's next pause for breath, then made his best—indeed his only—offer.

"The Shiloh tract is the one I want, sir. And never mind a shilling—I'll pay ye half the land's price, at the rate promised in your note, as down payment. In hard currency." He swallowed and added, "By that I mean in gold. Today."

Judge Cooper's reaction was a study in contrasts. Though clearly disappointed in Ian's choice, he couldn't conceal his delight at the influx of capital on offer. "*Gold*, did you say? Guineas?"

"Aye, a few. But also gold unminted—if ye'll accept such in payment."

To say the man was thunderstruck would not have been overstating things.

"You're telling me you've acquired gold, raw from the earth?" Cooper asked, one hand rising to grip Ian's shoulder, eyes bright with speculation. "Now *that* I would very much like to see."

With the contents of Ian's small leather pouch emptied upon the desk, William Cooper began to speak of financing his fall election to Congress and the grand hall he meant to replace the house in which the family presently dwelled. "Its building goes slower than my wife should like. But with this . . ." The judge's eyes fairly glowed. "I regret you will not be joining us here but . . . well, I would say we've reached an agreement nevertheless."

Smiling broadly at Ian, Cooper proffered his hand.

Within the hour a fair copy of the agreement was made, a witness summoned for its signing, and the sale of three hundred eighty acres of land on Black Kettle Creek near the village of Shiloh—along with a schedule of payment to result in Ian's obtaining permanent title within three years—was a fait accompli.

Cooper had concealed the exchanged tender before the summoned witness came. Once he had gone, the judge brought out the gold again and spread the larger flakes and nuggets on his desktop. While Ian tucked away his copy of the agreement and retrieved his hat, William Cooper poked with evident fascination at the ore.

"You're certain you didn't obtain this in New York?" he asked, not for the first time.

"The gold was given me in payment some while back, as I pass it on to ye," Ian replied, also not for the first time.

"Payment for your Carolina land?" Cooper probed, but when Ian only smiled, the man desisted. "I see you wish to keep the knowledge close. But I've long harbored hope that such treasure lies beneath our Otsego soil, awaiting some fortunate soul's discovery." The man gave a hearty laugh. "Perhaps it lies beneath the land you've just purchased!"

"That would be something," Ian said, his mind teeming with the gathering of provisions and breaking the news that, at the wagon's speed and the conditions of the western New York roads, they had another week of travel ahead.

Before he could properly take his leave, the room's door burst open and a lad of about six years rushed in, dark-haired and exclaiming, "Papa! Papa!" stopping short at sight of Ian, having apparently forgotten his presence in the house.

"James Fenimore!" Cooper waved the lad over before Ian could admonish him to further discretion about the gold. "See this, my boy? You're looking at gold come straight from the earth, untouched as yet by fire or hammer. What think you of that?"

"Is it ours, Papa?" the boy queried, reaching a fingertip to poke the nearest flake.

"Indeed, it is," Cooper confirmed, whereupon the lad peered up at Ian with keener interest, until his father added, "Now, back to whatever it is you're meant to be doing. I've not yet finished my business with Mr. Cameron."

James Cooper cast Ian a last appraising glance, then scampered from the room. When the boy was gone and the door shut, Ian cleared his throat. "I'll take my leave as well, sir. There's much needing done to see those in my care secure for the winter and little time for doing it. Before I go, might I beg a favor?"

"Of course," Cooper said, rising from the desk to see him out. "You've but to name it."

He hoped the man meant it. "Would ye keep word of where ye came by the gold—indeed the gold itself, can it be managed—between us two?" *Three*, counting young James. Ian doubted Cooper's son would remember his name, but the judge, he had come to realize, was fond of telling tales. "At least here, in Cooperstown?"

The man took a moment to think through the request, before grudgingly nodding. "I shall in any case need wait until I've returned to Philadelphia before attempting to exchange the gold for coin." Cooper shot a regretful glance at the ore on his desk, as if he would fain keep it in its present state, had he no pressing expenses of his own.

Ian left William Cooper with the man's good wishes and his own resolution to secure permanent title to the land on Black Kettle Creek as swiftly as possible—should that narrow vein on John Reynold's land not fail.

23 August 1796

To Seona Cameron
Beachum Lane
Boston, Massachusetts

Dear Seona—

I have written Da, detailing our Journey to Cooperstown and our dealings here (be sure he shares that Letter) and have procured our Winter provisions. The morrow begins the final leg of our Journey, back toward the Mohawk River, then north along West Canada Creek to Black Kettle Creek. Our destination, Shiloh, is situated some Miles above their confluence. I am thankful for the Almighty's mercy in seeing us safely thus far, for preparing the way before ever I saw the need.

Naomi, Malcolm, and Ally say their time with you proved too brief. I find myself in full agreement. From the moment I set my gaze on Gabriel and he permitted my embrace, I wished to never let him go. At our parting I fought the urge to cling to him, who knows me not as

Father. Or could it be he does? When you bade him, "Say goodbye to your Daddy," and he said the word I've most longed to hear—"Da!"—my Heart did claim it, whether I have the right. It was a wrench, parting from my wee Lad again.

Mandy misses her Brother, having asked for him daily the first week of our Journey. They got on well, those two, more like twins never parted than half siblings who could not possibly recall one another. Though I would rather have remained near Gabriel and, by your leave, behaved toward him as a Father, I value this chance to establish a Place, a home that will outlast me and benefit my Children. There is more I could say on that, as there was more I wished to say that day on Copp's Hill. Could you sense it? I felt your holding back as well. Much has changed in a short time. Perhaps you find your head (and Heart?) reeling more than a little. Mine do. Still I was pleased to find you making a life in Boston and am sensible that, at present, I have little to contribute to its betterment. God willing, that will change.

Meantime, will you write and tell me all that is happening with you? Tell me of Gabriel, how he grows, what new skills he masters. What words he is learning to say. What delights him. I would know my Son, as you allow. He and you are much in my prayers. By them I remain Your Most Obedient Servant—

Ian Cameron
Cooperstown, New York

13

SHILOH, NEW YORK
September 1796

While Cooperstown had been a carefully plotted affair, all straight lines and right angles, the village of Shiloh resembled nothing so much as a scattering of forest mushrooms; structures sprouted wherever nature's whimsy decreed or the hilly terrain proved amenable. The final mile to reach its cabin-dotted outskirts was some of the roughest they had encountered. Malcolm and Naomi, Mandy astride her hip, had alighted to walk it while Ian went before, leading Ruaidh, calling guidance to Ally to bring the wagon safely over the stony track, while the rush and tumble of Black Kettle Creek kept them company.

With the sun past midday, they reached the village proper, nestled in a hollow surrounded by wooded slopes. A cleared level ground was shared by a low-roofed trade store and smithy, both built of square-hewn logs, shaded by the same great oak, and several cabins, also log-built. The track they followed swept up to where a mill sat astride the creek, taking advantage of a waterfall's natural force. Its weathered timbers marked it of an age with store and smithy.

From the latter came a hammer's ringing, a tinny clanking on the warm late-summer air. The smithy seemed as good a place as any to stop and gain their bearings. Other tracks led away from the village besides the one snaking up past the mill. Ian didn't want to make a wrong turn so near their destination.

On the trade store's porch, an old man in a rocker smoked a pipe. In a cabin-yard some ways off, a woman tended a wash kettle. In the same yard, a boy chopped wood. All shot glances their way as Ally set about watering the wagon team from a nearby well, though none forbade them its use.

Ian left Ruaidh hitched to the wagon's tail to receive his share, but before he could cross the yard to the smithy, a rider came into the village from a track that wound over the wooded ridge to the west. At first it seemed the man meant to pass on, up the rise to the mill. Catching sight of wagon and team, he reined his mount in Ian's direction.

While the smith's hammering and the *thwack* of wood-chopping filled the air, Ian watched the man's approach. His horse, a dark bay roan, was showing its age but seemed in good condition. The man was dressed in linen breeches and a well-fitted broadcloth coat, with a felt hat nicely cornered. What could be seen of the hair tailed back from a clean-shaven face was nearly black, though gray-streaked.

He dismounted and walked his horse to the wagon, where Ally held a bucket for their horses to drink in turn. Ian for the first time noticed what else the old horse bore: full saddlebags, with a small wooden chest tied between that put Ian in mind of Lily's simples box, only larger. The trappings of a country doctor?

"Passing through Shiloh, are ye?" the man inquired. His eyes were very blue, with creases gathered at the corners. His accent was markedly Scottish and reassuringly amiable as he added, "Though to where, I've no notion, save it be Canada."

"Not passing through," Ian replied, hearing his own faint lilt deepen in response to the other man's. "We've lately come from Otsego County, where I purchased land here. From William Cooper."

The name sparked recognition and interest. The man's gaze looked Ian up and down. "Oh, aye? Land whereabouts here?"

"To the eastward, along Black Kettle Creek, which I'm guessing that track up along the mill ought to follow. I cannot tell from here whether it takes a bend in that direction."

"It does. Creek and track both bend eastward above the mill and head on up into the hills for a bit." Upon shifting his horse's reins to his left hand, the man proffered the other. "Neil MacGregor, pleased to make your acquaintance."

"Ian Cameron, likewise." They shook; then with a nod toward the man's saddlebags, Ian asked, "Is it *Doctor* MacGregor?"

"It is," the man said with a broadening smile. "But *Neil* does as well."

MacGregor. The name niggled at a memory. At last Ian bethought himself of Judge Cooper's map and his chosen tract with its lake and spring and the neighboring farm labeled with the name just spoken. "I think I've bought the parcel of land adjoining your farm. If ye're the MacGregor who lives out east along Black Kettle."

"Wi' a wee lake between?" Neil MacGregor asked.

"The very one." Ian turned to indicate Ally, standing now with Ruaidh's muzzle deep in the water bucket, listening with unabashed curiosity, and Naomi, Malcolm, and Mandy, peering through the wagon's canvas. "We're just up from Cooperstown, where the sale was made. Before that we came from North Carolina, by way of Boston."

"Then I daresay ye'll be ready to end your journey," the doctor said. "'Tis but two miles to my farm, half another at most to yours. I'll keep ye company if ye're of a mind to conclude your adventure now."

"Yes, sir, we are!" Naomi answered for one and all. "Mister Ian, back in Carolina you asked did I want to see the world. I done traipsed over enough of it now for *seven* lifetimes. I'm ready to sit me still."

Had he not been of similar mind, Ian would have made himself so after that declaration. Assured the track beyond Shiloh was none so difficult as that last stretch leading into it, Ally drove the wagon up the slope past the mill, with Ian and Neil MacGregor riding ahead.

"Keppler's Mill," Neil named it. "And that," he added as the road bent eastward past a new-built cabin, "is where my daughter, Maggie, will commence to teaching school, once harvest is past."

Proving an amiable guide as they rode the winding forested track, the man spoke of Shiloh's history before and after the war. Ian gathered that the late conflict with the Crown had been hard on the folk thereabouts. As well as losing sons, husbands, and brothers in battle, they had suffered the depredations of invading British armies. And their allied Indians.

"And ye? Have ye been settled here so long?" Ian asked over the steady clop of their horses' hooves and rattling wagon coming along the gently climbing track.

The simple question yielded Neil MacGregor's story in brief. A physician trained in Edinburgh, he had come into the region some twelve years back as the dust of war was settling, sent by the American Philosophical Society in Philadelphia as a naturalist. His aim being to create a field guide to the flora of the Adirondacks, he had encountered some unspecified misfortune that stranded him in Shiloh.

"Where I found both place and people so diverting," he added with a flash of humor Ian was certain disguised a far more complicated tale, "that in the end I couldna tear myself awa'."

"Did ye never complete your field guide?"

"I did. Over the next three years. I've a copy at the farm should ye fancy a keek."

Ian assured the man he did, but as they rode the track, creek flashing through the trees on their right, he was keen to observe the living flora itself. He recalled Cooper waxing eloquent about New York's northern forest, how his cabinetmaker's heart would rejoice at the sight. The man had not been wrong. Mighty shading chestnut, oak, beech, and maple met his gaze, spiced through with the white of birch and poplar, graced by the somber notes of pine, spruce, cedar, and hemlock, all scenting the warm summer air.

They had traveled nigh two miles to Ian's reckoning when Neil pointed out a particular stand of maples, their broad trunks sprouting plugs Ian recognized before the man declared the stand his wife's sugar bush, where she harvested sap each spring for boiling syrup.

"I helped with such when I lived with an uncle," Ian said. "Among the Chippewa near the western lakes."

From his saddle Neil MacGregor cast him an appraising look but didn't remark; they had emerged from the wood to find themselves at the edge of a broad field of corn, planted in a manner Ian, with no small surprise, recognized as native—not in uniform rows but in mounds, with beans coiling up the stalks and broad-leafed squash vines shading the earth below. Along its edge sunflowers grew, tall and yellow-headed. Neil MacGregor scanned the bladed stalks beyond. They rode but a short way farther before he halted his horse and called, "Willa! I've brought ye and the bairns a surprise. *Neighbors.*"

As Ally brought the wagon to a halt and climbed down to help the others out of its bed, voices called back from various parts of the field. First to emerge from between the sunflowers was, Ian presumed, the woman Neil had called—his wife, Willa MacGregor—and much like a sunflower she was in appearance herself. Nigh six feet tall, Ian realized once he dismounted to greet her, still slender as a lass, though her face bore the freckling of years of fieldwork and her reddish-brown hair showed white in its rusty hue.

More arresting than her height were her eyes. One was brown, the other predominantly green.

Ian had but a moment to be disconcerted by the striking oddity before two lads came bursting from the cornfield. Ian mistook them briefly for twins, but turned out they were two years apart in age, which the elder, Jamie, was keen to clarify. "This is Liam. He's only nine."

Liam gave his brother's ribs a nudge. "Almost ten—but tall for my age!"

Both had their father's dark hair and blue eyes. Ian presumed the same of the two who next issued from the standing corn, a young man in his early twenties and a lass about Catriona's age, until they drew near enough for Ian to see plainly they were both dark-eyed, their complexions darker than the rest of the family's. The lass's was a pale-fawn shade, her brother's a slightly darker copper. The cast of their features marked them Indians, though Ian didn't think them full-bloods.

His heart gave a squeeze; the sight of them minded him of Seona. It had been nearly a month of thinking of her, days in the saddle wondering what *she* was thinking, having seen him after so long only to have him leave again with vague promises of going off to settle in the hope it might benefit her and Gabriel . . .

But now Neil MacGregor was introducing this second pair as his son Matthew and daughter, Maggie—the one soon to be teaching school in that cabin above the mill. No explanation was forthcoming of their familial connection to the elder MacGregors, who clearly had no Indian blood between them.

Swallowing back his curiosity, Ian introduced himself and his wee girl, then the others. "Malcolm and his family chose to come north with me," he added, wanting their status to be clear from the start. "To make a life for themselves as well."

His companions were greeted as the free persons they were. Ian watched with pleasure as Willa MacGregor engaged Naomi in conversation and Maggie coaxed a shy smile from Mandy.

With an invitation to return and sup with the family that evening—gratefully accepted—they bade the MacGregors farewell, save for the doctor, who swung back into the saddle to accompany them down the track past his well-tended fields.

Neil MacGregor's house soon came into view: framed and solidly built, modeled like Judge Cooper's but with a stone foundation and deep veranda giving it a greater sense of permanence. Then the track led on through forest again, roughening for its general disuse, precipitating such a jolting ride that Naomi, Malcolm, and Mandy again alighted to walk.

Ian was about to dismount as well when he caught sight of sheeted water glinting between the trunks of red pine lining the track, the first feature he recognized from Cooper's map, besides the creek. The lake was smaller than Otsego but of a similar limestone green, with a fringe of cattail reeds along its irregular shore and an islet there at its southern end.

"Where," Neil MacGregor informed him, "my wife, as a lass, was wont to retreat wi' a book to read. The land was once her father's."

Ian halted Ruaidh. Neil followed suit, while those on foot and Ally, with the wagon, caught them up. They were not yet past the lake, but Ian knew what lay beyond. So did his new neighbor, who said, "Welcome home, Ian Cameron. And may the grace of the Almighty be upon ye and yours."

10 September 1796

To Seona Cameron
Beachum Lane
Boston, Massachusetts

Dear Seona—

We are come to the Adirondack foothills and have at last seen our Land, indeed are settled upon it. By lantern glow I take up pen as, for the first time since leaving Mountain Laurel, Mandy sleeps enclosed within our own squared walls. As yet they are but waist-high, hewn of unchinked log, our floor bare earth, our roof a span of stars. Naomi and Malcolm sleep nearby. Ally does not, having declared some while ago, "I'm meaning to sleep out by the stock again, Mister Ian, till all them beasts is settled in their spirits."

I have been eager to tell you of the Family who claims the farm west of us. We met Neil MacGregor upon our arrival in Shiloh and had his company the last leg of our Journey. Along the way we met his wife, Willa (of striking interest are her eyes, which do not match in color, a thing I have never before seen), and their four Children, two of whom are, I have since learned, of Mohawk Indian blood. The eldest, Matthew, is well-grown at twenty-two and a great help with the farming when not training Horses, for which skill he has a high reputation. Maggie, a quiet lass, three years younger than her brother, begins this Autumn to teach a village School. Two younger sons are called Jamie and Liam. Neil MacGregor came to the frontier as a Naturalist, sent to create a Field Guide to the mountain flora (perhaps Da knows of this book?), and serves as Physician hereabouts as well.

Judge Cooper's map did not prepare me for what greeted us as we emerged from the wood surrounding the lake between our land and MacGregor's. Timbered slopes roll up to the ridge that bounds the tract to the Northward, while the creek bounds it to South. Between these extremes lie Acres ready for pasturage or planting, well-drained for the most part, though in need of grubbing. More Acres lie beneath forest that might one day be planted, but I mean to manage these trees with care. The Chestnuts I shall let stand for mast, should we acquire Hogs. Some of the Maples we will tap for sugar. Others I will preserve for future projects (cabin furnishings to begin with). We have the creek, lake, and their feeder streams for Fishing, which I am assured is plentiful. While Beaver and most fur-bearing game are gone from the area, I am told Deer, Turkey, even Bear are still to be found. Expected soon is the arrival of the Geese that stop yearly on the lake in their Autumn migrations. Since our coming here, I have lain awake each night listening to the watery calls of Loons, unheard since my days in Canada. When first I caught that wild melody on the air, it filled me with a sentiment I could not name, until I described it to Malcolm, who pondered briefly and said, "Ye've come home, Mister Ian. Your ears ken it. So does your heart." A place of belonging. I pray that it will in time prove just so.

Yesterday I acquired the beginnings of a Cattle herd, got in trade from one Elias Waring, County Magistrate, former Colonel of Militia, a stooped old soldier who walks with the aid of a cane. Occupied in the main with the breeding of Horses, he was pleased to have two of our half-draft team in trade, Mares of foaling years. Another I traded to the blacksmith for a milch Cow and the promise of the Horses remaining to me reshod as need arises. We are left with Ruaidh and Cupid, last of the wagon team, which shall serve Ally for a saddle horse and, I hope, to pull a plow come Spring. Three of the Cattle I earmarked for Ally, the start of his own herd.

"These be my *cows?" he asked when I told him, as if he thought me not in earnest, but it is the least he deserves.*

His arms, too, aided William Cooper on that road in Pennsylvania, not to mention all he is owed for his years of servitude. I find myself keen to see what Ally will do with Cattle of his own. He may well surprise us.

I shall close this Letter that, despite my efforts, falls short of conveying my contentment with this Place. Doubtless I will pepper you with more on the subject, but I desire to know how things are with you and Gabriel. I trust you received my Letter sent from Cooperstown and hope, as we agreed on Copp's Hill, that you will write to your Most Obedient Servant—

Ian Cameron
Shiloh, New York

28 September 1796

To Ian Cameron
Shiloh, New York

Dear Ian—

I got both your Letters. I am sorry for causing you pain the day you left. I knew before your first Letter come telling of it. I saw it in your eyes when Gabriel called you Da. I told him to bid you goodbye not thinking it would hurt. It hurt me too. Then you gave me that Arrowhead you carried since the day Gabriel was born under that old creek Willow and said my words back to me, spoke to you that day we parted long ago. "Keep it for me." I would have burst into tears had you not taken your leave right quick. You asked to know what Gabriel does for the first time. He never has called another what he called you that day, and of course you have the Right to claim him. I would not deny my baby his Daddy. That pain will not be his.

Mister Robert asked me to pen the News for my own

practice at this Letter writing and bade me say we are "Thankful to Almighty God for your safe Arrival and Settlement in a Place so much to your Content." His words, but I mean them too. Dùthchas—that is a Gaelic word your Daddy spelled out for me and says you might recall. It means a sense of belonging to a Place, also to the People that have lived there before you. It seems this is what you mean to create.

I like the sound of your Farm and those MacGregors. They put me in mind of the Reynolds with their kindness. At least that Neil MacGregor puts me in mind of John. I have not yet heard enough of his Wife to know if she is another Cecily. Those eyes you say she has, two different colors! It must be strange to see. Catriona took interest in that Family and is penning a note to go along with this. I will let her say what she will about them.

Mama and me sew most days until our fingers are sore, saving what we earn. Gabriel is cutting teeth and cranky with it. Now Summer is past with its sticky heat I am in better Spirits. I so admire Boston's Autumn. Do the leaves turn colors where you are like they do here? It makes me want to drop everything and paint a picture. Some days I do.

Your Brother has not called much since you left. We all wait to hear of Penny. Mister Robert thinks Ned should go to Deerfield and mend things if he can. Miss Margaret misses you and Mandy, Naomi—everybody. Many are the partings in this Life. Too many together bruise the heart.

There is something I must ask and do not know how to come at it but straight on. What did you want to say to me on Copp's Hill that you did not say? Could you write it? Seems like we can read each other's Words this way and maybe make a better answer than we would have done that day when neither of us knew our minds or what we were meant to be feeling.

That is all for now except to say I am happy you and

everyone—give them my and Mama's Love—will be warm in your cabin this Winter. And Ally has cows! What you wrote made me and Mama laugh like we were standing there when he said it. In your writing I can hear folk talking clear as Boston's bells. I do not know how to make it seem a person is talking on the page, but I will write again regardless—

Seona Cameron
Beachum Lane, Boston

28 September 1796

To Ian Cameron
Shiloh, New York

Dear Brother—

Thank you for gifting Seona and Lily with Juturna (and her dam) before you left. She is the sweetest Filly and Seona kindly lets me ride her to the Common whenever I wish.

Da found a copy of Dr. MacGregor's book and it is lovely, but your News of Shiloh raised many questions, foremost among them: how do the MacGregors come to have a Son and Daughter who are Mohawk Indians? Have you uncovered this Mystery? If not, do so for me as a particular Favor, then write and tell me all!

Give Mandy many kisses from her Auntie. I miss her sweet face. And all of you. It is lonely since you left. Your Most Affectionate Sister—

Catriona Cameron

14

SHILOH, NEW YORK

16 October 1796

To Seona Cameron
Beachum Lane
Boston, Massachusetts

Dear Seona—

I was delighted to receive your Letter dated 28 September (along with Catriona's), but must hasten to assure that you need apologize for nothing, much less my conflicted sentiments at our parting. It is my most precious Memory of Gabriel, his calling me Da. I think of it with Joy, even if the distance still between us wrenches. Each time Mandy says a new word or masters some skill, I rejoice in my Daughter's growth—and grieve over missing the same in my Son. How complicated a thing is Parenthood! While I celebrate each advancement Mandy makes, with it comes a pang at seeing her take another step away from me. Letting go, even in small measure, is bittersweet.

In answer to your Query, the trees here did color up, as dazzling to the eye as those of Boston. Would that I could have painted a scene and posted it to you, but you would laugh at my efforts (recall that Lobster I attempted to sketch?). But do cease disparaging your writing. Have you any notion how improved is not only your Penmanship but your skill with Language? Please practice those skills, not only with News of my Family and Son, but also of yourself. Tell me what you think and feel. Even should it disappoint or wound me, I would know.

Being mindful of Catriona's interest in Matthew and Maggie MacGregor, I have some news to share on that front, related by Neil whilst he, Ally, and I spent several days splitting rails and putting up fencing to create a larger paddock for the Cows. Having lost both their white Father and Mohawk Mother, the pair were adopted by Willa and Neil the year they married, 1784. How this came to be is a Tale of which I have as yet but the broadest strokes, but Catriona may be interested to know their Names in their Mother's Tongue translate to Owl (Matthew) and Pine Bird (Maggie). Though shy in conversation with most outside her family, Maggie manages to stand before a cabin full of Children to teach. She has a fondness for Goats and makes a fine cheese from the produce of her herd. Matthew is a different sort, never shy to speak his mind, usually to be found with some Colt or Filly, gentling it to the saddle. The Lad can all but talk a Horse into doing his bidding.

You asked what I refrained from saying that day on Copp's Hill. As you expressed it, sometimes there is no way to come at a thing but straight on. Had I known the truth of your disappearance from Mountain Laurel after our handfasting, or that you carried my Child, I would not have married Judith. Yet she was my Wife. While in Boston, I knew I needed time to mourn her passing but found myself lost for words to express this to you. Why is it possible to tell you so with ink when, standing before you, I could not? Perhaps, as you say, we have time to consider before giving answer, though honesty compels I admit that here I am at the table I built yesterday, in our Cabin (roofed, daubed, doors and shutters hung) writing to you the very day I fetched your Letter home from Shiloh, where I took corn purchased in Cooperstown to be ground.

Leaving Boston was painful, but you write that my leaving hurt you as well. In what way? The last thing I want is to cause you further Heartache, yet how could I have done otherwise, appearing unheralded, with Mandy a reminder of Judith, who I placed between us? There was never going to be an easy way through this, but I thought it best I remove to New York, to give us time to come to terms with things as they now are.

Mandy has marked her second Year. She follows Naomi around the cabin-yard, liking best to feed the Chickens, each of which she has named. While I sit here scratching with my quill, Naomi has put her to bed (with a sleepy kiss for her Da). Ally has gone out to check the Stock, returned, and dropped into his bed. Malcolm has long since sought his, though I am not sure how well he sleeps with the pain his old bones give. Naomi bids me greet you all. She misses "that great sprawl of a Kitchen" at Beachum Lane. I shall have to build her one as grand, I see.

My candle gutters. My own quilts call. Let the others read the parts of this Letter you feel at ease sharing, but keep the rest, those Matters of our Hearts, between yourself and your Obedient Servant—

Ian Cameron
Shiloh, New York

Ian was late rising the morning after reading Seona's letter, thanks to sitting up into the night, penning a reply. The evidence of insufficient sleep was reflected in the glass hung beside the cabin doorway, but as he scraped clean his stubbled cheeks, the stream of morning sunlight through the open door also revealed his undiminished satisfaction.

With Ally and Malcolm both seeing to chores, Mandy out with Naomi gathering eggs for their breakfast skillet, he didn't bother tamping down his grin.

As he rinsed his razor in the basin, his gaze slid to his letter, left on the table. He had been too weary to melt the sealing wax last night. Good thing, he realized, as a cow's lowing reached his ears. He had forgotten to share one of yesterday's doings. Ally had acquired a fourth member of his herd, from Neil MacGregor, a newly weaned male calf he meant to raise up for a stud bull.

Ally had broached the subject after hearing their neighbor talk of selling the calf. Approving the notion, Ian encouraged him to approach Neil, make an offer, and settle the details of the transaction. Having accepted Ally's offer of labor in trade, Neil had brought the brindled calf with him yesterday when he came to help finish their fencing project. The calf seeming content with its lot, Ally had turned in for the night in the cabin, rather than sleeping out with the herd.

Finished with his ablutions, Ian decided to snatch a moment and add the account to his letter, thinking Seona would appreciate hearing of Ally's burgeoning entrepreneurial initiative. He had made the first careful trim of the quill with his penknife when the ruckus outside the cabin started up.

The new calf's bawling began it, joined by a cow's deeper bellowing, with Ally shouting above the din.

Ian abandoned knife and quill. Before he reached the door, there came a sound that all but froze him with dread: Mandy's terrified cry.

Outside the cabin he was met by pandemonium. One of their cows had broken free of the new paddock. Ally was lunging about, attempting to secure it. Or so Ian thought at first glance. A second disabused him of the presumption. It wasn't one of their cows but the new calf's brindled dam, loose from MacGregor's pasture and rampaging about their yard, attempting to reunite with her offspring on the other side of the rail fence.

More alarming was what Ian saw outside the henhouse, mere steps away from the frantic cow's lethal hooves—Naomi bending to scoop Mandy off the ground.

"Angels, save us!" she cried. Faster than Ian would have thought possible, she sprinted for the cabin, Mandy screaming in her arms. Ian's brain screamed too—for him to get out there and halt the unfolding calamity. Fearing his girl trampled, his knees had gone weak.

A grip on his arm startled him. He hadn't noticed Malcolm's approach. "Mandy's no' taken hurt. But Lord help us with these cows!"

The old man's laughter jarred Ian from his paralyzing fright, just as Naomi reached them and he saw she and Mandy were dusty and shaken but whole.

"Mister Ian!" Ally bellowed from the yard. "Help! We got to catch this mama cow afore—!"

Even as Ally shouted, the brindled cow rammed the fence. Poles splintered inward, where her calf danced about, inciting further demonstrations of maternal devotion. Ian sprinted into the scene, mind racing for a solution, but in the end neither he nor Ally proved nimble or daring enough to get between that plunging cow and her calf.

"We gonna lose the fence and all them cows!" Ally shouted. "What we—whoa!"

In a black-and-white blur, a soul both nimble and daring had arrived on the scene—Neil MacGregor's collie, Scotchbonnet, though of her master there was nary a sign. Halting their ineffectual dodging about, they stood back as the collie waded in.

Ian had seen such dogs at their work before, with sheep as well as cattle, and knew what they could accomplish with a creeping stalk, a steady gaze, and a force of will wholly out of proportion to their frames.

Normally a slender creature, Scotch was heavy-bellied with a litter of pups soon to whelp. Her impending circumstance notwithstanding, in seconds she had the cow backed off the fence far enough for Ian and Ally to get between and set to right the cracked rails, preventing the calf and the rest of their agitated herd from spilling into the yard. Ally did his best to talk calm into bovine brains, while Scotch proceeded to force her errant charge back toward its proper abode, with Naomi, Mandy, and Malcolm watching from the cabin door-yard.

It was then Neil MacGregor arrived, alerted to trouble upon riding in from a medical call. "Which took me from home in the wee hours," he explained once the dust had settled, crouching to give his good dog's ears a fondling. "I spotted Scotch here heading down the track and, surmising what must be afoot, rode after my canny wee lass."

Naomi slipped the dog a strip of venison, smoked days ago. Then Neil and Scotchbonnet took their brindled escapee home, Neil promising to secure her until maternal anxieties abated. *"An rud a théid fad o'n t-sùil; théid e fad o'n chridhe,"* he said in parting, at which Ian and Malcolm chuckled but Ally and Naomi gave puzzled looks.

"Out o' sight, out o' mind," Malcolm loosely translated.

"Or heart," Ian added, smile fading when thought of Gabriel tightened his chest. "Let's shore up that fence, Ally."

As the smell of frying bacon wafted from the cabin, they set to replacing the damaged rails.

Pausing for Ian to lift the final rail into place, Ally swiped off his hat to mop his sweating brow. "This'll teach me to let a critter lie out on its own, first night away from its mama."

"That's sound thinking in general," Ian replied. "But somehow I doubt it would have made a difference had ye let that calf lay its head in your lap the night through."

Pursing his lips in thought, Ally shoved a leaning post upright while Ian packed its base with earth.

Ally stood back, blew a gusting breath, and with the first tone of rebuke Ian had ever heard him use, added, "You never warned me how taxing it be, Mister Ian, being my own master. Means *I* the one got to think of every little thing, don't it?"

"Aye, Ally, it often seems so," Ian agreed, just managing not to laugh. "So what shall we do to prevent this happening again?" He fully expected a commitment to sleeping out with the calf from then on.

Screwing up a frown, Ally gave the question a ponder; then his broad features brightened. "I'm gonna get me one of them collie pups, soon as it's born. Their mama's smarter than us two put together."

Ian did laugh then. He couldn't help it. Nor had he the heart to tell Ally that collies weren't born as canny-wise as Scotch but must be taught the business. Still, as they made their way back to the cabin for their breakfast, he slid the man a sidelong glance, deciding Ally was equal to the challenge—and that he had just been handed a far more entertaining postscriptum to share with Seona.

After receiving a letter from John Reynold and another payment in gold, Ian had undertaken a hasty trip to Cooperstown before snow fell in earnest, making the roads impassable without a sleigh, a conveyance he had yet to construct. With William Cooper attending Congress in Philadelphia, he had dealt instead with Moss Kent, a young lawyer lodged with the family, who afterward invited him along the village street to a nearby tavern.

Cradling a cup of cider at the tavern's counter, Ian spoke over nearby conversations and a game of dice raising the noise level in the public room. "Mrs. Cooper seemed a mite thin, from what I recall. Is she unwell?"

"I've written Cooper repeatedly," Kent said, "at Mrs. Cooper's request, enjoining the man to come home before Congress adjourns. She has no wish to spend another winter here and pines to be gone before snow flies." He shook his head. "She'd uproot them all and go back east, but I think it would break the younger boys' hearts. Will, Sam, young James, they adore this country. It's gotten into their blood."

Ian was about to admit of being like-minded when the level of noise in the room spiked; the dice game had broken up in a quarrel. The loudest voice, slurred with drink, belonged to a wiry, slope-shouldered man, reddish hair and beard dulled by grease and gray. Another man, younger, scraped back a chair to stand facing the gingery drunkard. "Ye're naught but a sore loser, Crane. We been casting these dice for years. Not a soul would back a claim they're weighted in my favor."

"Be off with you," another man said, turning on the one called Crane. "Don't play the game if you cannot take a loss."

Gazing blearily around the taproom, the man Crane took in the faces turned his way, expressions ranging from irritation to open hostility. He snarled something too mumbled to catch, then snatched up a battered hat and slunk from the tavern, his steps surer than Ian would have expected, given the state of his speech.

A wafting of cold night air swept through the room, bending candle flames and shivering over the back of Ian's neck.

"One good thing about winter coming," Kent muttered at the banging door. "Snow will send that ne'er-do-well back up to his haunts on the Mohawk—at least until spring."

Ian swiveled on his stool to face his companion. "Not an isolated incident, I take it. Who was that?"

"Aram Crane, and a sorrier excuse for a man I hope you never encounter."

"The village drunkard?"

"Not ours, thank Providence. He's been living half-wild in the hills north of the Mohawk for a decade at least, bothering folk up there. He comes down to Canajoharie, Cherry Valley, or Cooperstown—more's the pity—a few times a year. At best he's a nuisance. At worst . . ."

"A man to be avoided," Ian supplied when Kent let the statement fizzle. He sipped his cider, thinking it time he returned to his hired room in a quieter inn and the bed awaiting him there. Even on Ruiadh it was a two-day ride back to Shiloh, pushing hard.

"If you would know my opinion on the matter," Kent said, "it's time for Judge Cooper to step aside from politics, let minds with deeper learning take the lead. His crude form of backwoods justice leaves much to be desired when men like Crane are free to roam, slapped on the wrist for their crimes."

Crimes. Was Crane guilty of something worse than being a troublesome drunk? And what was Kent about, disparaging Judge Cooper when he lodged in the man's house, managed his affairs, penned letters for his wife?

Ian set down his cup. "I wouldn't know about the man as judge or congressman, but he's been exceedingly generous to me. And as I've an early start to make in the morning . . ." Leaving coin on the counter beside the cup, he took up his hat. "I expect ye'll see me again come spring. Until then, I wish both ye and the Coopers well."

Though clearly disappointed by the abrupt leave-taking, Kent thrust out a hand. "All right, Mr. Cameron. At least now I know Cooper's claim of the gold you paid for your land was more than his wishful thinking."

Alarmed at the mention, Ian grasped Kent's hand briefly, then made for the tavern door, clapping his hat on his head. Outside in the starlight, the air was chill, though not yet with the bite of winter.

With hands balled into fists, Ian strode from the tavern. Passing an adjacent row of shops, he cast a look back, assured to see no one had followed him from the establishment. Perhaps no one had overheard the mention of gold. He hoped Kent would keep his gob shut on the matter and share no further details.

"Let me go!"

The outcry shattered the peace of the village street as Ian turned back to watch his path—not quick enough to sidestep the small figure that bolted from between two shops. Ian caught the child by slender shoulders to steady . . . *him*, apparently, for lack of a petticoat.

"Lad? What's got ye bothered?"

The boy struggled briefly, then stilled, face lifted. "Mr. Cameron?"

"Aye." Ian squinted, at last recognizing Judge Cooper's youngest son. "James, is it? What are ye doing out in the streets at this hour?"

"Nothing," the boy said with the haste of the guilty. He looked back down the alley from which he had bolted. "That man—he asked did I have any coins in my pockets. When I said no, he tried to see for himself. I don't! I only have—" The boy gulped back whatever he had been about to admit and asked, "Did you bring my pa more of that gold?"

"Hush now." Ian's grip on the lad tightened in warning. He heard the shuffle of someone still in the alley. It sounded like whoever had accosted the lad was retreating. "What are ye about, wee James? And what *do* ye have in your pockets?"

"I told you. Nothing . . ." Even as he said the word, from the vicinity of the boy's breeches there came the shrill chirp of a cricket. Probably the season's last—and destined for a sibling's bed or hair or porridge bowl, come morning.

"Get ye home," Ian said, grinning at thought of a day when—God willing—he might have such a conversation with Gabriel. "Afore some other rascal finds ye out."

The boy darted into the night, in the general direction of the Cooper residence. Ian decided to follow, to be sure he made it home. He had barely reached the next gap between two darkened structures when a shadow stepped out, moving across his path. A shadow larger than a child's.

Ian halted, hand brushing aside his coat, fingers curving around the handle of his belt knife, as out of the darkness came a voice he recognized, though it wasn't as slurred as last he heard it.

"Cameron's the name, is it?"

"Who wants to know?" Ian asked, though the man's silhouette confirmed what his ears had already discerned.

"No one," said Aram Crane, bumping Ian's shoulder as he passed into the night.

12 November 1796

To Ian Cameron
Shiloh, New York

Dear Ian—

Mama and me laughed over your telling of Ally and that Cow you tried to catch until the tears rolled down our cheeks. It minded me of the Pig at Mountain Laurel—that Shoat John Reynold bought that kept running back to us. You caught it in the stable-yard, no help from any collie dog, but I am happy you had that smart dog of Mr. MacGregor's to sort out your Cow problem. Mama says tell Ally that's why we have each other, too, to help us think of all the things.

I did laugh about that Cow but later, thinking on it, I cried. I did not know what was making me sad when first I thought it funny, but Mama knew. She said that Cow come seeking her Calf was like you coming back to Boston for Gabriel. That made me cry more since you had to leave him again. Gabriel misses Mandy. He asks for her like he used to ask for Ned's boys, back in Winter. He does not ask for Robbie and Eddie now. I do not want him to stop asking for his Sister.

It will be a fine thing to have a collie dog helping Ally with the stock. I reckon by now it is born. I like hearing about Shiloh and the doings there. You cannot tell me too much of that. Mister Robert told me what that Gaelic you wrote down that Neil MacGregor said means. "That which goes far from the eye goes far from the heart." Maybe that is true for Cows but not for me. Is it for you? Is Gabriel still in your heart? He has a passel of new words since you left. He does not talk as clear as Mandy but is putting more of his words together now. I do feel a pang of sadness watching him grow, even though his learning makes me proud and I would not trade being his Mama for anything. Which makes me all the sorrier for your Brother, who had this joy, then lost it. Ned means to spend Christmas in Deerfield. We pray good comes of it.

I want to tell you what I should have wrote in my first Letter, that I pray for you and Mandy, Malcolm, Naomi, Ally, even your neighbors you have named. Every day. There is something else I want you to know. You asked in what way did your leaving hurt me. I thought surely you could guess.

I have sat here with my quill hovering over the paper, unable to set down what I meant to say about that. I do not know what can be done about this pain between us. Or maybe I do but am afraid of it. I am trying to be truthful. That is all I can bring myself to write for now—

Seona Cameron
Beachum Lane, Boston

15

SHILOH, NEW YORK

November's chill crept with evening shadow through the doors left open to the MacGregors' stable-yard, down the aisle to the second box stall, where the smell of frost and decaying leaves mingled with the pungent scent of puppies. Outside the box, in which Scotchbonnet's litter of six nested in straw, Ian and Neil leaned against the latched gate. A fortnight shy of weaning, the puppies—black-and-white fluffballs all, save one brown-and-white—were old enough to tumble about the box with Jamie, Liam, and Ally, who had come with Ian to claim his promised pup.

"Ye've your choice of the males," Ian told him, Neil having mentioned Colonel Waring, who owned the sire, had claimed a female before the whelping. "The girl pup is spoken for."

"That's still five of 'em!" Ally exclaimed, on his knees as the pups swarmed him with licking tongues and swatting tails. "They all as purty as their mama."

Peering over the lower slats, boarded to contain her offspring, Scotch wagged her brushy tail.

Ian turned to share his amusement with Neil. Catching a shadow on the other man's face, he pitched his voice low. "Ye're satisfied with the work in trade?"

He hadn't witnessed the stone-grubbing done in a newly cleared field the MacGregors meant to plant next spring, assuming all was well when Ally returned from his last day of work claiming his pup fairly purchased.

"What?" Neil blinked, then registered the question. "Oh, aye. The man works as hard as any two I've kent. It's no' that." He drew Ian away from the puppies' box, deeper into the stable. "Did ye ever meet the Colonel's son Francis?"

"Francis Waring? No. Heard his name in passing, is all."

Concern weighed Neil's brow. "Aye, well. He's been awa' to parts unknown since afore Scotch's pups came."

"Parts unknown?" Ian echoed.

"It's no' a thing unusual for Francis. He's . . ." Neil searched for words. "Prone to wandering the hills from time to time. Shy as a wild creature himself, more at home with the foxes than his own kin, ye might say. But he's ne'er been gone this long a stretch, and it getting on for winter. Maggie's gey worrit over him and—"

"Mister Ian?"

They turned back to the puppies' box to see Ally on his feet, looking distressed.

"I done narrowed it down to two—the brown and the freckled. But . . ." The big man's lower lip trembled. "Reckon it'll be nip and tuck can I choose. I can't handle thought of *not* choosing either."

A grin pushed back the worry shadowing Neil's face. "Och, Ally. No need for nip and tuck. Choose them both, if ye want."

Ally's trembling lip sagged. "Mister Neil . . . you mean it? I'd work double for 'em."

"Ye've already worked enough for two." Neil returned to the box to eye his sons. "Speaking of work—Jamie, Liam, there's boxes to muck afore the rest of the horses are brought in for the night."

With groaning compliance, the boys rose, shedding straw and puppies. The three exited the box, letting Scotch in without letting the pups out, a task requiring everyone's attention. Not until the gate was shut did Ian catch sight of the stranger standing in the stable doorway, tall and imposing.

"Neil," he hissed, registering breechclout and leggings, tomahawk and belt knife, long black hair worn loose. He was reaching for his own knife when his neighbor turned, saw the Indian, and grinned.

"Here ye are at last, man. Matthew was starting to think ye'd forgot him."

Smiling in welcome, Neil MacGregor strode past Ian to greet the Indian with a hand to a lofty shoulder, as the boys came rushing from the stable's depths with cries of "Uncle Joseph!"

Seated cross-legged before the hearth, the sleeves of his shirt pushed up to copper armbands—revealing tattoos encircling his forearms in a series of lines and elongated triangles—Joseph Tames-His-Horse still exuded an imposing air as he fiddled with a pipe slow to light from the glowing wood-splinter he held to its bowl.

While Ally had returned to the farm after choosing Nip and Tuck, as he had christened his pups, Ian had stayed and supped with the MacGregors and the Mohawk warrior, who, it turned out, was Willa MacGregor's clan brother.

"We're all Wolf Clan," Maggie had said, smiling across the supper table. "Except Papa. He's just a Scot."

"*Just* a Scot?" Seated at the table's head, Neil had pretended offense. "Need I remind ye, lass—MacGregors are a clan too. As are Camerons," he added charitably with a nod toward Ian at the table's foot.

"Even Jamie and I are Wolf Clan," Liam had added, giving his older brother a nudge. "It comes through the mother."

"So I've heard," Ian had said, familiar with the notion of matrilineal clans. "But, Willa . . . how did *that* come to be?"

"I was fourteen when taken captive," Willa explained, passing a dish of the spiced corn and beans called succotash. "From that islet in the lake, one day when I went there to read my book."

"It was *Pamela*, by Mr. Richardson," Maggie interjected, to answering grins around the table.

"It was a mourning raid," Willa continued. "The warriors were seeking captives to adopt. I was taken north over the mountains to the *Kanien'kehá:ka*—the Mohawk—who lived on the St. Lawrence River, and given the name Burning Sky." Willa gazed across the table at the tall man seated between Matthew and Maggie. "And met my brother."

Above the bosses of his cheekbones, Joseph's dark eyes teased, their corners creasing deep. "I found you in a cornfield, angry and crying and not much pleased to make my acquaintance."

"Not at first," Willa agreed. "I changed my mind soon enough."

The story had gone on around the table, told by one and then another, how Willa lived twelve years as a Mohawk before returning to Shiloh. There she found her parents dead—accused of being Loyalists to the Crown, their farm confiscated and scheduled for auction—and Neil MacGregor lying injured on the border of her land. Neil had been passing through on his way into the mountains when he had taken a fall and broken his wrist. Willa had sheltered him. While he healed, she set about proving her parents hadn't been Loyalists. All to keep her land.

It was during those days Joseph Tames-His-Horse had arrived on her cabin doorstep, seeking his missing clan sister. He had stayed for a time, doubting her choice to leave their people and live again as a white woman.

"And I wanted to be sure of this one," Joseph added, canting his head toward Neil. "That he did not mean my sister ill."

"Aye," Neil said. "And ye managed to put the fear o' God and man both in me, wi' barely a word exchanged on the matter."

With a rush of warmth for this family forged from brokenness, from loss and pain, Ian had longed for his own to be so. For Seona and Gabriel—Lily too, if she wished—to be present at his table, as they were already in his heart. He dared to hope in a future in which that vision could come to pass. But how?

After supper everyone save the boys, gone back out to the puppies, had seated themselves in the house's common room, a parlor made to feel more rustic than refined with a set of elk antlers resting along the wide mantel and bear pelts draped over furnishings, not to mention the packs, shot bags, rifles, and snowshoes arranged against the wall. Since his thirteenth year, Matthew had spent each winter hunting with his Wolf Clan uncle, who had come from his Canadian home with the

Mohawk in Grand River to collect the lad. They were leaving come morning.

The fire crackled. The scent of woodsmoke filled the room, in which everyone save Ian had a project going. Maggie had a book open, preparing school lessons by candlelight. Willa sorted through a bushel of late apples. Neil sharpened a set of scalpels with a stone, while Matthew, on the floor next to Joseph, cleaned a musket.

Ian realized he wasn't as surprised by the revelation of Willa's past as an Indian captive as he might have been. He had heard its evidence in her speech, seen it in their fields—corn, beans, and squash grown together, those Three Sisters he had seen grown thus by the Chippewa.

He mentioned as much from his chair near the hearth, opposite Willa's clan brother, who had been mending a winter moccasin before pausing to light his pipe, which appeared to be drawing to his satisfaction now. Ian half expected it to be passed around their circle, as he had seen done in the lodges up north—west, rather. He tended to forget how far north he was again living.

Joseph Tames-His-Horse raised his head. "Did you live among the Chippewa?"

"Aye, in a settlement of trappers and their families. My uncle's a fur trader. His wife is Chippewa."

Maggie looked up from the book open in her lap. "Do you have cousins like us? Like me and Matthew?"

"I do," Ian said, then ventured, "But how did ye and your brother come to be here, not living with the Mohawk up in Grand River? If ye don't mind my asking."

Maggie's gaze questioned her brother. "Shall you tell it or I?"

"You're better with stories," Matthew said.

"All right." Maggie turned back to Ian. "It was Uncle Joseph who found us—though first *we* found his mare, left in a thicket while he was hunting. Matthew and I were on our own, orphaned, and seeking our mother's people."

Joseph had tracked his stolen mare, found the children, and taken them to his clan sister, returned to her white father's farm. At first they hadn't trusted Willa, no matter she spoke their mother's language better than they did. But Willa won them over at last. Though Joseph had promised to take them farther west, to where the Mohawks had fled with their allies, the defeated British, they chose to remain with Willa.

"By then Papa wanted to marry Mama," Maggie said, face bright with the memories of their family's beginnings. "Mama agreed with the plan. So we adopted them as our parents."

"In a manner o' speaking," Neil MacGregor interjected, clearly tamping back a grin. But across the room, Matthew was shaking his head.

"I take back what I said about your storytelling, Maggie. You left out the exciting part. What about the burning cabin and Francis—"

After Matthew bit off his words, Ian blinked at the frozen expressions in the room, then followed their gazes to Maggie, whose face had drained of joy. She rose with her book and made for the door, pausing to murmur to their mother about preparing for the morning in solitude. She left without saying good night.

Awkward silence settled, broken by the fire's snapping, until Ian cleared his throat, turning to Neil. "Is that the same Francis ye mentioned before?"

"Aye. The same."

Matthew muttered something in what Ian took for Mohawk, then looked around the room, scowling in self-recrimination. "I'm sorry. I wasn't thinking . . ."

Joseph was watching their faces. "What is amiss with Francis?"

"Nothing, we hope," Willa said as Neil set down scalpel and stone and rose to add wood to the fire. "Weeks ago Goodenough and the Colonel noticed he was gone—on one of his hill rambles, we thought. But it has been over a month. He never stays away this long."

Still agitated, Matthew eyed the doorway through which his sister had passed, then shot up from the floor and went after her.

The air left in his wake stirred, unsettled. Joseph's pipe had gone out. He did not relight it. "I should have finished what I began that summer."

"No," Neil said, taking his seat. "The man hasna troubled us again."

"Who?" Ian asked, thoroughly confused. "Francis?"

A beat of silence passed before Willa said, "No. Another who did harm to us, the year the children came to us." Her mouth had tightened as she spoke, her gaze on her brother sharpened in warning.

"Aram Crane," Joseph said, ignoring it.

Shock rippled through Ian at the name. He straightened in his chair. "Crane? I met the man—or one going by the same name. In Cooperstown, last month."

Their startled looks had Ian telling the story of finding young James Cooper being accosted by Crane, after his disturbance in the tavern. The tale left them grim-faced, Joseph Tames-His-Horse most of all.

"Joseph, you are not to blame for every ill that man has committed these past twelve years," Willa said with surprising fervor, at which her clan brother raised his gaze in challenge.

"Am I not?"

"No. And as I have said, many times, better to let sleeping dogs lie."

"Crane was a British Army deserter," Neil explained for Ian's benefit. "He was the other reason Joseph came to Shiloh, twelve years ago. He was tracking Crane for the British, out of Niagara, and found him here."

"I had the man," Joseph said. "Had him in my hands, a prisoner. He escaped."

After another prickling silence, Neil said, "Cooperstown is a long way off. Let's dinna fash about Crane, aye?"

Ian opened his mouth to relate what Moss Kent had told him about Crane—that he expected the man to go back north of the Mohawk River before winter, far closer to Shiloh than Cooperstown—but hesitated to feed the tension in the room. He looked instead at the darkened window. It grew late. He wanted to start another letter to Seona before he slept.

One letter at a time . . .

As if the Almighty had dropped the thought into his brain, he knew it was the answer to how the vision he had had at supper could come to pass, that of the souls who claimed his heart regathered. With that vision uppermost in his mind, he rose and bade his neighbors a good night, thanking them for their hospitality. Joseph headed out to the stable to tend his horse. Ian clapped his hat on to follow, but Neil intercepted him on the chilly veranda.

"I ken ye're wondering about Maggie and Francis," he said softly, though all the windows of the house were shut. "While ye get your horse saddled, I'll tell ye."

1 January 1797

To Ian Cameron
Shiloh, New York

Dear Ian—

Today I pen the New Year for the first time. Did everyone in your cabin have a good Christmas in the wilds of New York? How deep is the Snow there? We have more than enough on the ground and bleak skies again this day, so more must be coming. Icicles on the eaves are big around as my arm! I long for the day my fingers do not sting when I bring in water from the pump or buy wood from the sellers. I never knew how blessed with wood for burning we were at Mountain Laurel until I came to a place it must be bought.

Our Christmas was quiet except for Gabriel. It is hard on him being cooped indoors when it is too cold to be outside. Sometimes he dashes about (Rambunctious your Mama says). Lest you think I am not raising him proper, most times he is a good Boy, though he is at his best on days he can be outside to run off his Rambunctious. How does Mandy do inside that cabin in Winter? Gabriel is saying about a hundred more words than when last I mentioned it but still has trouble with words with R in them, like his own name. Your Mama says you had the same trouble but now you can roll those Rs like a proper Scotsman when you want—which I know—so I am not bothered about it. We attended Christmas meeting, then made ourselves a Feast with a Turkey and trimmings. Ned is still in Deerfield but writes he will return by month's end, though Penny will not come back to the house where her Sons are no more. Your Daddy says it might be best Ned get shed of the place after all.

It is hard to warm the reaches of this House, as you know. We gather Evenings with our work in the keeping room. Sometimes we make up pallets by the fire, me, Mama, and Gabriel, then hang a quilt over chairs to make a tent. Gabriel says we are Bears in a cave. Your Mama read him a story with Bears in it. He has not stopped talking of Bears since. Do you have Bears in Shiloh? I promised I would ask.

Your recounting of how the MacGregors became a Family was something to marvel over. It filled up my heart with warmth and my eyes with tears in a way I am still trying to fathom. I am sorry to hear about that Francis Waring gone missing, and that Maggie MacGregor is upset over it, even blaming herself, like Mr. MacGregor told you when you were taking your leave that Evening. Though I doubt her confessing her love for the man, a love he could not return, is likely to have sent him off into the Wilds for so long, causing everyone such worry, even if he is as strange as was described. It must be something else. But I do not know these Folk, so I cannot say of a certain.

Catriona is saying she wants to write to Maggie MacGregor her own self. I suspect she has gone ahead with the notion and will be adding a Letter when I post this of mine. Your sister is behaving herself flichtie (your Mama's word again), down in spirit some days, flying high as a bird others. She will say she is fine when I ask, or claim to be missing you and Mandy, which I am sure is true. I miss you too, though I felt something different in your last Letter, a distance I did not understand. Then I reached the part where you asked why I could not tell you my thoughts in my last Letter, that you worried you had asked too much of me. You admitted there is pain between us, that you know what you want to do about it, but think I am not ready for whatever it is. Maybe I could be if I can put a Question back to you. Do you still have those Matters of the heart you once mentioned concerning me? I need to know, because one reason there is still pain between us is because I have those Matters and I do not want my heart broke again.

I like what you said about Gabriel, that his absence could never drive him from your heart. I hope to hear from you and that you will answer my Question—

Seona Cameron
Beachum Lane, Boston

PS: I laughed about Ally getting himself <u>*two*</u> *pups when he could not choose between. And those names he gave them. Nip and Tuck!*

16

20 January 1797

To Seona Cameron
Beachum Lane
Boston, Massachusetts

My Dear Seona—

Earnest Blessings to you, Gabriel, and all for a New Year begun in Peace. My own is made brighter having received your Letter. Two days ago I conveyed Catriona's to Maggie MacGregor in Shiloh, where she teaches those children whose parents allow it (though the Lass is as blue-stockinged as my Sister, there are those who withhold even the most basic learning from their Offspring on account of Maggie's Indian blood). Yesterday I had a visit from Neil MacGregor, who shared his and Willa's relief; not for Months had they seen Maggie so animated as when she arrived home bearing Catriona's Missive. Neil brought other news to share—Willa MacGregor is with child. All are astonished, none more than Willa, it being now ten years since their last, Liam, was born.

Winter is bitter here. Snow is deep, the cold unrelenting—I have reacquainted myself with the Art of Snowshoeing and have built us a sleigh that Ally's mare, Cupid, easily pulls. Mandy does well enough in the cabin but misses the Chickens, so Naomi bundles her warmly and takes her out to fetch in the eggs the Hens keep snug in their shed. I have done some hunting, though I do not like to be away above a night (tell Gabriel that, at present, all our Bears are snug asleep in their dens). We are well enough provisioned otherwise as I was able to purchase additional stores in Cooperstown in Autumn.

Whatever else newsworthy comes to mind I shall write to Da, for I wish to address a Subject with you and feel I must do so while both my candle and courage last—that being the answer to your Question. Have I no more Matters of the Heart concerning you? Seona, it is uppermost of all I have, has been since before I was made to believe you had abandoned me and run to Freedom with Thomas. I wish I could turn back time and see through the machinations of my Kin who spirited you away, find you long before I managed it. Then I see my sleeping Daughter and cannot wish her away. I love Mandy. I love Gabriel. And I love you.

My Heart pounds having written such bold words. Should I find the courage to seal this Letter and post it, know these lines are bathed in my Prayers that the Almighty might redeem our broken Hearts and grant us another chance at wholeness. I count the days until I hear from you on these Matters that so concern our Hearts.

Meanwhile remaining Your Devoted Servant—

Ian Cameron
Shiloh, New York

30 January 1797

To Ian Cameron
Shiloh, New York

Dear Ian—

I see you found the courage to post that Letter, written ten days ago by your Date and here I am reading it. It must have taken wing (an Angel's?) as it has reached me so fast, and with all that snow still to hinder. It is good to hear Catriona's Letter was so well received. I knew it already, for Letters have come from Maggie MacGregor.

There is much I want to say about those Matters of our Hearts. First I must ask one Question more, hoping you will answer and not fret over how I will take it. Did Judith know you never stopped loving me? Because she loved you from a true Heart. I saw that plain. While it hurt like a knife cutting up my own, I was glad at least you had the sense to choose her over her Sister, who I think has loved no one but her own self ever.

Now I will confess. When you left us last Summer, I almost begged you to stay. As you and that wagonful trundled off from the Chestnut Inn, I wanted to—

I got called away of a sudden from writing this Letter, and for something you will want to know about. I have seen Thomas Ross! He is alive and keeping on with what he started down in Carolina, which your Mama tells me not to write plain. Thomas came to the house and supped with us. He heard about you selling Mountain Laurel, then the lot of you heading off to New York. He wanted to know all you had told us of Shiloh. I asked after Esther, but he has not been back to Chesterfield and does not know anything of her or of Maisy and Jubal. After supper he went his way, not saying it outright, but I know he means to continue his Work.

Lest you think Thomas showing up has distracted me from what is between us, it has not. You said in a Letter some time back that there was never going to be an easy way through this. I cannot imagine it was easy for Judith, either. Not if she knew how you felt about me all the while. Did she know?

I wait for your reply, hoping again for Angel Wings—

Seona Cameron

Beachum Lane, Boston

17 February 1797

To Seona Cameron
Beachum Lane
Boston, Massachusetts

My Dearest Seona—

Perhaps there is an Angel winging our Correspondence between us, for while more than ten Days have passed between the dating of your most recent Letter and my receiving it, still it has arrived more speedily than I dared hope, yet I hardly know where to begin my reply. I shall start with those responses which hold my Heart most lightly.

Maggie MacGregor has indeed entered zealously into correspondence with Catriona. Willa informs me Maggie brings home a Letter from Keagan's store every few days. Having grown fond of the MacGregors, I am gratified by this further connection between our Families.

Onward to your News of Thomas. He lives—the wee gomeral—and you have all broken bread with him! I am relieved to know the Conviction that caused him to pursue his reckless course in Carolina has neither deserted him nor led to his untimely Death. Concerning Esther's situation, I will pray the more fervently for her Safety and Deliverance. My means are limited at present, but God's never are.

I come now to that Subject most gripping to my Heart. Aye, Judith knew of my love for you—from the day I asked her to be my Wife to the day our Son was birthed and they went together to be with the Lord in Heaven. But know, Seona, that during the time I was married, with you and Gabriel gone to Boston, I learned to cherish Judith, to value the woman she was, as a Wife and as Mandy's Mother. That I loved her were the last words she heard on this Earth. With no notion whether that is what you wanted or dreaded to hear, I can only assure you of its Truth, which is what I want between us, even if it brings with it a sting. Healing often does.

I have begun reading aloud Scripture of an Evening after we in our cabin have supped. Just now we find ourselves in the Book of Hebrews, the Twelfth Chapter. "Wherefore lift up the hands which hang down, and the feeble knees; and make straight paths for your feet, lest that which is lame be turned out of the way; but let it rather be healed." That part about straight paths reminds me of something I heard Willa MacGregor say, which she explains is a Mohawk way of thinking. It is this: I want the path between our Hearts to be made straight, cleared of all Obstacles. Cleared of hurt and misunderstanding, for our Healing. Do you desire that as well? Will you come to us in Shiloh, you and Gabriel, and make this place (and once more my Heart) your Home?

Tonight another snow is falling but I hope tomorrow the sleigh and our sturdy Cupid will deliver me the miles into Shiloh to post this Letter, in hopes our attending Angel will see it whisked to you with haste. Though thought of waiting even a Day for your reply finds no purchase in the Heart of your Devoted Servant—

Ian Cameron
Shiloh, New York

28 February 1797

To Seona Cameron
Beachum Lane
Boston, Massachusetts

Dear Seona—

Doubtless I am hasty in writing less than a Fortnight since posting my last Letter, but find I bear the waiting poorly, fearing what I wrote concerning Judith, or my hope of your coming to Shiloh, has caused distress. Is that how I should judge your Silence, or is it the vagaries of the Post and your reply merely delayed in reaching me? Or that I failed to mention Lily? I assumed she would accompany you. Forgive me that omission. Let me make the Invitation explicit: if Lily wishes to come to New York, she is welcome.

Now I must broach another Concern. Yesterday Willa MacGregor walked over to relate, with no small discomfort, that she read a Letter from Catriona found tucked into a book left behind when Maggie went into Shiloh one recent morning. She meant nothing unseemly by it; Maggie, so Willa thought, has been in the habit of sharing Catriona's letters with her. Plainly not all her letters.

Is there something amiss with my Sister concerning that man who caused Da and Ned such difficulty last year? The name Morgan Shelby was mentioned in the Letter in a manner that raises concern—that he has troubled Catriona as well. The precise nature of troubling was not made clear but seemed of a most serious nature, which is why Willa asked if I was apprised of the situation. I am not but wish to be.

No doubt this Missive will cross your reply to my last and my impatience will be soothed (and perhaps my Concerns for Catriona allayed) by the time you read this belated Postscriptum from your Devoted Servant—

Ian Cameron
Shiloh, New York

12 March 1797

To Seona Cameron
Beachum Lane
Boston, Massachusetts

Seona—

Winter shows Signs of easing its grip on the Wilds of New York, yet still no word from you! I have leapt over Impatience and slid headlong into Worry. It is not like you to go so quiet, even if what I asked was met not with Joy, as I hoped, but dismay. You asked for Truth. I ask only the same—

Ian

13 March 1797

To Ian Cameron
Shiloh, New York

Dear Ian—

I have just received your Letter dated 17 February. Did our Angel get himself turned about? I will write briefly and send this on its way in Hope that you do not wait so long to know my Answer. I do desire to come with Gabriel to Shiloh. Mama too. She and I talked of it before your Letter came. How ought we to go about it? Your Daddy says he will help but he must hear from you. I am in such a state of Nerves my hand trembles, and you may not make heads or tails of these my words, so I will end this and write more when I have better possessed myself.

I like being your Dearest—

Seona Cameron
Beachum Lane, Boston

9 April 1797

To Seona Cameron
Beachum Lane
Boston, Massachusetts

My Dearest Seona—

In a state of Nerves is precisely how I am rendered knowing you are coming to us. I will write to Da of the particulars of that Undertaking (you have Juturna and her dam, but perhaps another horse and cart could be procured?). I shall meet you on the Road, perhaps in Albany. But know that however the practicalities are arranged, you will not travel one step of the Journey unaccompanied by a trusted Guide, provisioned for every necessity—speaking of which, Naomi tells me Malcolm is desirous of a Bible of his own. On my next sojourn to Cooperstown, I may find one but feel the Gift would carry more substance did it come from our Family. Would you ask Da whether a Bible might be procured and bring it with you when you come?

I have read the few Lines you wrote countless times over, wishing for something more of your Heart, but it seems you have chosen to share such Sentiments in person. But did you not receive my second Letter? You make no mention of Catriona. What is afoot with that Sister of mine?

I have come into possession of some seasoned Maple which I deem suitable for Cabinetmaking and need to begin crafting some serviceable plenishings for our cabins—plural. Ally and I have, despite the muddiness of our thawing ground, begun building a second cabin for Naomi, Malcolm, and himself (and the Collies, who grow like weeds and are learning their Business among the Cows). So you see there will be room for all. I intend to build a proper House, this Summer if I can get wood enough cut and seasoned but more likely next. Much grubbing and tilling of earth remains to be done, readying our ground for its first Planting, before your arrival. Joyous Day!

I am the happiest of Men as I envision you here, sharing in this adventure of creating a Home, and could write reams on that giddy theme. I will restrain myself and seal this Letter and begin one to Da, remaining forever your Devoted & Faithful Servant—

Ian Cameron
Shiloh, New York

PART III

Spring 1797–Summer 1797
New York

17

ALBANY, NEW YORK
June 1797

The abovestairs room in the public house, away from the busy river dock, was so like others they had hired on their journey thus far, Seona barely took note of its particulars as she laid Gabriel, heavy as a sack of stones and clammy with fever, on the quilt overspreading the bed. She had known something wasn't right with him when they woke that morning in a similar room on the Hudson's east bank, ready for an early river crossing, with hopes of reaching Schenectady by nightfall.

Seona had spent days dreading the Hudson. Wanting that broad river behind them, she had reasoned away Gabriel's sleepy disinterest in breakfast, his crankiness. Well out on that choppy water, with her own belly surging to the ferry's dip and sway, her boy had vomited down her petticoat. By the time they set foot on dry land, with horses, cart, and baggage accounted for, Gabriel had been hot and wailing in her arms.

With no sign of Ian waiting at the ferry landing, and no more thought in anyone's mind of trying to make Schenectady, Ned Cameron had driven the cart up into the town of Albany, found the inn, and settled them in that room. If *settled* it could be called. Past wailing now, Gabriel was fretful and whimpering in his misery, blue eyes pleading, pricking Seona's own with tears.

"I know, baby. It'll be all right." *Lord, make it all right.*

Voices reached her through the room's open door, one her mama's.

"Here ye are, girl-baby," Lily said in her most comforting tone, coming into the room with Seona's spare petticoat over one arm, simples box tucked under the other. Behind her came a girl, short and slender, no older than sixteen. She carried a pitcher and was aproned like a kitchen maid, which it turned out she was. She was also as black-haired and copper-skinned as Lily.

"Hannah Kirby," she introduced herself, advancing into the room to pour water from the pitcher into a basin already provided. She set the pitcher to one side and bobbed a curtsy. "I'm at your service—between meals—to fetch for you and that little man of yours. Water's heating in the kitchen," she added, addressing Lily, who had set her box on a bench at the bed's foot and was rummaging through it. "I'll bring it up directly and you can brew your fever tea. Would he take a little sweetening in it?"

"Aye." Lily set out willow bark, yarrow, mint, other herbs. "Maple sugar, if ye have it to hand."

"Plenty—it was a good sugar boil this spring." Hannah paused by the bed to peer down at Gabriel's flushed cheeks. "You've traveled from Boston? That's enough to take it out of anyone. How's his breathing? I could chop onions for a poultice. Nothing like onions to loosen a chest."

"No . . . thank you," Seona said, grateful at least Gabriel's breathing held no rattle. "I think it's just the fever. He vomited once, as you can smell, but that might have been the ferry crossing."

Hannah wrinkled her nose but smiled, making a dimple appear in one rounded cheek. "I'll be back directly with the hot water."

From her perch on the edge of the bed, Seona watched the girl leave the room, long black braid swinging to her waist. "She's Indian."

"I reckon she must be, or part." Lily crossed the room to peer down at her grandson as Seona began to strip off his sweaty garments, which needed washing as badly as her petticoat. "Ye'll want to bathe him. Hannah left cloths for the purpose."

Seona took up one of the clean rags brought with the water and started bathing Gabriel to cool his heated skin. Like any child he'd had fevers of the milder sort in Boston, but she had dared hope they would reach Shiloh without having to deal with illness along the way. Somehow it struck a deeper chord of helplessness, caught halfway between the home left behind and the one they journeyed toward. Nothing familiar, the most basic tasks a hurdle to surmount. Everyone they met a stranger.

Lily, with her usual outward calm, measured willow bark and the other herbs for the tea, ready to steep it as soon as Hannah returned.

Gabriel tried to push Seona's hand away when she touched the wet, cooling cloth to his brow. "Mama . . . no-o-o."

"There, baby," Seona said, wishing she could take his misery and bear it her own self. "I know you feel all over achy. Granny's fixing something to make it better."

"Aside from tea brewing," Lily said, "not much to do but hope he sleeps. It's surely just a spring ague. I'm surprised Catriona hasn't come down with the like, ailing in spirit as she's been."

Seona felt her stomach churn as it had crossing the Hudson, but for different reasons. With so many letters crossing back and forth over late winter and into spring, some of them weeks delayed in reaching her, she had no way of knowing whether that last she wrote, giving Ian answer as to what had happened with his sister and that Morgan Shelby, had reached him in time to prepare him for their sudden change in plans.

Mister Robert had written to Ian of Ned's happier news. In March, weeks after Ian's brother returned to Boston, word had come that Penny, still in Deerfield, was with child. Intending to return to her, Ned had agreed to drive the cart Mister Robert had bought, at least across the Hudson River, before turning back for Deerfield, where he meant to remain until his child was born. Scarce three days later, Seona had dashed off another letter to Ian, full not of happy news but the distressing tale he had asked to know—all that had been going on with Catriona and Morgan Shelby.

I think while you were here last summer, Mr. Shelby was in New York, but already your Sister had got herself snared by the heart, despite my cautioning her against the man. Before you arrived from Carolina, she admitted to me how they chanced to meet and that she was trying to bring Mr. Shelby and Ned together to reconcile. She did not heed my Caution, only worked out how to be slyer about it. My understanding is that Mr. Shelby toyed with your Sister's affections through the Winter, whenever he was in Boston—meeting up with her in secret—until she was besotted enough to think he meant to ask your Daddy for her hand in Marriage. How she thought your Daddy would give his blessing, I do not know. I never did trust that man, not from the moment I set eyes on him. But let me tell the rest.

Mr. Shelby went away for most of April, then came back to Boston days ago and found your Sister to say he had married some rich woman in New York but wanted things to go on with Catriona as they had been—and more. That is when she finally saw him for the Rascal he is and told him she would be no Kept Woman, not to him or any man. Things might have settled down then and everyone gone on none the wiser if not for one of Catriona's so-called friends happening to see them together that last time. That girl told another what she saw. You can guess what followed. In the span of a day her reputation was besmirched as soot . . .

Seona had written that letter to Ian because she'd had to, but it hardly bore thinking on even now—save for the one good thing that had come of the wretched business. When the truth came out and Ian's parents confronted Catriona, things between Seona and Ned had gotten a needful airing too.

Until that point, Seona had been willing for Ned to guide them to the Hudson, despite not liking how he and Ian had parted. Then Ned showed up at the house, having heard the rumors about his sister and Morgan Shelby. Wading into what was already a right *stramash* between Catriona, Mister Robert, and Miss Margaret, Ned accused his sister of being "worse than *Ian*."

Seona had no words. Catriona found some. "Then maybe I'll just . . . go to Ian!"

She said it like one might declare they would go to the devil; then she burst into tears. Seona thought her mad enough to slap her brother for good measure. Not wanting to see things get so out of hand, she found her voice, shaking with anger of her own. "Ned Cameron, that is the last I will hear you speak against my baby's daddy. You best clean your mind of jealousy and whatever else you have against Ian afore it eats you alive and you're no good to Penny and that child that's coming."

Lily joined the fray then and led Seona out of it, saying Gabriel needed her upstairs. But later Ned found her and made an apology. He hadn't even known why he said what he did, because he no longer believed the worst of Ian. "Ye were right about my being jealous. But I'm working on putting that to death."

She had been glad to hear it, for while she had no idea how they would otherwise make it to New York safely, she had been unable to imagine traveling in company with Ned after what they had said to each other.

No one had taken seriously Catriona's tearful threat to *go to Ian*. But she proved to be in earnest. Tales of her and Mr. Shelby—embroidered with shocking details that never happened—had made the rounds of her friends and acquaintances and would not be easily set to rights. There were those who would believe the worst no matter how the family came to her defense. Robert and Margaret Cameron had weathered such before, with Ian, but Catriona was young enough to believe her world had come crashing down in pieces, never to be fit back together.

Nor would they, Seona knew. Leastwise, not as they had fit before. Catriona, despairing, had begged of her need for a fresh start—in New York. "But, Catriona," Miss Margaret had pleaded, "New York, 'tis sae far. What about Deerfield? Ned's going back there."

"Ned hasn't his own place in Deerfield," Catriona had argued. "And I couldn't bear it, going to strangers, if they'd even have me. But Ian will. I know he'll understand. Besides, Maggie MacGregor wants me to come. *Please . . .*"

Seona reckoned Mister Robert and Miss Margaret knew the

moment it was out of their daughter's mouth that New York was for the best. It was letting go their youngest, long afore they thought to do so, that wrenched—just as they had come to terms with bidding their only living grandson farewell. In the end they had managed it, though at what cost to their hearts Seona didn't like to think.

Having enough to fret over at present, she shook the memories away. "What about our trunks, Mama? Are they safe?" Always before, Ned had taken the precaution of carting their trunks to whatever room they had hired for the night.

"Your trunks are still on your cart," said Hannah Kirby, returning with a steaming kettle, a saucer heaped with maple sugar, and four cups on a tray. "Uncle's keeping an eye on them."

"Who's your uncle then?" Lily asked as Hannah set the tray on the room's table.

"The stableman here. He's looking after your horses too. Anything else you need before I go to work in the kitchen?"

Assured that they were fine, the girl left them, shutting the door. Lily got busy brewing the tea. As she transferred the leaves to a cup and poured steaming water over them to steep, Seona rose to change her petticoat.

"I'd thought Catriona and Ned must be seeing to the horses, but I guess not. Where are they then?" She untied the soiled garment, let it drop to the floor, then stepped into the clean one. Or cleaner. Nothing she owned was truly clean after so many days of travel.

"They're looking for Ian," her mama said, crossing to the bed to sit with Gabriel.

Seona's fingers fumbled with the petticoat ties. "Didn't Ned say we'd made such good time so far that we'd more likely find him in Schenectady or somewhere on the Mohawk?"

What if Ian was already in Albany? She had made this choice to go to him, *wanted* to go to him, yet thought of seeing him again set her nerves dancing.

I can do all things through Christ. She had read those words in the Cameron family Bible before leaving it behind but had forgotten the rest of the verse. Retying her petticoat, she thought of the Bible they had brought along for Malcolm, wrapped in oilcloth at the bottom of a trunk. She couldn't leave Gabriel to go fetch it.

What was wrong with her anyway, jumpy as a cat at thought of Ian? Maybe it was just as much about starting over again in a new place, with people strange to her—people who had no reason to accept the likes of her in the place a wife would claim.

Ian wanted her. That was the important thing, wasn't it? He had never stopped loving her, though he had done right by Judith. Now he wasn't married. She wasn't a slave. Gabriel looked set to have his mama and daddy raising him and his sister together. So why was she growing more uncertain of what awaited in Shiloh the nearer she came to it?

She thought of Catriona, who had ridden beside her on Juturna for days, sunk in her misery—reminder that a heart might break in an instant, but it was a longer road back to wholeness. To trust.

You won't let it all come to ruin again, Lord. Surely You won't.

18

COOPERSTOWN, NEW YORK

William Cooper, returned from attending Congress and in possession of one less parcel of frontier land, weighed the gold flakes offered in payment, measured out what was due him—the lion's share—and returned the rest to the pouch Ian tucked into his coat. With the gold spread across his desk glittering in the window's light, the judge bent over it, as fascinated as at their last encounter.

"Come now, Mr. Cameron." Cooper raised keen eyes to scrutinize Ian in good-natured doubt. "Am I to credit your having obtained *this* ore beyond the bounds of our fair province? Never tell me you've been off rambling back to Carolina, leaving your land untended?"

Though they were alone in the room off the main hub of the man's house, it was the one question Ian had hoped Cooper would refrain from asking. He hadn't planned on paying off his land for another year at least, but having received the gold from John days before he meant to set out down the Mohawk River, he had decided to give himself those extra days to swing south to Cooperstown on the way and be done with the business. What remained of the gold, and whatever John sent in future, would go toward building a proper house for his family.

His family. The notion was enough to distract him from Cooper's room spread with maps, ledgers, and legal papers—including the twice copied, signed, and witnessed land deed needing only to be divided, one half given into his possession, the other legally registered.

Cooper picked up the largest bit of gold, a pea-size nugget, turning it to the light. "I'm more inclined to believe you had it in your possession all along but chose not to purchase the land from me outright—for your own good reasons," he added. "Perhaps you held it back to make improvements?"

"That's not it at all, sir," Ian said. "Though I haven't neglected my land. There's a corn crop sowed, cabins raised, and my cattle are well-pastured."

"Cattle, is it?" Cooper frowned, dissatisfied with the evasive answer. "Ah, well. I cherish hopes that beneath these hills slumbers a wealth untold. Alas, many an ore sample brought to me has proved false. Until yours." His scrutiny sharpened. "I had the first of it verified—had to, you understand—in Philadelphia, last autumn."

"Of course." Ian smiled blandly. "I've not seen your lads about, sir. At their lessons, are they?"

Cooper blinked at the change in topic. "No lessons today. Over breakfast I heard the boys plotting to climb the ridge from whence I first glimpsed this country, up along the lakeshore."

"Mount Vision." Recalling his conversation with the man's lawyer last autumn, he asked, "They've taken to the frontier, your lads?"

"Like pigs to slop!" Cooper exclaimed as he retrieved a knife from his desk. With a glance at the closed door, he added in a tempered tone, "Their enthusiasm for this wilderness is illimitable. If only my wife's regard was half its measure." He proceeded to slit the sheet of foolscap along its center fold, separating the copies of the deed. "The grand hall now in progress should better please her—brick, you know, not timber—if I can build it quick enough to hold her here."

"I hope she'll find it to her liking," Ian said, his mind flown to Seona and her likings. After living under his da's roof, his homestead would seem primitive. Would she pine for Boston's comforts?

Whether or not, he wanted to lavish upon her all she was denied growing up a slave at Mountain Laurel. If she would receive it from him. It hadn't escaped his notice she had agreed to join him in New

York, bringing their son, without promising she brought her heart as well. He hoped his suggested reason for the omission was true: she meant to speak of such things face-to-face.

For himself, the love long-buried for Judith's sake had resurrected during their exchange of letters, rushing in to fill mind and heart until he was hard-pressed to set either on anything else—even the appalling news of his sister, in that last letter found waiting for him on his way out of Shiloh. He ground his teeth over what he would like to do to Morgan Shelby, then set his mind again on Seona, knowing he would have the full story from her. And so much more, he hoped.

He longed to provide her a life abounding in contentment. He wanted them to be a family, in the eyes of God and man. Was she coming to New York with something else in mind?

With his copy of the deed tucked safe in his coat, alongside the gold remaining, Ian crossed the street to retrieve Ruaidh from Cooper's stable, only to be sidetracked by sight of a nearby trade store and the notion of purchasing something for Seona. A gift fit for a wife. The first of many, he hoped.

The store smelled of new wood, pickled meat, oiled leather, and something scented of lavender that minded him of a similar shop where he had bought a comb for Seona's ringleted hair. He hadn't seen her wear the comb in Boston. He hadn't seen much of her hair, for that matter, pinned high and capped often as not.

"Good day to you," a voice said from among the shelves of goods. A man emerged, aproned and bespectacled, brushing his hands clean of something powdery before offering one to shake. "Hansen's the name. May I be of service?"

"Cameron's mine," Ian said. "I'm headed up to the Mohawk to meet the woman I mean to marry. I thought to get her a gift. I've no fixed notion what."

Beetled brows rose above the man's spectacles. "Something practical?"

"Actually . . . no. Not in the least." Ian's gaze fell to a display near the store's front, a shelf containing trays of small trinkets. "I bought her a hair comb once."

Hansen indicated the shelf with an outstretched hand. "Another?"

"Perhaps." Ian moved to the trays and sorted through their contents while Hansen watched, offering suggestions, until another customer entered the shop and he left Ian to paw through the selection—rings and bracelets, brooches and pendants, most copper or pewter, a few small silver pieces, all variously worn. There were a few paper fans. One, a beautifully painted, slightly spark-damaged specimen he thought from Japan, tempted him despite the imperfection.

In another tray he found strings of the purple-and-white shell beads the Indians called *wampum*. There was a row of small glass bottles containing scented oils, including the source of the lavender. But nothing made his heart click with recognition of the *right* gift. About to seek his fortune among the larger items displayed, he saw a thing he had nearly missed—a silver ring, its slightly tarnished edges causing it to blend with the pewter rings jumbled in a birch-bark tray.

He fished it out and took it to the store's window, where the light revealed the ring's design, an intricate series of woven vines and flowers. *Morning glories.* He made out the trumpet blossoms—tiny versions of those Seona had drawn at Mountain Laurel—as well as the sparkle of three diamond chips cresting the top of the band. An exquisite piece of work, despite the dimming tarnish. And, he judged, about the right size for Seona's slender finger, around which he suddenly had the earnest craving to slip it.

"Found something?"

Ian turned from the window to find the store empty save for himself and its proprietor. He held the ring out on his palm. "I have."

Hansen named a price Ian knew he could pay—with half the gold in his breast pocket. Uncertain whether he should, he made as if to inspect the ring again. "Where did it come from? Someone here in the village?"

Hansen scrunched his brows in thought. "Best I recall . . . it arrived with a tinker, come down from Fort Stanwix. The work of a silversmith there. The stones—such as they are—aren't paste. They're the genuine thing. And did you note the inscription?"

at the table for breakfast, which Ned and Catriona had taken in the inn's public room. "I'm daring to hope we can start for Schenectady today."

Another twenty miles, that would be. Seona sighed, then smiled at her boy's pale curls peeking from the quilt's folds. Gabriel had proved himself a good traveler, happy as his auntie Catriona in the saddle. Until this sickness.

"I'm glad for a day off a horse's back," Seona said, then frowned. "No—two days, isn't it?"

Lily eyed her over a cup's rim. "It's the third day dawning, girl-baby. Ye've been cooped up in this room too long." She sipped her tea. "Ned's down to the docks again, but Catriona's around somewhere. Finish up your breakfast and go find her. Get some air."

Seona's gaze went to the bed as she swallowed another bite, but Lily didn't let her speak the doubtful protest forming on her tongue.

"I'll stay with him." With a glance around the room, strewn with washing hung to dry, belongings scattered about, Lily added, "And start packing up our things. If ye see Ned while ye're out, tell him it looks like we should be ready to start well afore midday."

"Miss Catriona was in the kitchen with me after breakfast," Hannah Kirby said when Seona found the maid wiping down tables in the public room. "She's gone out to see that lovely filly—yours, she says."

"Juturna's mine," Seona confirmed. "But Catriona's twice the horsewoman I'll ever be," she added, at which the young maid gave a knowing smile. Doubtless she had seen far more of Catriona these past days than Seona had.

Thinking of the many times Hannah had climbed the stairs with a tray laden with broths or puddings to tempt Gabriel's appetite, meals for her and Lily, extra candles, water—all with nary a complaint—Seona placed a hand on the girl's arm. "I'm sorry for the extra work we've put you to, but thankful for your help with Gabriel."

"He must be feeling better," Hannah said with a quick flash of her dimple, "seeing as you're belowstairs."

"He's sleeping good," Seona said, stifling a yawn. "Mama thinks we'll be on our way today." She studied the maid with interest, wishing there were time for an acquaintance, one Catriona had no doubt made. "Is the stable out back or across the street? I didn't take note when we arrived."

With a final swipe of the rag, Hannah picked up an empty glass smelling of ale. "Cook's preparing dinner, but I've a moment to spare. I'll show you the way."

Out back of the inn was a yard in which their cart was parked, a covered well, a bakehouse, a capacious henhouse, and the stable. Seona trailed Hannah through its doors and down the aisle past several box stalls, most empty and tidied, a few hung with tack and occupied by horses munching feed.

They passed a man mucking out a stall. Hannah greeted him as *Uncle*. Seona caught only a glimpse, but a startling one—the man had graying black hair tied back into a long straight tail and skin a darker bronze than Hannah's. Seona had seen full-blooded Indians on the outskirts of Boston, selling their baskets, brooms, and wares. This man was clearly one such, dressed in breeches and a work frock of rough weave protecting whatever he wore beneath. On his feet were moccasins, worn and unadorned. He smiled at Hannah, met Seona's gaze briefly, then bent to his work as they passed.

Several boxes farther down, Juturna peered over a wall and whickered. Catriona stepped into the aisle, currying brush in hand. "Seona? Gabriel must be better—you're down from that room at last." Already slender, Ian's sister had lost half a stone before they left Boston. Her short gown hung a bit loose.

"He's better. Mama thinks we'll be leaving today. I came out to tell you."

"All right." Catriona stepped back into the box. Though Seona had noted the dark smudges under her eyes, she seemed in better spirits than she had displayed for weeks. "Did you meet Hannah's uncle, Oneida John?" Catriona asked. "He's taken care of our horses."

"Did I see him working?" A glance at Hannah confirmed it. "But what sort of name is *Oneida*?"

"The name of my mother's people," Hannah said. "One of the *Haudenosaunee*—the People of the Longhouse. Iroquois, you'd say."

"Like the Mohawk," Catriona added, stepping around to Juturna's opposite side. "I told Hannah about Maggie MacGregor, in Shiloh."

"A half-breed like me," Hannah said, then grinned, showing that dimple again. "The Great Longhouse once stretched from here to the lakes in the west with the Six Nations all in a row. The Mohawk were the keepers of its eastern door. Since the war they've mostly gone."

"To Canada," Catriona supplied, already having spoken more than Seona had heard at any one time during their journey. "Oneida John fought with the Marquis de Lafayette during the war. For our side."

"As did many Oneida warriors." Hannah's expression sobered. "Some of their families took refuge in Schenectady during the war."

"And never went back?" Seona asked.

"Most did," Hannah said. "Uncle took a musket ball in the leg during a battle. It never healed right. He couldn't go back to fighting or even hunting. But it was really because of my mother we ended up here, in Albany."

"I haven't heard that story," Catriona said, moving to brush Juturna's tail. "What about your mother?"

"By the time her family left Schenectady to rebuild their village, she'd married a white man and I was born. Uncle found work after the war and stayed too, then followed my parents here."

"Where are they now?" Catriona asked. "Your parents?"

"Dead. A few years ago. Uncle's taken care of me since."

While Catriona expressed her sympathy, Seona's mind swirled with half-forgotten snatches of that poem Ian's sister had been so taken with last spring. The one about the Indian student who traded his bow for book learning. Did Hannah's uncle miss the forest like that Indian in the poem had done? What did he think of folk like her, like Ian, coming to live in places his people once called home? Would she ever again feel herself at home in a place, not adrift somewhere between worlds? Or like an intruder? Impulsively she asked, "Was it hard?"

"Was what hard?" Hannah asked.

"Learning to live in the white world." Like she still struggled to do. Learning to live as a freewoman, one who passed for white but wasn't.

"I suppose it has its challenges, but it's the only life I've known," Hannah said. "It's harder for Uncle, finding his place in a world too often shifting underfoot."

Worlds shifting underfoot. Seona understood that well enough.

As if reading her thoughts, Hannah asked, "Surely you've experienced the same, you and your mother? Catriona told me you have Cherokee blood."

"I did," came Catriona's admission as she stepped out of Juturna's box and latched the door. "I hope you don't mind."

Seona shook her head. "I guess with Mama it's obvious. Or we think so."

"Think so?" Hannah echoed.

A glance between the two told Seona that Catriona hadn't shared all the details of their story. But Hannah was waiting, expectant, and the girl had been open with her. Face warming, not meeting anyone's gaze, Seona spilled out the truth. "My grandmama died birthing my mama, so we never knew her. We aren't certain if she had Indian blood, but we always supposed my granddaddy was Cherokee. My grandmama was found living with them. She spoke their tongue but didn't look Indian. Naomi said she was brown as a walnut. Skin, eyes, and hair. Curly hair. Not like any Indian she'd ever seen."

"Naomi?" Hannah asked.

"Naomi was enslaved at Mountain Laurel," Catriona said. "The plantation where Seona was born. Naomi's free now, living in Shiloh with my brother Ian—the one we're waiting on."

Hannah glanced from Catriona to Seona, brows pulled tight. "How did you wind up on a plantation if your grandmother was a Cherokee or became one?"

"My grandmama was taken from one of their villages," Seona said, "during the French War, and carried back east, big with child—Mama. Soldiers thought she was a white captive when they grabbed her during a dawn raid. When they saw she wasn't white, they took her for a runaway slave. Could be she was, but they wanted to be rid of her afore her baby came. Miranda Cameron—my other grandmama who I never knew either—bought her off those soldiers and took her in."

"One of your grandmothers *bought* the other?" Hannah's dark eyes rounded. "Then you and Lily are . . ."

A horse nearby gave a ringing whinny, greeting its owner, arrived to tend it. For a moment no one spoke.

"Were," Catriona said, breaking the silence. "Seona and Lily were slaves on my uncle's plantation in North Carolina. He made my brother his heir, but after Uncle Hugh died, Ian left Carolina to settle on the New York frontier. And now . . ."

"Now we're all free," Seona said when Catriona glanced at her. "We're headed to live with Ian and the others he brought north. Like Naomi."

"But isn't Gabriel . . . ?" Hannah glanced at Catriona. "Tell me it's none of my concern—it's only that Gabriel bears a likeness to you, and as I've heard you all called Cameron, I assumed this brother you've been waiting for was . . ." She looked to Seona. "Your husband."

Seona drew breath and, for the first time, spoke the hardest words of all. "Gabriel is Ian's son. But I'm not his wife."

"Not yet, you aren't," Catriona said as they made their way along the street above the inn. "But surely Ian means to marry you now."

Their conversation had been cut short when the inn's cook had called Hannah Kirby to the kitchen, but it had clarified something for Seona, a truth that had hovered at the edges of her thoughts, elusive as a firefly, winking out and drifting off whenever she grabbed for it. She had never had to explain herself or Gabriel at Mountain Laurel, nor with the Camerons in Boston. But they were journeying toward people who, like Hannah, did not know their history. People who would be their neighbors for years to come. All their lives, maybe. How would they look at her if they knew she had been a slave or Gabriel was born when his daddy was married to another? Would she and Lily be accepted by the likes of those MacGregors? Would they be equals among them or something less?

"Seona?" Catriona took her arm and slowed their pace along the street where ironshod wheels rattled and strangers glanced and children shouted in play. "You've nothing to hang your head over. Not like me."

Seona halted and drew Ian's sister aside, near a shopwindow. "Not you either," she stated firm, inwardly fuming at that Morgan Shelby for bringing Catriona so low she had felt forced to uproot herself from her home, her parents, the life they had envisioned for her.

They were all pursuing the same thing—she and Catriona, her mama, Ian, Naomi and her kin too. Seeking a place where they could plant themselves, then grow up toward the light and flourish. Was it best to come straight out with the truth about the past, risk other people plucking them up before they could take root, or hide what she had been, pretend her life began the day that wagon rolled out of North Carolina? Was Ian thinking on how he was going to explain her and Gabriel? She was still rattled from that conversation with Hannah Kirby, who wouldn't be the last to ask.

The bell over the shop's door tinkled as someone entered it, pulling Seona from her thoughts just as Catriona gripped her arm again. "Seona, look."

She hadn't registered the display in the shop's window when they'd paused. Books. Stacks of them.

Catriona's glance mirrored pain. "I've been thinking about that poem, the one I read in Da's shop that freezing day we wore our spring gowns like a couple of ninnies. Remember? The one by Freneau?"

"I mind it," Seona said, clasping Catriona's hand and giving it a squeeze. "But let's don't go inside. Every joint of me is cramped from sitting so long in that room. I need to walk."

Nodding agreement, Catriona led the way along the street, but she didn't hold her silence. "'From Susquehanna's utmost springs, where savage tribes pursue their game, his blanket tied with yellow strings, a shepherd of the forest came . . .'"

"You set it to memory."

"And it's stuck there." Catriona murmured what sounded like *and bless'd the copper-coloured boy* . . . before they turned a corner and ran smack into a tall, broad-shouldered figure striding from the other direction.

Seona took the brunt of it. The impact knocked her off-balance as a deep voice exclaimed in dismay. She felt hands on her shoulders, large and strong. They steadied her, but before the world had righted itself and she could look into the face of her assailant, now sputtering apologies, Catriona's exclamation filled her ears.

"Ian? Ian, it *is* you!"

Seona raised her head and met the gaze it seemed her very bones remembered for the jolt that went through them. Eyes like smoke across an autumn sky, wide with startled recognition and gathering joy, before they shifted from her, flaring even wider.

A second before his sister threw herself into his arms, with utter incredulity Ian Cameron said, *"Catriona?"*

20

With his arms inexplicably full of his sister, who hadn't ceased babbling since she threw herself into them, Ian couldn't tear his gaze from Seona. Those green eyes, thicketed in dark lashes, were the most captivating sight in the world. Even clad in her shabbiest short gown and with her hair mostly covered in a kerchief, she was beautiful, stunningly so, as if the memories he held from their days together in Boston had been but a ghostly echo of her reality. He couldn't speak or breathe, undone by the joy crashing over him while his sister was still talking and he not taking in the half of it. All he could think was *God be thanked . . . God be thanked . . .* for Seona was safe. In New York.

Then she dropped her gaze and uncertainty pierced his joy. People passed them along the row of shops where they had collided, but he barely noticed.

He breathed in at last, and it hurt.

"Ian? Have you heard anything I've said?" Pushing against his chest, Catriona stepped back, and Ian got a better look at her, the bones of her face grown too prominent, those of her collar sharply defined, her eyes underscored by bruises. A ghostly echo of his memories of her.

On the street behind him, a wagon clattered past. Something inside a nearby shop shattered. A woman's voice rose, shrill and aggrieved.

"What are ye doing in New York?" Ian asked, more sharply than he meant to.

Looking stricken now as well as shockingly thin, Catriona said, "You didn't get my letter?"

"No. I had one from ye, Seona." He turned to her, longing for an embrace, even a word. Needing explanation. "Ye wrote of that wretch Shelby, but I only received it on my way out of Shiloh." With the sordid details of that affair flooding back, he turned to Catriona, the hot tangle of bewilderment and outrage in him cooling. "I don't know all that happened but I'm sorry for it. Truly I am. And I'd happily thrash the man for ye, could I find him. But was it so bad ye had to leave Boston?"

"Oh, Ian. *Yes.* I did write to say I was coming." Catriona bit her lip as if to stop its trembling.

"But never tell me ye ran off without Da's blessing?" As he had done at her age.

"No, Ian," Seona said, speaking at last. "Your mama and daddy thought it best she come with us—and prayed you'd take her in."

"I'm sure you'll find a letter from Da waiting on you," Catriona hurried to add before he could reply. "Though there's nothing more to tell, really, than what Seona wrote."

"So," he said, needing to be certain, "ye've come to *live* with me? Us?" he amended with a glance at Seona and a smile he couldn't quell—and she didn't return—while his sister stood there on that Albany street, blue eyes brimming with shame and hope.

"If you'll have me, Brother."

Ian felt his heart wrench. "Of course I will. But . . . how long have ye been in Albany? Where's Lily? Ned? Gabriel?" He looked around as if they might appear there on the street. "Did ye meet with any trouble on the journey?"

"So many questions," Seona said, a corner of her mouth lifting. "We been in Albany two days—three, counting today."

He felt his brows soar. "Why so long?"

"Gabriel," she said. "He came over fevered during the river crossing."

His hand had curled around her arm before he could think to stop it. "He's sick? How bad?"

"Just an ague. He's better this morning. We were thinking to start for Schenectady, soon as Ned showed up again."

"Showed up?" He let her go. "Where is he? Did he leave ye here on your own?"

"Of course not," Catriona said. "He's spent nearly every hour we've been here combing Albany for you. No doubt he's off looking now."

Banking the fresh outrage that had started to build, Ian caught his breath and sorted through the present mental clutter to the most vital thing. "Gabriel . . . ye said he's well now?"

Seona nodded. "Better. Mama's with him. This is the first I've been out of that room since we got here. But you'll want to see him."

As much as he wanted a moment alone with Seona, he wanted to see his son as badly. He would get neither there on the street. "Lead the way," he said, meaning for his sister to do so but Seona walked ahead and turned the corner, leaving him and Catriona to follow.

The inn where they were staying was a few blocks away. They were inside, passing the door to the public room and heading for the stairs to the upper floor, when a shout brought them to a halt.

"Ian!" His brother left a cup on a table and knocked over a bench in his haste to intercept them in the inn's foyer. "Where did ye find him?" Ned demanded of their sister but barreled on before Catriona could reply. "Where have ye been, Ian? Why weren't ye there at the river to meet us?"

While Seona and Catriona tensed, looking between them, Ian attempted a smile. "Good to see ye again, too, Ned. Since ye ask, I was down in Cooperstown, paying off my land and securing the deed. I thought there was time for it, but I see I was wrong. Nevertheless, I'm here now."

"Aye," Ned said, features pulled into a glower. "And I'm ready to be—"

Ned flinched when Ian put a hand to his shoulder, as if he had expected to be struck. Did his brother think he was owed a blow? His smile felt more like a grimace as he said, "I understand Penny's waiting and ye're eager to be back across the river. Ye will be before the day's done, I promise. We'll talk in a bit, aye? Right now I need to see my son."

Gabriel slept, so Ian didn't take him into his arms either but let his son drink of needful rest, noting the changes the past year had wrought. He had written Seona of his ache at missing his son's growing up. Now he saw in the lad, nearly three years old, what he had missed: lengthening limbs; breeches and shirt instead of a gown; the softly rounded face of the toddler he had last seen subsumed by that of the boy he was fast becoming. An ache lodged in his throat so tight it took more than one swallowing to clear it and address Seona's mother.

"Lily, I haven't even greeted ye proper, I was so eager to see him," he said in a hushed tone, nodding toward his sleeping son. "Are ye well?"

Lily paused her folding of garments meant for the trunk open at her feet. "Oh, aye," she said as softly. "And glad ye found us finally. I think Ned's ready to bolt for that ferry boat."

He crooked her a sheepish smile. "So I noticed." Glancing aside at Seona, who had stood looking on while he devoured their son with his gaze, he added, "I best go speak to him. Would ye come out with me?"

Leaving Gabriel with a lingering glance, he strode into the passage, pausing at the head of the stairs. He turned to face Seona, who had followed him from the room but drew up short before they could collide as they had done on the street.

She took a half step backward. "You told Ned you paid off your land. So soon?"

"*Our* land," he corrected, noticing she could not, or would not, meet his gaze. As on that day atop Copp's Hill. As if they had never expressed the things they had in their letters. "And aye, I left Shiloh nigh a week ago—I went to Cooperstown. I have the land deed."

Patting the breast of his coat where the document was tucked safe, along with the ring he'd bought her, he scrutinized Seona's face, wishing he saw excitement there, or pleasure, not merely surprise.

There was a window at the top of the stairs. Her eyes caught the late-morning light and glowed like jewels in her sun-kissed face, and still it was all he could do not to bend his head and kiss her thoroughly. His every fiber ached for the tender reunion he had imagined each mile

of the journey east. Instead he mirrored her restraint. "Seona . . . are ye all right?"

She nodded. "Are you?"

"Me? Aye, I'm relieved. *Happy.*" Uncertainty tempered his grin as she searched his face.

"You're not angry at your sister's coming west with us?"

"No." He could understand Catriona's desperation to escape her heartache, the shame Shelby—and the gossipmongers—had left her to bear. Hadn't he similar cause for leaving Boston at her age? *Eighteen.* But his poor mam and da, left to weather the loss and scandal as they had when he fled to Canada. "I'm sorry for the need. This cannot be what she wanted."

Her gaze flashed to his face, then away. "I reckon what we want don't always figure into things."

He could think of nothing to say to that, though he wished he could. The constraint between them swelled. The ring in his coat pocket felt heavy as bullet lead.

"Are ye tired? Have ye managed to rest at all? Such a long journey, Gabriel falling ill . . ." He babbled on. "Ye'll be glad to reach Shiloh, aye? I cannot wait for ye to meet Neil and Willa. And see the farm and everyone awaiting ye there."

He waited for her to speak, holding his breath. Afraid she was fixing to tell him she had changed her mind about Shiloh. About him.

"Catriona talks of seeing Maggie MacGregor," she said. "I know that'll comfort her, but . . . do the MacGregors know about me and Mama? About Gabriel?"

"Aye," he said. "I've spoken of ye often. It's only Catriona who'll be a surprise . . . or maybe not," he amended with a sound like laughter that wasn't. "No doubt she's written to Maggie about her coming west."

Seona shook her head. "I didn't mean *that* about the MacGregors."

"What then?"

She chewed at her lip, hesitant. But why should she hesitate with him there to guide her, to shelter and protect? He would let nothing harm her or their son. *Never again.* "The MacGregors are good people. Ye'll like them."

"And if he wasn't," Ian continued, putting his hand to Ned's arm, "I wouldn't have blamed *ye*."

The taut muscles beneath his fingers eased. Ned held his gaze but a moment before squeezing shut his eyes and heaving a gusty breath. "I don't mean to quarrel with ye, Ian. I really don't."

Ian gave his brother's arm a firmer grip. "Old habit, aye?"

Ned opened his eyes, mouth twitching. "One I wish to break."

"That sounds good."

They gazed at each other, between them a shared lifetime—the lads they had been, the jealousies and judgments made. As if a wind had come and cleared them all away, Ian saw the man his brother was now, wounded, broken, raw with a newfound hope. "Seona wrote of Penny and a child on the way. I'm glad of it, Ned. Glad too for your bringing my son and his mother and the rest safely this far. I'll take them from here. Go to your wife, with my blessing—for whatever that's worth," he hastened to add.

"It's worth a lot, actually." Ned seemed as surprised by the utterance as was Ian. Then concern darkened his expression. "But Catriona—ye'll take her too?"

"Aye. She's welcome with me."

Pain had returned to Ned's face. Or maybe guilt. "It's my fault. Everything befallen her. I brought Shelby into our lives. And if I ever see the man again—"

"Ye'll turn and walk the other way," Ian finished for him.

Ned raised a brow. "Would ye?"

Ian held his stare. "God willing, we'll never know. Where is Catriona, by the way?"

"I'm here," came their sister's quavering voice from somewhere above. "Eavesdropping on my ridiculous brothers."

Ian turned as Ned looked up to an open second-story window, where Catriona looked down at them, smiling through her tears.

"Hitch that horse, Ned," she called to them. "Then come and bid the rest of us proper goodbye before you go."

21

MOHAWK RIVER VALLEY, NEW YORK

Seona wondered what the hawks circling the bleached sky above made of their party proceeding west along the river road, beset by sticky heat and blackflies, hemmed by thick woods that hid all manner of dangers she could only guess at. Bear, panther, wolf . . . wild Indian? For now the biting insects were enough to contend with. She was smeared hand and face with the brownish grease Ian offered when the pesky critters began their onslaught. Scented with pennyroyal, the stuff sat on sweaty skin like a mask Seona longed to claw away.

She glanced ahead at Ian, driving the cart with Gabriel snug beside him on the narrow bench. He took his hat off his head and waved it over her boy's curls, no doubt swatting flies. Gabriel laughed, flailing his arms.

Seona's breath caught. Before she drew another to shout, *Watch where you're guiding that horse!* Ian had the hat back on his head, both hands on the traces, eyes on the road ahead. Her heartbeat calmed.

Beside the cart on Ian's side, Catriona rode Juturna. Snatches of her chatter floated back to Seona and Lily, riding behind. Catriona had a flood of questions about the valley they traversed and seemed bent on sharing with Ian everything she already knew, learned from Hannah Kirby or from Maggie MacGregor's letters.

The New York frontier was a world strange and new, to be sure, but

Seona wasn't as eager to embrace it. People could look the same from one valley to the next, but every place had its ways of thinking and living. She had kept at arm's length the knowledge that she must again learn to comport herself among a people unknown, navigate ways she might be slow to grasp. Now that knowledge pressed in on her soul.

"Ye doing all right, girl-baby?"

Seona glanced aside at Lily, astride Ian's roan. "I'm fine, Mama. Hot and beset. Aren't we all?"

Though what awaited her at journey's end was a daunting prospect, she was ready to be done with reins in her hands, the smell of horsehair and lather, reading swiveling ears and bobbing head, watching for snakes and any other thing that might spook the creature jolting under her seat.

"Ye look troubled," Lily said, tilting the wide straw hat shielding her from the sun's glare as they passed through a break in the forest lining the river road.

Seona looked ahead, fixing Gabriel and his daddy in her sights. She had Ian to help her find her way . . . if he understood the things she needed to know.

It was different from heading to Boston. In Boston she hadn't been anyone's wife. Wasn't one now but knew that's what Ian wanted. She had tried asking him, back in Albany, how he meant to go about it but had been too overwhelmed just seeing him again to find the words. *Do you mean to lie about me and our son or tell folk the bald-faced truth? What will that mean for me and Gabriel? What sort of place will we have in Shiloh?*

"I'm fine," she said again, glancing aside at her mama. "What about you? You and Ian's horse getting on agreeable?"

Lily reached to stroke Ruaidh's cinnamon-sugar neck. "I mind this fellow well enough. He's a canny wee thing."

Ian's Indian horse, got somewhere up in Canada before he came to Mountain Laurel, wasn't as tall or pretty as Juturna or even her dam, which Seona rode. But he was steady, smart, and never seemed to tire.

"He's the second horse you've ridden on this journey. First Ned's while he drove the cart. Now Ian's while he drives it."

"Might've been simpler had I driven the cart," Lily said with a laugh.

Seona tried to echo it but couldn't. Her mama had gone from spare horse to spare horse without complaint. Like she had gone from change to change in their lives since Gabriel's birth, accepting each. Molding herself to it. Did her mama ever feel like the trunks on their cart—baggage brought along for its use?

Tears pricked at the thought. Hiding them with a tilt of her own hat, Seona said, "Reckon we'll all be glad to be done with horseback." Looking ahead as Catriona's voice drifted back, she added, "Most of us."

Lily followed her gaze. "Catriona's a born horsewoman. But I'll be glad. Just a few more days and this'll be behind us."

Finding small comfort in that, Seona said no more.

They were four days journeying to German Flatts, where West Canada Creek flowed down from the north. They didn't stay in the villages that spanned the shallow Mohawk River. Having daylight left, they crossed and rode up along the West Canada a few miles before making camp, as they had done since leaving Albany. Ian was being thrifty, but Seona knew he preferred sleeping under the stars.

The sun set while they pitched camp. Twilight cast purple shadows, lit by the season's first fireflies. The blackflies gave way to mosquitoes whining about their ears and to moths drawn by their campfire to dance too near the flames. Small night creatures rustled in the trees along the creek bank.

They would see Shiloh on the morrow, Ian had said.

Stewing on that, Seona minded Gabriel while Lily baked johnny-cakes on a stone and Catriona helped Ian raise the canvas shelter under which they would sleep one more time.

She had managed not to be alone with Ian since Albany. She was regretting that now, but Catriona lingered at the fire after supper, still chattering away to Ian and anyone else inclined to listen. Seona looked about for something to occupy her hands, but everything was scoured and stowed, ready for an early start. Everything but Gabriel. His granny was attempting one of those tasks with a damp cloth, seated on a stump across the fire with him squirming on her lap.

It had ceased to amaze Seona how fast a boy could dirty himself in the out-of-doors. Gabriel had outdone his usual efforts this day. Face, hair, and hands were smeared with grease, to which had stuck crumbled johnnycake, ashes, twigs, bugs, leaves, and a substance Seona could not identify. By firelight, it looked green.

"Seona, what did you make of Hannah and her uncle?" Catriona, sitting on the log beside her, asked.

"I didn't talk to her uncle."

"But you saw him. Were they what you expected western Indians to be like?"

Distracted by the struggle unfolding across the fire, Seona frowned. "Don't know as I expected they'd be—Gabriel!" His protests had escalated to thrashing, no doubt bruising her mama's legs where his heels struck. "Mama, I'll take him."

Lily hoisted Gabriel onto a hip, then swung him onto the log beside Seona, giving her the cloth. "I'll go wash my own self," she said, sounding winded from the fight. "I'm wearing half his mess now."

Gabriel clambered off the log, making for the fire's edge. Never one to pay mind to hearth fires back in Boston, he had grown enamored of leaping flames on their journey, wanted to hunker at the edge of every fire they lit, poking a stick at the embers, more than once a reaching finger.

Seona grabbed a fistful of his shirt. "No, baby. Don't play with the fire, it's hot—*ouch*."

"No . . . ," Gabriel echoed in a cranky whine, tugging at her grip. "No!"

Ian, who had got up to check on the horses, came back into the firelight, noted Gabriel's defiance, and caught her eye. Hanging on to their son, Seona read the question in his eyes. Did she want him to deal with this small rebellion?

It disconcerted her. A father ought not to ask whether he should address a naughty turn by his offspring but do what was in his mind to do about it. Now she thought on it, Ian hadn't once disciplined Gabriel in Boston. He had left it to her or Lily. Since their reunion, he had sought her permission first, the few times he corrected their son. More like an uncle might do.

She thought of Mandy. Was he expecting her to treat his daughter as her own right off? To discipline as well as nurture? Or would there be a gradual falling into the role, like she supposed was happening with him and Gabriel? So much to think through, talk over, find out what the other expected.

For the moment, Ian's arrival was distraction enough for their boy. She shook her head as Gabriel leaned back against her knees, then grinned up at her, pale curls burnished in the fire's waning glow. Once more the little angel.

A sleepy angel. His eyelids drooped. He let her scrub his face and hands.

When Catriona asked, Ian said he reckoned they would reach Shiloh by afternoon on the morrow. "Long as the cart holds together. The road ahead gets rough in spots."

Seona's arm snaked around her baby. "I'll take Gabriel in the saddle with me, come morning."

Ian settled on the stump Lily had vacated, across the embers shedding light. "I didn't mean to alarm ye. I know the road. Ally and I got the wagon over it last year."

"Do you think Maggie MacGregor will be at her schoolhouse when we arrive?" Catriona asked, then before Ian could answer, added, "Which reminds me, Hannah Kirby said there are missionaries among the Oneida attempting to attract more tradesmen to their villages to teach the warriors so they can make a living aside from farming, since many of the men see it as women's work and won't tend a field. Did you know that, Ian? Among the Iroquois it's traditionally been the women who tend the fields—*and* own all they produce—but white men look down on it and call the Oneida men lazy, the women drudges, because their traditions are different."

Seona sympathized with the hardships the Indians faced adapting their ways to changing times but couldn't suppress a smile as she again restrained Gabriel, this time from clambering over the log into the trees between their camp and the creek, where fireflies still drifted, winking their greenish-yellow lights.

"Did I say something funny?" Catriona asked, catching her smile.

From across the fire, Ian was staring at Seona's mouth. The look in his eyes she knew of old, and the feeling it sent through her—like sparks from a flint—she minded as well. Flustered, she waved her free hand. "No. I just haven't seen you this . . . *captivated* by anything in a long while. I've missed it."

A shadow darkened Catriona's face. "I would better understand the plight of the people among whom we're coming to live, is all."

"None of which are Oneida," Ian pointed out.

"Some are Mohawk."

"Aye. But I think ye'll find your friend Maggie is far more alike to ye than different. Did ye find that maid back in Albany that much different from ye? There's Lily, for that matter," he added as Seona's mama came back into camp, fresh from washing. "She's at least half-Cherokee."

"Half-Cherokee and ready for her bed," Lily said, making slightly more of her faint Scots accent than was normal. "G'night to ye all."

"We aren't far behind, Mama," Seona said as Gabriel pressed his face against her thigh, wiped his nose, and whined. She pulled him onto her lap and rubbed his back, hoping he would give in to sleep soon.

"I did and didn't," Catriona said in response to Ian's question as Lily ducked beneath the canvas. She went on to talk of Hannah Kirby and her uncle as Gabriel bestirred himself, whined again, then sagged boneless in Seona's arms.

"This boy needs his bed too." She got up from the fire, leaving Catriona to Ian, though she felt his gaze follow her to the shelter.

Since his weaning, putting Gabriel down for the night was a quicker affair. She kept quiet so as not to disturb Lily, already asleep under their blanket—a shield from mosquitoes rather than for warmth. She smeared grease over Gabriel's freshly washed face and neck, sighing at thought of the dirt he would pick up in his sleep. Grime and little boys came hitched like cart and horse. She wondered if Naomi was keeping Mandy clean, living on a raw homestead like Ian's letters had described.

Tomorrow she would see for her own self.

When she emerged from the shelter, Catriona was still talking, but yawns punctuated her words. Seona caught Ian's eye as she made to go down to the creek to wash. His glance said he wanted a few moments alone with her, too. She relished the breathless stirring it caused even as she dismissed the thoughts that came with it.

Talk was needed. Nothing more.

She took her time washing up, half her energy spent swatting until a breeze rose along the creek and blew the mosquitoes away. In the air between the creek banks, bats swooped, hunting larger insects, their shapes high and dark and quick against the starry sky.

Ian's boots crackled the brush when he came into the moonlight that sparkled on the rippling water and lit the creek bank bright as twilight.

"Catriona gone to bed?" Her question made him chuckle, a sound heard above the creek's chatter, minding her of another moonlit night on the path from the Reynolds' cabin, first time he ever kissed her.

"Finally," he said.

Seona laughed, hearing its nervous edge, which only made her more aware of herself, petticoat kilted. The air was cooling, reminding her it wasn't yet summer despite the warmth of the days. Gooseflesh prickled her creek-wet arms, but she thought that might be due to Ian, who slipped off boots and hose and came into the water to stand close. "You still glad your sister came along with us?"

"I am. I hope she can forget what's past, make a life here. With us, for the time being."

Seona heard layers of thinking behind those words. A man weighing his limited means against the need to provide for his own. Whether or not his means would match the need, he hadn't said, but he hadn't made his sister feel an unwelcome burden. "You didn't plan for her," she said, pressing a little.

"We'll be fine." The answer came with a readiness that warmed her. "Are ye looking forward to being home?"

A warmth short-lived. The breeze in the trees and water burbling over stones filled the silence. Another bat dipped low and was gone. Ian waited for her answer.

"I'll be glad to end the journey."

"Aye," he said, stepping nearer. "We . . . ye and I, we've hardly had a moment to ourselves to talk."

"I've noticed."

They were dancing around each other with their words, like those hunting bats. His hand closed on her arm, warm through her sleeve. "Seona."

After months getting used to allowing herself such thoughts again, she found herself craving his embrace, certain she heard the same craving as he said her name. How she wanted to yield to it. But giving in would distract them from what they needed to talk over. Things needing airing before they could go deeper into each other's hearts.

She stiffened. He let her go. Whatever he had meant to say he swallowed back. "So . . . what d'ye think of New York?"

The question dashed like the creek's water. Cool. Distancing. Safe. "I didn't know how much I missed the countryside till I got shed of Boston. But New York seems wilder than Carolina."

"Wilder than Mountain Laurel, this part of it." His face tilted to take in the stars while the breeze ruffled his shirt. "There's a wilderness on our doorstep. Mountains called the Adirondacks. We're all but in their foothills now." He lowered his chin, gazing at her in the starlight. "Does it frighten ye?"

It wasn't wilderness unnerving her. "No."

"Ye'll like the farm. And Shiloh."

"You think Shiloh will like us?"

"Us?"

She could see the line of his brows pressed down. "Me and Mama . . . Gabriel."

His hand trailed shivers down her arm until his fingers curled around hers. "I cannot think anyone I've met will take against ye, Seona . . . if I understand what ye're asking."

She didn't think he did. "I'm asking . . . what do they know?"

"What does who know?"

"Your neighbors. Have you told them about me? About Gabriel?"

"We talked of this, aye? The MacGregors know ye're coming."

"I'm not Mandy's mama."

He stayed silent for a bit, their fingers entwined, then asked, "Are ye wanting to know if I've told them our story?"

Her heart banged. "Yes."

"Not everything, no."

When he didn't elaborate, she asked, "What you *have* told them, was all of it the truth?"

He released her hand. "Have I lied—is that what ye're asking? Of course not."

This was turning out as difficult as she had feared. "Would you?"

"Why would I lie?"

So I won't be despised, and our baby with me. The words were on the tip of her tongue when she realized he might take them badly, as if she was speaking against the MacGregors, of whom he thought considerable much. Who was she to know what they might or might not think of her? But she cared. All the more the nearer to Shiloh they came.

"Soon as they set eyes on Gabriel, they'll know he's your son—same age as Mandy. But I'm not your wife and never was."

"In my heart ye were," he said, impatience and reassurance mingled in his tone. "And I know we're not married yet but—"

As if their talk had somehow reached him, Gabriel's crying rose above the creek's chatter. Lily appeared above them on the bank, her shift pale in the moonlight, holding their fretful boy. Seona went splashing out of the creek to comfort their son back to sleep, saying not another word. She couldn't seem to find the right ones anyway.

Maybe they wouldn't even see the MacGregors tomorrow or anyone else Ian called *friend*. Maybe there was time still to get their story straight.

22

SHILOH, NEW YORK

They reached Shiloh by early afternoon, cart intact, sooner than Ian had dared hope. Passing the first scattered cabins along Black Kettle Creek, they drew curious *hallo*s and stares from women tending kettles or children in their yards. Not from anyone with whom Ian was yet acquainted. Even the village proper, around Keagan's store, was quieter than usual, save for the industrious ringing of the smith's hammer and a few old men sitting in the oak's shade.

Ian returned their waves but didn't pause the cart. He was starting up the slope past Keppler's mill, the women following on horseback, when he spotted the dark-haired lass unhitching a gray mare outside the cabin where road and creek bent toward the farms. So did Catriona, who pressed Juturna forward.

"Ian, is that—?"

"It is," he said. "She looks to be done teaching for the day."

Before he finished speaking, Catriona had heeled Juturna into a trot, which carried her up past the mill, where Maggie MacGregor turned, reins in hand. Even above the mill falls Ian heard his sister's laughter as she swung down from the saddle and the young women embraced in the cabin door-yard.

"That's a sound I haven't heard in too long." Seona had ridden up close beside the cart, as she had done whenever the trail permitted—to be near Gabriel, who she had let ride with Ian after all, but not with her full trust. She was smiling more broadly than she had done last evening by the fire. The sight had mesmerized Ian then. It squeezed his heart with longing now.

As the cart crested the slope, Gabriel shot to his feet on the bench beside Ian. "Auntie Catweena!" he called.

Pulling back on the traces, Ian clutched his wobbling son. The cart lurched to a halt in the door-yard, where Catriona and Maggie MacGregor were talking over each other in their excitement.

Smile vanished, Seona dismounted and plucked Gabriel off the cart but forbore to remonstrate over his near tumble as Maggie and Catriona hurried over, arms linked. Their faces, so dissimilar—fawn-brown complexion to fair; dark eyes to blue; brunette hair to russet—shone with matching joy.

"I've counted the days, thinking you couldn't possibly arrive until tomorrow, earliest." Maggie's hair wasn't plaited down her back, as she wore it at home, but swept off her slender neck, pinned beneath a cap. "Going by what Catriona last wrote."

"So ye knew she was coming?" Ian replied.

"Oh yes!" Maggie laughed, happiness overriding her usual shyness. "You didn't receive your letter from Catriona before you left. Papa has it at our place—he's one of the few Jack Keagan trusts with a neighbor's post."

"Not that you need read it now, Ian," Catriona said, looking more like the lass he left behind in Boston than the heartbroken one met in Albany.

"Maggie, let me introduce my son, Gabriel, and his mother, Seona. And her mother, Lily." He turned to the women standing with reins in hand, Seona with Gabriel clasped to her hip.

"Welcome to Shiloh," Maggie said. "Naomi and the others are beyond excited to see you again."

"And we them," Lily said.

Seona seemed to gird herself with courage to find her voice. "I've heard of you from Catriona," she said, while in her arms Gabriel stared, bright-eyed and curious, catching Maggie's attention.

"He's a sweetie." She swung her gaze to Ian, then back to Gabriel. "He looks just like you, Mr. Cameron."

"Call me Ian," he said. "Or ye'll make me feel as old as your da. Ye headed home?" He bent a nod toward the mare.

"I am. I'll ride with you, unless you've business to keep you in town."

"I think we're ready to be done traveling." He tried to catch Seona's eye to be sure this was true. She evaded his gaze by handing Gabriel to Lily so she could mount up again. Answer enough, he supposed. But as she reached down to take Gabriel on the saddle with her, he caught Lily giving her daughter a questioning look.

"More than ready," Seona said with a smile that didn't hide the strain behind the words.

Riding behind Ian and the cart, Catriona and Maggie kept up a lively chatter, his sister asking about Maggie's school, her parents, their farm, Maggie bubbling over like a spring with answers. Then Catriona asked, "Have you seen Francis since last you wrote?"

"No one has," Maggie replied, joy draining from her voice.

Their conversation dropped in volume, or they dropped their horses farther back. Either way, Ian caught no more.

"Who are they talking about?" Seona asked, nodding toward the pair riding behind.

"Francis Waring. Someone I've never met." Neither the MacGregors nor the Warings could, by now, hold the faintest hope that his extended absence was just Francis being Francis, off wandering the hills. No one was. "He's a close friend of the MacGregors."

Seona slid him a glance. "I mind him now—from your letters."

Ian cast her a searching glance at mention of *letters*. Had she forgotten what else they shared over those months? It felt as if a wall had risen between them, one he couldn't find his way around. He thought he had begun to last night at the creek. Seona had voiced concern about the MacGregors, but Gabriel had interrupted the moment and there had been no chance to continue the conversation.

Riding ahead on Ruaidh, Lily looked back. Seona urged her mount up to ride beside her mother, spurring Ruaidh into a matching trot Lily was forced to rein in. The horse knew this track well and was no doubt eager to be home. But there would be no riding past the MacGregors' farm without stopping.

"Ian," Maggie called from behind, confirming his prediction as the forest hemming the track opened and fields came into view. "You won't ride past without seeing Mama and the boys? Papa, too, if he's there. At least for a moment?"

"I know we're all tired," Catriona added, bringing Juturna up alongside the cart. "But please, let's do? I'd like to retrieve that letter," she added with a laugh Ian couldn't resist.

"*My* letter, d'ye mean?"

"You needn't read it," his sister reiterated, reddening as he had known she would. "Really it's of no matter. It's much too . . . I mean, when I wrote it, I was—"

"Of course ye can have it back," he broke in. "And aye, we'll stop. If Seona and Lily are agreeable."

Whether Seona and Lily were agreeable or simply resigned, their faces didn't reveal as the younger women cantered ahead down the track between the sprouting cornfields, turning at the long lane leading to the MacGregors' farmhouse, pushed back almost to the first rising of the ridgeline to the north. Less imposing than his uncle's dwelling at Mountain Laurel had been, the MacGregors' house was still a substantial affair, with its stone foundation and broad chimneys and the deep veranda wrapping its two-storied front and the single-story wings to either side.

Catriona and Maggie turned their mounts in to the stable-yard, where Maggie dismounted and began unsaddling her mare. Horses grazed in a nearby paddock, one the old bay roan, Seamus. Neil was to home.

"Matthew isn't here," Maggie was saying as Ian halted the cart in the yard. "He left this morning, gone hunting or checking his traplines. Soon as he's back, I need to tell him Colonel Waring has two new colts to start."

"That's right," Catriona said, looping Juturna's reins over a rail. "I forgot he works with horses. Are those his?" she asked, indicating those in the paddock.

Maggie started to reply, but a voice calling from the house drew their attention.

"Ian Cameron, welcome ye home!"

Neil and Willa MacGregor were descending the steps, on their heels Jamie and Liam, who broke into sprints once their feet hit the ground. Before the tide of MacGregors sweeping from the house could overtake them, Ian moved to help Seona and Gabriel out of the saddle. Lily beat him to it, taking Gabriel in her arms so Seona could dismount. Then they were surrounded by MacGregors. Ian caught a flash of panic in Seona's eyes before Willa MacGregor, taller than all except Ian and Neil and now quite noticeably with child, came forward.

"You will be Seona. And Lily," she added, addressing the women correctly. Then her mismatched eyes took in the child in Lily's arms. "And this little one is your son," she said with a look at Ian that confirmed rather than questioned.

"Aye. Seona, Lily, let me present our neighbors, Neil and Willa MacGregor—and their sons," he added as the dark-haired lads bobbed near, grinning. "Jamie and Liam. And ye'll know who that must be," he said to Neil and Willa, turning to indicate his sister, still in conversation with Maggie as they tended her mare.

"Catriona Cameron," Willa called, attracting his sister's attention. "We are glad to welcome you at last. All of you," she said, her hand coming to rest on her belly. "Lily, I am told you are a midwife. I will be glad of having you so near."

"Ye're seven months along, I'm guessing," Lily said, and Ian saw on both his neighbors' faces surprise at her Scots lilt, no fainter than his own.

While she and Willa spoke of babies, and Seona stood by mute, Neil took Ian by the arm. "I was awa' to your place this morning. All's well, though I ken they'll be glad to have ye home."

"Thank ye for keeping watch. Now, can we drag my sister away from your daughter—" he raised his voice to carry—"we ought to be heading in that direction."

Seona was already turning to remount as Catriona joined them, leading Juturna.

"Are we leaving?" his sister asked after introductions were repeated. Willa gave her the sealed letter that hadn't reached Ian in time and wouldn't hear of it when Catriona tried to repay the postage.

Maggie, still glommed to her side, said, "Matthew is going to adore your filly, Catriona."

His sister stroked the horse's seal-brown nose. "She's Seona's really. But she lets me pretend Juturna's mine."

Seona's smile seemed pasted on as Lily handed Gabriel back up to her in the saddle. Willa glanced from Ian to Seona, then said, "We look forward to seeing you soon. Come visit once you are settled. Any or all of you are welcome, as Ian knows."

"Mama . . . my belly is hungwy."

Everyone turned at Gabriel's announcement, to see him kicking his small heels against Seona's thighs, pointing at his stomach.

"Soon, baby," she said. "I'm sure we're all hungry." She kissed the top of his blond head, her gaze meeting Ian's.

Memory stirred of Cherry Valley and Aram Crane and his need to speak to Neil about the man. Now wasn't the time.

"Right then." With a farewell to his neighbors, Ian made for the cart. "Let's be getting home."

Their arrival was a scene of pandemonium as Lily and Seona reunited with Malcolm, Naomi, and Ally, and Catriona gave Mandy kisses, before both bairns demanded to be let down, Gabriel's hunger forgotten as Mandy babbled about their chickens and did Gabriel want to see where they put their eggs? Nip and Tuck ran barking circles around their knees, making the horses roll their eyes. Eventually the excitement wound down as Gabriel, tired and overwrought, abruptly fell to crying for his supper, Mandy adding sympathetic wails.

While Ian and Ally saw to the horses, Naomi ushered the rest into the new cabin she shared with her menfolk. Somehow plates or bowls were found for all and spots to sit. She had fixed a venison stew—"We was about to sit to it"—in her most capacious kettle and set to making up another batch of pone. When he and Ally rejoined them, Ian found barely room enough to squeeze inside, as Naomi scraped the kettle and served up the last of the stew.

He spotted Seona in the press, wishing he could judge her first impression of the place. As they had ridden in, he caught her looking out across the lake dividing their land from the MacGregors', its shore lined with red pine save the northwest corner, just visible from the cabins. Past the lake the trees fell away to the acres of corn he and Ally planted a fortnight ago. Past those was the mixed stand of beech and sugar maple he had chosen for a building site, in the shade of which stood the cabins and stable. Beyond the grove the land dipped into a gentle roll of pasturage dotted with his and Ally's cattle, before rising again to the south-facing ridge, thick with virgin timber. The ridge marched eastward until it too sloped down, giving glimpse of the mountain wilderness beyond. The place still took his breath away, filling him with the deepest satisfaction knowing it was his now, paid in full.

Whatever Seona thought of it, she had taken pains to guard.

She glanced up at his entering, preoccupied with keeping their fidgety son still on the bed frame where she sat, clear across the cabin, spooning stew into his mouth. More than one conversation was happening in the space between, voices cutting back and forth. Naomi waded through the crush, seeing everyone had enough to satisfy.

Surveying them in the tight space, sunlight streaming through doorway and window, it occurred to Ian it would be no easy matter, finding places for everyone to sleep. He was pondering how to broach the matter when he noticed Malcolm, perched on a trunk just inside the door, bowl balanced on a knee, attention given to a book laid across the other. Its cover was the same rich brown as the big-knuckled hand laid reverently upon it.

"That the Bible Seona brought ye?" Ian asked and found it needed extra effort to swallow his next mouthful when the old man looked up, dark eyes wet with tears.

"It means more than I can say, Mister Ian, to have my own at last. Thank ye, wi' all my heart."

"Aye, Malcolm. Ye're welcome." Ian transferred his attention to the book. "I don't think Da bound this one. May I have a closer look?"

Malcolm lifted the Bible. Ian set his bowl on the windowsill, waved off a questing fly, and opened the book. On one of the front papers, his da had written an inscription. He lowered it so Malcolm could see, then read the words Robert Cameron had penned, touching each with a fingertip as he did so. "'Presented to Malcolm Cameron this 30th of May 1797, by Robert and Margaret Cameron of Boston, Massachusetts.'"

Malcolm stared at the page. Around them conversation had fallen off. Ian glanced up to see every eye upon them, Naomi's on the verge of tears.

"Malcolm Cameron," the old man said. "Will ye show me those names again?"

Ian pointed to each. "That's your name, right there."

"I've always desired a Bible of my own," Malcolm said, fingering his name on the page. "Now I need only learn to read it."

Catriona, seated beside Seona with Mandy on her lap, said, "Maggie invited me to help with her school. Why don't you come along, Malcolm? Let her teach you."

Laughter filled the cabin at thought of the old man sitting among their neighbor's youngest pupils.

"There be time for sortin' that out," Malcolm said. "More pressing at the moment, to my thinking, is where we'll all be beddin' down tonight."

"My thoughts were running along those lines," Ian said. "I'd thought Seona and Gabriel—and Lily—would sleep in the cabin with me and Mandy."

"Where does that leave me?" Catriona asked.

"Aye. Ye." Ian raised a brow at her but smiled.

"Lily could come on in with us," Naomi said. "Help thin out your crowd."

"Oh, Mama," Seona said, frowning. "I don't know."

Ian wondered what she found disagreeable—being separated from Lily or sharing a cabin with him?

"You can't all fit in here," Naomi said. "That's plain to anyone with eyes."

Ian was about to suggest they divide themselves by gender, males in one cabin, females in another—though that would have separated

Seona from Gabriel—when Ally said, "Why don't we put up another cabin? Reckon we got the hang of it by now. Won't take us long."

"A third cabin?" Ian asked, wondering why he hadn't thought of it himself.

Seona leaned close to her mother, whispering. Lily straightened and looked at Ian. "Ye've taken days away to meet us and see us here safe. Have ye work waiting on ye—more urgent than raising another roof?"

"Corn's in the ground," Ian said. "The cattle have spring grass for pasture. The stable needs a bit of work. Actually, I ought to build a bigger one before autumn . . ." They had just increased the number of their horses by three. "But we could do it, especially if Neil and his sons lend a hand."

"No," Seona said. "Don't go putting yourself and your neighbors to such trouble for us."

Everyone turned on her looks of disbelief. Ian felt the prick of her words like a splinter in his heart. "It's no trouble, Seona. I mean to build ye an entire house, after all." He laughed to cover the fleeting hurt. "I want us all comfortable, meantime. Winters hereabouts are long."

A dozen cabins couldn't lend the sort of comfort he truly meant, but he was feeling just a little desperate to understand her hesitancy. Was she regretting having come to Shiloh, now she had seen the place? And him, again?

It was Lily decided the matter. "A third cabin would be perfect. Thank ye, Ian. We'll help however we can."

Not until Seona nodded assent did it strike him how her mother had addressed him. It was the first Lily had called him by his name without *Mister* or *Master* fronting it. "That's settled then. We'll raise a cabin straightaway." He and Ally could sleep out-of-doors while it was going up, leaving Catriona, Seona, and Lily with the bairns. Seona and Mandy could grow accustomed to each other. A good thing.

"I've but the one question more." He addressed it to Seona, pretending no other unanswered questions lay between them. "Where would ye like it to be?"

23

She chose his favorite of the beeches.

After supper in Naomi's cabin, he had led Seona through those magnificent hardwoods to choose the new cabin site. With their broad trunks spaced so widely a wagon could be driven through their ranks, abundant sunlight shafted through the leaves, warming the beechnut-scattered ground. Birds' trilling filled the boughs.

Threading through the trees, they reached the final beech, corded roots spread wide, standing sentinel at the grove's north edge. Seona had walked its circumference, trailing fingers over its grooved trunk, now smoothly pale, now carpeted in moss. From its shelter the view of the lake's northwest corner was unobstructed. Would be until the corn planted between grew high.

"Here," Seona had said, taking in the view he meant their house to share. "I might have seen all this before, you described it so well in your letters."

"D'ye like the place?"

She had turned, smiling softly, eyes haunted with some feeling he couldn't read. "It's beautiful."

He had wanted to take her hand, seal the moment with a kiss, but simply marked the corners of what would be her cabin with sticks driven into the ground, then walked her back to where the others were sorting themselves. He had set up a shelter in the yard, then fetched a shovel to start breaking ground while the light lasted.

Four days later the new cabin's walls were raised, chinked with debris from the notching, roof timbers set in place, door and window framed, a hole cut for hearth and chimney. The progress was thanks to a spate of dry weather and the help of all available hands, including those of Neil MacGregor and his youngest sons, Matthew having not yet returned from hunting.

Presently it was himself and Neil perched high on the roof beams with piles of split shingles they were hammering into place, using mostly black locust thorns, long and hard as nails. Before leaving Mountain Laurel, Malcolm had advised collecting as many as he could. They had yet to spot the trees so far north.

Malcolm and Liam were muddied to the shins in the pit dug to work the daubing, a mixture of clay, shredded cedar bark, and dried horse dung. Liberally watered, it squished between their toes as they trod the pit, making man and boy laugh.

"Listen to you both," Seona called from below Ian's perch. "Giggling like girls."

Lily and Naomi were minding the children so Seona could help with the cabin raising, since Catriona had gone into Shiloh with Maggie to aid at the school—from which the boys had been excused. Ian looked down to see her at the pit, come to gather another basketful of daubing. Locust thorn clamped between his lips, he set a shingle in place and watched her.

The day was warm but not overly sticky. White-billowed clouds sailed a blue sky. Seona's plaited hair bared her neck. Her short gown and petticoat were those she had worn in Albany when they met on the street. He remembered them from Mountain Laurel. Grown threadbare in spots, dotted with spark holes, they fit her still. She rose with the basket and returned to the cabin, glancing up as she neared. Their gazes caught before she passed out of view to continue her work.

Ian pounded in a thorn, then reached for another from the bag tied to his belt, but awareness of her made him call out, "Seona?"

She stepped back from the cabin wall to look up at him, hands covered in daubing.

"See that lone maple?" He nodded toward the westernmost tree comprising the hardwood stand, rising between them and the cornfield sprouting shoots in tidy rows. Set higher than the rest on a slight rise of land, its branches spread in a pleasing symmetry, leaves shimmering in the breeze. In the autumn, he knew, it would blaze into a conflagration of oranges and reds. "I aim to build our house next to it. I situated the other cabins so they can one day serve as dependencies of the big house."

Her shoulders flinched at the term—what his uncle's family, and their slaves, once called the main house at Mountain Laurel. He made mental note never to use it again.

Seona looked up, a question gathering in her eyes. She glanced along the roofline to where Neil MacGregor hammered shingles, then at the pit where Liam and Malcolm tromped the clay. Question unasked, she returned to the daubing, he to fitting shingles, wondering about their letters. Had she kept those he wrote through winter? He had kept hers. Treasured them. Ought he to bring them out, see if they might find their way forward by looking back?

If a moment to do so presented itself. He had tossed each night beneath the canvas shelter, knowing she wasn't at ease there but never a chance to speak alone, with so much needing his attention. Nor had he approached Neil MacGregor in private about the subject of Aram Crane. Other things had fallen by the wayside. He had intended to go on with his reading of Scripture of an evening, as he had done before Seona's arrival, but corralling them all into a cabin at once was proving nigh impossible when some had chores calling and others were already abed or getting the children to sleep.

"What of Gabriel?" Seona had asked that first evening while he marked off the new cabin's corners. The westering sun had bejeweled her eyes. "You mean him to sleep in this new cabin with me and Mama, or in with you and Mandy and Catriona?"

Had she forgotten his promise never to take her son from her? Not even for a night, could he help it. "I'm sure he and Mandy would get on fine, but he'll stay with ye and Lily until . . . we're all more settled."

Until we're wedded, he had wanted to say, but it felt too soon.

". . . then Maggie tried to make me go to school today," Liam was telling Malcolm down in the daubing pit, voice grown loud enough to intrude into Ian's thoughts. "Mama and Papa agreed that since Jamie's been helping, I could too, now there's this I *can* do."

Ian cast Neil MacGregor a look. In the eleven months since he had met the boys, Jamie had shot up in height, adding nigh six inches to his nearly thirteen-year-old frame, leaving his younger brother feeling abandoned in childhood.

"D'ye no' fancy it," Malcolm replied, "having your sister as a teacher?"

Liam scrunched his nose. "It's not enough I pay her heed at school. Evenings at home, she's after me to study *more*."

From the roof's opposite slope came a snort from Neil MacGregor.

Malcolm leaned on the stick he used to steady himself as he trod the daubing. "As a laddie, I hadna the means to read or write or study aught but what I could see o' the world wi' my eyes, hear wi' my ears, and touch wi' my hands."

Liam crumbled more cedar bark into the pit, then added clay and water to the mixture. "Because you were a slave?"

"Aye. I've always hankered at least to read. Move o'er a mite, lad. Let me help tread in that new bit."

Liam moved aside so they could work in the additions together. "Some men who were never slaves don't read." The boy glanced at the cabin's roof. "Papa doesn't."

Malcolm stopped his treading. "Your daddy's a doctor. Surely he reads."

Liam shook his head. "He can't."

Neil stopped his hammering to call down, "It's true, Malcolm. I canna read—on account of a blow took years ago." He tapped the graying hair tailed back from his brow, where an old scar traversed his hairline.

"Like my Ally," Malcolm said, straw hat bobbing. "Though he didna *lose* anything when that ol' mule kicked him as a lad. Just never grew past a child in his mind."

"I once hoped it would come back to me," Neil said, catching Ian's gaze. "That doesna look like happening, but I'm gettin' along all right, with Willa and Maggie's help."

"Mine too," Liam said.

"Aye, lad. Ye pen a bonny hand when ye put your mind to it. Though it'll be a few years before I let ye record my case notes—at least the more gruesome ones," Neil added in a lowered tone. The man had a vast capacity for memorizing the details of his patients' maladies and his treatments, routinely recited for his wife or daughter to write in his casebook—the same way he had written his field guide, he'd explained to Ian.

Seona had approached the pit for more daubing when an outcry from Naomi's cabin pierced the air—Gabriel's. She peered in that direction, no doubt evaluating the tone of the crying as Ian could do Mandy's. It didn't take long acquaintance with his son's cries to hear the anger in it now. When it ceased, Seona filled her basket. They returned to their tasks.

After some while Neil called down, "If ye wish to learn to read, Malcolm, I'm sure Maggie would teach ye—and ye dinna need travel all the way into Shiloh or sit in wi' the bairns. She'd come to ye here. Some evenings, perhaps."

Before Malcolm could answer, Gabriel's cries erupted again.

Seona had been pouring water into the pit. She set down the bucket and frowned toward the cabin where Naomi, Lily, and the children were ensconced. When silence fell once more, she turned to Malcolm and said, "Soon as we get this cabin raised, *I* mean to teach you to read that Bible, Malcolm. And—"

She broke off as Gabriel's crying commenced a third time, soaring on a note of pain. Abandoning the daubing, Seona snatched up her skirts and raced for Naomi's cabin.

"D'ye need me?" Ian called after her.

Seona didn't break her stride to answer.

Lily found her in Ian's cabin, holding her boy, who had finally cried himself to sleep after putting his hand to the embers Naomi had raked beneath her spider pan to fry up ham for their dinner.

"Everything all right?" she asked, pitching her voice soft at the sight of Gabriel sprawled limply across Seona's lap.

How many times had she been asked that question since Albany? How many times had she ducked it, saying she was fine? She nearly did so again before realizing her mama meant Gabriel.

Seona rocked him, sitting on the edge of Ian's bedtick, hands still spotted with daubing. Gabriel sagged in her arms, lashes tear-spiked, brows puckered. The pain of his burns trailing him into sleep. "The salve helped."

Lily peered at the slack little hand dangling from Seona's arm. "No blisters raised?"

"No." Three of Gabriel's fingers were scorched an angry red, but no skin had broken before Naomi caught him at her fire—gone behind her back for the third time in a half hour.

Lily sighed. "He won't do it again."

Seona regarded her boy with tender exasperation. "He's stubborn."

"So were ye," Lily said. "But ye didn't do it a second time."

Seona raised a brow. "When did I ever put a hand in the fire?"

"Ye were smaller than this boy," her mama said, fingers brushing Gabriel's damp curls. "Toddling around the kitchen at Mountain Laurel. Charmed by those pretty embers, just like he's been of late."

Seona shifted Gabriel on her lap, freeing her right hand to view the patch of shiny skin on her middle finger, across the center joint, the hint of one on the third. "Is that where these old marks come from?"

Lily took her hand to study them. "Likely so. I've wondered did ye hold the memory."

"I don't." Lily released her hand. Seona laid Gabriel on his daddy's bed, then whispered, "Did you ever?"

Lily shook with silent laughter. "Naomi says I did. Ally too. Must be the same, back to Cain and Abel playing at Eve's fire. Part of being human—and fallen. We all put our hand to the flames at some point."

"I wonder if Mandy's done it." She had toted Gabriel between the cabins, bawling his head off, in part so Naomi could calm Mandy, who set to wailing when her brother was burned.

"Naomi says she's stayed clear of the hearth. So far."

Maybe Mandy would learn from Gabriel's mistake. Maybe her tempting flames would be another sort. What that might prove, Seona hadn't a clue. Though Judith's daughter was starting to warm to her, it was still Naomi's comfort she wanted in such moments.

She had been thinking more about Judith since coming to Shiloh, looking after her daughter along with Gabriel. They might be gathering eggs, fetching water from the springhouse, or just sitting on a coverlet in the shade, and she would catch a glimpse of Judith in the child—a look in her brown eyes, a shy cant of her head, the sound of her laughter—and feel a pang. Judith was missing her growing up, looking like a perfect little blend of her and Ian.

But if Judith had been there, where would *she* be? Back in Boston, she, Lily, and Gabriel, maybe making a go of living on their own by now. Gabriel never knowing his daddy.

She wasn't regretting coming to Shiloh—despite the blackflies that pestered them if they dared go near the creek any time but midday. They had about run their course for the year, Ian assured her.

What hadn't run its course was her shyness with Ian, though she liked catching sight of him about the farm, working on the cabin, coming from the stable, headed off to tend the cattle with Ally—and Nip and Tuck. Ally went about his work with those dogs with a confidence he had never worn at Mountain Laurel. She admired Ian for trusting Ally with his own herd to build, was proud of Ally for rising to the level of that trust. They were taking meals in Naomi's cabin or sitting in the shade around it. It felt almost like being at Mountain Laurel again, but better. A body could rest when she needed without fear of some overseer coming along to scold her, or worse. And there was laughter. She ought to be content as a cat in cream.

"Ye talk to him yet, girl-baby?" her mama asked.

"When he wakes, I mean to, though I think you're right. He won't go messing with a fire again."

"I meant Ian."

Seona moved to the cabin door, where the sun shone bright and the breeze made little puffs of dust in the swept yard. Lily followed. They stayed on the side of the cabin facing away from the one being raised. She could hear Ian and Neil MacGregor hammering away.

"Too many people around, too much to do." She always had a little one clinging or a task to get done whenever Ian was by. Maybe a time or two she had only pretended to be so busy . . .

"Finding time and space isn't the problem," Lily said. "Looks to me the pair of ye are too chary of each other to bare your hearts. What I'm wondering is *why*—when ye shared so much in your letters?"

Seona hesitated for words. "I . . . guess I'm feeling shy of him. Scared. And I know what you're going to say next."

"Ye do." Lily slipped a hand around her shoulders. Pulling her close, she kissed her temple where the curls sprang loose of their pins. "No need to fear. The Lord's looking after our lot."

Somehow it had been easier to let the Lord be in control—or take comfort from the thought—when they had no say in matters, big or small. They had freedom now to choose. That meant they had to look after themselves to a point, didn't it? Shouldn't she be looking ahead to see trouble coming, doing what she could to head it off? She saw trouble coming when more people started putting together that she and Ian shared a son but not a daughter. That they were never married save for that handfasting business. But which was best, pressing Ian again about how he meant to handle things or waiting to see how she was treated, accepting whatever came of his choice—a lie of omission or the plain truth?

She had talked some to Neil MacGregor the past few days, and his sons, and caught no undertones of disdain. But it was the womenfolk—Willa, Maggie, others in Shiloh she'd yet to meet—who would make her and Lily's lives bearable beyond the bounds of the farm Ian was building. Seona had sensed no disdain from them either, but Willa MacGregor had lived all those years as a Mohawk Indian and adopted two Mohawk children. There couldn't be many like her.

Seona thought of Maggie, teaching white children in the village. Some of them. Some parents wouldn't let their children attend because of Maggie's mixed blood.

She hadn't let that stop her trying.

Maybe she should talk to Maggie . . . which meant leaving the farm, going to visit, risking rejection, which could be far more subtle than anything she thought Ian understood. A person could smile with their mouth, say the right words, and cut you with their eyes. Cut you right out of their hearts.

"Don't you trust him, girl-baby?" Lily asked.

Uncertain if her mama meant the Lord or Ian, Seona made no answer.

Ian and Neil MacGregor were sweating in their shirtsleeves as they finished up the roofing in solitude. Seona hadn't returned from tending Gabriel. Malcolm had gone to his cabin for a rest. Liam was off helping Ally and Jamie cart in chimney stones collected out beyond the cornfield to the north.

"I heard ye pointing out the house site ye've chosen," Neil said, clambering over the roof crest to Ian's side and taking up a shingle from the pile. "If ye put in rooms abovestairs, ye'll have a lovely view of the lake."

"I hope Seona thinks so," Ian said before Neil could bang in the locust thorn he set into place.

"How is it, having her here?"

The question was nonchalant enough Ian might have deflected it with a matching reply—if he hadn't caught his neighbor's gaze and read a concern at odds with his tone. "I'm not sure I know."

Neil's brows rose, deepening the lines in his forehead. "I've seen these past few days how she is with ye and how she is with Malcolm, Naomi, even Ally. I've been wondering, were she and Lily your uncle's slaves as well?"

Exactly what had his neighbor seen? The same reticence Ian had witnessed? The distance?

"They were both enslaved when I came to Mountain Laurel," he said. "My half cousin, Aidan, was Seona's father—he died before she was born. Uncle Hugh freed them just before his death."

"Your uncle kept his own granddaughter enslaved?"

"Aye. But it was more complicated than ye could imagine." Ian meant to say no more but, in the face of his neighbor's quiet attention, found himself still talking and talking, until he had told Hugh Cameron's story, Aidan's and Lily's, as well as his and Seona's from his arrival at Mountain Laurel to her leaving, the long months apart, then Judith's death and their brief reunion in Boston, the letters shared over the past winter. The hope of a second chance. "Ye mind I went to Cooperstown on my way to meet them, paid off my land?"

"I do." Neil reached for a shingle, then shifted along the roof timber he straddled. Ian handed him a thorn from the bag at his belt.

"While there I found a ring. I bought it thinking to give it to Seona when first I saw her again. Propose proper-like, aye? But when we met at last, I sensed . . . something amiss."

Neil hammered in the new shingle, then sat back and asked, "What? She'd changed her mind, after coming all that way?"

"No," Ian said reflexively. "I don't think so. But I decided it wasn't the best time for asking her to marry me. She was exhausted. Gabriel had been poorly. Besides, I thought it was understood from our letters we meant to marry, raise our children, make a home together. I'd told her I still love her."

He glanced at the smoke going up from Naomi's chimney; the scent of cookery was making his stomach rumble.

"Have ye told her since?" Neil asked.

"I tried. Once. She talked of . . ." He felt Neil's expectant gaze. "She talked of ye and Willa. Seemed worried about ye, what ye'd think of her. We were interrupted before I could get to the bottom of it."

By the son still interrupting them and likely to go on doing so. He pounded in another shingle, as did Neil before he cleared his throat.

"I'm reminded how it was meeting Willa. I thought her distant at first, unfeeling, until I came to understand all she'd lost. Then I kent her coldness for a shield. She was afraid of loving, of risking her heart again, ye ken?"

Ian nodded. How many ways had he missed the mark with Seona, assuming she saw the world as he did? Responded to it as he? She hadn't. Didn't. Maybe never would. Did that mean they could never find a place of trust, of understanding?

"I'm no' suggesting that's what's going on wi' Seona," Neil was quick to add. "I've a hard enough time of late with Maggie. Women are . . . complicated."

Ian barked a rueful laugh. "But Willa married ye. How did ye manage to build a life together after such a rough start?"

"At first I thought we wouldna," Neil said. "The day I asked her to marry me, she bade me go awa' and leave her. It broke my heart to do so. Soon enough God made it clear I was to go back and try again, despite Willa's stubbornness. So I did—went back to Shiloh and bunked behind the smithy, let Willa ken I was there and didna mean to leave."

"That's all?"

"No. I prayed. Fervently. After a time, the Almighty made it clear what I could do for Willa—to *show* her my love. And I did it. Helped save her land, rode all the way to Albany to fetch back her father's old letters that proved he was no Loyalist. I asked Willa to marry me again when I brought her the news." Neil's eyes, intensely blue, softened with the memory. "She was more agreeable to the notion the second time."

"I haven't asked once yet," Ian admitted. Not since that day in the orchard at Mountain Laurel, when he had asked Seona to be handfast with him, thinking he knew her mind, her heart. "Should I now?"

Neil was silent, thinking. Or praying. The silence held no strain. Ian was minded of how he had often felt in John Reynold's presence. Comfortable with the waiting. The sun passed behind a cloud, then out again. The air stirred, warm on his skin, a whisper in the beech leaves.

"It was one of the hardest things I've ever had to do," Neil said at last, "establishing myself in Shiloh apart from Willa, waiting for a way to show her my intentions, since speaking them hadn't worked."

Ian pondered that. Did he know Seona's mind any better now than he had that day in his uncle's orchard? Not as well as he wished. What was it Neil had just said? *Waiting for a way to show her my intentions . . .*

"I should court her." It hadn't issued as a question, and he sensed it was, at last, a course of action he felt some confidence in following. He needed to step back, slow his impatient heart. Get to know the woman Seona was now. Let her know him. They had spent less than a fortnight together in Boston, after all, and writing letters wasn't the same as being together, day to day.

"I think there's wisdom in that," Neil said. "Can ye manage it?"

Ian started to smile at the teasing in his neighbor's eyes, when Seona finally left his cabin. She crossed the yard to Naomi's, looking his way briefly. His breath caught with longing at the sight of her lithe figure, the grace with which she moved.

"With your prayers and God's help," he told his neighbor. "I mean to try."

24

After dropping off a broken bit with the blacksmith for mending, Ian reached Keagan's store, ready to complete his business in the village and head back to finish laying the new cabin's chimney. He, Ally, and Neil had planned to do so that morning, but Liam had brought word that his father was called away in the wee hours to physic a sick child—but would any of the women like to come dip candles with Willa and Maggie, who wasn't holding school that day?

Then Ally had come up from the pasture saying one of his cows had dropped a late calf overnight, then proceeded to drop a second, only to decide one was enough and refuse to mother its twin. After failing to interest another nursing cow, they penned the calf in a corner of the crowded stable where Ally was attempting to feed it with a bottle of its mother's milk, capped with a makeshift teat.

The business with the calves had reminded Ian: the herd had increased by six earlier in spring. Ally's two made eight new calves. He would need to bell them when they were weaned.

Keagan's store was the oldest structure in Shiloh, though an addition had been built to serve for a tavern. Voices reached Ian from the taproom, but the store side was deserted. He decided to have a look round for bells. He needed a good hide, too, to make summer moccasins for Gabriel and Mandy to run around in.

Seona, Lily, and Catriona had ridden with him as far as the MacGregors'. It was the first time Seona had left the farm since their arrival. Naomi had remained behind with Malcolm and the children. On the short ride between the farms, he had asked if Seona needed anything he might obtain in Shiloh, hoping she would request something. What he wanted to give her, the poesy ring, remained tucked in a pocket on his person. Just in case. *I should court her,* he had told Neil yesterday and had barely ceased thinking of how to go about it.

"Cameron? I'll be right over." The proprietor, Jack Keagan, peered from the taproom, clutching full pewter cups. He set them on a table where two men brooded over a checkered game board.

Ian found four cowbells tucked away on the shelves. He was setting them and a rolled hide on the counter when the tall, graying Keagan came in announcing he had a letter come for Ian. He went behind the counter—not to where he normally kept the post brought in weekly by rider, but into his room in back. Emerging, letter in hand, he explained, "I'd normally not keep a letter tucked away private not directed to me. But look at this."

Ian took the proffered letter, once wax-sealed, stamped with the sender's signet. The seal was broken in half.

"Come up from Cooperstown," Keagan said. "Looks like Judge Cooper's seal."

Ian had unfolded the sheet and seen the letter's signature. "Aye." He handed over coin for purchases and post, wrapped the bells in the hide and secured them with string Keagan donated, but decided to read the letter before heading out to Ruaidh, hitched at the smithy. He skimmed the judge's erratically spelled missive. The man was checking up on Ian, hoping all was well, then—

> *Despyte your Protestashuns that the Gold with which you compensayted me for your Land was not discoverd under New York earth, I have not relinkwished Hope that such a Vane may be found beneath Otsego Grownd—*

Ian bit back the impulse to swear. Spotting Keagan puttering about, wiping down shelves, he asked, "D'ye know who might have seen this, besides yourself and the rider who brought it? It *was* the usual rider?"

Keagan returned to the counter. "I presume so, but I didn't see. It was in with the regular post, waiting on the counter when I came back from the mill, three days back. Might have broken in the satchel. They do."

"What's broken then?" Neil MacGregor asked, coming into the store. "Saw your roan at the smithy, Ian. Figured ye were over to here."

Ian was careful in explaining the broken seal, not wanting Keagan to think he held the man to blame, but caught the troubled look the store proprietor and Neil shared, full of things unspoken. "Clearly ye're both thinking something about this letter. What is it?"

Neil looked suddenly tired and haunted. "I dinna recall whether I've told ye about Colonel Waring's son—his eldest. Richard Waring."

The name drew a blank. "I don't think ye've told me anything. It's the first I'm hearing of a *Richard* Waring."

Keagan glanced toward the taproom at the name, as if a ghost had been conjured and might come gliding through the doorway.

Neil dropped his voice. "Richard stole a letter directed to Willa, one that would have proved her parents' loyalties during the war—when such evidence was needed to save her land—and spared *me* a trip to Albany and a shooting by Aram Crane."

Aware that his jaw hung slack, Ian shut it. What had they told him, back in autumn, about their history with Crane? That the man, a British Army deserter, had done them harm. Not that he had gone so far as to *shoot* anyone. And one of the Warings had been involved?

"Had I not handed the letter over to him like a fool, you mean," Keagan was saying in response to the comment that had silenced Ian.

"No," Neil said. "Ye had no reason to mistrust Richard's motives. Not then. Ye thought he meant to take the letter to Willa."

"Anyway," Keagan said. "Richard's gone beyond tampering with anyone's post—cabins and children and anything else."

Cabins and children? Before Ian could respond to that bewildering statement, Neil asked, "But Crane? Have ye seen him?"

"I have not," Keagan said with unmistakable fervor. "Was he to show his face in Shiloh again, I'd be liable to shoot it off, ask questions later."

"All right," Ian said, impatient to understand. "Explain why this Richard Waring would have troubled ye and Willa so. Was he in league with Crane?" He had yet to tell his neighbor the tale of meeting Crane again in Cherry Valley. Seona and Gabriel's arrival, the many needs that pulled at him, the work needing done, his concerns over Seona, had pushed the encounter to the back of his mind for days. It came roaring to the forefront now.

"Reckon 'twas more the other way around," Keagan began, but Neil cut him off with another glance, then met Ian's gaze.

"I'll tell ye, Ian. But not here. Ride wi' me, if ye're bound for home."

"I am," Ian replied, taking up the hide-wrapped bells. "And I've a thing I need to tell ye, too."

"This has been such *fun*," Catriona said, spreading her arms above the rows of tow-wicked tapers dangling from drying racks laid between straight-backed chairs. "I've never dipped candles before."

Every woman in the MacGregors' kitchen paused in an act of tidying to eye her. Anni Keppler—the miller's wife—burst out laughing. "I hadn't harbored a doubt on that score!" She studied the tapers Catriona had dipped, notably lopsided compared to every other batch. "I'm guessing your family bought their candles?"

"We did," Catriona replied, unbothered that her misshapen tapers were a source of poking fun. "From a seller around the corner. Right, Seona?"

Slightly panicked when the weight of all their gazes fell upon her, Seona forced a smile. "In Boston we did. Back in Carolina we dipped tallows every fall—didn't we, Mama?" Like the passing of a plate at table, she fastened her gaze on Lily, thankful when those of the MacGregor women and Anni Keppler—who she hadn't known would be joining them—swung to Lily and away from her.

"Just after the hog butchering," her mama said.

They had also dipped beeswax candles, but those had gone to the big house. They were never allowed the best candles in the kitchen or cabins. Most times just an old Betty lamp with a tow wick. Or a pine knot. She and Lily shared a look in which those memories stirred, but Seona mentioned nothing to connect her to being a slave in the minds of these freeborn women.

She was still uncertain what Willa and Maggie knew about them. No chance of asking with Willa's plump, fair-haired friend present. Not even if Anni's blue eyes shone amiably as she said, "We've dipped our share of tallows too, but beeswax is easier to come by since Goodenough started keeping bees—mainly for honey to use as sweetening and for poultices."

Though Willa had had some beeswax on hand, it was Anni who had brought most of what they had melted at the hearth. They had propped the kitchen door open to the back veranda, emitting a breeze. Even so caps were off and temples gleaming from working over a hot kettle, though Willa had remarked on the grayness of the day and feeling a storm coming. Perhaps some cooler air with it.

"Poultices?" Lily said, ears perked to healer-talk.

"That's right," Anni said. "Goodenough is a midwife."

Best Seona could grasp the connections of these Shiloh folk, Goodenough had been the slave of Anni's father, Colonel Waring, back when Anni was young. Goodenough was free now, as was her son, Lemuel. Though Seona had heard talk of them—Catriona had met both while helping at Maggie's school—they hadn't come to the MacGregor farm this day. Only their beeswax.

Willa looked up from scraping a hardened drop off the table. "So is Lily, a midwife," she said, then flicked the bits of wax into the dying hearth fire and eased herself onto a chair, a hand on her swollen belly.

"Are ye well after all this work?" Lily asked, drawn to Willa like iron to a magnet. "Ye've been on your feet all the morn."

"Beeswax candles *are* so much nicer than tallow," Maggie said, resuming the conversation while Lily and Willa fell to talking of aching backs and swollen ankles.

"The smell for one thing," Anni, who had declared herself done with birthing babies after two sets of twins, said. "And beeswax burns so much brighter. I was thrilled when Goodenough started raising bees and putting out more honey and wax than she could use."

Seona glanced at her mama, talking with Willa. They had had no beeswax to contribute, though Anni and Willa insisted they take home the candles they had dipped. And Catriona hers. Not that anyone else coveted *those*.

Ian's sister seemed at ease in the MacGregors' home. But then she had spent nearly as much time with Maggie as she had at Ian's farm. Their companionship made Seona think of Judith, of what might have blossomed between them by way of friendship had Miss Lucinda not come between.

Hoping no one would notice her silence, she tried to look busy gathering up the leftover tow wicking, wishing she had remained at Ian's farm after all. Naomi alone had stayed back to mind Mandy and Gabriel, and Malcolm, still abed but awake when they gathered for breakfast.

"We can start on those reading lessons, Malcolm," Seona had said. "I don't have to go."

Naomi had insisted she would rather watch babies than dip another batch of candles. Besides, Catriona wouldn't hear of her staying. "Seona, you must come. Maggie and Willa want to get to know you. And Lily," she added, quick to include the one person who seemed to understand why Seona might balk at what should have been an enjoyable visit with their neighbors.

"Ye cannot hide here from the world," Lily said once Catriona went out to saddle Juturna. "Don't even start down that road."

"Listen to your mama," Malcolm had said from his bed. "There's time aplenty for ye to teach this old man his letters."

Which had put an end to her heel digging.

"The beeswax we had on hand came from a wild hive," Maggie was saying. "Matthew found it on the ridge last spring, following the beeline from our apple trees. He smoked the bees and harvested some honey and wax."

"And a dozen bee stings!" Anni added with a grin.

Seona was thinking about apple trees, minding those of Mountain Laurel and wondering where on the farm the MacGregors' might be, when Catriona asked, "What's a *bee*line?"

Seona knew the answer but let Maggie tell it. "The path a honeybee takes heading back to its hive. They tend to fly straight there, so if you see one taking off from a flowering tree in spring, you can follow it."

"Easier if it's more than just the one bee," Anni said. "They're fast."

Catriona was fascinated. "Have either of you ever followed a bee-line?"

"Willa and I tried as girls," Anni said. "We never found a hive."

"It takes practice," Maggie said. "Though I don't think it took Matthew long to pick up the skill, once Uncle Joseph taught him."

"So your brother's an accomplished hand with horses *and* bees?" Catriona asked.

"Horses being the easier to wrangle," said a deep and unfamiliar voice from the kitchen doorway.

They turned to see a tall, lean young man standing there, one who looked enough like Maggie to be her brother—which Seona assumed he was—though his hair was darker, crow black as Lily's, long and straight and tailed at the base of his neck. He was dressed in buckskin leggings and moccasins, with a blue shirt belted low on his waist, open at the collarless neck. Rolled sleeves bared lean, bronzed arms. A knife and tomahawk were thrust through the belt, reminding her of Ian, the day he arrived at Mountain Laurel. *Looking like a wildcat out the woods,* Naomi had said.

Though two men could not have been more different in looks, this one had something of the wildcat about him too. His mouth curved as he took in the sight of his mother's kitchen crowded with petticoats and pinned-up hair, but it was his eyes Seona noted in the seconds before the greetings commenced.

They were dark, and there was anger in them.

25

"Matthew!" Maggie exclaimed. "We were starting to worry."

"Is something wrong?" Willa said as conversations paused, making Seona think she too had seen that anger in the young man's eyes, from clear across the kitchen. Willa started to rise from her chair, awkward with her big belly.

"Don't," Matthew MacGregor said. "I've the horses and the meat to tend. I . . ." His agitated glance roved the kitchen full of women staring back at him. He seemed fit to burst with something wanting said, just not in front of strangers. Then, with a reckless light in those dark eyes, he threw caution to the wind. "Half my traps were violated again. Sprung and robbed. This time I know it was Aram Crane did it."

His lean face took on a ferocity that made Seona flinch, though she didn't recognize the name he had spoken. Not the case with Anni and Willa, who exchanged a look sharp with alarm.

Maggie's face had taken on a grayish cast. "You *saw* him?"

"No," Matthew admitted. "But you know what they say he does around Canajoharie. Pilfering traps. Taking shots at other hunters in the woods."

Maggie shook her head. "But Canajoharie is—wait, did he shoot at you?"

"No. And Canajoharie isn't *that* far away."

"Sixty miles," his sister said.

"Less as the wolf runs."

"Matthew," Willa said firmly. "You have yet to meet our neighbors, Ian's family, arrived while you have been gone."

Introductions duly made, Matthew MacGregor—visibly reining in his temper—nodded and said, "I saw your horses in the paddock. Which of you claims the tall filly?"

"That's Juturna," Maggie said. "She's Catriona's."

"Actually she's Seona's," Catriona corrected. "Though I mainly ride her."

"She's a beauty." Matthew stared at Catriona, whose color deepened until Anni Keppler took him by the arm and steered him toward Willa.

"Do you truly think Aram Crane has been hanging about—near enough to pilfer your trapline? I ask, Willa," she added, catching her friend's disapproving look and dropping her voice to a near whisper, "because of *Francis*."

"Francis?" Maggie asked. "You didn't see him, did you, Matthew?"

"Not a sign," her brother said. "Sorry, Maggie."

As Maggie MacGregor's eyes welled, Catriona frowned and said, "Let's go out to the yard. I think your mother's right about the weather. Don't you feel the cooling?"

She grabbed Maggie's hand and towed her toward the doorway, with a sidelong glance at Matthew that Seona read as wary. He lingered only briefly before following them out. Seeing to his horses, Seona supposed, and whatever meat or hides he'd brought back from the hills.

"I'm sorry," Anni said to the half-emptied kitchen. "I didn't mean to upset Maggie, but he's my *brother*. Though I may have control of my tears, I'm worried half to death over Francis." She turned to Lily and Seona, standing near the hearth. "I don't know whether you know?"

"Ian's told us," Lily said. "Your brother's gone missing, a long time now."

They knew more than that. Maggie MacGregor had long loved Francis, who didn't return her love. Or wasn't the marrying type. Ian had written that he wasn't comfortable around folk, instead was wont to wander the hills, sometimes for weeks. But never for months.

"I'll make some tea," Anni said briskly. "Do you mind, Willa?"

Willa waved a hand. "You know where it is kept."

Lily joined Willa at the table, but Seona left the kitchen, wandering half-heartedly after Maggie and Catriona. A parlor of sorts spanned the front of the house just off the central passage. She stood at the window, spotting Maggie carrying something into the barn. Closer to the house, Catriona stood at the paddock, where their horses had grazed while they dipped candles. Just inside the fence, Matthew MacGregor bent, running a hand over Juturna's foreleg. He turned his face in profile, mouth moving. Catriona appeared pleased by whatever he said. He stood with a supple grace, tall and dark compared to Ian's sister, as he stroked the filly's neck.

He led their horses out of the paddock and hitched them to a rail, ready to be saddled for the ride home.

"I thought ye'd gone out to them," Lily said, joining her at the window. She looked sidelong when Seona merely shook her head, then glanced through the window and pointed. Not at Catriona and Matthew, but the lane leading to the road.

Two riders were approaching the house, recognizable even through the wavy glass. Neil MacGregor and Ian.

Ian and Neil helped Matthew unload his packhorse of hides and meat, while the girls returned to the house. He had asked Catriona whether Seona was inside and if she had enjoyed their time candle-making. She was and had, Catriona reported, but in truth he was still distracted by the conversation he and Neil had had on their ride home from the village and what he had learned about Richard Waring, what the man had done to Willa, how he had died, and—most pertinent to Ian's mind—his connection to Aram Crane. Doubtful if Crane would have figured into the MacGregors' lives at all were it not for Richard Waring.

Having coveted Willa's land, thinking he could brand her parents as Loyalists to the Crown to get it, Richard had been the cause of their deaths years before Willa returned from living with the Mohawk. He had covered the crime by letting everyone in Shiloh believe her parents had fled, driven away by their supposed Loyalist sentiments—hence the confiscation of Willa's farm by the time she returned to it.

When she contested the accusation, Richard had enlisted Aram Crane, working for Colonel Waring as a groom, to harass her in every way possible, going so far as to truss Matthew and Maggie, then but children, inside her old cabin and set the place aflame. The children had been spared a horrible death by Francis Waring, hardly more than a boy himself, while outside, Willa was saved from Richard's attack by Joseph Tames-His-Horse, who fought the man hand-to-hand by the light of that burning cabin. A fight in which Richard Waring fell upon his own knife and died of the wound. Joseph was taken into custody by Colonel Waring but released when Francis came forward and revealed all that his elder brother had done.

"As for Crane," Neil had said, "he escaped his reckoning and fled into the mountains—not before attempting to murder *me*—where he's been living all this while."

"Except when he's in Cooperstown," Ian had replied as they came within sight of Neil's farm. "Or Cherry Valley. Where, as it happens, I had a run-in with the man on my way to meet with Seona." He had told his neighbor about the encounter that came after he paid off his land in gold. "Mined in Carolina," he had said, "though I'll ask ye to keep that quiet. I've not told Cooper where I came by it or another soul in New York. Seona doesn't even know of its existence."

"And ye think Crane got hold of the letter from Cooper?" Neil had asked.

"Knowing now what Richard Waring did with Willa's letter—and those two in league then—I think it possible."

"If rumor's to be credited," Neil had said, "Crane's murdered more than one man and never been brought to justice for it. Even without Richard having set the precedent, I wouldna put tampering wi' the post past him."

When the three were at last alone in the barn, Neil turned to Matthew and, to Ian's surprise, said, "Right then. What's going on wi' ye?"

Preoccupied as he was with his own concerns, Ian hadn't picked up on the tension behind Matthew's outward calm. He caught it now as Matthew hefted a saddle onto a rack and turned to face them.

"Aram Crane," he said.

Ian and Neil exchanged startled looks. Before Matthew could explain why *he* was angered over Crane, Seona, Lily, and Catriona came down the veranda steps and crossed the yard, ready to head home, having left the candles they had dipped to harden overnight.

"I'll come fetch them tomorrow," Catriona said as she swung onto Juturna's back, Matthew having gone to hold the reins.

Perched behind Lily on Juturna's dam, Seona looked down at Ian. "You coming with us?"

"I'll be along soon. I want to hear how your visit went." His smile felt strained; the conversation about Crane might have been interrupted, but it wasn't finished.

When the women were away, Matthew turned from watching them go and told them about the traps that had been sprung. "I know it was Crane, Pa. He took the hides and left the carcasses in the traps. No animal does that."

"But why d'ye think it Crane and not some other?" Ian asked. "Did ye ever catch him doing such a thing before?"

"Not me." Matthew hesitated, glancing at his father. "Francis did."

Neil MacGregor's surprise made it clear this was the first he was hearing of such a thing. "Francis saw Aram Crane robbing one of *your* traps?"

"He did."

"When did he tell ye so?" Neil demanded.

"Last time I saw him."

"Clear back in autumn? Why did *ye* no' tell anyone?"

As if he had long known he would face the question, Matthew's answer was ready. "Francis was adamant I didn't. Only later, after he was gone so long, did I wonder if he'd some notion of catching the man on his own. You know Francis."

"Aye," Neil conceded with evident reluctance. "Meek as a kitten but stubborn as a mule."

An alarming combination, Ian thought, pitted against the likes of Aram Crane.

"Anyway," Matthew went on, "after we started to miss him, I didn't want to alarm anyone unnecessarily. Then Uncle Joseph and I left for the winter hunt and . . ." Matthew trailed off, looking wretched.

Neil shook his head. "I ken ye and Maggie are especial friends with Francis but—"

"Maggie doesn't know," Matthew cut in.

"Ye should have told *me*—and Elias Waring—what Francis told ye he saw."

"I know that now!" Eyes dark with self-recrimination, Matthew stalked down the stable's aisle, headed for the open doors.

"D'ye mean to go after him?" Ian asked, ready to mount up and leave Neil to deal with his offspring, but his neighbor shook his head.

"No. I ken my son. Best to let him cool off first."

Ian followed Neil to the stable doors, where the man stopped, gazing out at the clouds thickening over the ridge to the north. A cooling breeze was blowing, carrying the damp, fecund scents of growing things. "This puts another shade on matters. Crane's being seen hereabouts back in autumn."

"If Francis's word can be relied upon," Ian said.

"It can."

Ian felt in his pocket for the letter from Judge Cooper, pulling it out to stare at that broken seal, as if the thing itself might give up its secrets. "If only Cooper hadn't written about the gold . . ."

He turned to look at Neil. Just behind him, in the shadow of the stable door, Matthew stood. Well within hearing. Neil turned, following Ian's gaze.

"What else has Crane done?" Matthew asked, stepping into the overcast light, eyes dropping to the letter. "Tampered with the mail, like Richard Waring did?"

His father raised a cautioning hand. "We dinna ken. The seal was broke on Ian's letter before it came into Keagan's hands, but what it speaks of is no one's business but Ian's. Understand?"

"I won't mention what I heard. I'm not even sure I *know* what I heard. But what if whoever broke it—?"

"*If* anyone did. The seal might have been broken any number of ways."

Matthew opened his mouth to argue, then shook his head and left them in the stable doorway. They watched him cross the yard and go into the house.

Ian swallowed. "So ye don't think Crane had anything to do with the letter's seal being broken? I thought ye did."

"Oh, I do," Neil said. "I just didna want to fuel the lad's hatred of the man. Joseph does enough of that. I dinna blame him, really. Joseph blames himself for letting the man escape." He sighed. "While we've no solid evidence Crane tampered with your letter, with what ye've told me today . . . the suspicions are piling up."

"And *if* he read the letter, he knows my whereabouts—if he didn't already." Ian unhitched Ruaidh from the paddock fence. "But he's been back in these parts—so Francis Waring said—when he'd been gone for how many years?"

"Nearly thirteen now."

The look they shared before Ian took his leave made it clear Neil MacGregor didn't believe they had heard the last of Aram Crane.

No more did Ian.

The morning after the candle dipping, as the sun streaked the clouded eastern sky with pink, Ian stood at Seona's cabin door, a bouquet of wildflowers in hand. As he raised a fist to knock against its freshly planed wood, a screech rose beyond it. Then Seona's harried voice: "Gabriel! Stop that . . . Mama, look out—"

A crash of wood. Water spilling. Lily's gasp: "Caught it—thank goodness."

Seona's dire warning: "You're getting a spanking right now, young man!"

His son: "Sah-wee, Mama. *Sah-weee* . . ."

Ian stifled the laugh wanting to burst forth, certain it wouldn't be well received just then. He didn't need to see whatever havoc his son had wreaked to know that between himself and Seona, he'd had the easier time of child-rearing. Until now.

While his boy loudly protested Seona's disciplining, Ian knocked and, deepening his voice, demanded, "Everything all right in there?"

Lily opened the door, looking no more than mildly ruffled, though the entire front of her petticoat was soaked and her grandson was screaming bloody murder, bent over Seona's knees, getting his bum swatted.

"Good morning, Ian. Are those flowers for me?"

He felt his face redden at her teasing. "Ah . . . well." He peered past Lily to the new bedstead, where Seona, gowned for the day but hair unbraided, was now cuddling their crying son, patting his back for comfort. She eyed him over Gabriel's tousled head, looking as harried as she had sounded. Brazening it out, he held up the flowers. "I wondered if ye wanted to take a wee walk with me, before breakfast?"

"I was heading over to help Naomi—before this one did his mischief."

"Girl-baby," Lily said, "I'll mind that boy 'til breakfast—and his sister. Catriona can help Naomi. Get ye gone."

Seona obeyed, hair streaming in ropy ringlets down her back, forgetting a cap as she bolted for the door. While Gabriel pouted on the bed behind her, she set off walking with her back to the rising sun.

Ian handed the flowers to Lily and hurried to match Seona's step along the narrow track that cut between their cornfields to the lake. After a bit she slowed her pace. "Tough morning?" he asked.

"First in our new cabin and he's already into trouble."

"A new place. He's curious."

"Mister Mischief, Mama calls him. He's living up to the name today."

Ian thought to halt her, make her take in the sunrise, but when he glanced back, what color the clouds had reflected was passing swiftly into gray. He hoped it wouldn't rain. While Seona, Lily, and Gabriel had moved into the cabin the evening before, he still had work to do on that chimney.

They walked in silence past the edge of the red pines to the lake, where blackbirds alighted on swaying cattail stalks, then flitted away with flashes of red amid their wing plumage.

At the edge of the reeds where the lakeshore opened, a heron waded the shallows, stalking its breakfast. Seona stopped to watch its gangly progress. Ian watched her, the flutter of her lashes as she blinked, hair unbrushed and tangled from sleep, until he thought of how best to address her still-knotted brow.

"Ye've done well with him, Seona. A boy can be a handful, I know—I was one. But I very much like the lad he's becoming."

The corner of her mouth twitched. "Even after what you just saw?"

"He'll have to do a good deal worse than tip a washstand to disappoint his da."

She met his gaze, biting that full bottom lip. "I been watching Mandy these past days. She's got that sweet spirit I used to see in . . ."

Looking disconcerted by the near mention of Judith, she walked on around the stand of cattail reeds and stopped with a gasp.

Out beyond the heron, a mist rose off the water in a hundred skinny tendrils that swirled and dipped and swayed. As they watched, the rising sun found a chink in the clouds and bathed the scene until the misty tendrils glowed as if lit from within.

Seona drew a breath and let it out on a sigh. "It's like angels . . . angels dancing on the face of the water." She tore her gaze from the glorious sight. "Ian . . ."

He would long wonder what she might have said—and what might have followed—had there not come in the distance, back at the cabins, a crash of something breaking.

Seona sighed again, then grasped his hand and pressed it to her cheek. "Thank you. This was just what I needed." Leaving him breathless, she started back toward the cabin at a run, only to turn and call, "And thank you for the flowers!"

Grinning, he gave the misty angels a lingering look before he followed her, determined that *he* would deal with his son that morning. More than deal. He would keep Gabriel by his side that day, let the lad help him finish the chimney. Even if doing so made the task take ten times as long.

26

July 1797

The sweet corn was ripening. Ian, Ally, and Malcolm were out in the field in the morning sunlight, picking what was ready before the day's heat could gather its strength and drive them to more sedentary work. Seona felt wrong leaving them to it while she tagged along with Lily to visit Willa, despite Naomi's readiness to mind Gabriel and Mandy.

"You minded them last time. The day we dipped candles."

Naomi dismissed that with a puff of breath. "How long ago was that? Two weeks?"

"Two or ten, it's not fair. Don't you want to go visiting?"

"I'll get off this farm again in good time," Naomi countered, sharing a look with Lily, waiting at the cabin door. "You need to go today."

"I *need* to?" Seona asked, wondering if everyone knew what Ian confessed to her after the day their cabin was finished—that he had told Neil MacGregor the story of Mountain Laurel and her and Lily being slaves there. Though relieved he had hidden nothing, unashamed of her and Gabriel, and assured that Neil hadn't taken against her in the slightest, she thought surely by now he had told his wife and daughter.

And others?

"Seona," her mama said. "Catriona's invited ye to Maggie's school and elsewhere half a dozen times since the candle dipping. Ye always find an excuse to say no. Not today. Put on your cap and let's go."

Ending the debate.

Having dismissed her students for the harvest season, Maggie was home when they arrived at the MacGregors'.

"She plans to go in and clean up the cabin in a few days," Catriona said as they dismounted in the yard and unsaddled the horses. "Bring home the books and such. I'm helping. You should too, Seona."

Seona managed not to roll her eyes. Why was everyone trying to get her off the farm every time she turned around? Wasn't this visit enough?

"Ye should, girl-baby," Lily said after the horses were in a paddock and Catriona and Maggie had gone into the cornfield, laden with hip-baskets, to pick sweet corn enough for everyone's dinner—including Goodenough and her son, Lemuel, whom Willa spotted coming down the lane, each mounted and leading an extra horse.

"Colonel Waring's colts," she said, having donned a pair of soft moccasins over swollen ankles to join them in the yard. "They are for Matthew to gentle to the saddle."

Seona was more interested in Goodenough than the colts. She wasn't sure what she had expected of this former enslaved housemaid of Colonel Waring's, but it wasn't this tall figure with her head of graying hair carried proud as she dismounted in the yard. Though Goodenough's skin was showing its age, the bones beneath were strong, beauty in their lines still.

Lemuel—*Lem*, they called him—was a handsome young man, of an age with Catriona and Maggie. Aside from his height, he barely resembled his mother, with dark, waving hair tailed back from an unguarded face no browner than Matthew's, who came over to inspect the new colts, a black with a white-starred forehead and a dark blue-roan.

"What do you think?" Lem asked. "Colonel reckons they're ready for the saddle."

"Two years old, born a week apart," Goodenough said, handing over the reins of the roan. "Same sire, different dams."

Seona tensed, thinking how the same could be said of Ian's children. But no one else, even her mama, seemed to make that connection.

"Black and Blue, I call 'em." Lem's sunny grin was infectious. Lily returned it, but Seona watched Matthew as he spoke in low tones to the colt called Blue, letting the horse nuzzle his hand before he rubbed between its eyes. The colt was edgy, surrounded by new smells and voices. Its ears twitched back.

Jamie and Liam appeared from the stable.

"Will you water these two?" Matthew asked his brothers. "Then stable Black. I'll take Blue into the paddock right after and get acquainted."

"Where's Maggie?" Lem asked as the horses were led away. "We saw the school shut up on our way here."

"Fetching in corn for dinner," Willa said. "You both will stay and eat with us?"

"Yes, ma'am!" Lem looked ready to head off in search of the girls when Catriona and Maggie emerged from the hillocks—still a strange sight to Seona, used to corn planted in rows. The girls stepped nimbly over the pumpkin vines encircling the stalks, each clasping a basket heaped with fresh sweet corn in the husk. Lem ran to take Maggie's basket, then hesitated as if realizing politeness demanded he take Catriona's too. She laughed and shook her head.

"Put it on the porch, Lem," Maggie told him.

Catriona deposited her basket there as Matthew led the roan colt toward an empty paddock. "Oh, he's going to work now. Shall we watch?" Taking Maggie by the hand, Catriona hurried to the paddock, Lem trailing after.

Goodenough watched them go. "That boy of mine's been puppy-dogging your girl around since the day they met," she said to Willa. "I just hope . . ." Her brow furrowed. "Don't know *what* I hope."

Seona didn't take her meaning until Willa replied, "I know. I want Francis back, but he will never be what Maggie hopes for."

"Ain't that the truth." Goodenough sighed. "But Lem's young yet, more boy than man, for all the work he do. Give it a year or two. Maggie might start to see him different."

The women went onto the porch to better watch the proceedings in the paddock, a fenced circle, its ground well trampled. Matthew let the colt nose along its fence while he stood at the gate talking with Lem, the girls listening. Abruptly he broke off conversation and moved toward the colt, halting in the paddock's center, shoulders squared—an aggressive stance.

The colt thought so. It took flight, breaking into a canter around the paddock, staying close to the rails. As far from Matthew as it could get.

"See how he uses his body, his gaze, to make the horse retreat," Willa said. "It is the way a wild mare, the matriarch of a herd, would drive away a colt if it had misbehaved. Matthew is telling it he is the one in charge and he wants it to go away."

"Why would he want that?" Seona asked.

"A horse does not want to be driven from its herd," Willa said. "Watch and see."

In the paddock's center, Matthew turned a circle, always facing the cantering colt. One hand gripped a coiled line taken off a fence post. He uncoiled it and flicked it at the colt, snapping the air. Seona felt the tension in the paddock as Matthew pressed the colt away. It went on for several minutes before she caught a shift in Matthew's gaze. She thought he looked away from the colt, or maybe just away from its eyes, and was surprised when the animal slowed its pace. When Matthew's eyes shifted back, the colt resumed its cantering like it wanted to fly away.

"Watch its ears," Willa said. "That is what Matthew is doing."

Gripping the veranda rail, Seona watched as Matthew lashed the line out, hitting the air, making the colt run. Six times it circled the paddock before its inside ear swiveled toward Matthew and fixed on him. When the colt ducked its head and ran along with its nose near the ground, Matthew turned sideways to it, coiling the line.

The horse slowed, came off the fence, and stood blowing breath. Then, like some invisible line drew it, step by step it approached Matthew, stopping at last with its nose just behind his shoulder, nostrils flaring, taking his scent. Matthew must surely feel its breath, but seeming to ignore the horse, he walked a slow circle away from it.

The colt followed, nose to shoulder. Matthew stopped, faced the colt, and gave it a stroke between its eyes. When he headed for the paddock gate, the horse followed him.

Willa smiled with pride. "He just made that colt want to be with him."

"Puts me in mind of someone I once knew." Lily caught her eye, and Seona realized with a start her mama was thinking of Aidan Cameron, who tamed a deer and taught a raven to speak. And captured her mama's heart.

"Matthew will do that again," Willa said. "Next time he will have a saddle and bridle ready, and the colt will let him put both on. He will be riding it before an hour has passed."

All through her childhood, Seona had seen Hugh Cameron break horses to the saddle, but never like this, so swift and gentle. "How did he learn to do that?"

"Some of it he learned from Joseph, my brother," Willa replied, "who was not called Tames-His-Horse as a young man for nothing."

Thinking of Willa's Mohawk clan brother, whom Ian had written about in his letters, Seona watched Catriona, Maggie, and Lem step back to let Matthew lead the blue-roan from the paddock. Catriona's mouth hung open with the same stunned admiration Seona was feeling. Ian's sister started toward the stable, following Matthew much as the colt had done.

"I doubt Neil will ever make of him a farmer," Willa said with affection for her adopted son. "He never shirks the work asked of him, but right there—" she bent a nod toward the colt Matthew led into the stable's depths—"that is where his heart is—when he is not hunting with my brother."

"Elias wants him working full-time over to our place," Goodenough said, "soon as Matthew's of a mind to take up the offer."

Elias. Colonel Waring's name. Remembering when Ian first bade her stop calling him *mister*, Seona wondered how it had happened for Goodenough and the Colonel. She had assumed Lem had a white father but . . . Elias Waring?

Willa arched her back, rubbing at it and wincing.

"All right," Goodenough said in a tone brooking no argument.

"Time to give those ankles and that back a rest. Let's get this corn shucked—except for you," she told Willa. "You listen to your midwife and sit."

Seona caught the disappointment that briefly crossed her mama's gaze as they followed Goodenough and Willa to where the sweet corn waited. *Two midwives.* Goodenough had just asserted her place as Willa's.

They dragged the corn baskets to a set of benches. Willa lowered herself onto a padded chair set beside the door. "I was never made to rest before while carrying," she said in amused protest, "but worked right up to the day."

"You're ten years older than last time," Goodenough countered as Seona settled on the top porch step. "Don't tell me you aren't feeling it."

Glad for a familiar task to occupy her hands, Seona helped empty the corn into a pile. They worked for a time in companionable conversation, warm air and warm skin taking on the familiar scent of torn green husks, until Goodenough went inside to get a kettle on the boil and Maggie left the others at the stable to join them on the porch, sitting opposite Seona on the steps.

"What did you think of Matthew and the colt?" she asked.

"I've never seen the like," Seona said. "When did he first try such a thing?"

"Uncle Joseph brought him a horse when he was Jamie's age. A half-wild filly. He told Matthew she was his, if he tamed her to the saddle. For days he just watched her in the pasture with the mares we had then, watched how they treated her, how she responded. He had her saddled and was riding her in the space of an afternoon." Maggie smiled, remembering. "Colonel Waring heard of it and had Matthew come to his farm to see if he could get a horse no one else could manage to accept a rider. That one took a day."

Goodenough came back out. Maggie took the shucked corn into the house. Seona was about to get up and help when Goodenough said she had heard tell Lily was a midwife too.

"Was it your mama taught you or your mistress?"

Silence followed the revealing question. Not only did the MacGregors know she and Lily had been enslaved, Goodenough knew.

Her mama had reached the same conclusion. "My mistress, who raised me more like a daughter, taught me until I was nigh grown," Lily said. "After her death, I learned on my own. I never knew the mother who died birthing me."

Goodenough had taken her seat again, but it was Willa who asked, "But you know who she was, your mother?"

Lily shook her head. "My mama was found by soldiers who went west to fight the Cherokees, back in the old French war. She got caught in a raid, mistaken for a captive. They got her away, only later realized she was mixed blood. African, white, maybe Indian. We don't know because she never spoke English. Only Cherokee."

Willa nodded. "She would have been with them a long time. Maybe a captive once, but one of the People then. How did she end up at . . . Mountain Laurel, was it called?"

Strange hearing the name spoken, so far from Carolina. If her mama thought it so, Seona couldn't tell.

"When the soldiers passed," Lily said, "the mistress took in my mama—for a price. A runaway slave, they were calling her then. I came along days later and thrived. My mama didn't. Afore she died, she said a word over me they thought was meant for a name. It was shortened to Lily, but what she said was *Tsigalili*."

"That a Cherokee word?" Goodenough asked.

"We think so."

"*Tsigalili,*" Willa said, gazing at Lily. "The name my Mohawk mother gave me means Burning Sky. Do you know what *Tsigalili* means?"

"I've never met anyone who speaks Cherokee."

Willa brightened. "My brother has mentioned a Cherokee man who came north and settled at Grand River and taught him some of that language. Joseph will come to us again in the autumn. Perhaps he can tell you."

With everyone gathered on the veranda to eat the freshly boiled sweet corn, the conversation was lively. Lem and Matthew talked of the

horses. Catriona talked of wanting to paint Matthew while he worked with the horses. That made Jamie and Liam roar with laughter until Maggie explained what Catriona meant.

"Would you like to, Seona?" Catriona turned, grinning, to ask. "Maybe Ian will make new easels for us."

They had brought their paints and brushes to New York, but not their easels, too bulky to transport so far.

"Oh, Seona," Maggie said, looking at her with deepening interest. "You're an artist too?"

"I like to draw. Painting's still new to me."

"Don't be modest," Catriona said. "You're already better than I am, and I've been painting for years. But look." Seona nearly dropped her last ear of corn half-eaten when Catriona nudged her and pointed down the track that led to the MacGregors' house. "There's Ian coming to join us."

Maggie, Goodenough, and Lily had gone inside. Seona was about to follow when she heard Willa tell Ian, at the foot of the veranda stairs, that Neil was up in the high foothills north of their land. "An old man, Hector Lacey, lives up there alone."

"Is he ill?" Ian asked.

"He was. A bad cough he could not shake. Neil means to talk him into moving down into Shiloh before winter."

Seona tried to slip inside the house to help clean up after their feast, but Ian spotted her and mounted the steps. "Seona, I'm heading into Shiloh. Will ye ride with me?"

Her chest tightened at his hopeful gaze. "I best head home. Naomi has the children and Ally's calf to tend."

"Ally was feeding the calf when I left. The bairns were napping."

"It'll need feeding again and Ally has work to do."

Feeding the calf was a task Malcolm could handle. The thought was there in Ian's eyes, but he didn't voice it. Seona heard the door behind her open and knew her mama had stepped outside.

"Can I have at least a moment?" Ian reached for her arm. Seona let him lead her off the veranda, down to where Ruaidh waited. Turning her to face him, he asked, "Is that truly why ye don't want to go with me?"

"No." It wasn't, but she couldn't find words to explain.

He looked at her, searching. "Did I do wrong, telling Neil about us?"

"You didn't. I just . . . want to go home. I'm sorry."

She watched his throat work as he smiled. "Nothing to be sorry about. I'll see ye at supper, aye?"

She was still watching him ride away when her mama spoke behind her.

"Why didn't ye go with him?"

She turned. "Mama, don't start—"

"No," Lily said. "What I aim to do is finish this, if I can."

"What?" Seona was too startled to resist when once again her arm was clasped and she was marched back to the house, past Maggie, Catriona, Matthew, and Lem, on their way out.

"Where did Ian . . . ?" A look at their faces, Lily's determined, Seona's stiff with apprehension, stifled Catriona's question. "Never mind."

Lily guided Seona down the passage to the kitchen, where Goodenough was scouring the table and Willa sat watching, bidding her to stop and sit down. She fell silent when they entered, then asked, "Lily? What is wrong?"

Lily released Seona to stand in the middle of the kitchen. "What's wrong is this child of mine, keeping the man who loves her at arm's length and hiding out on his farm, too scared to live this life she's been given."

"Mama," Seona said with barely enough mortified breath to protest. "I'm *here*, ain't I?"

Willa glanced at Goodenough. "Sit. Work can wait."

They all sat, Goodenough at the table's head, nearest Seona. She took Seona's hand in her worn one. "Little sister, what's got you afraid?"

Seona opened her mouth, but tears choked her. *Sister.*

Her mama saw and seemed to suppress a sudden smile. "How if I tell it plain, the way I'm seeing things?"

Tell it plain. How Seona longed for someone to do so, to make sense of the conflicting thoughts she had battled since coming to New York, to Ian, to this bright, free future he was offering. She nodded.

Goodenough squeezed her hand and released it.

"My girl-baby finds herself caught betwixt and between two lives," Lily said. "The one we knew in Carolina and the one we're making here. She cannot find her footing and is afeared to take a step—with feet or heart—until she knows where she and my grandson stand. Who they are. Maybe who they are to *ye*." Lily looked across the table at Seona, who felt the tears come burning. "Am I right?"

"Reckon that hits nigh the mark," Seona said, thumbing away a tear.

There was silence in the room. Waiting. Willa MacGregor had her eyes closed. Goodenough made a humming noise, then said, "Reckon either you or I could speak to this, Willa. Who's it to be?"

"True." Willa opened her eyes, brown and green. "I once did not know to which world I belonged, white or Mohawk. But I was never enslaved."

"All right," Goodenough said, as if accepting a mantle handed her. She looked Seona in the eye. "I'm going to tell you why you ought not fret over what I think of you or what Willa thinks or anyone else in Shiloh. But first you tell me something. What have you heard about me and my Lem?"

Seona glanced at Lily, who urged her on with a nod. "You were enslaved to Anni Keppler's father, the man who owns those colts you brought."

"That's right. But we're more than former slaves to Elias Waring. Lem's his son as much as he's mine. And before you ask it, no, I am not Elias's wife—save by common law."

Seona bit her lip, wondering why Goodenough thought that helped. "He freed you and Lem but never married you? Is it not allowed?"

It was Willa who answered. "Goodenough and the Colonel could marry in New York. No law forbids it, as in other places."

"No *written* law," Goodenough clarified. "But we all know there's what's legal and what folks will stomach."

Seona looked at her fingers gripping the table's edge. "I came here thinking to marry Ian, but I was his uncle's slave." Her own grandfather's slave. "Why would it be accepted for us to marry but not you and Colonel Waring?"

She had journeyed farther than she once imagined possible—not far enough to outdistance slavery's shadow. It lay over her still.

Goodenough's full lips spread in a smile. "I was enslaved to the Warings as a girl. Everyone in Shiloh knows that. There's some still think it their place to remind me of it—just better never let Elias hear 'em," she added, a mischievous gleam in her eyes. "That man respects me. Needs me. Loves me, too. He treats Lem as a son and makes no secret of it. We eat at his table. I sleep in his bed. It took time for even Anni to accept it, but she has done. Others too. As for marrying, Elias and I spoke our vows before God, years back, witnesses looking on. That's married enough for me."

"I was one of those witnesses," Willa said. "As was Neil."

Goodenough cast her a smile, then addressed Seona again. "You hold your head high in this place. Be who you are becoming. But don't ever pretend the first Seona never existed. That girl's with you still. From time to time, she'll need her wounds healed. But God Almighty loves every broken piece of you."

"From what I saw on his face today," Willa added, "so does Ian Cameron."

Seona's tears came fresh, but she nodded.

"Another thing," Goodenough said. "All Shiloh need never know you and your mama were slaves. But if tongues wag, you pay them no heed, for they aren't the ones worth troubling over. If you want to raise your boy with a mama and a daddy—sister, too—then do it. Never you mind another blessed thing."

Lily reached across the table. Seona met her hand with her own, clasping tight.

"Mama," she said, tears flowing hard. In Boston she had thought herself free, and in many ways she had been. But the house on Beachum Lane had been a place between. A halfway point of shelter. Of waiting.

Goodenough had it right. She felt like two souls in one body. The girl who was a slave. The woman who was free. Or learning to be. Could she find some solid ground for both to stand on long enough to know herself again?

Goodenough had done it. Willa MacGregor too. Each in her way. Done it right there in Shiloh. Surely she could too.

27

Back from Shiloh with Ruaidh freshly shod, Ian found Gabriel and Mandy crowded into the pen he had built for Ally's calf, along with Lily, who held a canteen for it to suckle. "Helping Granny feed Ally's wee bull, are ye?" he asked as he unsaddled the roan.

Helping amounted to each child keeping one small hand on the canteen, alongside their grandmother's, the other fondling one of the calf's ears, while between them Lily kept the canteen tilted so the milk flowed, holding in place against the calf's vigorous sucking the rag stuffed into its opening for a teat.

"His name's Blackie," Gabriel said.

"His name is *George*," Mandy said.

Ian had worried for the creature and the blow to Ally's confidence should it die. While smaller than its twin, it appeared to be thriving. It also appeared his children were having the first serious disagreement he had ever witnessed.

"No, Mandy. Not Geooge . . . Geowage . . ." Abandoning the struggle, Gabriel glowered across the calf's bobbing nose. "Blackie!"

"Ally told them they could give it a name," Lily said. "We've yet to settle."

"George's eyelashes are loooong," Mandy said, hands stuck fast to canteen and calf. "Like a girl cow."

"Blackie is a *bull*," Gabriel said.

"Aye," Lily agreed judiciously. "A baby bull with long, pretty lashes."

"Ganny," Gabriel protested, "bulls awe not *pwetty*."

Ian listened to the ongoing debate while he gave Ruaidh a brushing in his box, then opened the door to the paddock, where feed and water waited. He found the calf still suckling, Lily patiently enduring the children impeding the business with their efforts to help.

He paused at the pen. "D'ye know where I'll find Seona just now?"

"Naomi's cabin. Last I saw."

He caught a message in Lily's gaze as he turned away, one he couldn't decipher. Seona's near-panicked withdrawal when invited to go into Shiloh still troubled him.

Since that one brief excursion to the lake, cut short by Gabriel, he had failed to accomplish anything remotely resembling the courting he had intended. The demands of the farm—crops, building projects, stock to tend—ate up his days. Seona's were spent minding the children or helping with laundry, cooking, mending, sewing, the endless chores of living. The sweet corn was mostly in, but the field corn for grinding meal and next year's seed still dried on the stalk, awaiting harvesting later in the season. Other needs pulled at his thoughts as he crossed the yard to Naomi's cabin. Its door stood wide in the warmth. Hearing Malcolm's voice before he reached it, he paused, hesitant to interrupt.

"'Esther had not shewed her pee-people nor her kindred: for Mor . . . Mord . . .'"

"You managed it yesterday," Seona said. "Sound it out again."

"Mor-deh-cay-eye."

"There you go. Now read the next verse. Then I got to help Naomi with the wash."

Ian had known Seona was spending her spare moments teaching Malcolm to read. This was the first he had caught them at it. He looked about, not wanting to be caught himself listening, but saw no sign of Naomi.

"'And Mor-deh-cay-eye walked eh-ver-ee day before the court of the wo-man . . . women's house, to know how Esther did, and what should become of her.'"

"Good . . . ," Seona praised, though she sounded distracted.

"'Now when every maid's turn was come to go in to king Ah . . . A-has . . .'"

Ahasuerus, Ian silently urged, willing the old man to decipher the name.

When Seona failed to speak up, he peeked around the doorframe. Malcolm sat on a bench at the table, Seona beside him, back to the door, gazing out the window.

Malcolm raised his head. "Something on your mind, *mo nighean*?"

Seona leaned toward the old man until their shoulders touched. "More'n I can shake a stick at," she said, minding Ian of how she talked at Mountain Laurel. "Just now I was thinking of our Esther."

"I think on her too," Malcolm said. "And her mama and daddy."

Seona's profile was shadowed as she stared through the window again, the oiled hide that covered it at night rolled up, now the blackflies no longer pestered. The day was grown hot. He could see the sweat that rolled down Seona's neck.

"How is it fair we're here and she's back where that man . . . ?"

She didn't speak the name; still Ian knew and remembered like it was yesterday what Gideon Pryce—*that man*—tried to do the day he cornered Seona alone, on a visit to Chesterfield, his plantation. Esther lived there now, day in and day out. How old would she be? Twelve? Thirteen? Was there anyone to stand between her and Pryce, as Ian had for Seona? He had done what he could for Mountain Laurel's slaves, but Esther and her parents had belonged to Lucinda Cameron. Not his uncle.

"Ye been praying for her?" Malcolm asked.

"I have."

"Keep praying. The Lord sees Esther. He'll keep her, see her through whatever comes. Just like the Esther in this book."

"I wish she didn't—" Ian must have made a noise, for Seona swiveled on the bench and saw him there.

Embarrassed to be caught skulking, Ian stepped inside, intending to apologize for interrupting. The change in Seona's expression stopped him. A light had come into her face when she saw him. She didn't look away. A smile was forming.

"Seona, I—" The patter of feet coming at a run reached him seconds before two little bodies scooted past and into the cabin.

"Mama, Mama! I fed Ally's baby bull Blackie." Gabriel all but slammed into Seona, who caught him in time to soften the blow.

Mandy halted short of her, giving place to Gabriel, but couldn't seem to resist correcting, "Baby bull *George*."

Still smiling, Seona shifted her attention to Mandy. "Did you feed Ally's calf too, girl-baby?"

Like a puppy thrilled to be noticed, Mandy wormed her way in and leaned into Seona's side, burying her face there. "Yes, Mama."

Ian's breath caught. It was the first he had heard Mandy call anyone but Judith *Mama*. By the look of her, frozen still and blinking at his daughter, it was the first Seona had heard it too. His heart thudded as she took one hand from Gabriel and, almost shyly, stroked his daughter's curls. Mandy lifted her face and smiled. Seona's features trembled. Then crumpled.

Ian jumped when behind him Lily said, "Go on, Seona. I'll mind them."

Somehow Seona rose without knocking over bench or either child, found a passage through the crowded doorway, and was out of the cabin before Ian realized she had burst into tears.

"Seona?" Ignoring him, she headed deeper into the beech grove. He started to follow, but Lily caught his sleeve. "Don't stop me, Lily. I need to know what's going on inside that head of hers."

"I hope she tells ye," Lily said. "But there's a thing *I* need to tell ye first."

Seona had come to feel affection for the old beech tree behind her cabin, its heavy branches reaching wide, trunk rumpled at its base as though someone had draped a mossy quilt around it for a skirting. And it was broad enough to hide her from peeping eyes. In its cooler shade, with her back wedged into one of those folds, she cried into the petticoat bunched around her raised knees, hardly knowing how she had got there. Hadn't she just been sitting at the table, giving Malcolm his lesson, about to go help Naomi?

Then Ian had come. She had caught her breath at sight of him in the doorway, tall and lean, with that panther's grace she so admired, the light behind him making a halo of his hair. She had gotten it nigh sorted in her head, the things she wanted to tell him soon as he was back from Shiloh. She and her mama had talked it over as they rode home from the MacGregors', where Catriona had stayed behind.

"D'ye still want to be Ian's wife?" Lily had asked.

Still prone to tears, she had heaved in a quavering breath and said, "I do. Why hasn't he asked me?"

"He's not blind, girl-baby. He can tell ye've things to get sorted in your head. Heart too."

"He must not know what to make of me." She had been so much surer, writing to him over the winter. The things they had told each other had felt right and good. Even the things not quite said. With all those miles between them, they could bare their souls to one another. Face-to-face was a struggle. "I know I been fearful, hiding out on the farm. I don't want to be that way."

"Good," her mama had said as their horse clopped along the wagon track between the farms. "Ye'll find a way to let Ian know ye've got those things sorted now?"

Say what ye feel. Not what ye think I want to hear. Ian's plea, long ago at Mountain Laurel.

Truth was what she had meant to give him, next chance that came. She thought it had come, there in Naomi's cabin, until Gabriel and Mandy rushed in, which might have been all right had Mandy not chosen that moment to call her *Mama* for the first time ever, looking up with her sweet smile and her real mama's tea-brown eyes warming with love. It made everything tangle up inside Seona again, stabbed through with an ache of loss and guilt.

So she had run from it all. Again.

"No more." She pressed a wad of petticoat to her face, then planted her hands on the tree's sheltering roots, determined to find Ian . . . who stepped around the tree and found her first.

She hadn't heard him coming.

"Seona?" His eyes were pained, his hand outstretched.

She took it and he raised her up. She didn't think too hard about it before she wrapped her arms around his lean waist. His arms encircling her was the sweetest thing she had felt in too long.

"I'm sorry," he said, voice a rumble beneath her ear, breath warm on the crown of her head. "I've been thinking so much about what *I* hoped for, I lost sight of how hard this would be for ye, coming to a strange place, braced for people's judgment. I want ye to have a place in Shiloh. Not just here on the farm with me. But I've been impatient for it. And with ye. Will I ever learn?" Sliding his hands to her shoulders, he held her away so he could see her tear-wet face. "I'm an idiot. A *gowkit* simpleton."

Seona couldn't help it. She laughed. "Mama talked to you, didn't she?"

"She did." He smiled, but ruefully. "I understand now, how it might have seemed these past weeks. Like I didn't see ye struggling or was too busy with all that needs doing to care. I *do* care, Seona. I want to give ye a life here where ye can grow like this bonny tree." He took one hand from her and laid it on the beech's trunk. "Strong and reaching for the sky, with Gabriel and Mandy flourishing in your shade."

She could still hear Mandy's sweet voice calling her *Mama*. See Judith looking out through those eyes. She slid her hands up over Ian's chest. He wore no hat and had shed his coat before coming to find her. The linen of his shirt was soft and a little damp, the man beneath it nigh as warm as the summer heat. A faint sheen of sweat gleamed across his brow and upper lip.

"Can ye forgive me?" he asked, fingers tracing her cheek.

She pressed her face to his hand. "I can. I do. If you forgive me not telling you what's been troubling me."

"Ye'd have done so could ye find the words, aye?"

"I almost had them; then Mandy . . ."

"Come here." He drew her down to sit with him, their backs against the tree, facing the cornfield stretching toward the ridgeline, the sky above grown thickly clouded since the morning. "D'ye not want her calling ye *Mama*?"

"I do. It melted my heart. Then she looked up at me and . . . I saw Judith!" The name came out half-choked. "How can I just step into her shoes, let Mandy love me in her place?" Even if that was what she wanted.

Ian's breath released on a sigh. Seona risked a look at him—knees raised like hers, hands clenched around them. Staring out over the cornfield.

"I told ye, in our letters, that I loved Judith, but I've wondered . . . did I ever truly know her? She'd a strength and faith it took a deeper heart than mine to fathom." Seona wanted to protest the part about his heart not being deep enough, but he went on, "Before she died, she tried to tell me something about *grace*. 'It is enough,' she said. I thought she might have been speaking of Mandy. Or maybe she was offering grace to me, yet again. I'm still not sure what she meant, but . . ." He turned to her. "Ye knew Judith as well as I. Maybe better—ye knew her longer. What do ye think she'd want for us now?"

The safest thing to say would be *I don't know*. But Seona did know. "She'd want us to take the blessings given us. Not refuse them."

Ian shifted to face her, blinking. "That's not what I expected ye to say."

"What did you expect?"

"I don't know." He laughed softly, no more than a breath, but it made her smile, hearing the words she had been tempted to say. "I do know that ye and I see the world through different eyes. Maybe we always will. But that doesn't mean we cannot learn to look through the other's, if we try."

Ian pushed himself to his feet and reached down. She took his hand and let him pull her to her feet. Thoughts of all that needed doing crowded into the peace they had found beneath the beech tree. Babies to tend. Water to fetch. The wash . . .

"How do we try?" she asked.

"With honesty."

"It was easier in letters."

"It was. But we'll get there again. With practice."

In his smile she glimpsed the rawness she was feeling. And the relief.

She heard Gabriel's laughter, somewhere off through the trees. Mandy's too. She was about to head toward them, more by instinct than choosing, but Ian stopped her.

"Seona." She turned back as a breeze chattered through the leaves overhead. A light like inspiration lit in his eyes. "Tell me one thing that's true—a thing ye haven't already said. One thing you need me to understand."

She blinked. "Just one?"

He grinned. "For now, aye. One true thing. No need to explain or defend whatever it is. I won't ask ye to. Just tell me something true."

Again she didn't let herself think overlong. "I feel like my soul is split in two. One half is a girl enslaved. The other is a woman free. Or trying to be." Sometimes one, sometimes the other got the reins in her hands, but he could never know which just for looking.

He was studying her now, tenderness in his eyes. "It helps me to know it. And ye need to know that I love both, the girl and the woman." He paused before asking, almost shyly, "Shall I tell ye one true thing of me?"

His features blurred as she nodded.

"I eavesdropped on your conversation with Malcolm, a bit ago."

Seona burst out laughing, shedding tears.

Ian laughed with her, then sobered. "Ye spoke of Esther. I thought, if ye want, I could write to John Reynold, ask him to inquire. I don't know can he learn anything but—"

"It can't hurt to ask!" Overcome with gratitude, Seona did the last thing—of all the unlikely things this day had held—that she had seen coming when she opened her eyes to the morning. She took Ian Cameron's face between her hands, drew down his head, and kissed his mouth for the first time as that woman who knew herself to be free.

28

That kiss did as much to bridge the distance between her and Ian as all the tears and talking had done. Two days later, in their cabin, Seona and Lily were cleaning up the children, all fed their breakfast, which Lily had brought across the yard so as not to crowd Naomi's cabin. Ian found them there, washing up.

Mandy slid off Lily's lap to scoot across the cabin. Ian scooped her into his arms, gave her cheek a smacking kiss, then licked his lips. "Somebody tastes like maple syrup," he said, reaching for the rag Lily had been using to tidy his daughter.

"She won't take corn mush without sweetening," Lily said. "I miss a spot?"

Ian scrubbed the rag over Mandy's cheek while she squirmed in his arms. "Got it. Outside with ye, wiggle worm."

He swung her down as Seona finished with Gabriel, who grinned at Ian before darting after his sister. Lily rose and started after them but paused at the door when Ian spoke, her gaze on her grandchildren in the yard.

"Catriona plans to go into Shiloh today to help Maggie clean the school cabin. She wants to know if ye'd like to go along, Seona. I would," he hastened to add, "but Ally and I need to expand the crib before we're overcome with corn ready for it. Our yield looks to be more than I planned for."

Seona made a show of wiping down the table, feeling the pull of his gaze. They had taken another walk along the lakeshore the evening before, with the children romping about. There was a pair of birds on the lake like Seona had never seen, with striking black-and-white plumage and eyes red as holly berries. They were raising a brood of fuzzy black chicks that rode around the lake on their backs. *Loons*, Ian called them. Their eerie cry gave her shivers, first time she heard it, but she had come to like the sound, especially on those mornings mist shrouded the lake.

Last evening had been sunny and warm. While they watched the children play in the golden light, they had talked about the house Ian meant to start on next spring. He had wanted to know all her wishes and wants. They had stolen quick kisses when the children weren't looking and stayed out until the fireflies drifted bright along the edges of the cornfield, watching the children chase them.

It felt like they were a courting couple, getting to know each other again. All so different but familiar too. Her heartbeat knew this dance, though it sometimes made her blush, going through its steps this time for everyone to see.

Finally she looked up, crumbs wiped, not quick enough for Lily to note her hesitation. Still looking out into the yard, her mama said, "I need to visit Keagan's store. I'll go into Shiloh with ye, if ye want."

"Ye could take the letter to John for me," Ian suggested.

Lily left her listening post in the doorway. Seona dropped the rag and crossed to Ian. "You wrote about Esther?"

"I did." His eyes lingered on her mouth. "I'll mind Gabriel and Mandy. They can help me and Ally work," he added wryly. "Go spend some time with Catriona and Maggie. And Lily."

She bit her lip until a smile released it. "Mama's welcome to come along, but I wasn't going to say no."

They stopped at the MacGregors' for Maggie. Matthew joined them too, leading the roan colt he was done starting to the saddle, meaning to return it to Colonel Waring.

"Black needs more time," he said as they rode the track into Shiloh. "Blue's the more biddable in spirit. Aren't ye, *mo laochain*?" he asked the riderless colt, keeping pace at the end of its lead, while Maggie and Catriona rode beside him.

Riding behind them with Lily, both astride Juturna's dam, Seona saw Catriona's gaze fix on Maggie's brother and hang there as though startled at hearing the Gaelic endearment from the lips of one who looked nothing like a Scotsman.

Seona thought of Malcolm, her mama, even Willa MacGregor, whose way of speaking sounded different from any white person she had ever met. On account of living with the Mohawk, Seona supposed. No surprise her adopted half-Mohawk children might sometimes talk like their Scottish father.

We come to sound like who we're nearest.

A body's way of talking wasn't all that got molded by kin and company. Ways of thinking, of viewing the world and others, could change. The color of a person's skin was the only thing couldn't.

Deep in her thoughts, Seona half listened to the talk between the trio riding ahead until a sudden outcry startled her.

"What? Matthew, *look* . . ."

Maggie's voice jerked Seona from her ponderings to see they had nearly reached the place the track turned down past the mill and the school cabin that stood there. It wasn't in the tidy state it had been in the day they arrived in Shiloh. The door listed, as if someone had wrenched it nigh off its hinges. The window was a dark square speared by shards of glass.

Maggie heeled her gray mare to a canter and reached the cabin-yard first, her brother and Catriona seconds behind. "Wait!" Matthew called, but his sister had dismounted and darted inside.

Seona and Lily heard further outcries as they all followed.

The school cabin was wrecked. Benches, tables, slates, books. In the center of the ruin Catriona stood, hand across her mouth, while Maggie stumbled about, touching the halves of torn books, turning over broken benches as if looking for something whole. After a glance around, Matthew pivoted on a bootheel and headed for the doorway. He paused at his sister's voice.

"Matthew? Don't make a fuss over this."

"Maggie . . ."

"I mean it. Don't make it worse. I just want to clean it up."

Matthew didn't answer. One look at his face suffused with fury, and Seona and Lily stepped back to let him pass, then followed him out.

"Who would do this?" Lily asked his rigid back.

Matthew turned sharply at the question. "There's a dozen ways people have made it known they aren't pleased to have my sister teaching in this village. But not like *that*." His dark eyes blazed. "I'm going to Colonel Waring. He needs to know of this."

He strode toward Blue. The colt shied at his coming, snapping Matthew out of his rage. He halted, looking at the ground. Even from behind, Seona could see the steadying breath he drew, the easing of his stance.

Then someone else called, "Matthew? Is something wrong?"

They turned to see Anni Keppler coming up the track from the mill, a basket on her arm. She halted as the damage to the cabin door and window registered, her round face flushed bright. "Oh no . . . We didn't hear a thing across the creek—of course we wouldn't with the falls. Charles is away to German Flatts, so the mill's been closed since yesterday. This must have happened overnight. Is it bad inside?"

"I doubt there's anything worth salvaging," Matthew said.

Anni glanced downslope toward the village. "We should ask Jack Keagan. Someone must know something."

"No need. Besides, Maggie said she doesn't want to make a *fuss*."

"*I* want to make fuss," Anni retorted, then frowned. "What do you mean there's no need? You know who did this?"

"Maybe," Matthew said. "Aram Crane."

Seona did not recognize the name but Anni seemed to. She was wagging her capped head. "Crane? He hasn't been seen near Shiloh in years."

"He robbed my traps less than a fortnight ago," Matthew said. "Pa thinks I'm wrong but I'm not. Ian Cameron suspects Crane followed *him* from Cooperstown up to Cherry Valley last month. And Francis . . ."

Startled at the mention of Ian, Seona was slow to notice Anni's color had drained until behind her, Maggie spoke. "What about Francis?"

She and Catriona had emerged from the cabin. Matthew winced as Anni Keppler echoed the question, each word emphatic. "What about Francis?"

Matthew looked like a cornered critter deciding between fight or flight. Unlike the horses he knew so well, flight was not his way. He drew himself straight and said, "Francis saw Aram Crane robbing one of my traps."

Anni's mouth hung open.

Maggie, already on the verge of tears, asked, "Is that why he hasn't come home? Did Crane frighten him . . . or . . . ?"

"No, Maggie, that's not what I meant." But the uncertainty in Matthew's eyes stole whatever reassurance he meant to offer.

"Matthew," Anni said, flush faded, face white and rigid. "How could you keep such knowledge to yourself all these months? Does my father even know?"

"I mean to tell him today—now." Looking penitent but still furious, Matthew turned to his sister, who appeared more crushed by this news of Francis Waring than over her ruined school cabin. "Maggie . . . I'm sorry."

"What if Francis got it into his head to try and catch Crane?" Features twisting with fear and grief, Maggie turned back toward the cabin.

"Go see the Colonel—now," Anni told Maggie's brother, as firmly as if Matthew were her child. "You'll stay with Maggie?" she asked Catriona, who nodded and vanished into the cabin, from which drifted Maggie's half-muffled sobs.

"This is a little something I put up for our blacksmith's wife," Anni said in a shaky attempt at normalcy, holding up her basket as she walked with Seona and Lily down past the mill into the village. They drew near the log building Seona recalled Ian pointing out as the trade store. "She bore their third child last night. A girl. Would you like to meet them when we're done here?"

"Come just last night?" Lily asked, brightening with interest.

"Goodenough got there barely in time to catch her," Anni said.

Lily frowned, then shook her head. "I reckon not. I need a bit of muslin for the children—new nightshifts. Then Seona and I should head back up to the school to lend a hand."

Anni didn't blink at her mama's refusal, but Seona nearly stopped in her tracks in the store yard, under a big old oak tree. A brand-new baby and her mama wouldn't spare a moment's visit? After all that talk about *her* not wanting to meet folk in Shiloh?

But Seona held her peace as they passed through the door Anni held open. Inside, they were confronted with a counter, a wall behind it. To the right and going back a ways, shelves, casks, and tables held an array of goods, including bolts of fabric, which Lily made for. The place had a strong smell, a myriad of odors competing for the upper hand. Beeswax and leather, spirits and tobacco, cured hides and smoked hams.

A tall man of late middle years stood behind the counter. He nodded as they entered, blue eyes tracking Lily with curiosity—until Anni demanded his attention.

"Jack Keagan," she said, indignation returning in force. "Have you any notion what happened to the school cabin? Or *who*, I should say."

Mr. Keagan's expression turned grim. "You've seen it then?"

"I just found Maggie MacGregor there, discovering it for herself. And you didn't answer my question."

"Every soul come through the door this morning has told me of it, Miss Anni, but not a one knew who did the deed."

"Or admits knowing."

"Aye," Mr. Keagan acknowledged. "I'm sorry for Maggie. You know I got nothing against her teaching."

Anni sighed. Seona thought she might mention her brother Francis or that other name, Aram Crane, but she didn't. "This is Seona Cameron. She has a letter to post. You'll be all right, Seona, letting Jack help you with it?"

Seona nodded and, as Anni crossed to her mama, swallowed down a surge of nerves and approached the counter, encouraged when Jack Keagan smiled. "I've a letter going out from Ian Cameron."

"You'll be his kin, lately come to join him?"

Seona nodded. Strictly speaking, she was kin to Ian already. "And that's my mama, Lily," she added, turning toward the women looking over the man's stock of muslin.

Mr. Keagan took the letter bound for North Carolina, gazed at the direction on the cover, and snapped his fingers. "I've a parcel come for Ian Cameron. Perhaps you can tell him?"

"Or maybe I can take it?" Seona asked.

Keagan pursed his lips. "I make it a policy not to hand over the post to anyone but the addressee."

Anni Keppler had keen ears. She abandoned Lily and returned to Seona's side. "With exceptions now and then, Jack. Let Seona have the parcel and save Ian the trouble coming in to fetch it."

Jack Keagan frowned. "Is she his wife at least?"

"She will be before long," Anni said, at which Seona blinked, then nodded agreement when the man looked her way.

"All right then." He handed over the parcel and named the postage. Seona hadn't any coin on her person. Ian hadn't thought she would need it sending a letter but couldn't have anticipated receiving one. She felt a rise of panic. Then Lily was there, producing enough tender to pay for her yards of muslin as well as the parcel's postage, from coin saved from her work in Boston. The parcel was wrapped in oilcloth and tied with twine, thicker than a letter but still small enough to slip into the pocket tied at Seona's waist.

Outside the trade store Anni asked, "You're sure you won't call on our smith's wife with me? It won't be an imposition."

"No," Lily said again, her refusal firm. "But thank ye."

"All right but . . ." Anni turned to Seona. "What was it Matthew said about Ian? He saw Aram Crane in Cooperstown?"

"That's what Matthew said," Seona replied. "But it's the first I'm hearing of it."

Ian hadn't shared anything about this Aram Crane, whoever he was. A man Matthew thought had been pilfering his traps—that was all she knew of him. Why would such a man have followed Ian, of all people, from Cooperstown? And why hadn't Ian told them of it?

Back at the school cabin, Catriona had helped Maggie search for anything salvageable. Maggie clutched the results—a single primer. Telling them to leave the mess for now, she swung astride her mare and started for home. The rest mounted too, Seona riding behind the saddle this time, parcel in her pocket, bundled linen clutched under one arm.

Catriona cantered Juturna to catch up to Maggie.

Lily's silence on the ride back puzzled Seona as much as her refusal to go visit the smith's wife and baby. Clutching the newly purchased muslin, free arm around her mama's waist, she leaned to the side to say, "What's on your mind, Mama? The school or Ian and that Aram Crane person?"

Lily kept their mare at a walk, letting the other two outdistance them. "Both."

"Anything else?" Seona prompted, certain there was.

"Just something I've noted," Lily said. "Shiloh has no need of another midwife."

"You reckon one is good enough?" Seona asked, trying for a little levity. Her mama didn't respond to the play on words. "Maybe they do need another but just didn't have one 'til now. Regardless . . . I need you, Mama."

There was silence as the summer-heavy forest passed by either side, striped with sun and shade, the muggy air alive with birdsong and the buzzing of insects. The horse's hooves clapped thirsty earth, raising little puffs of dust among the weeds.

"There something ye want to tell me, girl-baby?"

Her meaning took a beat for Seona to grasp. "No, Mama. I didn't mean . . . Ian and I aren't . . ." She shook her head and laughed, not admitting how much she had been thinking of him in that way again. "Someday there'll be more babies, I hope. I'll need you by to catch them."

"Want maybe, not need," Lily said in a tone so final Seona tightened her hold as a frisson of nameless alarm raced through her.

"Not true, Mama. I'll always need you."

29

Malcolm had lent a hand with extending the corncrib, putting old skills to work planing wood planks and helping fit the new doorframe, then gone to his cabin for a rest. When Ian decided to take a break and see what Naomi had on hand to fill an empty belly, he detoured past the beech-shaded springhouse, built over the waters that bubbled from a hillock out behind the stable, and found Malcolm seated on the log bench outside it, elbows on knees, eyes shut. He started when Ian crouched by the spring to wash, nearly toppling before Ian caught his arm with a wet grip—an arm little bigger than a child's, beneath its shirtsleeve.

"Dozed off, did I?" Malcolm blinked heavy-lidded eyes. "Reckon I'd have gone on wi' it had ye no' come along."

"I worked ye hard today. Ally and I can finish the crib tomorrow, let ye get back to your garden." With an eye on Malcolm, he drank from the spring and, refreshed, held out a hand to help the old man rise.

Malcolm indicated the bench. "Sit wi' me awhile?"

Ian did swift inventory of pressing chores, one ear cocked for his offspring—napping under Naomi's eye, judging by the quiet. Seona hadn't yet returned. While he was glad she had finally ventured into Shiloh, he longed to see her again. Kiss her again. Saying nothing of that, he sat and leaned back against the stones. "Something on your mind?"

"Seona."

"She's on mine too." Ian caught the old man's eye and grinned.

"The pair of ye are keeping your counsel close. D'ye mind my asking, when is it to be?"

"When's what to be?"

The creases deepened around Malcolm's eyes. "Mister Ian, ye ken what I'm asking. When are ye and Seona to marry?"

"I haven't actually asked her yet." Ian's heart still set to pounding at thought of presenting the ring to Seona, asking her to be his wife. Silly that it should. He had asked her once before, with the gift of a hair comb, and she had accepted. They had a son together—a daughter too; he could see that bond growing between her and Mandy . . .

Malcolm's chuckle drew his gaze. "Mister Ian, forgive me saying it, but ye're one backward white man when it comes to matters o' the heart."

Heat smote Ian's face as a rueful laugh slipped out. "Backward, am I?"

Malcolm sobered. "Ye loved a woman who couldna be your wife. Then married a woman ye'd barely remarked until the moment ye proposed. I ken ye came to love Miss Judith," he added when Ian flinched. "I also ken ye never stopped loving Seona. Or pining for Gabriel. There's nothing keeping ye from them now, nor they from ye."

"I didn't want to rush things . . . again." How different their lives might be had he been patient the first time. How much easier, for Seona most of all. He hadn't had the Almighty then. No guide for his reckless heart.

He had both now. And he had this man, one of the many treasures fallen to him by none of his own deserving.

"If ye'd ken an old man's mind on the matter," Malcolm said, "I'm thinking what Seona's struggling wi' now is no' about her feelings for ye. 'Tis no easy thing, learning to walk this earth free after a lifetime of bondage."

"Aye," Ian said. "We've talked of it."

"Good. Keep talking. 'Tis no' a thing to be settled in a moment but grown into, day by day—same as we grow in Christ, aye?"

Ian nodded, though conviction stabbed. "What of ye, Malcolm? Naomi? Ally? Are ye having the same struggles?"

"Naomi keeps too busy looking after us to worry o'er such things, though in time she may come to it. Ally . . . well, ye've done more for him already than I ever thought to see, giving him a herd to build—and the wee dogs. Ye ken he'll be happy as long he has beasts to tend."

"I hope ye know I'll be here—God willing—to help however they need." A lump formed in Ian's throat, speaking of a day when Malcolm would no longer be with them. A day he hoped was still afar off.

The old man gave his knee a pat. "I've lived to see my daughter and grandson free. And the thing I longed to do before I stand before my Lord—read His words to me—I'm learning to do. Lily doesna worry me overmuch. She's found her way through far more difficult days than these. But Seona has a life as a freewoman stretching before her and the need to learn to navigate it."

"I mean to help," Ian said, the words hoarse with feeling. "With all my heart."

Malcolm nodded. "Let's talk to the Almighty about it, since my opinion isna the one that matters."

"Aye, let's do."

"Father in heaven," the old man began, "'tis Your will we seek. Your blessing we need. Your hand to guide our hearts as well as our heads. We canna always see what thorny patches lie along our way or the foes arrayed against us, but we ask for Your protection in this place we've come to settle . . ."

Ian's eyes flew open to scrutinize the man beside him, drawing breath to go on with his prayer. In that brief pause, he sensed both light and shadow reaching for his soul. For all their souls.

". . . that Ye'd be the rock this man chooses to build his house upon. Give him courage to go where Ye lead and do what Ye tell him to do." In the next pause for breath, there arose the rumble of two empty bellies. Malcolm ended his prayer with a chuckle. "And give us this day our daily bread or whatever my good daughter has prepared to sustain us. Amen."

"Amen," Ian echoed, sounding shaken enough Malcolm peered at him.

Ought he to tell this man about the gold and Cherry Valley and the letter with the broken seal? Matthew's violated traps. Francis Waring having witnessed Crane's pilfering. But Malcolm was looking far too tired and old to be laying such a burden on him.

"Come on." Ian stood with outstretched hand. "Let's see what Naomi has for our dinner."

Mandy and Gabriel were sprawled on Naomi's bed, drugged by the day's warmth. After a quiet dinner at her table, Malcolm lay down to rest. Ian and Naomi stepped out into the yard. He looked through the beeches toward Seona's cabin, knowing she hadn't returned, then nodded at the cabin where Malcolm's snores rumbled. "Does he seem to ye more tired of late?"

Naomi nodded. "He be eighty, give or take a year." She sighed and crossed her arms beneath her bosom. Below her kerchief, sweat beaded her brow. "Daddy been strong a long time. In spirit and body. Only the one ever gonna fail him."

Even with his aching joints, Malcolm had put in a full day's work at Mountain Laurel in the time Ian called the place home. Since then he had more than pulled his diminishing weight. Their vegetable garden flourished, with enough produce coming in to put up excess for winter.

"This past year," Naomi added, "he seen his share of blessings. Learning to read that Bible. *Freedom.*"

"What about ye, Naomi? Ye've not been off this farm in months."

Naomi's gaze took in the beech grove, the fields, the ridge to the north. "Daddy's not up to traipsing the countryside and I want to stay by him." Moisture gathered in her eyes as she swung her eyes toward the line of trees marking the track to Shiloh. "Speak of blessings, here come one of yours."

Seona and Lily had returned.

They dismounted in the yard. Lily went straight to their cabin, a bundle of new muslin tucked under her arm. Ian took the mare's reins from Seona. "Did Catriona stay over with Maggie?"

"She did. The children inside?"

Naomi had gone back into the cabin. "Sleeping. So's Malcolm. Are ye hungry?"

"Ian." Seona placed a hand on his arm. "Maggie MacGregor's school cabin . . . someone got into it overnight and busted up stuff. Door and window, benches, desks, books. Pretty much everything."

He took her hand in his, shocked by the violation, grieved for Maggie. Some families had denied their children schooling by a Mohawk lass, but what Seona described went beyond disapproval. It was outright spite.

"I'm sorry ye had to see it. Sorrier it happened. Poor Maggie."

"Catriona means to stay overnight at the MacGregors'. Maggie's distraught. Matthew was furious. He went with us, taking the blue colt to Colonel Waring, so he saw it all."

The mare whickered, recalling Ian to her needs. "He'll have told Waring what happened?" he asked, leading them toward the stable.

"He told Anni Keppler he would."

"Anni lives on that rise above the mill. She didn't hear or see anything? Did anyone?"

"Anni came with us to Mr. Keagan's store and asked. He seemed sorry for what happened but didn't know a thing. I don't know who else she might have talked to."

In the stable, Seona stood outside the box while Ian removed the mare's saddle, gave her a brushing, then opened the paddock door for her to go out to graze. He hung saddle and bridle to clean and oil later.

Seona fished through the slit in her petticoat and pulled from her pocket a parcel, wrapped and tied. "Mr. Keagan had this for you. Mama paid the postage."

"I'll repay her." Ian took the parcel, letter-size but thicker. He looked it over, checking for signs of tampering. "This is how it looked when ye got it? Ye didn't tie it up proper or rewrap it?"

"I didn't. Why?"

He could have bitten his tongue. From the front of the stable, the calf bawled, wanting its bottle. "I meant to feed George before ye got back."

"I think they're calling it Blackie," Seona said. "Where's Ally?"

"Down at the pasture. He'll be back soon for his dinner, unless he found fencing to mend. But never mind. I'll feed wee George—Blackie—whatever he's called."

Ian grinned, but a frown marked Seona's brow. He hadn't distracted her with talk of cows. She had drawn breath to speak when the doorway darkened. Lily had come with the feeding bottle.

"I heard one too many arguments about this calf's name," she said as they joined her at its pen. "Yesterday I taught those babies the meaning of a new word—*compromise*—and their first letters of the alphabet. They settled on calling it G-B."

Seona grinned. "Ian was about to feed him, Mama."

"I'll take care of G-B." Lily eyed the parcel in Ian's grasp and told them to take whatever it was and open it while the children still slept. "Might be your only chance today."

Under the beech tree by her cabin, seated shoulder to shoulder against its trunk, Seona seemed preoccupied, picking at a broken fingernail. He hadn't opened the parcel but suspected it was from John and contained some amount of gold. If so, it would be wrapped apart from whatever missive he had sent. He could ask Seona to read the letter aloud and slip what else the parcel contained out of sight . . .

"Who is Aram Crane?" Seona asked.

That name on her lips sent shock flooding through him. He leaned away from her and stared, thoughts of subterfuge juddering to a halt. "Did Matthew say something to ye about Crane?"

"Not to me. In my hearing. After he saw what was done to Maggie's school. He thinks this Crane person had to do with it."

"Why would he think that?" Ian asked, though the sinking in his gut made him realize he already knew.

"I don't know, but he thinks Aram Crane's been messing with his traps. What upset me most, he said something about that man following you, at a place called Cherry Valley." Her eyes pierced him, green and steady. "Was he not meant to say that?"

He read her preoccupation more clearly now. She knew he had been keeping a secret from her—a troubling one. And with all his talk of honesty.

"Here," he said, handing her the parcel. "Open it. If it contains what I think it does, it will help me explain."

He sensed her bottled questions as she took the parcel, worked loose the twine, then the oilcloth wrapping. Inside was a letter, as well as another piece of oilcloth wrapped around something small. He took the letter. "That's the bit I want ye to see," he said of the other item. "Open it. Careful though. Don't want to spill it."

Seona set the small parcel on her lap and unwrapped it to reveal a scattering of gold flakes and a few small pieces of quartz stone, veined with gold.

"Oh," she breathed, then covered the gold with a sheltering hand when her breath stirred the smaller bits. "I don't know what I expected." She raised her hand, peering again. "Not this."

"D'ye know what it is?"

She touched a flake with a fingertip. "I've seen something like it. Ally found a rock like this once, but bigger. About the size of a hazelnut."

"Did he?" Ian asked, surprised. "When?"

She stared out toward the corn standing high, thinking. "I must have been seven, maybe eight. You mind me telling how Ally used to give me things, like the arrowhead I found the day Gabriel was born?"

He grinned. He had given that arrowhead back to her in Boston, when they parted. "D'ye still have that?"

"Not on me, but yes."

She smiled back, and he felt the tension in his chest uncoil a little.

"Seona . . . what ye've got in your lap there is *gold*. That's how it looks, come straight from the earth." He told her of the discovery across the creek on John and Cecily Reynold's land. "We kept it secret until I returned to Boston. Da knows. And Neil MacGregor. Matthew, too, though I didn't mean him to hear of it. Now ye."

She was quiet, shoulder no longer pressed to his, eyes fixed on the substance in her lap. "This is how Mister John's been paying for the land you sold him?"

"Aye. Which is where the trouble with Aram Crane comes into it. Remember I told ye I'd paid off this farm before I met ye in Albany? I paid with gold—as I did when I chose this tract." He gazed out over his land, but it was Crane he saw, those predatory eyes watching him leave that morning in Cherry Valley. "I never told Judge Cooper where the gold came from, though he tried his best to pry the knowledge from me. He's fixated on finding ore on his own landholdings. I hoped he'd drop the matter—employ some discretion about it at the least."

A hint of alarm clouded her expression. "Judge Cooper told people?"

"To be fair, it mightn't have been the judge who set Aram Crane's nose to sniffing after me to start with. Cooper's wee son saw the gold. As did his lawyer. Perhaps his wife did, too, or a maid that dusted the room. Could be it was my own fault. I made a particular purchase in Cooperstown and paid for it with gold."

He had that purchase in his coat pocket now.

"Somehow Crane must have got wind of the gold and linked me to it. I've no other explanation for why, when I left Cooperstown to come to ye, the man followed me to Cherry Valley."

Seona's eyes widened. "Did he follow you to Albany? Was he nearby all that time, while we were coming to this place?"

"I never saw him again after Cherry Valley," he said, wishing it meant Crane hadn't merely done a better job of eluding his sight. "I'd hoped that was the end of it. Then a letter came from Judge Cooper. It arrived with a broken seal. Which mightn't have worried me had Cooper not written of the gold."

"You're thinking Aram Crane got hold of your letter; he's the one broke the seal? How can you know that?"

"I cannot *know*. But taken together with what Francis Waring saw, evidence the man has been hanging about Shiloh again, and now Matthew . . ." He stopped, noting how her face had paled. "Seona, I can see you're worried—"

"Worried?"

"Afraid," he amended, feeling wretched. "It's why I haven't told ye this until now."

She rewrapped the gold John had sent and thrust it at him. "Scared witless or not, I need to know what threatens me and Gabriel—all of us. So I can be on my guard, not go riding off to Shiloh again or anything foolish."

"That's just it. I didn't want ye to be afraid here. It's the last thing I want." Setting the parcel and unread letter aside, he took both her hands in his and rose to his knees to face her. "Whatever threatens us, I will protect ye. It's what I mean to do and all I want to do. Protect ye, provide for ye."

"Ian." She gripped his hands, leaning toward him, eyes pleading for his understanding. "When I was at Mountain Laurel, I had ample cause to fear. But I could generally tell where the meanness would come from. If I couldn't, Mama could. Or Malcolm. Sometimes I could hide myself, let it pass. But here . . . I don't know this place, these people. I don't know where to trust or where to keep up my guard."

"Trust *me*. Let me guard ye." Ian let go a hand to touch her face. They were both older now, more life lived, griefs borne, but she was as artlessly beautiful as on the day they collided in his uncle's upstairs passage, with her coiling hair and creek-water eyes, that mouth he still wanted to kiss every time he saw it.

"Seona . . . will ye marry me? Let me be a covering to ye in every way, as I've always wanted to be." Her eyes held his while his heart slammed. He kept talking. "I know it was understood we would marry when ye came here with Gabriel, but I want to do this right." He dug into his coat pocket and found the ring. "I've wanted to give ye this, as a sign of my love and my pledge, since Albany. Will ye accept it? Will ye be my wife?"

The tiny diamonds set into the morning glories entwining the silver band glinted in a dapple of sunlight. Seona took the ring, turned it, noticed the words engraved around its inner surface. Words he had memorized.

"'I Am My Beloved's.'" She looked at him.

He smiled, hopeful. "I didn't have those words engraved but they speak my heart for ye. I am yours. Forever. Can ye trust me to keep ye safe as well as to love ye? For as God sees me, I do love ye, with everything I am. More than even at the first."

Her eyes were all the world. Wide and green and welling with tears. "You've told me so many true things. Can I tell you just one?"

"With all my heart I wish ye would."

"I trust you. I'm choosing to do so."

She held on to the ring while he kissed her. A long kiss, deep and stirring. Both were breathless when it ended. Smiling. A weight of stones had flown off his soul. She trusted him. *Lord, let me be worthy of it. Don't let me fail her . . .*

Her attention fell back to the ring. "How do you keep finding things with morning glories on them? I still have the comb . . ." She looked up at him, eyes glistening. "Which finger do I wear it on?"

He took the ring and slipped it on the proper finger, pushing it over her knuckles, relieved when it fit. "I will lay down all I have and ever will have—my very life—before I let harm befall ye or our children."

As she had once before beneath that old beech tree, Seona took his face in her hands and kissed him sweetly. When she stopped, she said, "I'll tell you one more true thing, Ian Cameron."

He kissed the tip of her nose and whispered, "What's that, *mo chridhe*?"

"I never stopped loving you either."

PART IV

Summer 1797–Autumn 1797
New York

30

August 1797

Muggy July flowed into sweltering August. Rains came, sometimes with thunder. More often gently, soaking the earth without ruining the corn drying on the stalk.

Mandy and Gabriel frolicked between creek, lake, and beech wood.

Malcolm tended the garden and read his Bible, determined to make it from cover to cover while the Almighty lent him breath.

Naomi and Lily kept busy putting up what the garden produced—and with the milking, mending, churning, washing, and cooking, Seona helping when she wasn't looking after the children.

Ally tended the cattle, walking among them each day, studying eyes and shaggy coats, the udders of nursing cows, noting their appetites and whether their calves grew strong. He and Ian worked at building a more substantial stable, harvested grasses for winter feed, leveled the site for the house, where Ian drove stakes into the earth, marking off rooms, then walked Seona through them so she could change the arrangement if she wished.

They talked of when they might wed and where. Shiloh had no minister, but there was one in German Flatts. "We could go there, soon as the corn's in the crib," Ian suggested, and Seona found blushing boldness to say, "If we can wait that long."

Ian hadn't blushed. He had kissed her soundly.

There was no more talk of Aram Crane. The idea of him—to

Seona, a faceless haunt—was pushed aside whenever he came to mind, bringing fear that this life they were building was more fragile than she dared believe.

But no. Ian was strong. Capable. He loved her. She wrapped the strength of his promises around her heart like a shield.

Six days after Ian slipped the ring on her finger, Seona was in Naomi's cabin with Malcolm and the children, at the tail end of breakfast. The rest had scattered to their business. Lily to feed Ally's calf. Catriona to meet Maggie and Matthew and spend the day cleaning up the wrecked school cabin. Ian and Ally were down at the pasture. Naomi had gone to the yard to start a wash kettle boiling. Malcolm sat at the table with his Bible.

Seona had taken Mandy on her lap after Gabriel insisted on feeding himself the eggs and toast with strawberry jam she was coaxing them to finish. Mandy was a biddable girl, like Judith had been—which still brought a bittersweet reminder, though the child was calling her *Mama* now, and in her heart of hearts, Seona had embraced it.

"Girl-baby, did you help pick the strawberries Naomi put in this jam?"

Mandy had crammed a piece of toast into her mouth. Sticky-faced and chewing, she bobbed her head and swallowed her mouthful. "Afore you came, Mama. Afore *he* came," she added, peering across the table at her brother, making a bigger mess of his food than she probably had at half his age.

Seona stroked the child's silky hair, thinking it nigh long enough to put into braids. "Those blackberries over by the springhouse are ripe. We could have berries and cream with our dinner. Who's gonna help me pick?"

Mandy bounced on her lap. "Me!" She narrowed her eyes across the table. "And Gabriel *if* he puts berries in the basket, *not* his mouth."

Gabriel paused his chewing to grin at his sister, showing off a mouthful of eggs—most of which fell out onto his plate. He scooped them up and crammed them back into his mouth.

"Oh," Malcolm said, frowning at his Bible, oblivious to the mess being made beside him. "Now there be a word I'll no' have come across."

"Spell it for me," Seona said as Mandy reached for her plate and neatly popped a bite of egg into her mouth.

Malcolm spelled the word, then sounded it out. "Luh-vie-ah-thon. D'ye ken what that is?"

Seona had opened her mouth to tell him she had no idea when from the yard Naomi let out a screech of fright.

Malcolm sat frozen, head erect. Gabriel stopped chewing, blue eyes gone round.

Seona swept Mandy off her lap and onto the bench beside her. "You two stay put at this table and I mean it," she told the children. "Malcolm, keep them inside this cabin."

She bolted for the door, thinking *snake*. Thinking *panther, wolf, bear* . . . never for a second what it turned out had Naomi cowering behind the kettle she was heating over the fire—an Indian in their cabin-yard, sliding down off a winded dun mare. A tall, broad-shouldered Indian with his black hair loose about his shoulders and his thighs bared by a breechclout and leggings tied with scarlet garters at the knee. He wore a faded-blue shirt, belt thrust through with tomahawk and knife, and sleeves rolled high, showing forearms traced with tattooed lines ending in points like claws encircling his wrists. Another knife hung from a leather cord around his neck. He didn't touch the weapons as he strode forward, but Naomi lost her nerve regardless, making a dash for the cabin.

"No!" the Indian called. "Please."

Seona stepped into the sunlight. Naomi, eyes rimmed in white, stopped and faced the Indian with her.

He was nearly upon them before he halted, hands lifted, palms out. "I am looking for Lily," he said. "My sister is in need."

For all his imposing stature, the Indian looked nearly as frightened as Naomi. Though he was lean and well-muscled, his movements lithe, he wasn't young. Closer up Seona caught the glint of silver in his hair, lines fanning the corners of his frantic eyes. Still he radiated the power of a man in his prime.

His words penetrated her shock. "You . . . Are you Willa MacGregor's brother?"

Relief flashed in the dark eyes. "*Hen'en*—yes. There is no one at my sister's house to help. Everyone is gone away. I am to bring Lily. Where—?"

"I'm here!"

Seona turned to see Lily running from the stable, long braid flying, holding the canteen they used to feed G-B. Seona was startled by her mama's swift appearance. So was Willa's brother apparently. He stood gaping before he spoke again.

"My sister's baby comes. She said you can help. Will you help?"

Lily reached them and, without evidence of fear, touched the Indian's tattooed arm in reassurance. "Willa told us your name, but I've forgotten."

"I am Joseph Tames-His-Horse."

"All right, Joseph. Let me get some things. I'll ride with ye." Sparing of words, she ran for their cabin.

The Indian stared after her for a frozen second before jogging back to his horse.

Lily emerged from their cabin with her simples box. Joseph led the dun mare to meet her—a striking horse and comely, with its creamy hide a contrast to black mane and tail, legs encased in dark stockings pulled high. Joseph swung onto its back and, letting Lily use the stirrup, hauled her up behind him as if she weighed nothing.

Seona and Naomi stood breathless in the cabin doorway, Malcolm and the children clustered around them peering out, watching as they rode past. With one arm her mama clutched her box. The other hugged the Indian's lean waist.

"Come quick as ye can, Seona!" she called as Joseph Tames-His-Horse heeled his mount into a canter, long black hair blowing back across Lily's shoulders.

Seona arrived at the MacGregors' farm half an hour later to find Willa's Mohawk brother pacing the veranda, while through an open window on the upper floor the air was pierced by moans.

Joseph Tames-His-Horse descended the stairs and took the reins of

Seona's mount. "I will tend her," he said, clearly relieved for something to do.

"Thank you." The man looked only slightly less frantic than at their farm. Perhaps her mama hadn't wasted breath on reassurances.

Seona found them in a bedroom abovestairs. Sweaty hair braided, Willa MacGregor squatted over an oilcloth spread on the floor, straining and red-faced, while Lily gripped her arms. The baby's head was crowning. Seona grabbed a short stool, put it behind Willa, sat, and slipped her arms under the straining woman's sweaty shoulders, pressing her knees under Willa's elbows to lend support.

Freed to catch the baby, Lily kept her focus on Willa. "All right. Give a push with the next urge, and we'll have this baby out."

Seona felt Willa bear down, grunting through clenched teeth. She braced against the force of it with knees and gripping hands.

Lily crouched low. "Head's out. Cord's up around the neck. Don't push again 'til I see it's not too tight."

Willa groaned with the effort it took *not* to push. "Is she all right?"

Seona could picture her mama's fingers feeling between the pulsing loop of cord and the baby's tender skin. A cord around a neck was common enough, usually no worry . . .

"Aye," Lily said, relief flooding her tone. "It's not hindering. Let's finish this, Willa. One more push should do it."

It did. Seona felt the sag of Willa's weight. She lowered her to sitting. Lily had the baby on folded cloth, unwinding the cord from its neck. Two loops, another around its arm, no hindrance to its first lusty cries. Seona got a look at its nether regions.

"You knew it was a girl?"

"Almost certain," Willa replied, exhausted, exultant. "Maggie will be happy. And Neil, of course. The boys wanted another brother."

"Won't they be surprised to find a sister when they get home from fishing." Lily looked up and smiled at Seona, a knowing in her dark eyes.

"You knew too, Mama?"

"I may have."

Seona hadn't thought of it in a while, how her mama always guessed right about the babies she caught.

After the baby was washed, the afterbirth delivered, Willa tucked up in her bed with her daughter, Seona and Lily tidied the room, then made their way down to the kitchen to boil water for washing and to fetch something for Willa to eat.

"See, Mama," Seona said as she pushed soiled linen down into the kettle with a battling stick. "You're needed here—by more than me."

"I'm just relieved it went well," Lily said as she sliced bread from a loaf set out on Willa's table. "I was thinking all the way over about the last birth I attended. Rebecca Allen's."

Seona found a water pitcher and a cup while her mama buttered the bread and put it with a bit of cheese she found. They headed for the stairs, silenced by recollection of the harrowing birth that claimed the life of one of Mountain Laurel's neighbors and the babe that died with her, leaving its surviving twin motherless. Had that sorrow weighed on her mama all this time?

As they ascended the stairs, through a window on the landing Seona glimpsed Joseph Tames-His-Horse coming back from the stable. "Her brother's still out there waiting on word."

They entered the room, warmer now than when they had arrived. Lily set the plate on the bed. Seona poured water and handed the cup to Willa, who drank deep.

"Can your brother come in? He was mighty worried."

"He will not come in," Willa said. "It is not the Mohawk way. But he will want to know he has a namesake."

"Ye'll call her Josephine?" Lily asked.

Willa nodded, beaming at her tiny daughter.

"I'll tell him," Seona said.

Straightening from smoothing the bedcovers around Willa, Lily said, "No, Seona. I'll go."

The rising sun speared golden rays through the fir and spruce foresting that elevation, higher than the ridge that bounded Ian's farm to the north. They had set out at sunrise, he and Joseph Tames-His-Horse, after Jamie MacGregor arrived in the predawn asking if Ian would accompany Willa's brother to fetch Neil home.

Gone before Willa's labor began the previous day, Neil had ridden several miles north to visit Hector Lacey, the old man living alone in a squatter's shack on a mountainside. Willa presumed Neil had found Lacey in some need, for he hadn't come home.

"Pa stays overnight with folk plenty times, but he doesn't even know Josephine's been born," Jamie had said. "Matthew needs to take the black colt back to Colonel Waring today, so Uncle Joseph's going for Papa, but Mama doesn't want him riding out alone."

"Aye," Ian had said as he saddled Ruaidh by lantern light, recalling Joseph's history with the Warings—Elias Waring hadn't held him responsible for his eldest son's death, considering it self-defense, but had issued a warning, forbidding Joseph from showing his face in Shiloh again.

Ian had found Joseph astride his dun mare, rifle balanced across his thighs, waiting outside the MacGregors' stable. After Matthew relayed directions to Lacey's isolated cabin, they had headed north along a trail that passed a tall boundary stone set on a hillock grown with laurel, then on into the rising terrain. Though still the height of summer, the morning was cool. Ian was glad of his coat, knowing he would shed it soon enough.

At a point where the track allowed riding abreast, Joseph told him Goodenough had come to the house yesterday afternoon—at which point he had concealed his presence. "My sister says the woman was surprised to find the babe already come. I was glad I had only to ride to the next farm to find help."

Though Seona had returned home after the birth, Lily had spent the night at the MacGregors', helping Maggie care for Willa and the baby.

"She is a skilled midwife?" Joseph asked.

"Goodenough? From what I hear."

"Lily, I meant. Goodenough gave place to her and went back to the village."

"Lily is, too," Ian said, uncertain how much the man knew of their complicated connections. "Seona could be as well, with practice."

"That one is your woman?" Joseph said, gaze trained on the trail ahead.

"Aye. Soon to be my wife."

"I did not think of Lily as one of the grandmothers when I saw her running to me at your farm. She is young." They reached a split in the trail. Joseph halted his horse. "Here is where we head east to Lacey's cabin."

Ian took the lead. For a mile of twisting trail that wound up stony ridges and descended again, they rode in silence. Then a section of the path shot straight under trees wide-spaced. Joseph brought his mare alongside Ian's roan.

The man cut a striking figure on horseback, handsome but stern of feature, black hair falling past his shoulders, rifle at the ready. He had been a warrior in his youth. Now he was a carpenter. He farmed, too, though Ian had the notion his kin did most of the work on their land at Grand River, leaving Joseph free to hunt and roam for furs and skins to trade. And to visit his adopted sister and her family.

"Lily's also handy with a needle," Ian said, picking up their earlier conversation. "But living out on the farm as we do, I don't know she'll have much call for the skill, beyond the needs of our own clan."

Joseph nodded, leaving Ian to wonder had it been a good thing for Lily, leaving a city like Boston, where her skills could have been readily employed. Seona said her mother once spoke of finding a place where they could be independent, surviving on those very skills. Yet Lily had come along to New York as Seona predicted she would. Was she happy with that choice?

The trail steepened as it climbed another slope. At its top, faced with a thread of trail along its crest, they decided to dismount and walk their horses from there.

"Shouldn't be much farther," Ian said as he shouldered his rifle, reassured by its familiar weight. "If I mind Matthew's directions."

"Another mile past the ridge where we would decide to dismount." Joseph's mouth twisted slightly at the accuracy of Matthew's prediction. "He is glad for a new sister. Though not half as glad as little Pine Bird—Maggie."

Ian recalled it was Joseph who found Matthew and Maggie—calling themselves by their Mohawk names then—alone, astray, in need of mothering, and brought them to Willa, who had been alone and, if not astray, in need of being a mother.

"Have ye seen your namesake?" he called ahead to Joseph, now in the lead.

"Lily brought her out to me. Twice I have held her."

"Ye didn't go in to see Willa?"

Joseph slowed his pace. "In my lifetime much has changed for the *Kanien'kehá:ka*. Still I see wisdom in our traditions. A Mohawk woman who bears a child is secluded for a time. No man comes near her. Only women. But I will see my sister soon."

Ian wondered what Joseph would think if he told the man he had acted as midwife in his own son's birth.

Talk of sisters made him think of his own. He had left Catriona sleeping in their cabin that morning but recalled she had come home subdued after returning from Shiloh to find baby Josephine arrived. She had eaten little supper, gone to their cabin, been asleep before he could discover what might be amiss.

It had been a hard thing that sent her westward. He realized he had counted on her friendship with Maggie to supply her solace. And if that wasn't enough? So focused on the farm, on Seona, Gabriel, Mandy—and the unnerving distraction of Aram Crane—he had neglected his sister, who doubtless needed more than a roof over her head and food in her belly.

Perhaps he could remove one of the distractions pulling at him. Or get a better grip on it. "This morning Jamie reminded me what happened here with ye and Willa," he said as a solitary raven's harsh cry issued from the trees above them. "In part because of Aram Crane."

He noted the tensing of Joseph's broad shoulders as they passed through a sunlit patch. "That is one man I regret . . ."

Ruaidh's hoof kicked a loose stone on the trail. Its rattle covered whatever Joseph said, if he had even finished the statement. "What d'ye regret?"

Joseph glanced back. "I was going to say I regret never killing the man, but it is not true. I would have taken his life if forced to it. But I do regret his escape, for all the harm he has done since." He walked on, leading his horse. "You have seen the man. I remember you said so."

Around them the forest had awakened with birdcalls. Up ahead came the crashing of a deer bounding away, startled by their voices.

"And not just the once, last autumn," Ian said. "I saw him again in June."

They had reached a rock outcropping Matthew had described, its contours shaped like a turtle's head, skirted by the trail, the final landmark to show the way to the place they sought. From there the trail ascended along a ravine to where Hector Lacey had built a ramshackle cabin, squatting on land Judge Cooper might well own.

Joseph halted his horse. Gripping his rifle, he bent to study the trail. "Here are marks of Neil's horse heading in, not out." He stood and faced Ian, who had halted the roan. "Where did you see Crane this time? Cooperstown again?"

Ian planted his rifle's stock on the path and told of his last visit to William Cooper's village at the foot of Otsego Lake, of thinking himself followed on his way to Cherry Valley, then spotting Crane at the inn where he stopped. "I slept in the stable, on my guard. The man didn't trouble me in the night, but he was still there come the morning."

"What did he say to you?"

"Not a word. But he made a point of staring me down as I rode out."

Unease gathered on Joseph's brow. "This was in June?"

"Aye. I'd paid off my land and was heading east to meet Seona and the others in Albany. I haven't seen Crane since I rode from Cherry Valley but . . . have ye spoken yet to Matthew about the man?"

"I have," Joseph said, his tone making it clear he had been appraised of the recent suspicions involving Matthew's traps. "But why would Crane take such interest in you?"

Ian debated telling him more. This was a man deeply trusted by both Willa and Neil. One Ian wanted on his side, should Crane prove a threat to something beyond his peace of mind. "As it happens, I'd come into possession of some gold. Not coin. The raw thing, straight from the earth. I used it to pay off my land. I've reason to think word of it's gone round in Cooperstown."

"And to Crane's ears? Matthew did not speak of gold to me."

Good, Ian thought. He said, "He's still worked up over Crane, wanting to go after the man?"

"No more than I." Joseph gazed along the winding path leading past the outcrop. "I will stay near Shiloh for a time, I think."

"Because of Crane?"

"I have my reasons," Willa's brother said, features inscrutable as he turned to Ian. "Crane is one."

Matthew, no doubt, was another. Joseph wouldn't want him getting reckless notions about Crane any more than Neil and Willa would.

They started up the final ascent to Lacey's cabin. They were higher in the mountains than Ian had yet been, even hunting. The creek running noisily below the steep ravine on their right precluded conversation. On their left the equally steep but forested mountain rose another few hundred feet. In the distance, through the scrim of trees along the ravine's edge, could be glimpsed the higher peaks of the Adirondacks, stretching northward.

At last the slope on their left curved away, and a tight but nearly level spot between it and the ravine opened. They had no more than glimpsed the mossy roofline of Lacey's cabin, half-hidden behind a ragged patch of corn, before out of that corn, Neil MacGregor emerged, leading his old horse, Seamus.

"Joseph!" Startled by the sight of them, he drew up short. "Ian? Is it Willa?"

Ian was quick to reassure. "Willa's fine. But, aye, the bairn's come. A girl."

Astonishment, then a blazing grin, broke over Neil MacGregor's tired face. "The Almighty be praised—though I wish I'd been with her. Was Goodenough? She wasn't alone?"

"I arrived after you left for this place," Joseph said. "We must have just missed each other on the trail. Willa sent me to this one's farm—" he nodded at Ian—"to bring the one there who is a midwife. All is well. The girl is called Josephine."

"That's right. We'd agreed on the name for a daughter. 'Twas to be Joseph otherwise." Neil's grin doubled. "I've another wee lass. Maggie will be pleased."

Joseph granted one of his rare smiles in return. "She is."

"What about here?" Ian asked, finding their joy infectious. "Did ye manage to talk the old codger down from his hermitage?"

"Stubborn goat," Neil said, still grinning. "I came here on account of feeling something was amiss. An impression from the Lord, I take it now. Lacey cut his foot chopping wood and the gash wasn't healing. I caught it in time to save the foot, I think, if he'll stay off it long enough. I'll come back in a few days and check. But never mind it now."

"Aye," Ian said as he and Joseph turned their mounts to head back down the ravine. "Ye've a daughter to meet."

31

September 1797

Though most of the faces lit by the fires burning in the cabin-yard were different than in years past, Seona felt as if she had lived moments of this corn shucking before. The MacGregors were there, including Willa and baby Josephine, on her first outing. Joseph Tames-His-Horse had come, as had the Keppler clan from the mill, with Lemuel Waring in tow. But the biggest difference was having two of her own to look after. Thus far Seona had scarcely gotten her hands on an ear of corn with the children flitting between fires, from one group of shuckers to another, all filling up baskets and barrels with the field's bounty, mounding up husks for winter feed.

"Let me watch them, Seona," Catriona called, getting up from the smallest fire—with Maggie and Anni Keppler's daughter—to intercept the pair. "Come here you two. It's time you learned to shuck corn."

"Now that we've taught *you*." Maggie grinned at Ian's sister. "But the best way to learn is to teach."

"Auntie Catweena!" Gabriel cried, clutching at her skirt. "Take us to see G-B!"

"Yes, Auntie. G-B!" Mandy chimed, jumping in place, brown curls flopping.

They hadn't lost their attachment to the orphaned bull, recently introduced to the other weaned calves. With G-B no longer in the old stable, the children were strictly charged that someone accompany them down to the pasture to see their favorite baby bull.

"In a bit," Catriona promised. "Now it's time to shuck corn. You can do just *one* ear apiece. Next year, when you're bigger, you can do *two*."

"I'm big," Gabriel insisted. "I can shuck two!"

Seona gave Ian's sister a grateful smile and took her chance to sit at the fire where her mama held baby Josephine in the crook of her arm while Willa, Naomi, and Anni Keppler shucked corn around her. "You've had that baby long enough," she said, settling on the log Lily shared with Willa. "It's my turn."

Seona looked to Willa, busy filling up a basket with the stalk-dried ears. When she nodded, Seona took the baby in her arms, amazed how compact and solid in her wrappings she was, how soundly she slept amid the noise they were making, especially over at the largest fire where the men and a horde of gangly boys were busy working, though not without outbursts of ribbing over matters Seona only half heeded. Of that group, Ian was seated nearest their fire. More than once Seona had caught his gaze fixed on her while she followed Gabriel and Mandy or helped Naomi, Lily, and Anni set out cider and supper for when one or another took a notion to eat.

She liked hearing Ian's voice raised among the other men's, giving and taking his share of the fun. It reminded her of the shucking four years past when he found the red ear. John Reynold and Charlie Spencer had made him blush with their teasing and she had thought—for a heart-stopping instant—Ian would ask *her* for a kiss in exchange for that pretty ear of corn. In front of everyone.

He had asked tiny Ruthie Allen instead.

For the past little while the younger males had seemed bent on teasing Matthew. Over what, Seona wasn't sure. Matthew was taking it stoically while Willa's clan brother watched it all, face inscrutable as he worked—about as deftly as Catriona was managing.

"He has never shucked corn before," Willa said, following Seona's gaze. "I am surprised he was willing."

"Mohawk men don't shuck corn?" Lily asked.

"Not if they keep the old ways. My brother grows broad-minded in his old age."

Seona thought Joseph Tames-His-Horse far too striking a figure to be called *old*. Especially with the firelight burnishing those long-muscled, tattooed forearms, bared by shirtsleeves turned high. As if he heard Willa's comment, despite the noise the young men were making, he glanced their way and noticed them staring. Seona caught a flash of white teeth before he looked away.

"Still sharp-eared," Lily murmured.

The sound of Gabriel's voice at the neighboring fire reached Seona: "Please, Auntie! Can we see G-B now?"

"Let me finish shucking this pile; then we'll go."

Seona turned a quick maternal eye on her boy, but Gabriel settled back to tugging at the husks of an ear laid across his knees.

Willa's daughter gave a tiny burp in her sleep. Seona dropped her gaze to the baby, whose cap of fuzzy hair promised to be her mother's shade.

Her attention was soon drawn back to Ian's sister. Maybe seeing her with Maggie made it dawn on Seona that Catriona had spent most of her days at their farm lately. Not their neighbors'. She wondered why. Nothing appeared amiss between her and Maggie, that Seona could see.

Lily, who had taken up the task of shucking with practiced ease, leaned her shoulder against Seona. "Wanting another?"

Jarred from her thoughts, Seona asked, "Another what, Mama?"

Lily nodded toward Willa's baby. "One of those."

Seona started to say she did, eventually, but caught Ian, across the yard, watching her holding the baby. Seemed she read the same question in his eyes. And more.

Soon as the corn's in the crib. It was all but there now. She felt his longing, and her own, down to her bones. Then Josephine MacGregor awoke in her arms, looked up at her with startled eyes, and screwed up her tiny features in a wail.

Seona laughed.

Anni Keppler, who had been talking to Naomi, said, "I was going to ask for a turn with her, but it's you she wants now, Willa."

As Seona handed over the baby to Willa, the noise at the men's fire erupted in volume, this time led by Ian: "What—ye've never heard about the red ear? Not a one of ye?"

Other conversations around the fires ceased as all craned to see Matthew, the center of attention, an ear of corn newly shucked in his grasp. Instead of the usual yellow or white, it was mottled in shades of red.

"What of it?" Matthew asked warily.

Ian laughed. "In Carolina it's tradition. Any man who shucks a red ear may ask the woman of his choosing for a kiss, in exchange for it. So who is it to be?"

The center of jovial taunting, Matthew stared fixedly at the red ear. He didn't so much as smile, which Seona thought strange. Strange as well there had come no sound of giggles from the eligible young women present.

Matthew never looked their way. He thrust the ear at his youngest brother, seated on the log beside him.

Liam MacGregor, barely eleven years old, gaped at what was thrust into his hands as at something ten days dead. "Let a *girl* kiss me for this?"

He shoved the ear down the line at Jamie, old enough to entertain the idea. He shot a half-shy look at the girls, then lost his nerve. Blushing furiously, he handed off the red ear to Lem.

Seona glanced at the girls to see how they were taking this play and caught the distress on Catriona's face, which she tried to hide by turning a pasted-on smile to the children, watching the goings-on at the men's fire.

"Ready to go see G-B?" she asked with a false brightness lost on the little ones, who jumped up with instant zeal. Maggie said something to Catriona, who shook her head furiously, took her niece and nephew by the hand, and led them off into the beech shadows, down through the dark toward the pasture.

The crowd at the men's fire had closed off sight of Matthew. Half the boys were in a tussle over the red ear now—whether to claim it or be rid of it was anyone's guess. None had noticed Catriona's departure.

Matthew sat with shoulders rigid, gone back to husking corn.

"Mama?" Seona began, but Lily was already nodding, handing her the shawl she had set by earlier.

"I think ye should."

She found them at the paddock on the near side of the pasture, where the weaned calves grazed, watched over by their mamas on the other side of the fence. Gabriel and Mandy were pressed to the rails, petting G-B. Catriona stood nearby. They were shapes in the moonlight until Seona neared with a blazing pine knot taken from the fire. Catriona averted her face, wiping at her cheeks.

"Mama," Gabriel said, turning toward the light. "Pet G-B."

"All right, baby." Seona gave the calf a scratch between the ears, then turned her attention to Ian's sister. "What just happened back at the fires?"

Catriona raised a hand to muffle a sob. The children didn't notice, laughing over the calf, which was licking Mandy's face. Seona hadn't seen Catriona this upset since Boston. Her heart gave a squeeze.

"I think you know—or guess," Catriona said. "Maggie isn't the only reason I spend so much time at the MacGregors'. Spent, rather."

"You want to tell me about it?"

At first it seemed Catriona wouldn't or couldn't. She pressed her lips tight, then in a pained whisper managed, "I love him."

"Love?" She had spoken louder than intended, but the children were oblivious.

"Will you put the torch out?" Catriona asked, eyes welling again.

Seona dropped it on the ground, whipped her skirts aside, and gave it a stomp to put out the flame. Away from the fires, the risen moon shed light enough to see each other.

"It's not like Boston," Catriona said, the nearest she had come to mentioning Morgan Shelby since they left that city.

"I don't expect it is. Matthew MacGregor is another sort of man. A good man. Still . . ." Seona thought of that Freneau poem and its fanciful notions of Indians on the frontier.

"I know what you must be thinking," Catriona said, frustration in her tone. "That I'm just infatuated with my own 'copper-coloured boy.' It's not like that either."

This was going to take some talking through. "Gabriel, Mandy," Seona said, "you two stay right here and talk with G-B. I need to speak with your auntie. All right?"

Mandy spoke for the pair. "All right, Mama."

Not yet over that warm, sweet feeling she got whenever Mandy called her *Mama*, Seona took Catriona by the arm and moved her a few paces down the fence, still within hearing of the children's voices. From the pasture one of the cows lowed. In the distance she could hear the others at the shucking, glimpse the light of fires through the trees. She wrapped her shawl more warmly about her shoulders.

"Does Matthew not feel for you like you do him?"

He had refused to seek a kiss, finding himself in possession of a red ear. Or had he not wanted to make a display of his affections in front of a crowd?

"He does." Catriona's sigh was bone-deep. "I wish I could tell you the moment I knew I loved him, and he me. Neither of us can recall. It started with the horses. What else?" she asked with a small laugh. "He's so wonderful with them, but you know. You've seen."

"He's right impressive."

"Isn't he?" Catriona's voice warmed with admiration. "I thought I understood them, but what he does, *how* he does it—it's like he reads their souls. I couldn't get enough of watching him work with Colonel Waring's colts. In the beginning I had a perfect flood of questions, but he was happy to answer. He let me in the paddock to work with him after a while. We'd go riding together on the days Maggie was teaching . . ." Her voice caught. "Then *that* day happened."

"What day?" Seona asked.

"The day we found the school cabin broke into. That's when everything changed. Matthew changed."

"I mind he was angry. But why did it change things for you and him?"

Behind them in the darkness, the children giggled.

Catriona sniffled. "At first I didn't notice. I was too focused on Maggie. But after that day Matthew grew distant. He avoided being alone with me. Finally I caught him in their stable grooming one of the horses when no one else was near. I asked him to tell me what I'd done wrong, how I'd upset him."

"Did he tell you?"

"I hadn't done anything. He told me he loved me and wanted to ask me to marry him—but he wouldn't. Marriage to someone like him wasn't the life for me. Because he's Mohawk, and I should understand that without his having to say so after what happened at Maggie's school—" Catriona's voice choked off.

With one ear tuned to the children, Seona put her arms around Ian's sister and listened while she told the rest in snatches, how Matthew had used what happened at the school as evidence of what Catriona would face if they married. He couldn't do that to her nor bear to watch her love die in the face of such bigotry.

"He's *wrong*, Seona. I don't care what anyone thinks about us. Or what they say. We'd face it together, our families around us. But he's too stubborn to listen. He thinks he's sparing me pain, but denying our love is a worse pain than anyone else might inflict. I cannot make him *see* that."

"What about Maggie?" Seona asked, releasing her. "She hasn't given up being your friend."

"She has more sense. Or courage." Catriona crossed her arms, hunching around them. "I don't mean that. I think Matthew exceptionally brave—for himself."

"He's afraid for you," Seona said. "Afraid he'll bring you harm. That might be a pain too great for him to bear."

Catriona groaned. "I don't want to live my life afraid. Afraid of loving, of taking the risk—if it is one."

Nor do I, Seona thought. Ian had promised to protect her and their children, but was any man, whatever color his skin, able to hold back all harm from the ones he loved?

She reached to rub Catriona's shoulder. "Give Matthew time. Better yet, give the Almighty time." The words sounded good, but it felt like someone else saying them.

"If it's meant to be, it will be?" Catriona unlaced her arms. "I just wish it didn't hurt so much, the waiting. But you're right. I can pray. I *will* pray."

Seona heard a note of strength in Catriona's voice, a steadiness that hadn't been part of her makeup back in Boston.

"So will I," she promised before they rounded up the children and went back to the fires, knowing now this situation with Matthew was nothing like Catriona's former infatuations. This felt grounded in something more than fancy. Which she knew didn't make it less painful. Rather more so.

32

Seona awoke the morning after the corn shucking to find Lily had risen and taken Gabriel to breakfast in Naomi's cabin. Carried him off asleep most like. Gabriel did not greet the day quietly.

She lay thinking over yesterday's doings, rubbing hands sore from shucking, calling to mind Catriona's tears. Heaviness filled her for Ian's sister, heartbroken again in this place she had come to find healing. Her rubbing fingers found Ian's ring. Stretching out full on the bed, she thought how it would be to reach out and find Ian lying beside her. The corn was in the crib now. Most of it.

Risen at last, she was rummaging for a petticoat to put on over shift and stays when she moved aside a pile of garments needing washing and found the red corn ear.

"Up at last, girl-baby?" her mama said from the doorway, coming into the cabin with nary a clinging child. "Working on their breakfasts," she said before Seona could ask. "Catriona's helping."

Seona held up the red ear. "Mama, how'd you end up with this? Don't tell me *you* kissed Lem? He's the last I saw with it."

"Of course not," Lily said, lighting her a grin that nearly outshone the sunlight streaming into the cabin. "With all the awkwardness over the first, what would a second have done?"

"It's another?" Seona supposed her mama had found it, then slipped it out of sight before anyone noticed. "Likely for the best." She put it back to continue her hunt for a petticoat.

"You never told me what Catriona said when you went after her last night," Lily said. "Though reckon I can guess. She's in love again?"

Seona found the petticoat she was looking for, stepped into it, then tied it at her waist. "Truly this time. With Matthew."

"That much was clear. Don't know to how many—best keep whatever else she had to say between ye."

While Seona fastened her workaday short gown, she studied her mama standing in the doorway, radiating happiness. "I 'spect everyone else is dragging their bones about, but something's got you aglow this morning."

Her mama clasped her hands before her heart, looking giddy as Catriona in one of her brightest moods. "Sit down, girl-baby. I got something to tell ye."

"A sit-down something?"

Seona let her mama lead her to the rumpled bed. They sat side by side on the tick. Lily grasped her hand. "I wanted ye to know afore I tell anyone else—I been waiting for ye to wake. Last night after ye went off with Catriona and the babies, I had a chance to speak to Willa's brother. Ye mind her telling us months back he might know some Cherokee, could maybe tell us the meaning of my name?"

Seona caught a breath. "I'd forgot."

"I hadn't. I been thinking of asking him nigh on a month. Last night I found my nerve."

"Did he know?"

"Aye, he did. *Tsigalili* . . . it means 'chickadee.'"

Seona laughed, partly at the name, mostly at her mama's evident joy. "Oh, Mama. That's downright pretty—and perfect. Your mama called you her chickadee. Reckon you had a little black cap of hair, too."

Tears welled in Lily's eyes. They coursed down beside her nose, over her irrepressible smile. "When Joseph said it—the way he said it—I could sense my mama smiling down on me. I could almost feel her touch."

Seona pulled her into an embrace. "Now if only we knew *her* name," she said into her mama's neck.

"*Sadie* is all we have to go on," Lily said as they parted. "And that's just what Naomi thought it sounded like."

"You could ask Joseph if it sounds like any Cherokee name he's ever heard," Seona suggested. "If not, he could maybe ask whoever it is he knows up in Canada and write it to you in a letter—can he write?"

"He says he can."

"And is he leaving soon?"

"October sometime." Lily's smile wavered. "He and Matthew will be gone deep into the winter, hunting. It's what they do."

"They do," Catriona echoed from the doorway, making Seona start. Ian's sister looked tired, though not as if she had spent the night weeping. "I told Ian I'd help Lily watch the children this morning. He wants to spend it with you, Seona."

She felt a rush of pleasure, then recalled a snatch of overheard conversation the night before. "Didn't I hear Maggie say she wanted to teach you to make cheese from her goats' milk? She could come here, show Naomi, Mama, and me as well."

"I'll ask when I see her again," Catriona said. "Ian's having breakfast. You should join him."

They had gotten most of the corn into the crib, where it would finish drying though the autumn. What little was left in the field they could bring in today. Or tomorrow. Though Neil MacGregor warned winter could come in a hurry, there on the edge of the Adirondacks, the weather looked to be holding. Still bone-tired from days of harvesting, then hosting yesterday's shucking, all Ian could think of was his next main objective: making Seona his wife. Legally. Before God. And every other way.

"I wanted to talk about our wedding," he said as they walked along the lake after breakfast, hand in hand. "Now the corn's put up."

The day had dawned with a few thin clouds. Seona had wrapped herself in a shawl. Out on the water, migrating geese swam through a faint blanketing mist, while off at the lake's southern end, toward which they strolled, came the eerie call of the loons that had nested on the islet where Willa MacGregor used to read her books.

Seona bumped her shoulder against his arm. "You aren't letting any moss grow."

Her hair fell braided down her back, hastily bound before arriving to breakfast. Her skin looked flawless in the morning's light. She seemed rested, a stark contrast to his sister, who had offered to watch Mandy and Gabriel.

"'Better to marry than to burn,'" he quoted and waited for understanding to color her cheeks. Then he stopped and pulled her close and covered her mouth with his in a kiss that left him very much in danger of desire's flames.

They both pulled away smiling, promise in their eyes.

"Before we get too far down that trail," Ian said, "and I forget . . . what's amiss with Catriona? She left the fire last night and never came back, not even to say goodbye to everyone. I saw ye go after her." Once again Catriona had been abed when he dropped onto his own in the wee hours. Sight of her face that morning, pale and set, had discouraged his asking her straight-out.

They continued walking, passing beneath the tall red pines fringing the lakeshore, where their children's feet had worn a footpath through the carpeting needles. They were past the pines and in among the maples he had tapped last spring before Seona answered, frowning at the ground.

"She was upset about the red ear Matthew found."

"Because he didn't ask her for a kiss?" It had been Lem who found the courage to ask for a kiss in exchange for that red ear, passed hand to hand like a potato off the embers. Lem had gotten it, too. From Maggie MacGregor.

Seona halted beneath a young maple, its boughs tipped with scarlet. "Catriona told me why she left the fire, but she spoke in confidence."

Ian's amusement lifted like the mist off the water, visible through the trees. "Is it serious between them, her and Matthew?"

Some while back he had observed the pair out in the MacGregors' paddock and had a vague notion something more than a shared love of horses was developing between his sister and Neil's adopted son. With no definitive proof, it had been easy to dismiss.

"It is," Seona said, most definitively.

"*How* serious?"

Seona heaved a sigh. "Ian . . . her heart's broke."

"Again?" Ian asked, stunned to find the thing had gone on under his nose without his grasping the half of it. "Matthew doesn't seem the type to carry on with a lass without speaking to her next of kin—*me*. And Catriona . . . is she so foolish as to make the same mistake twice over in a few months' time?" He had worked himself from surprise to affront and had all but forgotten his purpose for this morning stroll with Seona. "I best talk to her."

Seona stopped him with a hand to his arm. "Ian. Don't."

Though gently spoken, her opposition was unexpected enough to bring him up short. "Why? Seona, what is going on?"

"Nothing they have cause to regret. No wrong done."

Ian frowned. "What are ye saying? Either it's serious between them and he's done something to hurt her, or it's not and . . . why is she upset?"

He hadn't meant to corner her, but he had. He saw it in her eyes as she said, "I hope she'll forgive me telling you. No, I hope you'll let things be so she never knows I did. It is serious, like I said, but your sister isn't the same girl who fell prey to Morgan Shelby. And Matthew is an honorable man. As I said, they've done nothing wrong."

"All right," Ian said. "What have they done?"

"Fallen in love. Not so unlike how it was with you and me, at the start."

"How so—aside from the secrecy?"

She blinked at that, not quite a wince. "Something you—*we*—ought to understand better than most. Secrecy aside, you and I bonded over a thing we did together: making Catriona's desk. Me drawing, you working the wood. Don't you mind it?"

"Of course I do." Her eyes, wide and green, searched his. Melting into them, he half smiled with the memories stirred. The spice of fresh-cut wood and beeswax, Seona seated on the low stool drawing morning glories. "So with those two it was the horses. Aye . . . but what went agley?"

"Maggie's school cabin. After that happened, Matthew pulled away."

He didn't need Seona to tell him the rest, though he let her do so. How Catriona confronted Matthew over his distancing. How Matthew, in a moment of frustration and pain, confessed his love, his wanting to marry. And his absolute refusal to do so.

"To spare her pain." Ian felt his heart squeeze not with anger now but sympathy. His sister loved a man who saw himself standing on the other side of a line he could never cross. "Or cause a little pain now rather than a lifetime of it."

"But, Ian," Seona said, taking his hand, "Catriona's not despairing. We talked it through last night. She's hurting, but she's praying and waiting for the Almighty to work things out for her and Matthew. She's not trying to force something into being."

As he had done at Mountain Laurel. He touched the face of the woman whose heart had shown its courage, crossing its own lines. Because of him. For him. He pulled her into his embrace again, thankful beyond measure for their second chance.

"All right," he said, cheek laid atop her head, breathing in the scent of her that mingled with the morning smells of earth and water. "I'll let it be. And I'll trust Neil and Willa to counsel their son. Leastwise to listen as ye did to Catriona. Thank ye for that, *mo chridhe*."

Only then did it hit him. What he had allowed to happen last night, that foolishness over the red ear. He had compounded his sister's hurt.

"You were just funning," Seona said, pulling away to look at him when he confessed as much. "Like they did to you at the Reynolds' shucking. You couldn't have known. I only figured it out from the way she reacted. You had your back turned and didn't see."

"Still," he said, unwilling to be let off so easy, "I should apologize—if she gives me opening. I won't let her know we talked. But I'm glad to know of it."

In that bold way he loved, Seona stepped close and, going up on her toes, kissed him. He got his arms around her quick enough to kiss her back. It was some time before they continued along the lakeshore.

They were nearing the point where the track to Shiloh passed before he asked, "Have ye thought about whether ye'd like a minister to marry us? Down in German Flatts?" Thought of leaving the farm shot a bolt of uneasiness through him. They would be vulnerable, traveling downriver. So would whoever stayed behind—should Aram Crane choose to cause mischief. Or was he fretting over nothing?

"I don't know," Seona was saying. "I'm not sure everyone could travel so far. Not Malcolm. He's been so tired of late."

Ian leaned back against the trunk of a tree fronting the lake, watching the loons glide around the far side of the islet. "Wish I could say I hadn't noticed."

"Is there another way?"

"Colonel Waring is still a magistrate. He could marry us. At his house. Maybe here at the farm."

By her brightening he could tell the notion was more agreeable. "I want them all with us. Mama, Naomi, Malcolm, everyone."

"Everyone?" he asked with a grin, then pulled her close for another kiss before she could say a word. They were thus engaged still moments later when he caught movement from the corner of his eye. His hand dropped to his belt knife, then stilled.

"What?" Seona pulled back to ask.

He had a finger to her lips before she barely got the word out. There was someone on the track, heading away from the farm. He glimpsed a petticoat.

"It's Mama," Seona whispered as the figure passed an open spot and he caught sight of a long braid, raven black, falling below a linen cap.

Lily was alone. Heading for the MacGregors, he presumed.

Neither said a word until she was past hearing; then Seona turned, a smile blooming on her lips. "She told me something this morning. Last night she got a chance to speak to Joseph. He knows a man up in Grand River. A Cherokee man. Willa told us some time back Joseph might know the meaning of Mama's name, Tsigalili."

"What does it mean? Did Joseph know?"

"Chickadee!" Seona laughed, and he with her. "Isn't that the sweetest thing? Maybe Mama's going back to ask what we thought of this morning, whether the name Sadie sounds like any Cherokee word he knows."

Ian nodded. "That's what Naomi and the others called your grandmother."

"You remember?"

"Of course. I hope Joseph can satisfy her." And that she reached him safely. It wasn't quite half a mile to the MacGregors' door but he didn't like it, Lily going off alone on foot, no doubt unarmed.

He ground his teeth, wishing that if Aram Crane was in fact lurking somewhere, he would show himself. He couldn't ask them all to hole up like refugees in a fort. "Now the corn's put up, I need to fill the smokehouse, since we cannot be slaughtering all our cows. I mean to get a deer—better an elk, if I can find one."

Seona's face clouded. "When?"

"Today," he said and felt his stomach tighten.

"How long will you be gone?"

"As short a time as possible." He forced a grin when she pushed out a pouting lip, then kissed the pout away. "When I'm home from the hunting, we'll go talk with Colonel Waring and choose a date to wed."

33

Ian didn't hunt with Ally, whom he had tried to interest in the notion, thus far without success. Instead Neil MacGregor came along.

"Ye chose the rare day I'd nothing else pulling at me," Neil told him as they made their way into the hills rising north of their farms. "Save the need to fill my own smokehouse."

Ian held aside a fir bough to pass a tight spot on the trail they followed. "I thought Matthew kept ye well supplied in meat."

"He does, for the most part. But once he leaves with Joseph, we'll no' see hide nor hair o' him 'til after the New Year. It's up to me, and Jamie, to supply us for the winter. Unless ye mean to slaughter some cows to sell beef to your neighbors?"

"One," Ian said. "If that. I cannot spare more until the herd's grown."

"I've heard Ally talk o' those cows," Neil said. "*To* them, for that matter. They're like pets, aye?"

Ian shook his head as they passed through a stand of beeches, carpeted in rich mast on which a herd of pigs would have happily gorged. "What Ally means to do with *his* cattle, aside from naming them, is a conversation I need to think through."

They tramped on in silence after that, using their breath for the steep terrain. After spotting a distant herd of deer, they spent half the morning stalking it, never getting near enough for shooting before something spooked the animals into bounding away.

The day was mild after a chilly start, clouded without rain. After the corn harvest, at both farms, it was good to be out with only Neil for company, though Ian's thoughts turned often to Seona, their wedding, and all that would come after. Building a home. Filling it with children, he hoped, though if all they ever had were Gabriel and Mandy, he would be content.

At midday they climbed a ridge and spied a big, straight poplar fallen along its crest, still firm and green. Leaning their rifles against it, they took a seat and a drink, then broke into the provisions each carried in a knapsack, sharing what they found there.

"So," Neil said after a time. "Matthew and Catriona."

Ian shot his neighbor a look. "Ye've talked to Matthew then?"

"I have." Neil gave him a smile full of the knowledge of his son's pain and Catriona's. "They've my blessing, for what it's worth."

"A lot." After a moment Ian added, "They've mine, too, but I've been thinking I should write to my da . . ."

"Maybe wait on that," Neil said. "Could be it isna what the Almighty has for them, a life together. Though I ken the lad loves your sister."

"And she him, apparently."

Neil chewed a piece of jerked meat, swallowed, said, "She truly isna put off by what concerns Matthew? Given what I ken of human frailty—and wickedness—such bigotry isna like to end anytime soon, unless the Lord return and set up a more perfect Kingdom on this earth."

Ian smiled at the notion. "According to Seona, my sister would take Matthew and whatever comes with him, rather than not."

Neil hadn't spoken in some time about the violation of his daughter's school cabin. He had been justifiably outraged by it, every bit as much as Matthew, though his was the cooler temper, the more bridled tongue. Still . . . "Maggie's school," Ian said. "Did ye ever get to the bottom of who did the deed?"

"Anyone who cares enough to expose the culprit doesna ken who to blame." Neil's jaw firmed. "Or *say* they dinna. And we both know who Matthew blames."

The name *Aram Crane* hovered like a haunt on the ridge where they rested. Had it anything to do with the man, or was Matthew ready to ascribe every evil that befell to the shifty, ghostlike Crane? Others in Shiloh might have done such a deed. He prayed it had been another, for if it was Crane, it meant the man was watching the MacGregors again—more than watching—and had surely taken note of their new neighbors. The thought made him itch to be back home, ready to stand between all threats and those he loved. As he had promised to do.

He didn't like this. It recalled too keenly his frustration, years ago at Mountain Laurel, when he couldn't be sure whom to trust, didn't know who was manipulating circumstances to their own ends. They had all been working at cross-purposes. Wheels within wheels. He and Seona—and Judith—had been caught in them and had their hearts ground. He whispered a prayer that it wouldn't be so for Catriona. For Matthew.

They moved on, rifles primed, but neither took a shot until evening when Neil startled a doe and brought it down cleanly before it could flee.

Early on the second day, Ian shot an elk cow.

Homeward bound, they were making use of meandering trails, dragging their meat on a travois, taking it in turns. In the lead with the burden, Ian caught a boot on something sprawled across the trail where it angled around a tall rock outcrop. He went down on his knees on the brushy slope, bruising himself on stones.

"Steady!" Neil called from behind, grabbing the travois to keep meat and hides from tipping. "All right, man?"

"Aye." Ian winced as he pushed upright. "Tripped on a limb."

He was about to rise when the smell hit him: an earthy odor, tainted with decay, perceptible near the ground. He looked more closely at what had tripped him, half-hidden among rocks. A limb it was, but not from a tree.

"Neil," he said, beckoning his neighbor forward.

Neil edged between the travois and the outcrop to see what Ian had discerned: a leg—the lower part of one, stripped of stocking and footwear, the flesh browned and hardened, drawn up tight to the bone.

Not just a leg, Ian discovered as he wrenched aside weeds downslope of the trail. An entire body, decayed and scavenged though still mostly articulated, lay among a thicket of huckleberry bushes tinged with autumn red, growing in patches below the trail. What was visible of the body wore the remnants of breeches and coat.

Ian lowered himself down the slope, parting shrubs, following the slender length of the corpse to its head. The hair plastered to the nearly fleshless skull was bleached pale, long but likely too short for a woman's.

"A man," Ian said, aware his neighbor had come down the slope behind him. "Took a fall, d'ye think?" He turned to look at the lip of the outcrop looming above, intending to judge its angle. Instead he caught sight of Neil MacGregor's face, gone ashen as no physician's ought, even at sight of a corpse gone empty-socketed, teeth bared in a rictus grin.

"Let me closer," Neil said. "Let me see him."

They exchanged places on the uneven turf, boots cracking branches. Neil dropped to his knees beside the remains, said something in Gaelic under his breath, then began tugging at the stiffened garments. He got his fingers inside the coat, furtled about, and pulled a small object free: a tiny wooden horse, polished smooth, had been protected in a pocket next to the dead man's heart.

"God have mercy." Neil MacGregor stared at the wee horse, shock and devastation writ across his face. "Matthew carved this. Maggie gave it to him."

"Him?" Ian asked, though with dawning dismay.

Blue eyes locked with his, Neil nodded. "Francis Waring."

Francis was laid to rest in the burial ground that contained his mother and four elder brothers. Of Colonel Waring's once-full quiver, only his daughter, Anni, and Lem, his son with Goodenough, remained. Elias Waring stood at the head of this newest grave, bent over a cane, looking alarmingly aged since Ian and Neil had brought him the grim news and his son's remains. A few came forward to speak of Francis, who for all his half-wild ways had been loved by many in Shiloh, the

MacGregors not least of which. Sandwiched between Catriona and Lem, Maggie wept openly.

Seona had accompanied Ian to the burial, then to the Warings' large stone house for a supper. They had refrained from speaking to the grieving man about a wedding ceremony. "Soon," Ian whispered as they mingled with guests in the parlor. "Not today."

"No," Seona agreed with a disappointment he found endearing. "Best we wait."

Spotting Anni and Willa, she drifted over to talk with them. Ian watched her offer Anni a comforting embrace. It tugged a tempered smile, seeing her at last forming friendships among the women of Shiloh. Deeper was a rooted unease. A sense that for all his building and gathering and planning for their future, it could all come crashing down in an instant. All Seona's trust in him turn to disillusion.

"I almost wish we hadna found him," said a voice at his shoulder.

Jarred from his thoughts, Ian turned to see Neil MacGregor with a glass of brandy in hand. Full, as though he had no more than sipped it.

"Better to know than go on wondering."

Neil caught Ian's glance at his glass. "I need to ride out after this, check on Hector Lacey's foot. Best I no' partake—much," he added, taking a sip. "I didna really mean what I said. 'Tis hard watching my lass grieve, is all."

Ian followed Neil's nod down the passage, in full view from the parlor doorway. Maggie stood at the other end, Catriona and Lem hovering. Ian's sister had an arm around Maggie, whose face was marked by weeping.

"Even so," Neil went on, "better she grieves now and find a way past this—for unless my eyes betray me, that young man has eyes for none but her."

With another glance at Lem, oblivious to all but Maggie, Ian asked, "Are ye inclined to favor such a match?"

"If she comes to favor the lad."

"They're young," Ian said.

Neil eyed him with a trace of amusement in his gaze. "And just how old are *ye*, young Cameron? I dinna think I've ever inquired."

"Today I feel fifty."

Far closer to fifty than Ian, Neil arched a brow. "The past days are weighing on me too, but in truth, man—what is your age?"

"Seven and twenty since the spring," Ian said as a group of mourners broke apart in the parlor, revealing Colonel Waring and Matthew in conversation by the hearth. Intense conversation by the angle of their bodies, the furrowing of Matthew's brow. The lad's outrage over Francis's death had been the least contained of anyone's. As well as his suspicion over who was to blame.

Recalling the scene when he and Neil brought Francis down from the mountain, Ian revised *suspicion* to *certainty*. Rather than entertain the notion it might have been an accidental fall, even a bear or a panther to blame—"Francis was too woods-canny for any of that!"—Matthew steadfastly maintained it was the work of their old nemesis, until Neil had commanded him to hold his *wheesht* about Crane and forbidden him to say a word of it in front of his mother and sister.

What Joseph Tames-His-Horse thought about the death, Ian hadn't a clue. While he had backed Neil in attempting to bank Matthew's rage, Joseph had not disagreed with the lad's assessment.

"Now I wonder what that's about?" Neil asked, spotting his son and Elias Waring by the hearth. The Colonel looked aside and caught them watching. The old man nodded, took Matthew by the arm, and steered him their way.

"Matthew tells me you intend riding out to Hector Lacey," Colonel Waring said when they reached the passage, his voice grief-ravaged but controlled. "Thank you both for being here and, again, for bringing Francis home."

"No' as anyone hoped, Colonel," Neil said. "I'm verra sorry for it. We loved him. But aye, I do need to be heading back into the hills to check on my most recalcitrant of patients."

Ian caught Matthew's gaze. The lad looked away but lingered at Waring's side as if he had more to say.

"We'll ride home with ye then, Seona and I," Ian said to Neil.

Waring turned a sorrowful gaze on him. "I hope all is well with you and yours, Mr. Cameron. It would seem your new additions are settling well in Shiloh." The old man shot a look at Seona, seated beside his daughter. "Though I've wondered you haven't spoken to me of changing that one's Miss to a Mrs."

Ian's face warmed. "Aye, sir. I mean to but didn't think today the time."

"Who among us knows what tomorrow will bring?" the Colonel asked. "Let us speak of it before you go."

They had done so, he, Seona, and the Colonel, while Neil and Matthew fetched their horses. A wedding date was set for early October. Colonel Waring agreed to come to the farm to officiate. By then Goodenough, Willa, Catriona, Lem, even Maggie had joined the conversation. All seemed at least to some degree cheered.

Though Catriona had avoided Matthew during the burial, supper, and the ride home to follow, she was solicitous of Maggie and wanted to spend the rest of the day with her. Seona headed inside the MacGregors' house at Maggie's invitation, promising to be back out shortly to ride home with Ian. Meaning to head out to Lacey's isolated cabin, Neil didn't unsaddle Seamus. Matthew volunteered to tend the other horses. "Catriona?" he called as his sister and Ian's mounted the front steps of the house. When Catriona turned back, he asked awkwardly, "I just . . . Do you want me to unsaddle Juturna?"

"I do, thank you," Catriona replied, then went into the house, leaving Matthew staring after her with longing. Schooling his features, he took up the leads of two of the horses and headed toward the stable, from which Joseph Tames-His-Horse emerged.

Willa and Neil frowned after their son. On the ride home, when Neil had asked Matthew what he and Elias Waring had been speaking about by the hearth, Matthew had brushed off the question, saying, "About the horses. A new filly."

"Waring does have a new filly," Neil granted, turning now to Ian. "But ye saw them. Did that look like talk of horses?"

"What talk?" Joseph asked, having come to fetch the other two needing stabling.

Willa took Josephine from the sling she wore and held the baby to her shoulder, gazing worriedly at her clan brother.

"Ian and I noted Matthew and Colonel Waring in a rather intense conversation after the burial today," Neil explained.

A burial which Joseph hadn't dared attend, though he owed his life to Francis. "Did they speak of Crane?"

"We couldn't hear a word," Ian said.

"But it is what you are thinking?" Joseph pressed.

"I fear Matthew will do something rash," Willa said, cupping her daughter's small head. "And if he convinces the Colonel it was Crane killed Francis, there may be two in favor of doing so."

Three, Ian thought, gazing at the tall Mohawk warrior with his jaw set.

"Would you think of leaving now with Matthew?" Willa asked her brother. "Going up to Canada sooner than planned?"

"Aye," Neil said. "That may be best. Get the lad awa' so calmer brains can prevail."

Ian wondered what exactly Neil had in mind for calmer brains to do about the problem of Crane, but Joseph's reply distracted him.

"I do not agree. But I will keep watch on Matthew. Closer than he will like."

Though it was all he said before he led the horses into the stable, it was enough to betray Joseph's concern. For all of Willa's family. None of them would rest easy, Ian feared, until Aram Crane was found and his threat—or the prospect of it—eliminated.

34

The clamor of hammer and saw awakened memories of Mountain Laurel. Malcolm in his cooperage. Ian working in that same shop. Good memories, in the main, but Seona found no comfort in the sound there in Naomi's cabin, planning her wedding with her mama while Naomi minded dinner. The children were outside with Catriona.

The woodworking noises came from the old stable, which Ian had left standing for a shop, with most of the horse boxes removed to make a larger space. Early that morning Joseph and Matthew had arrived, driving a wagonload of seasoned wood for new school furnishings. Undaunted, Maggie meant to reopen her school so long as any parent allowed a child to attend. Catriona would help when the fall session started up, teaching the youngest of Maggie's pupils.

Given how things were between him and Catriona, it surprised Seona that Matthew had come with his uncle.

"He's here for Joseph to keep an eye on," Ian had said, taking her aside.

To prevent his going after Crane. Ever since Francis Waring was found, Seona hadn't been able to shake the sense of being watched or the fear that, lured by rumors of gold, Crane was out there plotting how to get some. Ian planned to use the latest gold from John Reynold to buy fittings for the house he meant to build come spring. For the time being, he had hidden it. Exactly where, she didn't want to know.

She forced her attention back to the gowns spread on Naomi's counterpane. Brought from Boston, they were some of Lily's best work, though none without wear. They were deciding which to smarten up into a wedding gown. Her own sashed green, her mama's blue, or one of Catriona's, a pale-yellow calico.

"Catriona thinks the green." She had worn it only once since leaving Boston—for Francis's burial—and the straw bonnet with its matching ribbon. It was on the thin side for autumn, same as it had been for a March day in Boston. "Maybe add an overskirt cut away with some lace? Or turn my spencer into a pelisse? What do you think, Mama?"

Getting no reply, Seona turned to find Lily gazing out the window. "Mama?"

"What's that, girl-baby?"

Behind them Naomi clanked a spoon against a kettle's rim. "Ain't like you to go woolgathering, Lily."

Seona's mama snatched her gaze from the window. "Thinking I'd take dinner out to them working. If it's ready. As for the gowns," she added, "Catriona's right. Your green is best. Brings out your beautiful eyes. Let me worry about smartening it up. I should look at altering that spencer too. Might be a nippy day, come October."

As Lily moved to the hearth to ladle stew into bowls, Naomi said, "Best get those gowns put up afore hungry babies come tumbling in."

Seona returned each to its rightful cabin. Catriona was at the table with Gabriel and Mandy, dinners before them, when she came back. Seona thanked her for looking after the pair, noting the strain in Catriona's smile. It couldn't be easy, having Matthew there at the farm.

Lily came in from taking dinner to the shop.

"How's Daddy doing over there?" Naomi asked. "Any sign of Ally?"

"Malcolm's watching the work, taking it easy. Don't think Ally's up from the pasture."

Naomi set aside the biggest bowl. "He'll be along. My boy don't miss a meal."

Lily and Seona took over helping the children eat. When Seona's back was turned, cleaning up a spill, Catriona left her dinner untouched and slipped from the cabin.

Naomi turned from the hearth, spied the leavings, and clucked her tongue. "Let that be mine. I'll save the rest in the kettle for Ally. Hand me that bowl."

Though her own appetite wasn't robust, Seona ate what was given her. With the children still working on theirs and Naomi needing water for washing up, she took a bucket to the springhouse, nearer the new stable than the old. She was about to cut through its open doors and down the center aisle to the far door—the shortest route—when she heard voices from within.

"I don't see it at all. Neither do you. You're afraid. I understand."

"You don't, Catriona. You saw one instance—one of the worst, I'll grant—but you cannot know what it's like to live with it every day. I don't want that for you."

"Why not let me decide what *I* want for me?"

"Shiloh isn't the setting of one of your poems, and I'm no 'shepherd of the forest' or any such nonsense. I'm just a man with skin too brown for the liking of most, and there's no changing that."

"I wouldn't change it. Nor anything else about you."

"Catriona—why?"

"Why what?"

"Why do you want me so?"

"You already know. And there's no changing that either. Do you no longer love *me*?"

Matthew muttered something strangled, then . . . silence.

Seona wanted to hear no more of this fraught conversation. Before she could move, Matthew strode from the stable. A glimpse of his face revealed a contortion of unhappiness, laced through with a conflicting satisfaction. He was headed back to Ian's shop, where work had not yet resumed. Seona didn't think he had seen her.

She debated whether to check on Catriona or fetch the water like she was meant to be doing—taking the long way around the stableyard. Before she could decide, Catriona emerged, the corners of her mouth turned up, verging on a smile. As blind to Seona as Matthew had been, she headed for the cabins.

Seona fetched the water, then detoured to the workshop. Malcolm, finished with his dinner, had dozed off on a stack of baled straw inside the shop. Matthew was outside, standing before Joseph and Ian, who were seated on the ground, bowls in hand.

"I'm going, Uncle. Just for the day."

"Hunting for a few hours only?" Joseph stood and looked at the sun, already edging westward. "When you said you would help with these desks for your sister?"

"I'm not helping. If anything, I'm slowing you down." Matthew gestured at the pile of wood still in the wagon's bed. "And you're the one who promised to do it. Not me."

Joseph drilled his nephew with a look. "I promised my sister other things."

"To mind me—as if I were a child? I'm going hunting, Uncle."

Gathering up the bowls, Ian stood and headed toward Seona with an apologetic look. He took the full bucket from her. She took the bowls, about to suggest they leave nephew and uncle to sort things, when a bark announced Ally come up from the pasture, Nip and Tuck bounding ahead.

Inside the shop, Malcolm slept on, snoring softly.

Ally's broad face brightened at sight of the bowls, but he paused to say, "I'll go with you, Matthew, you don't mind me eating dinner first."

Ian set the water bucket down. "Ally, he means to go hunting."

"I heard," Ally said.

"And ye want to go? Why?"

Ally spied his dozing grandfather. "Look there. My granddaddy sleeping in the middle of the day again. It got me thinking, Mister Ian. He won't always be around, telling me how to do."

Seona felt a catch in her throat, glancing at the old man fast asleep. Ally spoke true, but his noticing made it somehow more real.

"I know it," Ian said, not without compassion. "But why does that make ye want to go hunting, of all things?"

Ally sniffed. "Mama be the boss of her kitchen. But she don't know other things. Cabin raising. Cattle tending. I need to know some things my own self."

"I agree," Ian said. "But hunting? Ye know what that means?"

Ally swallowed hard. "Killing critters for the table."

"Have ye even shot a gun?"

"Ain't never pulled a trigger. But when you go off places, you ask Mister Neil or Matthew to mind us. Better maybe I can do the minding when those times come up."

Seona wasn't sure if she was proud of Ally's turn of mind or saddened by the need. Ally didn't know about Aram Crane, but even he sensed something had Ian worried, reluctant to leave them unguarded.

"I don't have a gun to spare ye," Ian said.

"I've a musket you can use, Ally." Matthew turned to Joseph. "I'll teach him to shoot it. That satisfy you?"

Before his uncle could answer, Lily stepped from Naomi's cabin with the children, the pair wiped down for the moment. Spying their parents standing outside the shop, they came running. Gabriel collided with his daddy's knees before Ian swooped him up and held him upside down. While her brother whooped and chortled, Mandy came to Seona, who knelt to hug the little girl close.

Next she knew, Matthew and Ally were trudging off to Naomi's cabin, collies trailing. Joseph watched them go, shared a look with Ian, then pulled a plank of wood off the wagon's bed.

"Where are those two headed?" Lily asked.

"Going hunting, looks like," Seona said.

Lily's mouth dropped open. "*Ally?* Why not Joseph?"

"Joseph usually does some needful thing for Willa's family," Ian explained, "before he and Matthew leave for their long hunt. This time it's desks for Maggie's school. He's keeping his promise."

Lily gazed at Joseph, who had laid the plank over sawhorses inside the shop and was speaking to Malcolm, who had stirred from his nap. "He's a good brother," she said, then turned when the collies barked.

Ally, outside the cabin with a bowl in hand, wolfing down his stew, was talking to Nip and Tuck between bites, telling them they had to stay put so he could go off with Matthew and learn to hunt. The news wasn't going over well with either dog.

"I don't think they've ever been parted from him," Lily said. "We're going to have to tie those dogs to keep them home."

"Come on, babies," Seona said as Ian swung Gabriel to his feet and Lily took up the water bucket. "Let's go help Nip and Tuck be good dogs."

She stood. Ian kissed her briefly, bent to ruffle Mandy's hair, then went back to work. The rest trooped to Naomi's cabin, Seona wondering what, if anything, Ally would bring back from his first hunting trip.

On his way into Shiloh to visit several patients in need of doctoring, Neil came out to Ian as he was looping Ruaidh's reins over the MacGregors' paddock fence. The early morning was made the darker for a bank of clouds promising rain. Neil hailed him from the porch, but upon reaching Ian, his smile faded. "There's trouble in your look."

"Where's Matthew?" Ian asked.

"Gone back into the hills. Joseph's saddling up to go fetch him. I've a patient to see else I'd be riding too."

"How long has he been gone?"

"Willa and I didna even see him last night after he and Ally returned, he was gone again so quick." Neil paused, scrutinizing Ian. "Ally did come back?"

Ian nodded. "Ally's fine. It's only . . . I know why Matthew's gone back out."

"Hunting?" Neil asked hopefully.

"Not for meat." And now Ian was kicking himself for not riding straight to Neil late last night after Ally confessed what he had seen on the ridge with Matthew.

It was past sundown before Ally returned, having learned to shoot the musket Matthew lent him but with nothing to show for it. It had been like pulling teeth to get that much from him. Then Ian had asked what proved the vital question, whether Matthew had made a kill. They had been out in the stable with only a pair of lanterns for light, but Ian had seen the sweat bead up on Ally's forehead as he brushed Cupid, settling her for the night.

"Made a kill? Can't say as he done *that*."

Ian had stepped closer. "What did he do?"

Frowning at his big hand dwarfing the currying brush, Ally had worked his lips over his teeth, as if holding back words piling up on his tongue. "Mister Ian . . . I done promised."

"Promised what?"

"To keep it secret."

Alarm bells rang. "Ally, if there's something going on with Matthew, ye'd best tell me."

Ally's gaze pleaded. "Matthew gonna be mad."

"He can be mad at *me* because I need ye to tell me what's going on."

"Sound like maybe you know."

"I've an idea. If I'm right, there's danger here. For us all. Please, Ally."

In a rush of clear relief at the telling, Ally had spilled it all, and now Ian had to tell Matthew's father.

"They came across a rough camp about a mile north of your boundary stone. Matthew made Ally stay back while he wrecked it. Slashed a canvas, some bedding. Bashed in a pot or two. Scattered everything. Matthew wouldn't say whose camp it was. Not to Ally. Ye think it was Crane's?"

"Of course it was," Joseph said behind them, come from the stable in time to hear the tale. "Or Matthew thought so."

"He'd do no such thing to anyone else's camp." Color rushed into Neil's face and his jaw set hard. "The wee *gomeral.* He ought to have told us of it rather than provoking the man. What does he think he's doing now?"

"Flushing him out," Joseph said, his gaze on Ian. "It is not the worst idea, rather than waiting for Crane to make some move against one of us."

Neil huffed in frustration. "And I canna even ride wi' ye."

"I'll go," Ian said, after weighing the need to get Crane in his sights against keeping his farm and family safe. Surely doing the first would best guarantee the latter. "Ally told me how to find the camp. If ye'll have me," he added to Joseph.

"I will," the warrior said.

Before the portended rain fell, they found the ruined camp as Ally had described it. The better tracker, Joseph Tames-His-Horse scouted its edges while Ian waited with the horses, observing through the trees. The warrior moved with care, working his way outward around the camp's periphery. Even without the destruction Matthew had overlaid, Crane—or whoever—had camped there long enough to trample the area with coming and going.

Finally Joseph found a fresh trail heading northward. Whose, Joseph couldn't say. They followed it, leading their horses, Ian coming behind.

Having converged with one of the countless game trails crisscrossing the terrain, they were climbing slantwise up a wooded ridge when Joseph's mare kicked loose a stone. It rolled to the trail's edge, colliding with something that sprang out of the leaf mulch with startling violence. The dun mare shied on the slope, nearly losing its footing before Joseph calmed the animal.

Thinking it a snake, Ian called, "Are ye bit? Or the horse?"

Joseph crouched to run a hand over his horse's foreleg before turning to see what the stone had disturbed. "Not a snake."

Ian brought his horse forward and knelt, rifle planted on the trail. The thing lay there still, metal jaws closed. A sinister sight for all that. "Wolf trap."

Rain began to fall. Fat drops pattered through the changing leaves of birch and maple, the needles of cedar and fir. One hit Ian's hand, fisted around the rifle. While he covered the firing mechanism to protect it from the rain, Joseph took up a stick and scanned the ground around the sprung trap. Ian saw his gaze chill before he strode ahead a few paces and, with the stick, sprang a second trap set at the trail's edge, where man or horse might in a moment have stepped.

"How did Matthew miss them?" Ian asked, still searching the ground.

"I know how—and where—Crane sets his traps," said a voice above them.

Ian shot to his feet, holding tight to rifle and lead. Matthew MacGregor stood on the lip of the ridge, looking down at them. The noise of the rain had covered his approach. It was falling still, beading in their horses' manes.

"I knew Ally wouldn't keep it secret," Matthew called. "Thought he'd last a bit longer than this."

"I forced it from him," Ian called back, looking for a way up to the lad, finding none Ruaidh could navigate. Little more than twice a man's height, the ridge was nearly sheer, dangling the ends of roots where it wasn't choked with browning ferns.

"You have seen Crane?" Joseph asked, cutting to the point. "Or are you only guessing these traps are his?"

"I haven't, but I know it, Uncle."

"What of Hector Lacey?" Ian asked, moisture hitting his lifted face. "He's out in these hills living half-wild."

"I thought of that," Joseph said. "Lacey is in no shape for running a line unless that wounded foot has healed."

"You know it's Crane," Matthew called down.

Joseph raised his gaze. "I know you are foolish to go after him alone!"

Even yards below, Ian could see Matthew's jaw set. "I'm not doing this because I want to—not just. I was asked to do it, the day we buried Francis."

"Colonel Waring?" Ian minded the conversation he and Neil had observed. "*He* asked ye to find Crane?"

"He did. And before you say it, Uncle, I know you and Pa told me to leave it be, but that's as dangerous. For both our families," Matthew added, including Ian in his indignant gaze. "Crane's after your gold—or the gold he thinks you have. That's why he's back here."

There was gold now. Ian had hidden it—not in the cabins nor in any structure on the farm. He had scouted the beech grove until he found one with a crevice near its base. After assuring himself it was no nesting creature's home, he had placed the gold inside an old inkwell, corked it, wrapped that in oiled canvas, then put it inside the tree.

"That is not the only reason," Joseph countered his nephew's assertion. "You said yourself Francis saw him here last autumn. Crane did not follow this one to Cherry Valley, probably did not learn of his connection to Shiloh until spring."

"So we surmise," Matthew said. The rain was falling harder, darkening the shoulders of their hunting shirts. "Colonel Waring's still eaten up with guilt over harboring the man, giving him work, never knowing what he was. He wants him found."

"Did ye tell him it was Crane killed his son?" Ian asked.

"I told him what Francis said he saw. He reached the conclusion on his own. And so you know, Uncle, that trail you're following doubles back in about a quarter mile. It's a ruse."

Joseph nodded, unsurprised. "A thing Crane would do. Have you found a better trail?"

"No. Just a few more traps like those."

Joseph muttered something Ian missed with the rain's swelling patter, then called to his nephew, "Find a safe way down so we need not shout."

If the lad replied, Ian didn't hear it. His mind had juddered to a halt on *Just a few more traps like those.* How many more were scattered over these hills? Were there any laid closer to their farms? A horrifying image of little legs clamped between bloody metal jaws made him weak-kneed with thankfulness that Gabriel and Mandy weren't old enough to roam far. But anyone might step in such a trap laid on a well-used trail.

Ye canna see every trouble coming nor shield us from all suffering. No man can. Words spoken that morning filled his soul with dread rather than the comfort they were meant to convey.

Up early to ride to the MacGregors, he had led Ruaidh from the stable to find Malcolm wrapped in a quilt, sitting at a fire kindled in the yard. Unable to sleep, not wanting to disturb Ally and Naomi, he had come outside to read his Bible by firelight. Ian had given half an explanation for why he was off to their neighbors at such an hour—it was to do with Matthew.

Malcolm had merely nodded at that and dropped his gaze to his open Bible.

It had been too long since they read from the Scriptures together. Since Ian had even opened his Bible. "How far have ye gotten?"

"This morning I'm reading from Galatians."

"I thought ye were deep in the Old Testament still. Never tell me ye've skipped ahead?"

"No." Malcolm's teeth gleamed in the firelight, while in the east the heavy-clouded sky was graying. "I'm reading both. Old Testament at night. New in the morning. Like God's mercies."

"Seems fitting." Ian wondered if Malcolm was feeling pressed to hurry things along. "Would ye read me a bit, wherever ye happen to be?"

Malcolm tilted the Bible in knobby hands to catch the fire's gleam, then shut the book. "I was setting a verse to memory. Let's see have I got it. 'Stand fast therefore in the liberty wherewith Christ has made us free, and be not entangled again with a yoke of bondage.'" He grinned. "That sounded right."

"Bondage," Ian echoed, searching the old man's face, seamed with age and firelight.

"No' the sort under which I once labored. To my thinking, Paul's talking here about being justified by what a man does, rather than by faith in Christ Jesus. The bondage of works."

What a man does. But a man had to do for his own. Didn't Scripture also say a man who didn't do so was worse than an unbeliever? Where did responsibility end and a yoke of bondage begin? Ian had grasped the saddle and nearly mounted, but an overwhelming heaviness stopped him.

"Pray for me, Malcolm," he said.

Behind him Malcolm said, "That I do, daily. There something particular ye wanting me to speak wi' the Almighty about this morning?"

He hadn't told Malcolm about Aram Crane. Had Seona confided in him? If so, he had no need to explain. If not, he hadn't the time. "I'm all but sure there is. Though it's a muddle in my head just now."

"That's all right. The Almighty has it straight." Ian had swung into the saddle before the old man said those words still haunting him now: "Ye canna see every trouble coming nor shield us from all suffering. No man can."

But a man must see what he can and deal with it, he had argued silently on the ride to the MacGregors'. Hope that he had only imagined Aram Crane circling his family, a wolf beyond the firelight's bleeding edge, had died. The man was out there, and he must deal with it.

When Ruaidh ruckled a breath, Ian looked up to see Matthew making his way down to them. Joseph had turned his horse back the way they had come and taken up the sprung traps. Careful where he stepped, Ian turned the roan back as well. "I'm heading home. Hunting traps on the way. What will ye do?"

Joseph secured the traps across his saddle. "The same—and tie that one to this horse if that is what it takes to bring him back with us." He nodded at Matthew, coming along, scanning the ground, then held Ian's gaze. "But soon you and I must hunt for more than traps."

35

Ian had lain awake half the night, worry writhing in his gut, distress fisted around his heart. The worry was Crane. The heart squeeze was Seona. Alone in his cabin while the rain made a drumming on the shingled roof, he had told her of the camp Matthew ruined, the traps he and Joseph found. "Aram Crane's, we think."

Seona had clasped her arms across her middle and paced his cabin—as well as one might a space crowded with bed frames and trunks. The fire he had poked to life in the hearth crackled like the tension in the air.

"What does it mean? He's trapping game? Trapping *us*?" She faced him, cheeks drained of color. "Ian, our babies play at that wood's edge."

Seeing on her stricken face the vision he had had at sight of metal jaws beside the trail, he crossed the cabin, meaning to take her in his arms. She stepped back, warning him off with a hand.

"How close were those traps? Did you find them all?"

"They were a mile and more up in the hills. And no, I cannot say we found them all." He knew they hadn't.

"How can we live, afraid to step past the cabin-yard? This doesn't feel like freedom to me. This feels like . . ."

Bondage. She didn't say it, but he heard it clear. Thoughts whirled like dust devils, battering his heart with accusation.

"If it's Crane, I'll find him. But I cannot go haring off to comb the hills for a man who might be hiding in a hundred places, leaving my work undone and ye unguarded."

She looked, if anything, more frightened by his reassurance. "You can't guard everyone every moment of the day. Beside, you let a canebrake into the dairy shed, you don't go on milking. You root it out, kill it afore it strikes."

The mention of snakes jarred. As did her not so subtle laying of blame. Aram Crane might have returned to harass the MacGregors had Ian never set foot in Cooperstown with his gold to tempt the man, but he had let this threat into *her* world. No one else.

"I intend to, Seona. I'm not the only one wants the man caught. Joseph means to hunt him."

"Then let Joseph go after Crane. You stay out of it."

"Did ye not just say ye *wanted* me to go after the man?"

"I did . . . just don't go getting killed on top of everything. I don't want to be a widow afore I'm married!"

That made no sense. He had started to say so, but she fled the cabin, out into the rain. He had let her go. Neither of them was in a fit frame of mind for reasoned discourse. She hadn't said it, not in so many words, but he couldn't deny Seona was doubting him. And her choice to come to Shiloh?

The rain had let up soon after. Ally had headed down to the lower pasture to check on the cattle. At dusk he returned, saying the herd was uneasy. "Think a panther may be creeping round out there. Best I keep watch? I got that musket Matthew lent me."

Thinking it as likely a man doing the creeping as a critter, he had told Ally to bring the herd to the upper paddock. "The collies will let us know if anything troubles overnight."

Nip and Tuck hadn't sounded an alarm. No noises but the ordinary reached Ian from beyond the cabin as he lay staring at the roof's underbelly. When the window showed a hint of dawn, he rose and slipped on boots and coat, thinking to make a start on the school furnishings. Perhaps when Joseph arrived, he would be ready to load the wagon and head into Shiloh.

He paused beside Mandy's bed. Sight of his daughter's sleeping face, lit by dawn's half-light, so hollowed him with dread he hurled a prayer heavenward. *God Almighty . . . help me keep them safe.*

He took up a lantern, unlit, and opened the cabin door. Across the yard a growl arose. A low voice hushed it.

Ian exchanged lantern for rifle and shut the door softly. Above the trees the eastern sky had paled. With the rain cleared, the sky nearly cloudless, he discerned Ally standing in the yard, collies at his knees. All three staring toward the stable.

Ian heard what had alerted them. The kick of more than one hoof against timber. Muffled whickers.

"Something there," Ally said at his approach. "Horses troubled."

Ian cocked his rifle. "Keep the dogs back. We don't want them tangling with anything." *Beast or man,* he didn't add.

On their way to the stable they passed the smokehouse. Its door hung open, latch pried clean off. "Ain't no critter done that," Ally whispered as they paused, a dog tucked under each big arm, ears trained toward the stable as they squirmed to get free.

"Hold them, Ally. I'm going ahead." A warbler commenced a terse *twitchety-twitch* call in the beeches as he started along the paddock fence behind the smokehouse. The stable's lines grew clear in the coming dawn. Its doors were open.

A ringing whinny cut the air—Ruiadh's. Then Ian was running full out, rifle at the ready, boots thudding the earth, and nearly collided with the figure that bolted from the stable as he reached it. It was light enough to discern the bearded face seared into his mind since Cherry Valley.

"Crane!" he shouted, staggering as he whirled to follow the man fleeing through the beech grove. Toward Seona's cabin.

Fear sped his feet, but Crane didn't pause at the cabin. He ran flat out toward the harvested field studded with cornstalk sheaves, its farthest reaches shrouded in a mist drifting off the lake. As Ian reached the field, the collies streaked past him, vanishing between the sheaves. The light was swelling, but the mist lay low and creeping. Crane was lost to sight as Ian churned his way over broken ground, half-tripping on scythed stubs of stalks yet to be plowed back into the soil.

Ahead came a snarl. A high-pitched yelp. Behind came a pounding.

"No!" Ally cried as they came upon the dogs, one on the ground, the other milling about, nosing his brother. In that light Ian couldn't tell them apart.

"Stay with them, Ally!" Ian ran on, hoping it was in the right direction. Catching movement to his left—Crane darting into the pines that grew between field and lakeshore—he corrected his course but hadn't reached the trees before a rifle shot cracked. By instinct he flung himself behind the last sheave, though he saw Crane drop. Hit? Or taking cover?

Not hit. Crane was up again, staggering into the trees as Joseph Tames-His-Horse came out of the gray, bearing down from the north end of the lake.

"Hie, Joseph! I'm with ye," Ian called, but Joseph was intent on his quarry, who had reached a horse left hidden in the trees. Crane was mounted before Joseph reached him. Using his spent rifle as a club, the warrior came at the mounted man.

Ian didn't see where Crane had the long knife stowed. There was no outcry, save Crane's urging the horse into a gallop, leaving Joseph on his knees, clutching an arm. As Ian reached him, the warrior lurched to his feet. They looked after Crane, but Ian didn't get his rifle raised and aimed before mist swallowed man and mount, as they vanished toward the ridge.

"Let him go," Ian said on winded breath, hating the taste of the words as he lowered the rifle and turned back to Joseph. "Ye're hurt."

Joseph took his hand from his torn shirtsleeve. Red bloomed in alarming abundance.

Ally came out of the mist, a collie cradled in his arms. "Mister Ian, Tuck's hurt. I gotta get him to Lily!"

"Joseph's hurt as well!" Ian hollered back.

"Neil will tend it," Joseph said through his teeth and started back around the lake.

"Ally!" Ian shouted before he followed Willa's brother. "I'm going with Joseph. Keep watch 'til I get back."

Seona bolted upright in bed, a gun's report echoing in her ears. She reached for her mama to find Lily swinging her feet to the puncheon floor. Seona scrambled out of bed and went to Gabriel, awake and blinking. "Mama . . . ?"

"That was over by the lake," Lily said, crossing to the window to peer into the gray.

"One of the MacGregor boys hunting geese?" Seona hefted Gabriel into her arms. "There, baby. It's all right."

"I hear shouting from over that way," Lily said.

"Take him, Mama. I'm going to see." Seona pried loose Gabriel's clinging arms, then grabbed up her shawl and hurried out, feet bare on cold ground, hair curling loose down her back.

"Take care, Seona!"

Lily's admonition trailed her into the yard, where other voices met her. Naomi and Catriona, holding Mandy, had come out of their cabins to look off toward the lake. Naomi started her way. "What on earth? Ally!"

Seona rounded her cabin to see Ally coming at a run from the cornfield, something cradled against his broad chest. One of the collies raced ahead, streaking past her into the yard. The sun's first light hit Ally as he cleared the sheaves.

"Lily! *Help.*"

Seona turned back, saw Malcolm in his cabin doorway. Catriona, Mandy, Naomi. Everyone but . . . "Where's Ian?"

Ally halted in the yard with his armful of bleeding collie. "Mister Ian helping Joseph!"

"Joseph?" Lily had come outside, Gabriel on her hip.

Naomi reached them. "Boy of mine, you tell what's happening and tell it straight."

Ally sucked in a breath, big arms trembling. "We catched a Crane sneaking round, Mama—me and Mister Ian, Nip, and Tuck. Or that's what Mister Ian called the man. We run him off into the field and went after. Collies got him first. He cut up Tuck afore we got to 'em.

Then Joseph popped up from somewhere and shot at the Crane, but I reckon the Crane cut him too. Ian's gone with him for Mister Neil to stitch up. But, Lily, you got to patch Tuck!"

Seona was too stunned to move. "Aram Crane? He was *here*?"

"Who we talking about?" Naomi demanded, staring from one face to another. "Am I the only one don't know?"

A glance told Seona she might well be. Catriona's gaze held knowledge of the man. So did her mama's and Malcolm's. Seona guessed Maggie had told Ian's sister. How her mama and Malcolm found out about Crane, she didn't know. And who knew about the gold now?

"How badly is he injured?" Lily asked. "Joseph, I mean."

Ally shook his head. "Don't know. But *Tuck* . . ."

Though she looked torn between helping the dog and racing off after Ian and Joseph, Lily swung Gabriel to his feet. "Bring him inside, Ally; put him on the table. Catriona, light some candles."

Catriona passed Mandy to Naomi to do as Lily bade. Everyone else hovered in the cabin doorway while Ally held his collie and Lily examined the wound. Though she heard Catriona explaining to Naomi who Aram Crane was, distantly aware that no one else seemed to know what cause the man had for snooping around their place, Seona kept hold of the children, crouched inside the door, watching her mama work.

"Mister Ian bid me keep watch on everyone," Ally said while Lily parted the fur on Tuck's flank, following the bleeding gash. He raised pained eyes. "It bad?"

"It's clean, not too deep. A few stitches and a cleaning will do. Hold him now."

With the wound stitched, Tuck was able to limp out of the cabin. Ally went out with his dogs and his grandfather to discover the extent of Crane's meddling.

"Lord help us . . . guess we still need breakfast," Naomi said and went out, too, leaving Seona and the children in the cabin.

"Where's Catriona?" Seona asked, having no idea when she had slipped away.

"Dressing, no doubt," Lily said. "We best do the same."

Seona stared at a spatter of Tuck's blood on the table, another smear across her mama's nightshift. Mandy and Gabriel clung to her shaking knees. Lily, she realized, had asked no questions about Aram Crane.

"Mama, you knew—about Crane and the gold?"

"Joseph told me—I overheard talk between him and Neil MacGregor whilst I was there, so I asked. I'm guessing Ian has it hid somewhere?"

Seona nodded. "He was here, Mama—that man. I hoped at least on the farm we were . . ." She glanced down at the wide-eyed children clutching her shift. *Safe,* she didn't add.

Petticoat tied, Lily fastened a short gown. Still barefoot, she crossed to the table and took up her simples box. Instead of putting it away, she clutched it, staring at nothing.

"Mama . . . what is it?"

Lily looked up, worry in her gaze. "Maybe I should go."

Seona couldn't believe her ears. "To the MacGregors'? With that man out there lurking?"

"Bad man, Mama?" Mandy asked.

"The bad man huht Tuck!" Gabriel said, little brows drawn fierce over frightened eyes.

Seona put a hand on each of their heads, but dread made her voice shrill. "Neil's tending Joseph, Mama—you heard Ally. And you can't go off alone."

The cabin door opened. Ian's sister came in, dressed for riding. "I've saddled Juturna. Come with me, Lily. Nothing will catch us on her."

"It's time to end this, Pa!"

Neil MacGregor, intent on his work in a room off the kitchen that served for a surgery, calmly stitched the gash down Joseph Tames-His-Horse's left arm, while Matthew argued for riding after Aram Crane.

"How long will we let that wretch roam free to kill and maim?"

"Your uncle is hardly maimed," Willa, watching the procedure, said. "It is but a scratch." Despite her words—no doubt in part for the benefit of Jamie and Liam, crowded into the surgery door—tension weighed the look she shot Joseph, seated bare-chested on the examining table.

Matthew turned to Ian, standing inside the door, hands stained with blood. "Will Ally come with us?"

"He has his hands full with his wee dog. Crane wounded it." He hoped that was all.

"Matthew's right, Pa," Jamie said, looking scared but determined. "We gotta do something."

"Liam and Jamie," Willa said, "there is work in the stable waiting. Go see to it."

"Aw, Mama . . . ," Liam moaned, but his brother caught him by the arm and towed him away.

Joseph inspected the long row of sutures down his arm. "You are done?"

"Stitching, aye." Hands as bloodied as Ian's, Neil set aside a basin and red-stained cloths. "But sit ye still, big man. I mean to make a dressing and wrap the worst of it."

"Dress it, then let's *go*," Matthew said, taking up his brothers' post at the door.

An infant's hungry wail heralded Maggie's appearance, baby Josephine at her shoulder. "Somebody wants her mama." She winced as her red-faced sister squalled in her ear. "And I hope you don't mean to go *any*where," she added, fixing brother, uncle, and neighbor in a sweeping glance. "I mean to set up my school cabin—if not today, then tomorrow. You've yet to finish the desks. I've covered the window, but there's the door needing rehung."

Sharing a look with Neil, Willa took the baby and left the room to tend her. As the cries diminished, Ian noted Maggie's face, grief-lined but set with purpose.

Sympathy tempered Matthew's scowl. "Maggie . . . hold off opening the school. Let us catch this villain first. It's dangerous—"

"Of course it is," Maggie cut in. "But we can't stop living our lives. Catriona and I don't intend to. We're going to teach. I need desks and a door that fastens to do so."

"I'm no' as handy wi' a hammer as these two, *mo nighean*," her father said, nodding at Joseph and Ian. "But if my help can speed them along, ye have it."

How long was it, Ian wondered, since Neil had seen such a spark in his daughter's eyes? There could be no question of quenching it.

Maggie's smile was a candle's flaring. "I know, Papa. But weren't you saying just last night you meant to ride out to check on old Mr. Lacey?"

"Aye," Neil said with a wave. "Tomorrow, most like. I could help today."

"You've other patients." Maggie caught her brother's gaze. "Please, Matthew. Will *you* help them?"

Matthew compressed his lips, then loosed an exasperated sigh. "All right, but then—"

"Then," Neil said, fixing his son with an uncompromising stare, "ye'll go to Colonel Waring and get his blessing to raise as many men as will ride wi' ye to go after Crane. The more the better."

Matthew's scowl descended. "Pa . . ."

"Satahonhsatat," Joseph said in so commanding a tone Ian would have obeyed it had he grasped the word's meaning.

Matthew understood it. Still scowling, he gave a jerky nod. "I'll saddle the horses."

He strode from the surgery as the last person Ian expected to see entered—Lily, with her simples box. Looking past her, Ian asked, "Has Seona come?" He didn't want her seeing Joseph's wound. She was already terrified of Crane. How was she now, knowing the man had trespassed on their farm?

Lily shook her head, taking in the gash down Joseph's arm. "Aram Crane did that to ye?"

"He's survived worse," Neil said as Joseph reached for his bloodied shirt, crumpled on the table beside him. "I've sutured it, as ye can see. I mean to apply—"

"Honey dressing's good," Lily blurted, still clutching her box. As all gazes settled on her, she lowered hers. "Ally said ye were injured, Joseph. I didn't know how badly."

"Tsigalili." A corner of Joseph's mouth lifted as he raised his injured arm a few inches, the only evidence of the pain it caused a tightening around his mouth. "You see I am well enough."

The use of Lily's Cherokee name caught Ian off guard, but Maggie asked, "Did you come alone, Lily, or is Catriona with you?"

"We rode together," Lily said. "I don't think she came into the house."

"I'll find her." Brightening, Maggie went out in search of Ian's sister.

"Though I dinna suppose ye'll pay me heed," Neil was telling Joseph as he brought out honey from a cabinet, herbs to mix with it, "ye'd do well to give that arm a day or two to start mending before ye set your hands to anything reckless."

Lily glanced at Ian, question in her gaze. Thinking it best not to discuss the particulars of hunting their dangerous quarry in front of Seona's mother, he nodded at Joseph. "Ye'll find me in the shop. Take your time, aye?"

It was Seona he needed to speak to now.

Ian left the surgery as Lily inquired about the herbs Neil meant to mix with the honey. He found Maggie in the parlor, turning from the window. "Did ye find my sister?"

"She's in the stable. They brought your horse for you."

Ian frowned as Maggie headed toward the kitchen. With Seona on his mind, he went out to where Ruaidh was hitched but had barely reached the roan before he heard them.

"Let Joseph go after Crane," Catriona was saying, voice carrying from the stable's depths. "He caught the man once. He will again."

"We're already losing a day," Matthew said. "Pa says I must go to Colonel Waring and round up others for the hunt. Crane's trail will be cold. Don't you want the man caught?"

"Not at the expense of another life. Especially yours."

When Matthew spoke again, tenderness blunted his words. "I shouldn't matter to you."

His sister laughed. "But you do. And I'll not tire of saying it. I'm going in. Maggie and I have planning to do. You'll help Ian and Joseph finish the desks?"

"I said I would, though I think it's a mistake, opening the school now."

"If you're so worried, ride in with us and stand guard."

Matthew's voice was a low growl. "Catriona . . ."

But his sister had said all she meant to on the matter. Ian was still standing at his stirrup when she swept out of the stable, shawl about her shoulders, hair in a swinging braid. She saw him, stopped, then with a look of resolution crossed the stable-yard. "I suppose you heard that?"

"Most of it, I think."

She registered his lack of surprise. "You've been talking with Seona."

"Listen, Catriona—"

"No, Ian. You listen. I'm not who I was in Boston, and Matthew certainly isn't—"

"I *know*," Ian said, stopping her before she worked herself into a lather. "And for what it's worth, ye've my blessing, the two of ye. If God wills it."

Catriona opened her mouth, still on the verge of arguing. His words must have sunk in finally, for tears welled and she threw her arms around his neck. "Oh, Ian. I hope He does! And Matthew too."

Ruaidh waited patiently as Ian patted his sister's back. "If he has a scrap of sense in his stubborn head, he will. Matthew, I mean," he added as she pulled from the embrace. "Have ye written to Da and Mam?"

"I didn't see the point—yet. The day will come." She seemed to will the smile she gave him before heading for the house.

She didn't look back, didn't glimpse Matthew retreating into the stable's shadow, as Ian did when he turned to mount his horse.

36

It was late in the day before they completed the furnishings for the school. Matthew helped, smoothing the finished pieces with a rubbing of fine creek sand. In the afternoon Malcolm came out with his Bible to read while they worked. It was then Joseph asked about Mountain Laurel. "You spoke of your uncle and the farm he owned, that those with you—" he nodded at Malcolm, seated nearby—"were enslaved until you brought them north. Is it true Seona and Tsigalili were also enslaved?"

"It is," Ian said, wondering if Joseph knew more than he let on. "Hugh Cameron, my half uncle, was Seona's grandfather. His son, Aidan—Seona's father—died before she was born."

"Your uncle did not free his granddaughter?"

"He did, Lily with her. Just before Gabriel's birth, a few months before his own death. The day after I buried my uncle, Seona and Lily left for Boston to live with my parents."

"And this Aidan?" Joseph asked after a pause. "What was he to Seona's mother?"

Ian understood the concern behind the question. "By all accounts he loved her. He wanted her freed. He didn't live long enough to see it through."

"He wanted us all freed, did Aidan Cameron." They turned to Malcolm, who had stopped his reading to join the conversation. "But

Aidan was done to death by a wicked man, and we stayed in bondage, 'til the Almighty sent another with a heart like his."

Yet Ian's plans, like Aidan's, had been thwarted. "Seona and I were handfasted without the knowledge of my kin. I'd intended to see her free and safe to Boston, where I meant to join her, but she was snatched off the plantation and sold to strangers. I was made to believe she'd run from me, rejecting my plan to free her. By the time we found her again and I learned the truth—and that she carried my child—I'd already wed Judith, thinking to remain at Mountain Laurel, become my uncle's heir."

Joseph's expression remained unreadable. "The wife you took, she gave you the little daughter."

"Aye," Ian said, the grief still there but no longer near the surface. "We'd another wee girl who didn't live. And a son who died with his mother. Afterward, I came north. To Boston first. To Seona and Gabriel."

Joseph eyed Malcolm again. "You and your kin chose to stay with him?"

Malcolm nodded. "We might've kept to Boston, but farming is what we ken, no' a city crammed full to bursting with folk."

Joseph gave a shudder. "It is better you are here, Grandfather. And good," he added, addressing Ian, "that you and Tsigalili's daughter are to be joined at last. But when I arrived today, I saw she was much worried."

"Can you blame her?" Matthew cut in from across the shop, pausing his sanding.

While Ian had been watching Joseph's arm being stitched, Ally and Malcolm had discovered the extent of Crane's intrusion. After the man had broken into the smokehouse, undoubtedly in a search for gold, he had moved on to the corncrib and springhouse before trying the stable. While Seona minded the children, the rest had spent the morning setting things to rights until Joseph arrived with Matthew. Now Ian ignored the younger man's question and gestured at the pile of furnishings. "It's too late today for getting all this into Shiloh *and* getting the work there done," he added, knowing the pronouncement would strain Matthew's patience. "We'll load the wagon now. Catriona and I will be at your door at first light tomorrow."

Matthew and Maggie would accompany them, Matthew to ride to Colonel Waring while the girls saw the school sorted and Ian returned the emptied wagon to the farm. Matthew would escort the girls home. That was the plan.

"Then you and I have a man to catch," Joseph said.

"*We* do, Uncle." Matthew hoisted a bench and took it out to the wagon, while Ian began tidying the shop.

Malcolm headed for his cabin, from whence supper smells wafted. Joseph watched him go. "Once you have finished in Shiloh," he said, voice low, "hurry back. I will meet you and we will go after our enemy."

Arrested in sweeping sawdust, Ian asked, "Did ye not agree to Neil's plan?"

Joseph's gaze was firm. "He is cunning, that one we hunt. All his traps are set for men now. It would be unwise for many unknowing of his ways to go into those hills searching. But that one—" he nodded after Matthew—"should do as his father bade. While he is doing it, you and I will go after Crane."

"He'll be angry."

"But alive." Joseph's attention shifted past Ian, who turned to see Seona silhouetted in the doorway, fingers knotted in her shawl.

"What about you both?"

Ian couldn't read her shadowed face, but her tone was clear enough. Would they survive the hunt for Crane?

"I will help shift these things," Joseph said and hefted one of the narrow writing tables, biting back a hiss as it bumped his stitched wound. He had taken only willow bark for the pain.

"Ye and Matthew stay for supper," Ian called after him. "I can smell Naomi's cooking. Or maybe it's Lily's tonight."

Joseph halted in the shop's doorway—to refuse the invitation, Ian thought at first. Then he smiled, showing teeth bright against his skin. "I will stay."

When he was gone, Ian put aside the broom and crossed to Seona, whose eyes were full of the same dread that had his own heart gripped.

"We need to talk, Seona."

Seona found her mama after supper, sitting outside their cabin on a bench, stitching on what was to be her wedding gown. She had just given Gabriel a bath inside, as Catriona was doing for Mandy in Ian's cabin. Gabriel had run off wet-headed to his auntie and sister, warned not to dirty himself before bedtime.

Though Matthew hadn't stayed for supper, Joseph's pretty dun mare grazed in their paddock. Ian was likely still talking with him and Malcolm in Naomi's cabin. How long she would have alone with her mama, she didn't know, so she came straight at what she wanted to say.

"Mama, do you see any way we could go back to Boston?"

Lily jerked her head up and gasped—at what had just come out of her mouth, Seona thought, but turned out her mama had pricked a fingertip. She whipped it to her lips before spotting the gown with blood.

Seona had been drawing blood left and right, starting with Ian's before the supper she hadn't been able to eat, not after the conversation that had curdled her belly. The worst of it kept running through her mind, what they had said to each other after she pleaded with Ian not to follow Joseph's plan to go after Crane, just the two of them.

"I know ye're afraid," he had said, having led her to that very spot outside her cabin, away from listening ears. "Joseph knows the man's ways better than anyone. I trust him."

"We barely know Joseph!"

"Then for the love of . . . ," Ian had begun, only to continue more calmly. "Trust *me*, Seona. Ye must have, back in spring, to have come to me here."

She had stood twisting the ring he had put on her finger—*I Am My Beloved's*—while a wedge of geese flew over, heading for the lake, calling to each other. A sound that made her think of Mountain Laurel and plans gone awry. She stiffened when Ian touched her, then told him the one thing she had meant never to speak aloud. "I don't know anymore why I did."

The words had cut him deep. She had seen the color leave his face, the guilt and anguish fill it. "I cannot do enough to give ye peace, can I?"

Now her mama laid the needle aside, dangling from its thread. "Go back to wandering the wilderness when the Almighty gave us Canaan? Ye think nothing evil ever happens in Boston? Catriona might say different."

"Mama, this isn't the Promised Land. And I can't eat or sleep for fear of it."

"Aram Crane will be dealt with. Joseph and Ian—"

"What if it goes the other way," she cut in, "and Crane deals with them? We ought to have stayed back east, found a way to live, us three, like you wanted. Or maybe I should've let Mister Robert have his way?"

Lily was frowning and not in concern. "Seona, d'ye hear yourself talking? Forget Boston or any other place and scheme. Look around ye at where ye're standing. This farm is a gift to shelter and sustain ye. Work for your hands with no overseer to drive ye or your children into the ground. Look at that rise of land yonder and that pretty tree where Ian means to build a home to suit your every need."

Seona didn't look. "It could all vanish tomorrow!"

Lily's gaze fixed her. "It could. That doesn't mean we ought to quail at every shadow."

"What then?"

"Name our blessings. Hold them while we can. And, girl-baby, ye have blessings aplenty to name. Ian, for one. About to go hunting a wicked man to keep ye safe."

"I know, Mama," she whispered. "I know he wants to do right, but I just don't trust him anymore." She put a hand over her mouth, willing back the tears that burned her eyes.

"Is it only Ian ye've stopped trusting?"

Seona shook her head—in denial or agreement, she hardly knew—before she heard footsteps approaching. Fearing it was Ian, she thought to slip inside the cabin and shut the door. But it was Joseph Tames-His-Horse who rounded the cabin into the westering sunlight. He smiled down at Lily, taking in the gown draped over her lap.

"I have heard of your skill with the needle. Is that to be for the wedding?" he asked, looking up to include Seona in the question. His smile dimmed as he caught her troubled gaze. "You did not come for your supper," he said. "Is it because you fear what the morrow will bring?"

Seona couldn't speak. Mutely she nodded.

Joseph studied her, features bathed in golden light, fierce and nigh as beautiful as her mama's, who sat on the bench at his knee, waiting for him to speak. "This man we hunt was once before my quarry. Had I not lost him, much evil would have been spared many—my sister and her family among them. Now yours. I will not let him slip from my hand again."

"Thank ye, Joseph," Lily said. "How's that arm of yours?"

He looked down at her, mouth curving in a crooked half smile. "It will be fine. I will leave you now."

Seona found her voice. "Not on my account," she said, having heard the children in the yard, Catriona calling after them. "I best tend my babies afore they need another bathing." Which was one true thing, she thought as she left her mama and Joseph outside the cabin in the day's last golden light. Gabriel and Mandy were both her babies now. Whatever happened tomorrow, that couldn't be undone, no more than she could stop loving their daddy.

If only love alone could safeguard them all.

37

While Ian hitched the wagon in the dark of morning, Catriona took Seona aside to ask, "Why don't you come? Bring the children. Maggie and I can use the help. And it might be good to get off the farm for the morning." She glanced from Seona to Ian, aware all was not well between them.

Off toward the mountains came a faint rumble. The sky hung low beyond the ridge, though above them fading stars still showed in patches between the clouds. Their breath ghosted on the air.

"I don't know . . ." Thought of traveling the miles into the village kindled unease, but after yesterday so did staying put. Then she noted Ian, looking ready to object to the suggestion. As impulsive as Catriona for once, Seona asked him, "Why not? You wanted me to go into Shiloh. And it was never truly safe, was it? It's not safe anywhere."

She knew Ian hadn't ground to stand on to argue. His words from yesterday lingered in his eyes. *I cannot do enough to give ye peace . . .*

Before the sun had cleared the treetops, Gabriel and Mandy were in the wagon with their daddy, Seona and Catriona mounted. Strain marked the half mile to the MacGregors', where Maggie and Matthew joined them.

Neil MacGregor was saddling his old horse, Seamus, needing to visit several patients, including Hector Lacey, despite Joseph's protest that today was no time to be heading into the hills. But Neil had his own brand of stubbornness.

"I finally deduced the fellow's sticking point. He feared being tossed into gaol by Colonel Waring for squatting on land he doesna own, did he show his face in Shiloh. But I found someone willing to put up wi' the scoundrel for a few months—Elias Waring himself. So auld Hector has run dry of excuses. Besides," he added with a nod toward the foothills, "that's likely our first snow in the high country. He needs to come down today."

Matthew called to them, impatient to be away, still thinking Ian and Joseph meant him and half of Shiloh, could he raise them, to come along when they went after Crane. Seona was tempted to set him straight.

Catching Joseph's warning gaze, her nerve to speak up fled.

The morning seemed to darken rather than brighten as the rising sun lost its battle with the advancing clouds, but no rain fell in Shiloh, where a surprise waited. The school cabin had been swept clean, scoured top to bottom.

While Seona watched Gabriel and Mandy explore the schoolhouse where their auntie would soon help teach, Ian made quick work of the broken door hinges. Anni Keppler and her daughter came up from the mill—perpetrators of the tidying. They helped unload the furnishings into the cabin-yard while Seona tried not to catch Ian's eye. She heard him admonishing Matthew, set to ride to Colonel Waring to tell of a manhunt that would not unfold like he expected it to.

"By time ye're back, the girls should be done here. Promise ye'll ride with them to the farm. I don't want them on the road alone." Matthew promised and rode off on his errand. Ian stepped into the cabin doorway and spotted her within. "Did ye hear me, Seona? Don't start for home until Matthew's back."

She nodded, not meeting his gaze. Gabriel and Mandy gave their daddy a kiss farewell. Ian lingered in the doorway. "Seona, look at me."

With her face set like a shield, she looked.

"It's going to be all right," he said.

Hearing the others in the yard, she dropped her voice. "Wish we both believed that."

Never mind Aram Crane and what he might do to Ian, she had just wounded him afresh.

"I have to go."

"Go," she said, wanting to tell him *Godspeed.* Wanting to say more, she didn't know what. She took a step in his direction as Catriona nudged him out of the doorway, walking backward with one end of a table in her grasp, Maggie at the other end.

"Watch out, littles," she called. "We don't want to run you over."

Gabriel and Mandy stood against the log wall, wiggling with excitement as Anni and her daughter followed with another table. When the doorway finally cleared, Seona hurried out.

Ian was up on the wagon bench, slapping the lines over Cupid's back. The wagon lurched into motion. The sky in the east had darkened with clouds. Thunder rumbled as the curving track along the creek bore Ian out of sight.

"I expect you'll have some new pupils this autumn," Anni Keppler said as the last table was arranged to Maggie's liking. "Word's gone round Catriona is teaching, too."

Seona looked up from lifting Mandy and Gabriel onto a bench so they could pretend they were "getting schooled," as Mandy put it.

Maggie stood at the front of the room, surveying her domain. "You spread the word, you mean," she said.

"I thought it would be helpful for folk to know."

"It is." Maggie shared a glance with Catriona that spoke contrary things, gratitude and regret uppermost. "I'm thrilled you'll be teaching with me, Catriona. And glad more children may attend because of it."

"*I* wish people had better sense," Catriona said. "Regardless of my presence."

"You'll have these two," Seona said, standing behind her babies, who swung dangling legs, pretending to read an imaginary book spread on the table before their noses. "Likely afore I can blink twice."

Even as she spoke, she wondered, Would such a thing truly come to pass? It would be a few years before Gabriel and Mandy were ready for such learning. Where would they be then? Or by suppertime?

"Oh—Seona," Anni said, looking happy to change the subject. "I just recalled. You've a letter at Keagan's store."

"A letter for Ian?"

"Addressed to you, I'm told," Anni said, before she and her daughter left to see to their own chores.

"We're about done here," Maggie said once they had gone. "But we have to wait for Matthew. We could do some planning, Catriona and I, while you fetch your letter, Seona. Better hurry though. That weather's closing in."

Seona had a few small coins in her pocket, enough for postage, she thought.

Mandy reached for her, wanting to go, but Gabriel shook his head. "I'm getting schooled, Mama."

Catriona laughed. "We'll watch him."

Seona settled Mandy on her hip and gave Gabriel's curls a caress. "Mind your auntie. I'll be back."

"If Matthew doesn't get back soon, maybe someone down at the mill can escort us home," Maggie was saying as Seona stepped from the cabin. The rush of the nearby falls that turned the gristmill's wheel covered whatever Catriona replied as Seona started down the slope toward Keagan's store.

"Wonder who's writing to me instead of to your papa, girl-baby."

Mandy's feet, covered in the moccasins Ian had made, kicked at the folds of Seona's petticoat. "Papa drove the wagon home."

"He did," Seona said, wishing she could banish the memory of Ian's hurting gaze.

Turned out it was something more than a letter waiting on her. She took the bulging missive outside the store and broke its seal while Mandy sucked on a piece of maple candy Mr. Keagan had given Seona with her change. Inside was a letter and a folded bit of hide, thin and pliable. She unfolded that and nearly gasped. More gold, tiny nuggets like a scattering of sunflower seeds.

Why was it addressed to her and not Ian? Seona rewrapped the gold and thrust it into her pocket. With hands that shook, she unfolded the letter. Her gaze dropped to the signature and her heart leapt. Cecily Reynold.

Distracted by the surprise, she skimmed the lines written in an elegant hand. Cecily had news to share about their farm, the neighbors, her son, and a new baby girl they had named Angelique. Then Seona reached a part of the letter that riveted her attention:

> *John has word for you of Esther, for he met with her when Business last took him to Pryce's Sawmill. He contrived a few moments alone to speak with her. Rest assured, my dear Seona, that in the way I think matters most to you, Esther is well. There has been no interference from any unwelcome Quarter, for while she may not have said as much to John, there was another to whom she spoke more freely. It was in secret that TR came to us, not long after John met with Esther.*

TR . . . That would be Thomas Ross.

> *We do not know, and did not inquire, how T managed to speak with her, nor did we ever expect to see his face again, but are gladdened by it. John has agreed to help him, if ever help is needed, in a certain Endeavor I need not put into words for you. So while the worst you may have feared has not befallen Esther, still—oh, Seona—she cried most pitifully to John for missing you . . .*

A tug on her petticoat jerked Seona from the wrenching words.

"Mama . . . you sad?"

Looking down into Mandy's worried eyes, Seona folded the letter and blinked away tears. "No, girl-baby. I'm fine. Is that candy good?"

Mandy nodded, smacking sticky lips. Seona had a piece for Gabriel too. She tucked it and the letter into her pocket and took Mandy by a hand as sticky as her mouth. As they climbed the slope past the mill, she ached knowing Esther was so far away. Ached with regret for letting Ian go off to hunt the man threatening them, with nary a kind word. She couldn't speak to Esther, but she ought to have spoken to Ian. Said *something.*

We never know when that last time will be . . .

Thunder rolled again, deeper than before. Mandy squealed. Seona swung the child into her arms. Rain was coming, sure enough. They had best head home else be caught in it. Would Ian and Joseph still go into those hills with a storm brewing?

Seona pushed her legs to carry her up the slope. The mill wheels were grinding as she passed, but up at the school cabin, all was quiet under the lowering sky. The horses, hobbled in the yard, whickered at her, unsettled by the thunder.

Seona stepped inside the cabin. "Catriona?"

No one was there. The benches nearest the door were overturned, a desk shoved out of line. Had Gabriel got to roughhousing and the girls took him outside?

With Mandy growing heavy in her arms, Seona ducked back out, reasoning away a vague alarm. Had she walked right past them, down at the mill? Or had they gone clear across the creek to visit more with Anni and her daughter? She would check but first ducked round back of the cabin to a grassy yard, to be sure the girls and Gabriel hadn't gone there.

"Gabriel?" she called and nearly dropped Mandy in startlement when Maggie MacGregor came running out of the woods, petticoat hemmed in mud.

"I cannot find them!" She stumbled but righted herself as she reached Seona, long, dark hair tumbled from a cap snagged half-off her head, as if by a tree limb.

"Are they hiding?" Seona asked before registering the panic in Maggie's eyes.

"Only if it's a cruel joke! I went down to the mill to see if anyone was free to ride home with us. Everyone was busy, so I came right back. Now they're gone—and look!"

Maggie thrust a crumpled scrap of paper at Seona. It appeared torn from a book.

Seona set Mandy down and took what she saw was a note, handwritten on the margin of the torn page, but her mind was in a spin, eyes unable to focus on words that looked to have been scrawled with charcoal. A new dread had its claws in her.

"Where is Gabriel?"

Maggie shook her head with exaggerated force. "I don't know! That note was stuck to the door with a knife. *Read it*, Seona."

Seona looked at the paper, her brain finally making sense of the words written there, ill-formed and smudged though they were.

Give over the gold if you want them back. I will come for it.

38

While hailing a nearby cabin, spreading word about the hunt for Aram Crane, Matthew MacGregor had heard Seona scream. He and Lemuel Waring, armed with rifles, came racing their horses along a trail to the schoolyard.

Numb with shock at what the words on the paper portended, Seona couldn't grasp the questions hurled at her. *Was there sign of struggle? Did no one hear anything? How long had Catriona and Gabriel been missing?*

While Maggie gave answer, Mandy whimpered, frightened and confused. Seona did not remember putting her down but knew she ought to pick her up again, comfort the child. Her limbs were leaden. Where her vitals had been moments ago, an emptiness yawned, a cavern opened beneath her ribs.

Give over the gold . . .

Matthew snatched the note from her hand. Maggie stood before her, mouth moving over the same words twice before Seona heard them.

"What does it mean, Seona? What gold?"

. . . if you want them back . . .

Seona heard her own voice speaking as if from far away. "He . . . Ian paid for his land with gold. Not coin. Gold dug out of the earth. Aram Crane learned of it."

I will come for it.

"*Raw* gold?" Matthew asked. "That's what Ian meant? And . . . what? Crane thinks you have more?"

Mandy clung to Seona's legs, whimpers turning to wails.

"Whoever did this, we have to tell Ian and Uncle Joseph." Tears streaked Maggie's cheeks as she hoisted Mandy into her arms. "Mount up, Seona. I'll hand her to you."

"No one move!" Matthew thrust the note back into Seona's hand and dashed across the schoolyard. In seconds he gave a shout. "I have their trail! Someone's already trampled over it, but I see it still. I'll follow it from here."

He sprinted back to the horses.

"That was me, Matthew. I went a ways into the forest looking for them, but—"

Before Maggie could utter the protest they all saw coming, Matthew said, "I won't leave them in Crane's hands a second longer than I must. See them to Ian's farm," he told Lem, already in the saddle. "He and Uncle Joseph are waiting for me. Tell them where to pick up the trail."

Looking suddenly older than his years, Lem said, "I will."

But he wouldn't. Joseph and Ian meant to go after Crane on their own. Had already gone, surely. "Matthew. Wait—"

Ignoring Seona, Matthew led his horse into the trees. Lem grabbed Juturna's reins to lead the riderless filly. Sight of that empty saddle struck panic through Seona. She swung into the saddle, reached down for Mandy, then drove her heels against the mare's sides. Clinging to the child in front of her, she felt strong muscles quiver and bunch beneath her as the mare's hooves dug into the track.

She had never ridden a galloping horse, never seen a forest stream by so fast; still the miles between Shiloh and the farm seemed impossible to cover. Lem's horse caught her up, Maggie's just behind. Though the rain sheeted the hills in curtains of gray, the track before her had seen none yet.

Thought of Gabriel in Crane's hands, up in those hills somewhere, drew a moan that the mare's pounding hooves barely muffled.

They met Ian and Joseph on the track between the farms, Lem shouting ahead their news. Hat pulled low, draped in an oilcloth cape, Ian turned his roan across the track to head off Seona's mount. The horse came to a jarring halt as Ian grabbed the reins. Seona clutched at Mandy as the mare collided with Ruiadh, who withstood the impact, braced.

"What d'ye mean?" Ian demanded, taking in their stricken faces. "Catriona and Gabriel were *abducted*?"

"From the school cabin." Lem spilled out the details a second time until Joseph cut him off.

"Where is Matthew?"

"He found the trail," Maggie said. "We couldn't stop him."

Seona freed a hand from Mandy and shoved the crumpled note at Ian. She watched his face harden with dread as he made out the words, before thrusting it at Joseph.

"He's coming to my farm—if we don't find him first. He wants the gold."

"Have you any?" Lem asked.

"Aye. Some. He'll never find it." Ian looked to Seona, who knew he was debating going back for it.

"There is no time," Joseph said for her. To Lem he said, "Bring everyone to my sister's house. Stay with them there."

"You don't need me to ride with you?" Lem gripped his rifle, scared but ready to aid.

"No," Ian said. "Better just Joseph and I. We'll pick up Matthew's trail at the school." He met Seona's gaze.

"You should've gone after him sooner," she said, knowing it the opposite of what she had asked of him before. Knowing she was as much to blame for this turn, having taken her babies into Shiloh. Too terrified to care.

"I should have," Ian said. "I'm sorry."

"Just find them!" The words ended in a wail. She pressed her mouth to Mandy's curls to stifle the noise.

"I will. God Almighty help me, Seona, I . . ."

He had meant to say *I promise*, Seona was certain. But Joseph had thrust his rifle in the air and loosed a hair-raising shout. He kicked his horse into motion with a spray of dirt and the hollow drumming of hooves.

Still clasping Mandy tight, Seona plunged a hand through her petticoat's slit, drove it into her pocket, and wrenched out the leather-wrapped gold Cecily Reynold had sent with her letter. Ian's gaze fastened on hers, far too near to misread his desperation. His remorse.

She thrust the folded leather at him. "Give that devil what he wants."

He stared at it. "What?"

"More gold. Take it—go!"

Comprehension gripped his features. With a fist around the scrap of leather and the treasure it contained—enough to purchase two precious lives?—Ian loosed no shout but rode after Joseph in grim, determined silence.

Matthew's mount had left a churning in the earth; he had wasted no time pursuing Crane. Neither did Ian and Joseph. They didn't ride into the village seeking whomever Matthew had summoned for the hunt—now become a rescue—preferring speed and stealth over numbers. Rain had begun to spatter. It had been drenching the higher hills since before dawn.

Matthew's trail had obliterated much of the sign Crane had left, but not all. The man was afoot, leading his animal, the hoofprints deep enough to indicate the horse bore weight. Gabriel and Catriona. Bound no doubt. Conscious? Wounded?

You should've gone after him sooner.

He should have gone after Crane as soon as they found the traps. Or Francis Waring's remains. Clear back in Cherry Valley when first he suspected the man of trailing him.

Trace of hunter and prey left Shiloh and angled into the forested hills to the northeast. Even afoot Crane had moved swiftly, making use of beaten paths but more often the subtler trails of deer and elk, climbing ridges, bending ever eastward. Ian rode behind Joseph, letting the Mohawk scout the trail, exerting his energies toward unraveling the man's twisted mind.

Give over the gold if you want them back. I will come for it.

Obviously he meant to hold Gabriel and Catriona captive until he had what he wanted. If it came to bargaining, would whatever Seona had given him be enough? He hadn't had a chance even to glance at it.

Please. With half his mind he tried to pray. It was like casting a net of spiderweb, his faith too fragile to lay hold of hope. Grace was needed. Help from on high in a measure beyond what he could possibly deserve. What he deserved was what he had seen in Seona's eyes as she all but hurled the gold at him. Shattered trust.

Rain battered through scarlet leaves, striking his hat, running down the cape. The air chilled as they climbed. Though its firing mechanism was covered against the rain, he tucked the rifle under his cape for good measure. Last thing he wanted was a misfire, when the time came. If it came. Was there a way through this without bloodshed?

Thrust into his coat pocket, the gold burned like an ember. He would give it all to Crane and promise the rest hidden in that beech tree for Gabriel's and Catriona's lives. What was the man's plan? Did he mean to carry them back to the farm or secure them somewhere first? Should they have waited for Crane to come to them?

He couldn't have borne it. How was Seona bearing it?

Please.

His spiral of second-guessing was cut short as ahead on the trail Joseph halted and slid from his mount, moccasin-clad feet hitting the damp ground. Ian followed suit. Rifle clutched in reddened fingers, he led the roan forward until he reached Joseph, crouched on the path, the edges of his cape spilling rain.

"Ye cannot have lost the trail?"

"No." Joseph stood, face and hair beaded with moisture. "It goes on as before. Crane only, I think."

"Matthew lost it?"

"Or left it. Do you see where we are?"

The ridge they were cutting across rose steeply to the north. Slopes thickly wooded fell away south and east, blurred under darkened skies that rumbled as the storm rolled down toward Black Kettle Creek. They were near the trail they had taken the day they fetched Neil down from Hector Lacey's cabin, perched above that creek-cut ravine. "I do see."

Joseph caught his gaze. "My sister's husband meant to go there today. Maybe there are more in peril than we knew."

Did Crane know of that isolated place? Was he making for it as a refuge, a place to stash Catriona and Gabriel? Was Neil trapped up in that squatter's shack—and the old man too?

They led their mounts forward, looking for a way up the ridge the horses could manage, while keeping watch for traps. There could well be more, and other sorts, the nearer they came to Lacey's cabin or whatever den Crane was making for.

Was his son cold? Terrified? Had Catriona fought her captor? Was she injured?

The spiral sucked him down again, though he clung to the desperate hope that Crane wouldn't harm them, not if he meant to trade them for gold.

Please . . .

At last the ridge they flanked presented a gentler face where a side trail split away and climbed, a barely discernible impression angling up through the forest duff.

"Here." Joseph stopped. "If the deer climb it, so may—"

The crack of a branch snapping and thud of heavy feet had them whirling to where the slope fell away on the trail's opposite side, rifles shouldered, the stock cover of Ian's hastily yanked askew. Blood pounded in his ears as he scanned the trees, searching for a man's figure. Something to aim at.

Joseph's mount whickered as Ian spotted not a man but another horse picking its way toward them, coming up through the dripping trees. A dark bay roan, saddled, reins trailing. Seamus—Neil MacGregor's horse.

Joseph thrust his mount's lead at Ian and, with one mistrustful eye on the leaf-strewn ground, reached the horse and brought it up to the trail. Behind Seamus's saddle, Neil's doctoring kit was tied. Of the physician there was no sign.

As Joseph led Seamus near, Ian noted a hitch in the gelding's stride. Had that started before or after parting ways with its rider? No blood stained the saddle or tack. No evidence of anything amiss, save Neil's glaring absence.

Joseph's gaze mirrored Ian's confusion and dread. "Do we climb to the trail above or keep to this one?"

"Neil wouldn't have used this one to reach Lacey's cabin," Ian said, then added without conviction, "Maybe he found that last stretch along the ravine too treacherous in this rain, left the horse below . . . to come unhitched?"

Mounted or afoot, Neil would have taken his medical supplies up to the old man's cabin.

"I will see. Wait here with the horses." Before Ian could protest, Joseph was climbing nimbly up the ridge along the faint indentation that marked where deer had passed.

Ian grabbed Seamus's bridle before the horse could follow. He checked the gelding's feet, finding the reason for that hitching stride lodged in the right forehoof. Seamus had picked up a stone. With his knife, Ian worked it free. "There ye go, old man." He set hoof to earth and slid the knife back into its sheath, alongside his tomahawk.

Minutes crept by. Rain fell noisily through leaves well gone toward scarlet and gold at that higher elevation. Thunder cracked. For the first time, lightning flashed, bluish, surprisingly bright in the brooding gray. His and Joseph's mounts stood steady, but Seamus's ears flattened.

"Easy," Ian soothed, as his own fears screamed. *Gabriel . . . Catriona. Please, God Almighty, hurry. Hurry . . .*

At last he heard Joseph descending the ridge—sliding in soggy leaves, catching himself against trees, his caped form a glimpse through autumn foliage. When he was down onto the lower trail, breathing hard, he reached for Seamus's reins as well as his own mount's, hitching them together. "We must get the horses up there."

Ian balked. "Crane's trail goes along this way."

"We will follow it—later."

Rain was fast obliterating it. "Why not now?"

Joseph grabbed his arm, hard enough to command Ian's full attention. "Because I have found my sister's husband."

39

The trap had caught Neil's ankle, biting deep through boot leather and flesh. He lay on the ground, rain-soaked, white-faced—*dead*, or so Ian thought for a gutted moment.

"He lives," Joseph said.

Before returning to Ian, he had tied Neil's belt around his calf in a makeshift tourniquet, wrenched open the trap's jaws and removed the foot, but hadn't touched the mangled riding boot. Ian couldn't bring himself to look twice at what the gaping leather revealed. Rather he looked at his neighbor's face, still and sheened with rain.

"We must get him onto his horse," Joseph said, then eyed Seamus's load. "No, mine. Tsigalili will know what to do?"

Had Lily ever tended such a wound? Ian didn't know. "She'd try. But we cannot leave off following Crane."

Neither could they abandon Neil.

"*We* will not," Joseph said. "I will take him to the women and come back to you."

Relief swelled, though a new fear pierced it. He had counted on Joseph if it came to a fight. Lightning flashed. Its tail of thunder boomed. Rain pelted down. Ian held the dun mare steady while Joseph gathered Neil MacGregor into his arms, hefting him onto the saddle, face against the horse's mane. Neil roused with a cry as they eased his wounded leg over the horse's rump.

"We have ye," Ian said as the man struggled to sit upright in the saddle, injured foot dangling, eyes dull with shock. "Joseph's taking ye home. Lily's there to aid ye. Just hang on." To the horse. To life.

The shock in Neil's blue eyes gave way to bleak assessment. His gaze shifted to Joseph, steadying him from the other side while he slipped Neil's sound foot into the stirrup. He blinked again at Ian, eyes dilating with dawning urgency. "Catriona . . . Gabriel. I saw them."

Ian grasped the hand that clutched weakly at the reins. "Where?"

Neil motioned farther up the path, where, they now saw, it crossed the game trail they had been following below. "They passed . . . with Crane."

"Taking them to Lacey's?"

Neil nodded. "I never made it. Dinna ken whether Hector . . ."

"I'll see." Dead or alive, innocent or in league with a devil—Ian would sort out Hector Lacey with the rest.

Joseph swung onto Seamus and took his mare's reins to lead. "What of Matthew?" he asked Neil. "Did he not see you?"

Neil closed his eyes, grimacing. "Matthew? Where is he?"

"I'll find him too." Ian gripped his neighbor's hand, aware of his own shaking. He shared a look with Joseph.

"I will return," Willa's brother said.

Resolved to continue alone, Ian nodded. "Get him home. I'll find them."

The rain had closed in, falling steadily. For a time they had all crammed into Willa MacGregor's house, muddied around the edges and anxious for their missing ones and those gone to rescue them. Neil, too, out in that mess visiting the ailing. While Malcolm sat by the kitchen hearth reading his Bible, murmuring prayers, Naomi and Maggie fixed a dinner Seona knew she wouldn't taste. Lem, Ally, and the boys finally went out to tend horses and check on Tuck, healing from his knife wound.

Willa went to answer her baby's cries, leaving Seona and Lily alone in Neil's surgery. Lily had brought her simples box.

"In case there's need," she had said as they gathered up things to keep themselves and Mandy occupied for however long they would be away from home. She was sorting through it now, though she had its contents memorized.

Seona had held a teary Mandy, who hadn't stopped asking for Gabriel until she dozed off, then put her down on Willa's bed. With nothing now to do with her restless hands, her mouth took up the slack.

"Mama, I cannot bear this waiting. I want Gabriel." She wrapped her arms around that gaping emptiness below her ribs. "I *need* him."

Lily turned from her box, features pinched, her own need plain in her gaze. "Come here, girl-baby."

In her mama's arms, Seona wept, fear choking her words. "I didn't think it would be . . . like this."

Lily rubbed her back. "Ye didn't think what would be?"

"Being with Ian. Being free. Here. All of it. He *promised*, Mama."

Lily pulled away, holding her shoulders to better look at her. "What did he promise?"

"To keep us safe. When he gave me this." She wrung trembling hands, twisting the silver ring. *I Am My Beloved's.*

"Seona," her mama said with a slow shake of her head. "Did ye think freedom from slavery meant freedom from every trouble?"

"I don't know. But I never would have come here if I'd thought it meant losing *Gabriel.*"

"He's not lost. Ian's out there doing all he can to bring Gabriel home. Catriona too. So are Joseph and Matthew."

She knew that, and it ought to have reassured her, but this fear was beyond reason. "Even if we get him back—both of them—what's next?"

Lily didn't answer that. Instead she asked, "Why d'ye think Ian made ye such an impossible promise?"

Impossible. "I don't know!"

"I think ye do know."

Seona stared at the windowpanes streaked with rain. "Do I?"

"Would Ian have made such a promise if he wasn't desperate to see ye happy? To make up for all the hard things that happened to ye at Mountain Laurel?"

Seona turned from the window, arms laced. "You're saying it's *my* fault he promised?"

"No one's at fault—save that Aram Crane causing grief. Just don't hold Ian to a promise no man but one can keep. The one who's also God." Lily frowned as she said that last. "Have ye given up—?"

From the front of the house a door banged open. Men's voices spoke, a deep, urgent tangle, until one rose above the rest: "Tsigalili!"

Her mama's stare turned blank. "Joseph?"

Seona's heart nearly burst with hope, but Lily beat her to the surgery door. Filling the other end of the passage, coming at them fast, were Joseph and Ally, streaming rain, carrying between them an equally soaked Neil MacGregor.

Willa came from somewhere in the house, baby in her arms. "Neil!"

Joseph didn't speak until they had Neil laid out on the surgery table, white as linen, dark hair plastered to his skull. He seemed uninjured . . . then Seona saw his foot. So did Willa. Ally backed out of the way as she rushed forward, handing a startled Josephine off to Seona. Lily was down at Neil's boots, holding the gaping one open to better see the bloody mess within. Something—a belt—was cinched around the calf above it.

Maggie came rushing from the kitchen. "I thought it was Catriona and Gabriel back. What's happened?"

Lily got the ruined boot off, rousing Neil to groan. From the doorway Maggie echoed the sound. Seona figured everyone crowded into the little surgery was thinking the same. Neil's ankle looked like it had been chewed by a bear or . . .

"A trap?" Seona blurted and would have covered her mouth had her hands been free of whimpering baby. She jiggled the child unthinkingly as Joseph gave them answer.

"One of Crane's."

Willa caressed her husband's head. "How?"

"We found him caught. Near the cabin of the man he was going to bring down from the hills. We think that is where your son is," Joseph added, meeting Seona's gaze. "And Ian's sister, taken with him."

"Ian—did he come back with you?"

"And Matthew?" Maggie asked from the doorway.

"We have not found Matthew. Ian was heading up to Lacey's cabin when I left. One of us had to bring him home," Joseph said with a searching look at Lily, still examining the extent of Neil's wound. "I will go back."

Seona bowed her head over Willa's baby, restraining the scream wanting to come tearing out.

"Seona . . ." Neil's voice, but a thread, held them instantly riveted. "Crane had them bound . . . but whole."

"You saw them?" Seona stepped nearer.

"Aye . . ."

"But you . . . ," Willa said, features nearly as pale as her husband's. "How did this happen?"

"On my way to Lacey," Neil forced through teeth beginning to chatter. "Seamus . . . lame. I stopped to check . . . dismounted onto the trap."

He hadn't reached Hector Lacey's cabin. They hadn't found Matthew. Ian was left to face that trap-setting, child-abducting, gold-hungry villain alone. Seona pressed back a sob as Willa laid a blanket over her husband's upper body, leaving his legs exposed, then looked appealingly at Lily. "Is there anything you can do?"

Her mama's features were a mask of control as they all took in the ruin of Neil's ankle. Seona saw bone amid the bleeding flesh. So did Maggie, who was nearly fainting against the doorpost. "Where's Lem?" she asked weakly.

"On the porch," one of her brothers said in the passage behind her.

"Take me to him. And, Lily . . ." Maggie looked at Seona's mama, pleading. "I'll be praying."

She left the surgery. Joseph started after her but paused before Seona, touching her shoulder briefly with a hand still rain-wet. But it was to Lily he looked. She was looking back in a way that startled Seona—the kind of speaking look she and Ian had sometimes shared.

"You are certain?" Joseph asked.

A nod from Seona's mama drew joy across Joseph's face, brighter than the lightning that briefly lit the surgery window. He was gone before the thunder rolled, and Lily took command. "I need one more pair of hands."

"You could have mine, if someone takes this baby," Seona said, voice shaking as this new fear piled atop the others.

Already deep into Neil's medical supplies, Lily shook her head. "No, girl-baby. I need someone can give their all to this."

"Reckon that's me." Naomi had left the kitchen too and stood now in the surgery doorway, sturdy as an oak, holding a steaming kettle. "You'll need this. Tell me what else to do."

Seona held Willa's daughter close in trembling arms. "What do *I* do, Mama? I can't do nothing."

Lily fixed her with a gaze that took her back to their broken conversation. "Pray, girl-baby. That's what you need to be doing."

After Joseph rode down the mountain with Neil MacGregor, lost among the trees in a graying blur, Ian had led Ruaidh to where the game trail crossed the broader path. The rain had made a pudding of the trodden ground, but the need for tracking was past. He knew this climbing trail. There was no other shelter on that rain-swept mountainside save Lacey's cabin, at its end, but while everything within him screamed to race forward, fear of triggering another trap and rendering himself helpless held him in check.

Head bowed to the weather, he trudged on, leading his horse, rifle tucked beneath his cape. He left the leather ties of the lock cover loose. It was still in place over frizzen and pan, but the powder wouldn't stay dry long in that downpour. If it was now.

The path climbed steeply through hardwoods already in autumn array, the dark greens of pine and fir. Rock outcrops thrust through the earth, creating gaps in the forest shelter he crossed with care, watching for traps but also for Crane retracing his path. Having secured his prisoners, he would make for the farm. Unless he meant to wait out the storm.

As he neared the creek that twisted out of the mountains through the ravine, Ian encountered runnels crossing the trail that hadn't flowed in summer. All coursing downslope to spill into the creek, which he heard even before the trail steepened for its last climb along the ravine's lip.

At that point he hesitated. He and Joseph had led their horses along it back in summer. Not in such weather as this. He would go faster without Ruaidh.

A stand of fir offered the only shelter. He hitched the roan among them as a faint flash lit the mountainside. Ruaidh flattened his ears. Ian counted seconds until thunder rumbled. A longer delay. Rain still fell with battering force, but he dared to hope the worst of the storm was passing as he left his dripping horse.

The trail wound up, pocked with stones that broke from the saturated earth beneath his feet to go tumbling into empty air before striking the water below. Coming to a jut of rock where the view was unobstructed, he paused to look over the edge.

The ravine's face wasn't sheer. It broke into levels where stunted trees had found purchase. Some thirty feet below, what had in summer been a clear, burbling creek edged by stony banks surged high and brown, filling the narrow ravine.

The next stretch of trail hugged the forested slope. A mere six feet out, it fell away to frothing water. He was halfway across it when a crescent of earth at the trail's outer edge sagged away, sheared off by its rain-soaked weight. Ian dropped his rifle as he fell to his knees, scrambling to keep from plunging over an edge two feet nearer than it had been. He clawed his way to the base of the slope, reaching back to snatch his rifle before it went tumbling.

Heart banging, he sat in a patch of sodden ferns, staring at raw earth gaping as though a great mouth had torn away a bite. Then he took in the next few feet of trail he would have trodden had the earth not fallen away beneath him. A frisson of mingled alarm and relief shook through him.

The snare was simple. A slender limb laid across the trail was its trigger. Ian traced its line to the base of the slope and found the rigging. Tied with scuppernong vine, it blended with the matted ferns and saplings growing thick on the steep slope—except where a pile of deadfall, held precariously in place by two upright posts, waited to come sweeping across the trail, and anyone on it, when those posts came free. All it would take to unleash the avalanche was a careless boot, or hoof, kicking aside that slender limb.

He could spring the trap and leap to safety, was on his feet and seconds from doing so when he reconsidered. The weight of that deadfall crashing down might take out another chunk of trail, impeding Joseph's approach. Instead he found a slender stick, drove it into the soft ground square in front of that triggering limb, then with chilled fingers untied his neckcloth and fastened that to the stick, spreading the ends out wide, the linen pale against the sodden earth.

There could be no missing that. He prayed it would do for a warning as he stepped carefully over the limb.

Past the snare, the trail angled up through a stand of yellowed birches, then took a gradual bend away from the ravine, up into a narrow hollow. Ian proceeded with redoubled caution but discovered no further snares before the bottom edge of Hector Lacey's corn patch came into view.

The stalks still stood, brown and dripping, but Ian ducked low, not making straight for the cabin that squatted like a toad at the planting's other end, at the base of a jumble of massive stones that formed a near-perfect arc. With the wooded crest of the mountain rising behind, draped in cloud, those stones rimmed the cabin like a fortress wall. An irregular one. Though Ian minded them vaguely from his previous visit, closer scrutiny showed the stones jutted in places where a man might climb. Or hide. Though slackening at last, the rain's patter covered any sound there might have been from the cabin. Glimpses through the cornstalks revealed no movement.

He wanted to rush the place, go barreling in, take down Crane, and rescue his son, his sister—old Lacey too, was he held captive. Again he checked the frantic impulse. What he needed was a better view. Higher ground.

Ian crept along the field's ragged edge and up into the trees, making for those rocks, moss-covered and tree-grown at their crowns. He was nearly among them when the clatter of falling stones froze him, hunkered in the shelter of a rotting stump.

Cradling his muddy rifle across his knees, he eased the tomahawk from his belt, gripping its handle in a chilling clench. He had drawn back the weapon for a throw when a voice spoke, soft but alarmingly close.

"Ian?"

40

Matthew MacGregor was soaked to the skin, having worn no cape against the rain when he took off from the schoolyard. Concealed within a stony crevice among the rocks behind the cabin, he and Ian hurled questions at each other, low and urgent.

Were Gabriel and Catriona inside the cabin with Crane? The man's horse was hitched in a lean-to behind the cabin, so they must be.

Was there another way inside the structure? No, just the door in front.

Where was Hector Lacey? Dead, alive in the cabin, fled, who could say?

Had Matthew been spotted? Of course not. He had been careful!

"What of Uncle Joseph, didn't he come with you?"

It was a question Ian wasn't sure how to answer. Instead he asked, "Did ye not see your da as ye came up the trail?"

"I lost the trail when the rain picked up. I guessed Crane was headed here. I came at the cabin from the quickest way I knew. My horse is there." Matthew waved up past the rocks. Apparently there was another approach to the place. "Why would I have seen Pa? He talked of visiting Lacey, but he wouldn't have in this weather."

"Aye, he would. We found him caught in one of Crane's traps. Joseph took him to Lily to tend the wound." The lad's stunned and shaken face decided it. Ian was telling him no more, certainly not how gruesome a wound it had been. "Joseph's coming back . . ."

A desperate determination darkened Matthew's gaze.

"Ye know he will," Ian said, meaning to head off whatever reckless plan the lad was forming. "He has as much cause for taking down Crane as I."

"We all do. And that's useless to me." Matthew jerked a nod at his rifle, propped against the stone. "Your powder dry?"

"We're not shooting at the cabin with Gabriel and Catriona inside." Or Lacey. The old man might be a prisoner in there too.

Matthew drew his tomahawk. He narrowed his eyes at the one thrust into Ian's belt. "Can you use that?"

"I can."

"To kill a man?"

"If I must—listen. Crane will come out. Ye saw the note, back at the school? He means to collect his gold." Ian slipped a hand beneath his cape and took out the parcel Seona had given him. Hunched to shield it from the tapering rain, he unfolded the leather. They peered at the meager scattering it contained. He had advised John to send a little gold at a time in case it should go astray. Advice he regretted now.

Matthew wiped at the moisture trickling down his face. "Will that satisfy the man?" he asked doubtfully.

"I don't know." Ian folded the gold away and stowed it again. "I have to try—some way that won't further endanger anyone."

"Except Crane." Matthew's nostrils flared. "What if we don't count on the gold or Crane to give them up for it?"

"What? Ye mean, use it to lure him out and—?"

"Put a blade through him. Or two." Matthew was quivering as if on the verge of rushing the cabin in an onslaught of destruction.

Ian grabbed his arm, squeezing hard. "That's my son in there. And my sister—who loves ye, in case ye've forgotten."

Matthew pulled free. "I know whose lives are at stake and I . . ." His face contorted, regret sparking in his dark eyes before determination hardened them again. "I've been an idiot about Catriona. I know that. But this is something I can do. Let me help."

"I mean to, if ye'd hush and let me tell ye."

Matthew pressed his lips tight, then jerked his head, nodding.

Ian shoved out a breath. "Right then. Here's how it'll go. While ye come at the cabin from behind—quietly—I'll circle back and come straight at it through the corn, like I've just come up the trail. I'll call Crane out, let him know I have the gold he wants. He'll come out to me if he thinks I've come alone. If he does—"

"When," Matthew cut in.

"Get round the cabin. Wait until his back's to ye and I have his attention. Then slip inside." Seeing the lad's eyes brighten, he added, "I mean it. Wait until ye know Crane has come out to me. If ye get into the cabin, clean your pan and—here, take my horn, that powder's dry at least." He slipped his powder horn from beneath the sheltering cape. "Take aim at Crane in the yard. If ye get a shot . . ." He debated briefly, thinking of Joseph coming up the trail into the line of fire. "Take it," he finished. "Don't worry about me."

"I won't," Matthew said with a bloodthirsty grin.

"Follow the plan, aye? Watch for snares as ye go."

They went their separate ways, but Ian had barely reached the lower cornfield when his plan of rescue went awry. The cabin door banged open. Gaps between the shriveled cornstalks were wide, but too many stood between Ian and the cabin to gain a clear view. Presuming it was Crane, he strode ahead through the corn, mouth opening to reveal his presence.

From behind the dilapidated cabin came a ringing whinny. Seconds later Crane's saddled horse trotted into the yard. Ian was close enough to see it—a rather lovely black mare—and Crane, standing startled as the horse came at him.

Matthew had created his own distraction.

Swearing and lunging for the mare, Crane slipped in the muddy yard. The horse bolted for the cornfield, straight at Ian. As he assessed the oncoming mountain of horseflesh—and what to do about it—he caught sight of Matthew rushing from behind the cabin to plow into Crane, taking him back down into the mud before he regained his balance.

Ian nearly dove from the mare's path, then remembered the snare back on the trail, where the earth had fallen away. He stepped forward, hand and rifle raised, a flimsy barrier. "Easy, pretty lady. Easy . . ."

The mare, slowed by the crowding cornstalks, hesitated long enough for Ian to grasp a trailing lead. The mare halted, snorting and quivering. She was rain-draggled and in need of better shelter, but he stroked the sleek black face, let her blow nervous breath warm across his hand, all while a struggle was unfolding in the yard.

Fighting for calm, he turned the mare back toward the cabin, hearing shouts, grunts . . . an outcry.

Pointed in the right direction, Ian gave the mare's rump a slap. To his relief she trotted back toward Crane, who stood in the yard over Matthew's still form, in his hands a pistol he must have used as a club. There had been no firing. Matthew's tomahawk was on the ground.

Crane faced the cornfield from which his horse emerged. "Who else is there? Cameron?"

His name on the man's lips chilled him deeper than the rain had done. His mouth was dust-dry as he said, "I'm coming out to ye—to talk!"

Crane's gaze fixed on the sound of his voice. "Come out then. Hands and rifle where I can see." Rifle lofted high, Ian walked out of the stalks into the slanting yard fronting the squat little cabin. Crane raised the pistol. "Rifle on the ground. Don't even touch what's hanging from your belt."

A few strides from the man, Ian halted. Slowly he lowered the rifle to the earth, then straightened to stare down the pistol's barrel. "My son, my sister—are they in there?"

Satisfaction flickered in eyes Ian had not forgotten since that morning in Cherry Valley. Eyes like a hungry wolf. "They are."

"If I shout, will they hear me?"

"They will. You won't hear them." Aram Crane's mouth worked in a nest of graying beard, tongue licking lips. "I assume you brought something to trade?"

Ian kept the gut-churn of fear out of his voice as he called, "Gabriel! Catriona! I'm here, loves! Ye're coming home with me!"

There was no response. With no way of knowing if Crane spoke the truth, he ground his teeth and said, "I have your gold. I'm going to reach for it." He untied his cape and let it fall, then eased the folded leather from his coat. Crane's eyes lit on it. "Ye'll take this in trade for my kin?"

"And him?" Crane sneered at Matthew, who hadn't stirred. Blood trailed over his face from a gash somewhere on his scalp.

Ian's heart slammed. Shaking now with his own bloodlust, he feigned indifference. "I've come to bargain for my kin. Take what I offer and give back what's mine."

If he lived, that lad bleeding on the ground might well be his kin one day.

Crane took a step forward, pistol unwavering. "Show me what you think they're worth."

While her mama fought to save Neil MacGregor's ravaged foot, Seona gave baby Josephine to Maggie, who was watching over Mandy in the kitchen, then fled the house to find herself, pelted with rain and muddy-hemmed, in the MacGregors' spacious stable, where she let a sob slip free.

Ally, Jamie, and Liam all but leapt from the boxes they were mucking to stand in the aisle, staring. Tears tracked Liam's face. Jamie was red-eyed.

Pitchfork in hand, Ally studied her a moment, then said, "Joseph and Ian gonna get them back, Seona. Mister Neil . . . he'll be all right, like I been telling these two. God's working it out."

Hearing such simple faith expressed, Seona burst into tears. "Ally . . . I don't know."

Ally set aside the pitchfork and came to stand before her. "We all praying, ain't we?" Behind his back the MacGregor boys bobbed their heads. "You come to pray in here, Seona? We can let you be."

Tears clotted in her throat, pulled taut her mouth. Though she couldn't reply, still they went, leaving her with the horses . . . and a dark presence that clutched at her, tormenting. She stood in the stable doorway, watching rain strike puddles in the yard, making tiny rings that vanished as others took their place. The sky was bruised but the thunder had stilled.

Across the yard the house stood strangely silent for what she knew was going on within its walls. Her mama was surely praying with every breath she drew as she did what she could to mend broken flesh and bone. Willa and Naomi would be fighting beside her, Malcolm somewhere near, interceding for everyone. Even Ally was praying, while Seona's soul floundered, mired in fear.

When had she last sensed the Almighty's presence? Felt His love? What had happened to her faith? Her hope?

Spying a bench inside the stable doorway, she collapsed on it and said her baby's name over and over. "*Gabriel. Gabriel . . .*" Her hands rubbed her thighs until her fingers brushed the lump in the pocket beneath her petticoat. The piece of maple candy she had meant to give her boy. She bent at the waist, arms encircling herself.

"Please, God. Please, God. Please, God, don't take him. Or Catriona. Bring them back. Joseph, Matthew . . ." *Ian.* His name screamed inside her but wouldn't pass her lips. "Be with Mama; guide her hands . . ."

She faltered. Her prayers seemed to rise no higher than the stable roof, collecting in the dusty rafters. "Do You even see us? See *me*?"

"The Almighty sees ye, Seona. So do I."

She leapt up, turning to find Malcolm at the stable door, leaning on his cane. She wiped at her streaming nose. "Did Ally send you out?"

Malcolm made his way to the bench. His trip across the yard had taken longer than hers. His shoes were mud-caked. Rain patched his coat. Moisture trickled from his lambswool hair down his wrinkled brow into his beard.

The bench was wide enough for two.

"I heard ye pray for all in need this day," Malcolm said, planting the cane between his knees. "All but the man ye're set to marry, who's off facing down the one that's brought us harm."

"Didn't I?" She stared out the stable doors, feeling Malcolm's scrutiny.

"Ye're verra disappointed in Ian, I think."

She saw no reason to dissemble. "Wouldn't you be?"

"Aye. Was I looking to him as my savior, instead of the Lord Jesus." Malcolm placed a hand over one of hers clenching knots in her petticoat. "Seona, is it Ian ye feel betrayed by or the Almighty?"

The question unleashed a torrent. "Maybe I betrayed my own self. I thought making the choice to come here would be the hardest thing—but I ain't ever known fear like this."

Malcolm's hand gave hers a squeeze. She unclenched her fingers and twined them with his, feeling swollen joints between her own. They sat in ringing silence for a time, Seona hoping he would say something to make sense of the war in her soul.

"I've come a goodly way in my Bible reading," he said. "And I've noted a thing worth pointing out to ye. There's a particular commandment given us in Scripture o'er and again. Maybe more than any other. D'ye ken what it is?"

Seona wanted to let go his hand, to rise and pace and scream. She hadn't read the Bible since leaving Boston, save for helping Malcolm with his efforts. Ian had his own Bible, which he had said she was welcome to read, but there had been precious little time with all the work needing done, two little ones to tend.

She half choked on her feeble answer. "I haven't the faintest notion."

Rather than reprove her lack of knowledge, Malcolm smiled. "Nor did I 'til lately. It took reading the Scriptures through for me to see it. But from the time of the Old Testament to the New and surely still, the Almighty has been telling His beloved the same thing. 'Be strong and of a good courage, fear not, nor be afraid of them: for the Lord thy God, he it is that doth go with thee; he will not fail thee, nor forsake thee.'

"'Fear thou not; for I am with thee: be not dismayed; for I am thy God: I will strengthen thee; yea, I will help thee; yea, I will uphold thee with the right hand of my righteousness.'"

She was weeping again, eyes burning, a swelling in her throat. The stable, the wet yard, the house beyond blurred as Malcolm went on.

"'But now thus saith the Lord that created thee, O Jacob, and he that formed thee, O Israel, Fear not: for I have redeemed thee, I have called thee by thy name; thou art mine.'

"'Let not your heart be troubled: ye believe in God; believe also in me.'

"'Be anxious for nothing; but in every thing by prayer and supplication with thanksgiving let your requests be made known unto God.

And the peace of God, which passeth all understanding, shall keep your hearts and minds through Christ Jesus.'"

As the words washed over her, Seona's tears flowed. No longer burning. Cleansing, like rain. And then she heard it. Or thought she did. The voice her fears had too long muffled. *Thou art Mine.*

"I am my Beloved's," she mouthed, then sniffled, blinked teary eyes, and in no small wonder asked the man beside her, "You set all that to memory?"

"Scripture bids us meditate on the Almighty's words to us, get them down inside us," Malcolm said. "Then let your request be made known to Him and get the peace He promises."

She needed that peace as she needed air.

"Just now, though," Malcolm said, "I'd tell ye a thing about the verse from John's gospel that says, 'Let not your heart be troubled.' D'ye ken what Jesus was talking about, what made Him say those words?"

"I wish I did," she said, voice thick from weeping.

"He was talking about His *death*. Which tells me something ye've maybe lost sight of."

"What's that?"

"If Jesus could say those words facing the cross—and never think He wasna afraid of the suffering to come—then ye and I can do the same in the face of our own suffering. We can choose to let fear come in, take root, and master us, or we can choose to guard our hearts and give fear no purchase there. No power to rule our words and deeds."

Malcolm paused. Seona waited, raw and bleeding as the wound her mama was tending. Her words and deeds this day had been unguarded, to say the least. Ruled by anger, fear, maybe even spite. She had chosen to take the children into Shiloh, knowing Ian hadn't wanted her to do so. It was down to her decision that they were even at that school cabin.

"There will always be fears, Seona, for as long as we live in a fallen world. They stalk us. They roar. Make it hard to hear the Almighty, see His hand at work. But ye've the power to refuse fear a welcome into your heart. Ye're the master there. No one else."

Seona looked at Malcolm. Really looked as she hadn't in some while. Worn from a life of toil. Frail with years. Master of his heart. "You've always known that, haven't you?"

Malcolm shook with gentle laughter. "Not always. I learnt it, like all must do."

He sobered, and she saw that while he felt concern for those they loved in peril, his peace went deeper. His trust in the Almighty's love and strength was unshaken. He reached again for her hand, stared at it clasped in his own.

"I'm an auld man, *mo nighean*, my life all but spent. I willna always be here to remind ye o' these things. 'Tis time ye find the courage to fight for your own heart. For Ian's and your bairns'. Ye must remind them they've a mighty Warrior in the battle for their souls. Jesus."

"I haven't been doing my part." She had busied herself with so much doing and let her faith go unnourished. But it went deeper than that.

What was it Malcolm had said? That he would be disappointed in Ian too, if he had been looking to him as a savior. *An impossible promise,* her mama had called Ian's vow to keep her and the children safe from all harm. They were right, both of them. She had put a burden of expectation on Ian that no man was made to carry, but he had tried to bear it, bound to her by chains of love. How had she not seen it, she who had known the burden of slavery?

"When Ian's back," she said with sudden conviction, "we need to find a time—I don't know when but there's got to be a *when*—to just . . . plunge ourselves into the Word. Mandy and Gabriel too. I don't know if we can dive as deep as you been doing but . . ."

Her words trailed off. Malcolm was looking at her, fair to beaming. It jarred her into realizing she had uttered plans for their future as if Gabriel was coming back, as if they were going to watch him grow up with his sister. She and Ian, together.

I Am My Beloved's.

"I don't want to be afraid anymore, Malcolm."

Malcolm gave her hand a little shake. "Ye can feel afraid, Seona, and still trust the Almighty is working things for your good. Let Him be the first one ye lean into—not me or your mama or Ian. Remind yourself of all He supplies. Peace, wisdom, mercy, grace, hope, strength in time of need. Ye've already guessed how ye find those things. How ye find the One who *is* those things."

"Reading His Word," she said.

"Every day. Talking to Him about it as ye read—and after ye've closed His book. Your heart is a garden and His Word the seed. It'll grow there if ye sow it."

Seona sighed. If this man knew anything at all, it was gardening. And his Lord.

"I know what you're saying is true. Still I long for this day to be done. For them to be back safe, the danger past."

"Amen to that." Malcolm leaned close and kissed her brow, his old man's scent enveloping her. "One day all the troubles will be past, and we will count them as fleeting shadows in light of what we've gained by trusting Jesus. But even now our Father in heaven sees Gabriel and Catriona, just like He sees ye. Choose to trust Him, no matter what this day, or tomorrow, brings."

Malcolm sagged a little as he finished, as if their talk had drained him. Seona leaned against him, more to support now than to draw her own comfort. "I choose," she said—and immediately felt those fears clutching at her again. She closed her eyes and said it in her soul. *I choose to trust, Lord. I choose to fear not. Help me endure this waiting. I choose. I choose . . .*

She didn't open her eyes as Malcolm said, "The Almighty will never leave ye, child. Read His Word for yourself, every page of it. Then read it again. Learn who He is. Who He says *ye* are. That's how ye learn to trust Him, to love Him."

He prayed then for Gabriel and Catriona. For Ian, Joseph, and Matthew. For Neil and those working to mend him. He was still praying when Seona sensed a shining through her eyelids and opened her eyes upon a glorious sight framed by the open stable doors.

Somewhere over the mountains, sunlight had broken through a chink in the clouds to blaze out golden toward the east, where a rainbow arced in colored bands across the rain-swept sky, filling her scoured soul with wonder.

41

Matthew lay unmoving in the cabin-yard. Aram Crane stood between them, pistol aimed at Ian, demanding to see the gold hidden in the folded leather he clutched.

"Listen, Crane," Ian said, certain the man wouldn't be satisfied with the ransom he had to pay—yet something urging him to give the man a chance to walk away from this. "Ye don't have to die today. I've done ye no harm and won't, if ye let the ones ye're holding go, leave this place, and never show your face again to trouble me and mine or anyone in Shiloh."

Crane spat on the ground next to Matthew. "You want to talk harm? He's the one wrecked my camp."

"And ye pilfered his traps. Ye were seen at it." Crane was inches shorter than he, wiry of build, probably twice his age, yet there was about the man a sense of ruthlessness, a wolfish cunning Ian knew better than to underestimate.

"Seen by who? Waring's half-wit! I paid him at last for running his mouth all those years ago. Ruining what chance I had at keeping my place with Waring."

Rage at the offhand admission of Francis Waring's murder, and the irrational blame, clouded Ian's vision red. By the time Francis had spoken against Crane, that night Willa's cabin burned, the man had lost any hope of keeping his position as a groom with Colonel Waring. Had he forgotten Joseph Tames-His-Horse?

Ian hadn't but clamped his lips over the threats eager to leap off his tongue. Joseph would come. He had to trust that—without arousing Crane's suspicion that there was anyone left to challenge him, besides Ian. If he could delay a little longer . . .

"I'll see my son and sister before I give ye anything."

Crane drew back the pistol's hammer. "First I see that gold. I'm losing patience."

Ian's gaze flicked sideways as Crane's mare stepped close to Matthew, nosed his face, snorted a breath that elicited a faint moan. Relief crashed through Ian.

"All right." One measured step at a time, he closed the distance between himself and Crane, holding out what he had to offer.

The man gestured with the pistol. "Open it."

The rain had nearly ceased, but when Ian had the leather folds lying open on his palm, a fat drop hit its contents, making the bits of gold shine. Crane's eyes lit with surprise, as though until now he hadn't fully believed in the gold's existence, despite all he'd done to obtain it. He licked his lips. His head lifted. Grizzled brows drew down. "Where's the rest?"

"Ye'll let me inside that cabin before I promise ye anything more."

"That's not the plan. I want every bit you have. Then you're going to show me where you're getting it. What's in that cabin will keep."

Ian's heart thudded a hollow rhythm, realizing there would be no peaceful way out of this. Even if he managed to get Gabriel and Catriona away, Matthew too, Crane would never believe no endless source of wealth was hidden somewhere on his land. He would never stop threatening. They would never be safe.

A raindrop struck Ian's jaw, leaving a cold trail down his neck. Clouds sagged low and ragged over the pointed crowns of trees ascending toward the mountain's summit. Pistol aimed, Crane awaited his answer.

Ian doubted he could get his hand to his tomahawk, much less throw it, before the man shot him . . . unless he made a false move, invited fire, threw himself to the side enough to sustain a wound that wouldn't incapacitate him completely. Before Crane could reload, he would take him down. Or maybe Crane's powder was wet and the pistol would misfire . . .

Where was Joseph?

He made up his mind to risk it. An instant before he set his plan in motion, a noise from the cabin reached them. A rhythmic thumping, like someone kicking a wall. Another sound joined it. A muffled voice attempting a scream.

Ian's hope soared. "Catriona!"

Crane's face twisted with rage. With a shouted oath, he whirled toward the rickety shack and fired the pistol, the report like a final peal of thunder on the mountainside.

"No!" With horror tearing through him, Ian dropped the gold and charged through acrid smoke, plowing into Aram Crane before the man could turn, pulling free his tomahawk as they fell.

When they hit the earth, he rolled off the man and clubbed him over the head with all his strength.

Scrambling away from Crane's body, he sprinted the short distance across the muddy yard, where he yanked open the cabin door so hard it wrenched off its rotting hinges. He shoved it behind him, into the yard.

Three paces away, across a narrow span of earthen floor, Catriona and Gabriel huddled on a low bed frame, bound, gagged, overjoyed at sight of him. Crane's shot had penetrated the cabin wall but missed his captives, embedding in a log inches above Catriona's head. Particles of exploded wood sprinkled her hair.

Weak with relief, Ian took a step inside. Above her gag, Catriona's eyes widened. Violently she shook her head, emitting a muffled shout.

Ian understood a second too late. Yanked from behind with such force he lost his footing, he stumbled backward over the fallen door, landing flat in the yard with the breath knocked from his lungs. Crane loomed over him, face half-bloodied, tomahawk raised. Ian's own had fallen out of reach.

Sucking in breath at last, he rolled to the side. Crane's blade cleaved the saturated earth, missing Ian's face by a handbreadth. As Ian got to his knees, Crane wrenched his tomahawk free and came at him again, so fast Ian knew he would never make it to his feet in time to meet the blow.

Just shy of delivering it, Crane staggered to a halt, staring at something beyond Ian. Breaking off his attack, the man lunged instead for his mare, which had been cropping bits of grass in the yard. She bolted at his coming, kicking out her hind legs.

Cursing, the man dodged his horse's hooves and halted, gone still as stone, eyes widened in terror. Then he whirled toward Lacey's plot of corn and sprinted across the uneven ground as if the hounds of hell were at his heels.

Only one. Joseph Tames-His-Horse, tomahawk in hand, had come from around the back of the cabin at a run. He paused beside Matthew, still lying stunned in the yard.

Ian scrambled to his feet. "He's alive. But Crane . . ." The man had plunged in among the cornstalks, heading for the creek trail. "Did ye come that way—up the ravine?"

"No. From above. But that one will not escape." Face suffused with a terrible eagerness, Joseph bolted after Crane, leaving Ian torn. He needed Gabriel safe in his arms—and to see Crane taken down.

Conscious now, Matthew pushed himself off the ground. In a voice dazed and strained, he said, "I'll get them—go!"

Ian hesitated a second before memory of that deadfall trap, down along the trail, seized him. Joseph hadn't come that way, hadn't seen the warning Ian left. Crane would need none, but Joseph was running straight into that trap.

He snatched up his tomahawk and raced across the narrow yard into the cornstalks. Bursting out the other side, he saw Joseph disappearing around the first bend in the trail, where it angled close to the ravine.

"Joseph!" The rush of creek water drowned his voice.

Praying not to slip and fall, Ian ran, boots slogging, churning mud. As the mountain's slope on his right pressed the trail close to the ravine's edge, he glimpsed the creek thirty feet below, its storm-fed level higher than an hour past. Ian rounded the first bend in the trail. And saw no one.

He ran on, nearly losing his footing half a dozen times on the descending trail pocked with stones waiting to slide from under a boot before another bend brought him in sight of the warrior.

He heard Joseph's thunderous shout. "Crane!"

Several yards on from the running warrior, Ian spotted the yellow birches that marked the spot where Crane had set his trap, their slender forms clinging to both sides of the trail. Crane had nearly reached them. He must have heard Joseph's shout. He glanced back as if to judge the nearness of his pursuer.

"Joseph!" Ian called again and this time made himself heard. Joseph looked back, slowing his descent.

Crane faced the trail again and quickened his stride, taking advantage of Joseph's distraction to gain ground—and went down in a flailing slide as he reached the birches. He disappeared among their white ranks.

Ian heard a scream, cut off by a clattering rumble. Beyond the birches, the deadfall tore flood-like across the trail and hurtled over the ravine's lip, the form of a man glimpsed among the falling debris.

Joseph descended as far as the birches, where he paused. He was grasping a slender white trunk, leaning out to peer into the ravine, when Ian overtook him. Red stained his shirtsleeve where the gash Neil had stitched bled afresh. Below them the creek was silted brown, foaming over rocks, writhing its way out of the mountains.

Of Crane there was no sign.

"He's gone," Ian said, voice lifted above the rush.

Joseph met his gaze with fierce intention. "He will be."

"Ye're wounded," Ian argued, realizing what the man intended, but Joseph was over the side and gone before Ian's reaching hands could halt him. Certain the warrior had followed Crane to his death, Ian leaned out as far as he dared.

Joseph had found what might have been the only path down the ravine's face to the creek below. As Ian watched, he dropped off the final precipice into the churning flow, letting the swollen creek take him downstream.

Stunned, bruised from battle, Ian made his dazed way back up the trail with a sense of loss as great as his relief in knowing Gabriel, Catriona, and Matthew were alive. Joseph. Neil. The day's casualties crashed over his soul, knocking him off his feet. *Seona.* He would restore to her their son, but what of her trust?

He went to his knees on the trail, knowing once again he hadn't done enough. Wasn't enough. He bowed his head to his muddied fists.

Grace . . . it is enough.

The creek rushed on in the ravine below, but Ian was no longer on that rain-swept mountainside where death and violence stalked. He was far away at Mountain Laurel, on his knees at the bedside of his dying wife.

"*Your* grace is enough. That was all she meant. I could never be enough but *Ye* are. Ye have been all along."

A truth Judith had tried to make him understand so many times. The grace of almighty God went beyond his deserving as far as the east was from the west. Not just for salvation—for every choice, every situation, every moment that had followed. It had nothing to do with how hard he had striven or how wise he had been, whether or not he had foreseen every evil coming and safeguarded those in his care against it. He wasn't all-seeing. Nor was he powerful enough to shield Seona and their children from every hardship for all the years to come.

He didn't have to be. The grace of a good and loving God who *did* see all was enough to carry them through this veil of shadow, to weather whatever troubles it would bring—holding fast to all the joys—until they arrived at last in that Kingdom ruled by peace and righteousness.

With a cry of release, Ian Cameron rose from the trail and stumbled on, eager now to hold his son, embrace his sister, get them down off that mountain—clinging to the hope that grace was enough to safeguard his and Seona's hearts as well and give them a future.

42

"Ian!" His sister's voice reached him while he was still among the dripping cornstalks. They were outside the cabin when he emerged, Matthew with Catriona in his arms, Catriona with Gabriel in hers. The black mare had settled and was back to cropping the sparse grass browning in Lacey's cabin-yard. Where, he wondered, was that old man?

Then he reached them, took Gabriel from his sister, and relief swept all other thought away. Vociferously past his fright, Gabriel babbled about his adventures with his auntie and the bad man who took them away from getting schooled.

"Getting schooled, were ye?" Ian said shakily, rattled with the aftershocks of terror as he patted his son's sturdy little back.

"With Mandy! *She* went with Mama, and that's when the bad man took me and Auntie Catweena away and then . . ."

While his son recited his grievances, Ian opened his eyes to Matthew, bloodied from his head wound, and Catriona, pale and shaken, a bruise darkening on her swollen cheek. Ian ground his teeth to see it.

"Come here," he said, shifting Gabriel and holding out an arm.

Bedecked in his discarded cape, holding the hat that had tumbled from his head in the scuffle with Crane, his sister came to him, placed the muddied hat on his head, and leaned into his side. "He's gone?"

"Crane? Aye. Over that ravine into the creek."

"Dead?" Matthew asked as Catriona pulled away.

"Before he hit the water, maybe. He sprang his own trap. A deadfall. It knocked him off the trail." When Matthew stared blankly, Ian asked, "D'ye remember any of it, after the blow ye took?"

"I heard Crane admit to killing Francis. But you . . . you gave him a chance to walk away from this and live. He didn't take it."

"I didn't think he would."

Matthew frowned. "Still you offered."

"I think it was the Almighty offering it through me. A last chance to escape the fires of hell, maybe." All of them, even Gabriel in his arms, stared at him with widened eyes.

"I wouldn't have done it," Matthew said. Not in anger. Admission.

"Ye might have, had ye felt God's nudging ye to it."

"I did feel it," Matthew countered. "Right before I loosed his mare. I didn't heed it. Maybe had I done as ye bade me . . ."

"There's no looking back," Catriona said. "At least not to brood over what cannot be changed. There's only what we do next—repent if need be and resolve to do what we know is right."

She met Ian's gaze with a trembling smile that spoke of sorrows past and wisdom gained. Then she shivered, despite wearing his cape. Her cloak must have been left in the school cabin. The gown she wore beneath the cape was wet. All were wet through and the air behind the storm was biting. But it was Matthew most concerned him now, with those dazed eyes staring through his bloody mask.

"Can ye ride?" Ian asked him. "We need to round up the horses and get off this mountain."

"Of course." Matthew drew himself straight as Catriona snaked an arm around his waist. He turned his face and brushed a kiss against her hair, come unpinned to curl around her shoulders in rain-darkened hanks. "You are the bravest woman I've ever known," he told her.

Catriona suppressed another shiver. Not her blazing smile. "Brave enough to marry you."

Matthew closed his eyes. "Don't I know it."

"Do you? Good. Let's hear no more talk of who isn't suitable for the likes of me."

Matthew's blood-streaked lips curved. "Not a word." He opened his eyes and fixed Ian with a look of dawning concern. "Uncle Joseph . . . did I dream him?"

"Ye did not." Ian felt a plummeting in his gut, saw the same in Matthew's eyes.

"Where is he then?"

Hating to do so, he told them what Joseph Tames-His-Horse had done. Matthew's gaze questioned—ought they to search for Joseph?—concluding as had Ian that they needed to get Catriona and Gabriel home. "What of Lacey? Where is he?"

"The cabin was empty when . . ." Catriona's teeth had begun to chatter. "When Crane brought us here. He must have been scared off. Before today, I mean."

"Let's go," Matthew said. "Up to my horse. I'm taking this one." He crossed the yard to where the black mare grazed. Despite the smell of blood on him, she didn't shy. They found Joseph's mare hitched with Matthew's horse, which Catriona mounted, taking Gabriel up with her. Ian and Matthew led them down the mountain, horse hitched to horse, circling around by other paths and coming back finally to the sheltered spot where he had left Ruiadh.

They found the roan still waiting, happy for the sight of them.

The surgery door off the kitchen was shut. Maggie had finished cooking the dinner Naomi started before the need to tend Neil MacGregor drew her away. Mandy had eaten. So had Ally and the boys, then gone back out to the stable. Lemuel Waring had stayed, rifle propped nearby, baby Josephine asleep in his arms. She was starting to fret as Seona and Malcolm came into the kitchen. Lem jiggled her, crooning.

Maggie turned from the hearth and stilled, watching Lem holding her sister. A smile tugged at her mouth before she looked to Seona and Malcolm. "There's stew left. I can fix you both a plate."

Malcolm nodded, but Seona declined. Before that glorious rainbow faded, she had asked Malcolm to tell her those *fear not* verses again. Now she sat at the MacGregors' long table, pulled Mandy onto her lap, and looked through Neil's field guide, pondering the verses, feeding her spirit as she turned pages and remarked on drawings finer than anything she would ever produce. She would take up painting again though. Among other essential things.

"What's this one, Mama?" Mandy asked, her voice clear as a bell.

"It says here at the bottom. Bog laurel." *Thank You, almighty God, for this sweet girl-child. Keep Your strong arms around her brother until he's brought back safe to mine . . .*

"I was born at a Laurel," Mandy said, tilting her face up to Seona's.

"You were born at a place called Mountain Laurel, in North Carolina. So was I. So was your Granny Lily and Naomi, Ally—"

"Gabriel?"

Seona swallowed. *Let not your heart be troubled . . .* "Gabriel, too," she said, voice steady on his name.

Mandy tugged at her encircling arm. "Because we're family?"

Seona glanced at Malcolm, watching from his seat at the table. "That's right. By blood or by heart." All of them born at Mountain Laurel and elsewhere, linked by birth or choice.

She was about to turn another page in Neil MacGregor's book when Mandy's head bobbed erect. "Granny!"

Seona hadn't heard the surgery door open. Lily and Naomi filed into the kitchen looking wrung from their ordeal. Josephine, startled awake, let out a wail of need no jiggling could satisfy.

Maggie rescued Lem. She took her baby sister and whisked her into the surgery, closing the door behind her, muffling the baby's cries. They soon ceased.

Seona set Mandy on the bench beside her and rose.

Naomi went straight for the kettle, peered in at what remained, and started ladling stew onto two plates. "Thank the Lord there's leftovers. I'm give out for want of it. Lily, you too."

Seona rounded the table and took her mama by the arm. "Come sit." Nearly swaying on her feet, Lily sat on a bench across from Mandy. Naomi set a plate of stew and a spoon in front of her. "Mama? Is he all right?"

Lily pursed her lips and blew out a long breath. "He stayed awake through it all," she said at last. "Guiding me every cut, every stitch, the setting of every bone." She met Seona's gaze, then blinked at Mandy, Malcolm, Lem, the plate in front of her. "We saved his foot, I think. How much use of it he'll have, I don't know."

"Time will tell." Seona put an arm around the exhausted bow of her mother's spine. "He's overcome so much already, and his faith is stronger for it. I think, no matter what, Dr. Neil will be all right." She glanced at Malcolm. "We can release him to the Almighty."

Lily pulled her head back, staring, a crease between her brows. "Girl-baby?"

Seona had opened her mouth to tell her mama about the *fear not* verses, the rainbow, the talk in the stable, when from that direction voices rose—not just male voices.

"That's Catriona!" Lem exclaimed.

Before she could catch another breath, Seona was off that bench and through the house and onto the veranda, where she halted at sight of horses congregated in the stable-yard and three . . . no, *four* figures dismounting. Matthew, his face streaked with blood. Catriona, handing down their son to Ian.

"Gabriel!" She leapt down the veranda steps and flew across the puddled yard, where she halted and received her son, who clung crying not from harm—to her soaring relief he had taken none—but an exhaustion deep as her mama's.

"It's all right," she soothed, rubbing his back, eyes shut to keep the world at bay. "You're all right now. Mama's got you, baby."

"Aye, he is all right," Ian said, his voice near.

"So am I, in case anyone wants to know."

The edge of laughter in Catriona's tone made Seona's eyes spring open. She shifted Gabriel in her grasp and reached for Ian's sister, pulling her into a tight embrace. "I'm so relieved you are."

"Pa?" Matthew asked, looking toward the house.

"Willa is in the surgery with him," Lily said, having followed Seona out into the yard.

Seona turned to see Mandy in her arms. The child squirmed down and ran to Ian, who swooped her up and kissed her soundly. She looked at her brother, sagging in Seona's arms. "Where did you go, Gabriel? You made Mama worry!"

"Sahwee, Mandy . . . ," Gabriel murmured, half-asleep against Seona's shoulder.

Ian's gaze stayed fixed on them as he told Matthew, "Go inside; see your da. I'll stable the horses, put the mare in a paddock for ye to sort later."

Seona didn't ask where the black mare had come from. She only wanted to hold her boy, feel the strain of his weight as she pressed him close. Everything else felt far away.

"Let's see to that gash," Catriona said, taking Matthew's arm to tow him toward the house, adding over her shoulder, "Lily, could you have a look?"

Seona thought surely her mama had done enough, but Lily nodded and said, "I'll be right in . . ."

Seona turned to watch the pair cross the yard in time to see Catriona's grip on Matthew's arm slide down to his hand, which she clasped as they climbed the veranda steps. Matthew didn't pull his away.

"Is it safe to go home?" Seona asked, at last addressing Ian, her heart expanding toward him now she had fully absorbed the fact of Gabriel's safety—knowing she had so much to say. So much to explain. He was still holding Mandy. His eyes held longing. Pain.

"Crane is gone." He took a step toward her as if intending to say more, when Lily spoke again, her voice sharp.

"Where's Joseph? Did he make it back to ye?"

Until that moment Seona hadn't registered Joseph's absence.

"He did," Ian said. "And just in time. Crane had taken Matthew down and was about to do the same to me, but at sight of Joseph, he ran. There was a trap—a deadfall snare Crane set along a ravine. He fell and sprang it himself and was swept over the side into a creek raging high from the rain. The water took him." Ian shook his head and looked at Lily with haunted eyes. "I thought Crane surely drowned—if not killed by that deadfall collapsing on him—but Joseph wouldn't trust to it. He went down the ravine after the man. Let the creek carry him downstream too."

"With that wounded arm?" Her mama's face went gray. "How high was the water? Raging, ye said?"

"Aye, but Joseph's strong . . ." Ian's reassurance trailed off, for Lily hadn't waited to hear it. She had turned back toward the house.

"Mama?" Seona called.

Lily didn't pause. Nor did she go inside. At the veranda steps she veered away and headed toward the woods that grew between the MacGregors' house and the lake. The north end, nearest the ridge.

"Mama!"

Lily reached the trees and kept going.

"I have the horses to deal with," Ian said. "But we need to—"

"Ian," she interrupted, "what's wrong with Mama?"

"I think she . . ." Ian shook his head. "Seona, can we talk for a moment? Please."

The need for it screamed from his eyes. Seona was torn by the same need, but also by the dismay she had seen on her mama's face. She needed to tell Ian how wrong she had been for making him think her happiness—maybe even her love—rested solely on his efforts to keep them safe. But with their arms full of their children, she couldn't even embrace him. She managed to free a hand to grip his arm, meaning to reassure, but he flinched when she said, "We'll talk at home. Soon. Ian—I need to go after Mama."

43

Lily had reached the wood's far edge, where scattered pines opened to the lakeshore, before Seona, trotting along the rooted path with Gabriel nodding in her arms, caught up. "Mama, wait!"

Out from under the pines, Lily halted on the path that led around the lake to their fields and cabins. She was crying when she turned.

Catching her breath from the chase, Seona hoisted Gabriel higher on her hip. "What's wrong? Is Dr. MacGregor worse off than you let on? That must have been the hardest thing you've ever had to do."

Lily palmed away her tears. "Hard, but we came through. Barring any festering, we saved his foot. He'll walk on it again, God willing."

"Then what's got you crying?" Sheer exhaustion would be enough.

Her mama held her gaze, eyes brimming with more feelings than Seona could catch and name. "Girl-baby, there's something I need to tell ye."

Seona stepped closer. "What?"

Her mama's smile was a tremulous effort. "I aim to marry Joseph . . . if he comes back to us."

Under the storm-racked sky the lake water lapped in tiny ripples along its shore. Farther out a chilling breeze ruffled its dark surface. Seona had left her shawl in Willa MacGregor's kitchen, but she felt nothing—saw nothing, save her mama's earnest eyes as she spoke.

"It's been the same for him as me all these years. Grieving a love that couldn't be, never finding it elsewhere. Just waiting, loving the ones in our care. Then that morning he came seeking my help for Willa . . . he says he knew as I came running from the stable it was me he'd waited for. I took longer to know the same. But I do know now. We mean to leave afore snow comes. I'm going to Grand River with Joseph."

"What?" Seona bit her tongue before she said the words that sprang to mind—*Mama, this is no time for fooling.* Plain enough it wasn't fooling.

Not so long ago she had wondered if her mama had dreams or hopes apart from her and Gabriel, but since coming to New York, she had been so caught up with her own hopes and fears she hadn't thought about such things. She had fallen back into the habit of taking her mama for granted. But all the while, her mama's heart had quietly been opening to Joseph Tames-His-Horse. She meant to marry him. She meant to *leave.*

In all her planning and second-guessing those plans, Seona had never imagined a life without her mama in it. She wouldn't be in it much longer—if Joseph hadn't gone down that creek to his death.

Let not your heart be troubled . . .

"Girl-baby, listen." Lily touched her arm, the other hand on Gabriel's head. "Ye've had your doubts, especially under shadow of these terrible threats, and I know he hasn't done everything perfect, but ye're never going to find a man who loves ye like this boy's daddy does. One who would march into a lion's den for ye both—like he proved today." She stroked Gabriel's tousled curls, relief over his safe return plain. "Even so, he's just a man. Don't rest your deepest hope in him."

"I know that now, and I won't." Seona covered her mama's hand with her own. "I just never thought *you* would leave."

"Don't put your hope in me, either. I'm a woman, like ye."

Seona couldn't stop the tears welling. "Of course you are, Mama. And you deserve everything I hope for myself. It's just . . . I'll miss you when you go."

When, not *if.* Catching that distinction, Lily's dark eyes widened. "D'ye believe he's well then? Joseph? That he's coming back for me?"

"I do," Seona said.

Her mama's eyes flared wider as she looked past Seona to the edge of the forest that spread down nigh to the lakeshore, from whence a deep voice spoke.

"As should you, Tsigalili. For I have come back."

Seona caught the joy breaking over her mama's face before whirling to see Joseph Tames-His-Horse, bruised and bloodied, stepping from among the dripping trees. Lily ran to the forest's edge, straight into his arms.

Holding her sleeping boy, Seona took in the sight of the tall warrior cradling her mama to his chest—and felt her heart molding to this unforeseen turn. Over her mama's head, Joseph lifted his gaze and, with a striking vulnerability, silently sought her blessing.

Smiling at the man who, it occurred, had every intention of becoming her daddy, Seona nodded, receiving the unexpected gift.

Then she left them and went to find Ian.

His hands were shaking as he unsaddled Juturna's dam, preparing to put her into the paddock with Ruaidh. With Nip and Tuck trailing, Ally had ridden to the pasture to check on the cattle they had left untended since morning. Naomi and Malcolm were in their cabin with Mandy. Catriona had stayed at the MacGregors', while Willa saw to Matthew's gashed scalp. For Joseph he still prayed, hoping someone would bring word ere long. As for Seona, Lily, and Gabriel, he had yet to see them returning around the lake.

We'll talk at home. It was all Seona had said before racing after her mother. He tried to summon every nuance of her expression, but it had happened so quickly. She had put a hand to his arm and squeezed—he hadn't imagined that—and he had seen that she still wore the ring he put there. *I Am My Beloved's.*

Was she still? He wouldn't blame her if she returned to Boston with Lily and Gabriel after all this. They would be safe there. His da would make sure of it, one way or another.

He set the mare's saddle where it normally rested and returned with a currying brush, his constricted heart a painful throbbing in his chest. Had she found Lily? Were they all right?

Seconds later a notion so terrible swept him that he dropped the brush to clatter on the packed earth, causing the mare to snort. Had Crane set traps between the lake and the ridge? He and Matthew had sprung several more spotted on their way down the mountain. What if there were others?

Panic had him by the scruff. He unlatched the outer box door and gave the mare a smack on the rump, sending her out unbrushed to graze with Ruaidh. He left the stable at a run, heading for the lake.

He hadn't cleared the beeches before he saw Seona coming across the harvested cornfield, Gabriel in her arms, face composed—until she caught sight of him. He halted in her cabin-yard, for the second time that day gripped with relief so powerful it nearly doubled him.

Seona hurried her steps, rightly judging his state if not the reason for it. "It's all right," she said, a little breathless. "Mama's with Joseph."

"Joseph?" he echoed. "He's all right then?"

"Yes. I don't know about Crane or what he might've done to the man, but he and Mama—" She shook her head, and the most singular smile he had ever seen curved her lips, a smile with as much sorrow as joy behind it. Tears shimmered in her eyes. "They mean to marry."

That knocked every other thought from his head. "Each other?"

"Yes!" She laughed and hefted Gabriel, sagging in her arms. "I need to get this boy down afore I drop him."

Ian reached for Gabriel, relieving her of the strain. She followed him into the cabin and pulled back the blankets of the little bed, where he laid their son, still damp from his rainy adventure. Gabriel rolled onto his side, nestled his head into the pillow, and stuck a thumb in his mouth. Seona's breath rushed out at the sight.

"God Almighty be thanked," Ian said, which made her look at him.

"And you, for getting him back."

The calm statement was so *not* what he had expected from her, he hardly knew what to say. "Seona—I . . ."

"Outside," she whispered. Taking an old shawl off a peg by the door, one kept for work, she stepped out of the cabin. Still chafing in his rain-dampened coat and breeches, boots a muddy mess, hair drying in ropy curls, he followed her out, knowing he looked a wreck.

The air was chill. The storm clouds overhead were thinning, racing eastward on a shivering breeze.

Seona sat on the bench beside the door. "I completely missed it, Mama and Joseph. I've been so centered on myself, second-guessing everything both of us have done and said—oh!" she interrupted herself. "Mama's not just getting married, she's leaving. Going to Canada with Joseph."

Ian stepped away, mind spinning over what she had started to say. *Second-guessing everything* . . . "Joseph said nothing of it to me. But . . . don't ye think it's for the best?"

She blinked. "Why would you say that?"

Surprised she need ask, he said, "Ye'd be better off with them, ye and Gabriel, given all the ways I . . . I've failed ye." Her puzzled expression changed to something else. Disappointment? Blame? He pivoted before he could discern what and so she wouldn't witness his own heartache as he plowed on. "Ye'd be safe with them, aye? Joseph . . . he'll be your da once they're married. And if I know anything of Joseph Tames-His-Horse, he knows how to take care of his kin. He would—"

"Ian, sit down here beside me."

He clenched his fists, gazing stubbornly toward the lake. "Let me finish."

"No."

At that he turned. She had risen, shawl wrapping her shoulders, arms crossed. "I see the despair in you and can guess what you mean to say. I don't want to hear it."

Blood rose hot into his face. "Ye won't even hear me out?"

"I won't. There's no reason for it. Despair is for those who have no future, no hope. We have both."

Tears came like a tide-rush, burning his eyes and nose. "We do?" was all he managed before the swell took him.

She uncrossed her arms and walked into his, held him tight, and let him cry into her hair. He felt her fingers in his, gently stroking through the tangles the day had made. "We're going to be married in a few days' time. Aren't we?"

A strangled sound escaped him, not a sob nor yet a laugh. "I . . . I think I want to sit down now."

They sat outside the cabin where Gabriel slept, watching the changing sky as gray clouds parted and the westering sun peeked through, lighting up the ridge and lakeshore, faintly raucous with the calls of wild geese. Seona talked of what had happened in Neil MacGregor's barn while her mama fought to save their neighbor's foot, if not his very life.

"Malcolm made me see how I was letting fear rule my heart, how I'd put my hope in the wrong place—too much in you, too little in God. That wasn't fair, Ian. I went so far as to blame you for Gabriel . . . but it wasn't your fault. It was mine. I insisted on taking him and Mandy into Shiloh. I'm sorry, for all of it."

He groaned at her apology. "Seona . . . it's all right."

"It's *not.* I neglected things I shouldn't have, let slip what I knew was right to do, while under my nose I had the example of a man doing them—Malcolm, learning to read his Bible, then reading it through, day by day, setting his hope on things eternal. That's how a body guards their heart. I let myself get too busy doing all the things needing done, so my soul went unfed, my heart unguarded. I stopped hearing the Lord's voice and listened to fear."

Conviction drove through Ian, piercing as an arrow. He bowed his face into his hands, laid bare before the Almighty's revealing light. He was no less culpable than she. *Forgive me,* he prayed, then confessed to Seona how he had let himself believe it was up to him to anticipate every evil that might raise its head over the horizon, every need, and get ahead of it all. "But my fear was that I could never do enough to keep ye safe or provide all I want for ye and the bairns. It's given me no rest. No time for the things I intended us to do, like what ye said. Seeking the Almighty. Laying that foundation before I try and build upon it."

"I want that foundation," she said, gazing off to where he would in a few months' time begin laying another foundation, for a home. "I want to find the time to build it. Everything else—all those good things we want? They'll come in time if they're needed. But not if we're stumbling at every wind that blows."

He straightened and took her hand in his, felt her fingers grip his willingly, marveling that after all they had been though, she could want such things. Want him. "Find the time or make it, we will. So we never again need find our way back to the Almighty."

"Or each other."

"Aye," he said. "And what happened, Seona, it wasn't your fault. Crane would have taken Catriona alone or found a way to reach the children, or ye, here. But he's gone now. I know Joseph saw to that."

He closed his eyes against a shower of sunlight, feeling the ring on Seona's finger, rubbing against his skin. He blinked down at it. The tiny diamonds in the flowered band caught sunlight and sparkled like the rain beading the grasses at the yard's edge, dripping from the golden beech leaves of the mossy giant that sheltered the cabin at their backs.

Nothing was as bright as her creek-water eyes. He leaned his head and kissed her gently, feeling the jolt go through him, tender and sweet, when she kissed him back.

He smiled against her mouth, then asked, "D'ye mind what the ring I gave ye says?"

She pulled back to meet his gaze. "Of course."

"Ye're my beloved. And always will be." Though he couldn't summon courage to ask what he wanted to, she had mercy enough to tell him anyway.

"'I Am My Beloved's,'" she quoted, leaning in to rest her head against his shoulder. "And he is mine."

44

Early October 1797

The beeches edging the cabin-yard shimmering gold . . . leaves drifting down from spreading boughs, sparks on cool air, twirling in the grip of the gentlest breeze . . . a sky so cloudless blue it drowned the senses . . . the late-morning sun taking the edge off autumn's chill . . . across the harvested fields, the distant chorus of geese on the lake . . .

Ian Cameron judged his wedding day to be as perfect as if he had arranged it so. Even when a dozen geese rose to cut across the heavens in a dark wedge, calling as they flew, he could find nothing melancholy in the sound, though in the past it had struck him as most mournful. On that day the cries of the wild geese spoke to his heart of enduring companionship, of seasons lived in community, such as that gathered to celebrate his and Seona's nuptials.

The Kepplers were in attendance. Goodenough and Lem had come with Colonel Waring, standing now to officiate the ceremony mere moments from starting.

Along with Willa and their children, Neil MacGregor had come, having ventured from home for the first time since his injury on the mountain. With his ankle unable to long bear him up, even with the aid of a crutch, a chair had been provided him, next to Malcolm's. Neil's recuperation would be long, perhaps never full, but in keeping with his irrepressible spirit and indomitable faith, the man had determined to resume his doctoring, to everyone's relief. Willa's most especially.

The MacGregors had come not only to witness Ian and Seona's joining, but that of Lily and Joseph Tames-His-Horse.

Until three days ago, Seona's mother and Willa's clan brother had meant to journey to Grand River and Joseph's Mohawk kin to marry there, assuming Colonel Waring would refuse to officiate for them, Joseph's having been the hand that took the life of his eldest son. The old magistrate had surprised one and all, forgiving the deed and lifting the restrictions of his and Joseph's uneasy truce.

Now the two stood in each other's presence for the first time since that fateful night, neither completely at ease, though Ian guessed Joseph's nervousness—discernible only by the tension in his stillness—had less to do with Elias Waring than the reason for Ian's own.

Taller than any man present, save Ally, the man set to become Ian's father-by-law was a splendid sight in his native dress, bedecked in quillwork and buckskin fringe and sun-gilt silver, his long hair tied with the blue-gray feathers of a heron. A white blanket with red trim, folded long, was draped across one shoulder.

With their backs to Colonel Waring, Joseph and Ian watched the cabin where Seona and Lily had been, for the past hour, gowning up and having their hair arranged. Joseph cast a sideways glance at him, dark eyes betraying impatience. Ian grinned. The corner of Joseph's mouth quirked in response before he shifted his gaze past those gathered, to the door of the cabin from which their brides would soon—*very soon, please*—emerge.

A titter started among the Keppler offspring. It swept back across the ranks of witnesses, young and old. Ian had no attention to spare for their murmured words, though he shot his children a warm look, Mandy in Naomi's arms, Gabriel perched higher than them all, little legs astride Ally's broad shoulders.

Ian glanced again at Joseph in time to see the warrior's deep chest expand in an indrawn breath, his dark eyes light with anticipation. He whipped his gaze back to the cabin. Its door had opened.

Catriona and Willa were first to emerge, hurrying to their places,

Willa beside Neil's chair, Catriona to Matthew's side—like an arrow shot. Matthew greeted her with a look so blatantly besotted Ian looked away, not before he saw their hands clasp, not quite hidden in the folds of his sister's gown.

Then Seona appeared in the cabin doorway, dressed in her green gown, and all other thought fled his mind. She paused, framed in the opening, and met his gaze across the yard. Smiling full, she stepped aside for Lily to exit the cabin. Hand in hand, mother and daughter crossed a golden carpet of beech leaves to those gathered at the grove's edge.

Ian's breath caught somewhere in his throat and held there, while currents coursed through him like the blood in his veins. Joy, relief, wonder that this day had dawned for them at last and with such splendor. But no glory of nature on display could outshine Seona, dark hair held back from her face with the comb he had given her long ago, entwined with the morning glories that matched her ring, the rest left curling thick to her waist. Her head was crowned with a circlet of red huckleberry leaves. Her eyes were as vivid as the day.

Lily, similarly crowned, wore an amber gown the women had furiously stitched over the preceding days. With her face shining for her bridegroom, she took his outstretched hand as Ian reached for Seona's.

Lily released her with a smile already teary, both clearly eager to get on with things.

Joseph and Lily, they had decided, would be married first. But as Ian and Seona stepped aside so they could stand before Elias Waring and exchange those ageless vows to love, honor, and cherish, Ian caught Seona's gaze. They shared one of those looks that spoke without words.

The evening before, while they had shifted her and Gabriel's belongings to Ian's larger cabin, and Catriona's to Seona's—after today, Lily would go with Joseph to stay for a while with the MacGregors—Ian had unearthed the wee portraits of Miranda and Aidan Cameron, which Seona had kept since leaving Mountain Laurel.

Their faces were fresh in his mind as they stood beneath the beeches. Ian did not deem it too fanciful to believe that, more than on that day in the birch hollow, he had the blessing of his cousin, Aidan, now.

Not just for this union with his daughter—made right and true in this blessed second chance—but for Lily, who had at last found a man with whom she could safely rest her heart.

Seona squeezed his hand, her lifted face shining with the day's double portion of joy. Ian had to will himself not to bend close and kiss her before either could speak their vows. Instead they watched with full hearts as Lily and Joseph did the speaking and the kissing.

"I didn't want to cry today, Mama," she had told Lily as Catriona and Willa left off their arranging of hair and gowns and stepped from the cabin, leaving the door open to the blazing blue-gold of their wedding day. She had slid two fingers across her cheek. "Look now, I'm already wiping tears."

Her mama's eyes had shimmered too. "This day deserves its tears. Let them fall, girl-baby. They're joyful ones, aren't they?"

"My heart is so full," Seona had whispered and all but fell into her mother's embrace. Lily had held her briefly, kissed her cheek, then touched it tenderly. Never mind the fine lines netting the corners of her eyes or the bit of white threading her crow-black hair, woven in a simple braid and crowned in scarlet leaves, her mama had never looked so radiantly young, with a smile that could no more be dimmed than could Seona's own.

"Ye're beautiful," Lily had said. "Beautiful and whole. Shall we do this?"

Not a question. An invitation.

"Let's go get married, Mama." This time there would be no fragile, makeshift promises traded in secret. A real wedding, openly celebrated, as sure and true as the foundation she and Ian meant to build upon.

Seona stepped outside the cabin into the cool of the day and felt the sun's warmth lightly touch her shoulders. She paused for her mama to join her, clasping hands as they walked on scattered beech leaves, down the short aisle created as their guests parted to let them pass, each to the side of the man who had eyes for none but her. She spared the tall, bighearted warrior who was about to become her daddy a swift smile. Then all her attention was for Ian.

His eyes were a smokier blue than the sky, his hair a less vibrant gold than the leaves drifting down around them, but his smile rivaled the late-morning sun still rising in the sky. His hand held tight to hers as her mama and Joseph spoke their vows and joined their futures along with their hearts, while she tucked away for safekeeping impressions of the passing moments.

The warm pressure of Ian's fingers. His solid presence at her side. Geese flying over, calling to each other. The rattle of the breeze through golden leaves overhead. A brief, bright shower as some fell . . .

The sense of others looking on. Kin and neighbors—some of those neighbors becoming kin—but also those who had lived and loved and gone their way. Master Hugh, her granddaddy. Judith, whose daughter she would love and raise with stories of her mama as a girl. The father and grandmother she had never seen, save in their tiny portraits. Looking up at Ian only to realize he was thinking of Miranda and Aidan Cameron too . . .

Elias Waring finished with her mama and Joseph, pronouncing them husband and wife. There came the first kiss on the mouth Seona had ever seen her mama give a man. Joseph unfolded his red-trimmed blanket and draped it over his and her mama's shoulders. Lily nestled against the ribs of her new husband, sheltered beneath the blanket and his encircling arm.

Seona wiped a few more tears and held her mama's joyful gaze. Then it was her and Ian's turn.

No stumbling over words this time. She had memorized her vows to love, honor, cherish—until death parted them. So had Ian. Colonel Waring had but to nudge them along while they faced one another, hands clasped.

Her mama's turn to cry.

Seona already wore a ring. After the vows there was a kiss, chaste and sweet if not exactly brief, before the old magistrate said a prayer of blessing over them all.

While he prayed, Seona and Ian faced each other, hands still clasped between them, eyes closed. His breath warm on her brow. A breeze ruffling chilly fingers through her hair. The sun warming where it touched.

Something struck her left hand, cold, smooth, no harder than a finger tap.

She opened her eyes to find a perfectly formed beech leaf, yellow-gold, resting on their clasped hands, half on hers, half on Ian's. He had felt it too and was looking at her when she lifted her gaze—all other eyes save those of the littlest still closed in reverence as Colonel Waring's prayer went on. Again their thoughts converged.

The hollow with the waterfall . . . the canopy of autumn birches . . . Munin, her daddy's old raven . . . the tying of a hair ribbon around their wrists . . . the birch leaf they had trapped between their bound hands.

Bound now by more than wishful thinking and unanchored hope, they opened their hands just enough to let the beech leaf fall into their cupped shelter, then closed it safely away. She would press it in their Bible, to remember.

Memory. That was what that old raven's name had meant. Nothing to flinch from now, be they old memories or new, painful or joy-filled. For what was memory, after all, if not the trail of God's grace following them all the days of their lives?

Early that morning, once it seemed certain the fine weather would hold, makeshift tables, benches, and chairs had been set up in the cabin-yard for the wedding feast, some brought from the MacGregors', others from as far away as the Warings', enough for everyone to have a seat or at least a block chair set nearby.

One table groaned under the bowls, platters, and kettles that kept coming out of Naomi's cabin, some provided by Willa and Maggie—including a spiced ginger wedding cake that all but melted in Seona's mouth. More contributions had been brought by Goodenough and Anni Keppler, creating an abundance that left Seona and her mama once more on the verge of tears for everyone's kindness and generosity.

Pure thankfulness.

After everyone had eaten their fill and then some, there was dancing, none other than old Hector Lacey providing the tunes, having come by a fiddle from Jack Keagan's store, already possessing the skill to play it.

They had wondered for a full day about that old man, after the ordeal on the mountain with Aram Crane was ended. Turned out he had fled his squatter's shack at Crane's invasion, shortly before the man brought Gabriel and Catriona there, captive. Mr. Lacey had found his way eventually to the MacGregors and since been provided that promised home with Colonel Waring, Goodenough, and Lem, where he seemed content to spend the winter.

"After giving himself a thorough scrubbing, out back of the stable," Goodenough had been heard to say more than once. "But I cannot rid him of that mangy critter nesting round his neck—what he calls a *beard*," she added as her foot tapped time to the old man's fiddling and she watched the young folk and a few of their elders cutting circles in the cabin-yard. "Yet," she was quick to add.

Seona and Ian hadn't risen from their places at the table. Neither had Lily or Joseph, seated nearby, exchanging tender looks that made Seona want to cry—*again*—whenever she caught one.

They watched the dancers, Catriona and Matthew in particular.

"You already posted that letter to your parents," Seona said, leaning close to feel Ian's warmth, his thrumming energy. She knew he would be asking her to join the dancers before long. "But you didn't mention *them*."

She nodded toward his sister, being twirled among the dancers by Neil and Willa's adopted son. The two made a handsome, striking contrast. Seona had seen Catriona happy before—giddy, even reckless—but now her joy was settled, centered. Seona knew she wasn't the only one who had learned these past months where to place her hope. Or in whom.

Lord, that we never need learn this again. Establish it in our hearts. Evermore.

Ian had written to Mister Robert and Miss Margaret of their pending nuptials, and of Lily and Joseph's, and had given account of all that had transpired on the mountain—leaving out the more harrowing bits, including what had happened between Joseph's going over the ravine into that raging creek and his showing up again on the lakeshore to claim himself a bride. A thing of vital importance, as it turned out, dispelling all doubt as to Aram Crane's present situation, though they were left to wonder whether he perished by his own snare, drowned in the swollen creek after his fall, or escaped those perils only to be ended by human agency.

Joseph refused to speak of what he found downstream where the creek made a bend, nor in what manner he dealt with what he found there. Perhaps he had told her mama. As for the rest, knowing Aram Crane would never trouble them again was sufficient to render their sleep untroubled.

But Ian hadn't mentioned Matthew in his letter, though from the way that young man was looking at his chosen dance partner, Seona knew Ian had best give his parents due warning. And reassurance. Matthew had accepted the position Elias Waring offered, of training the man's horses full-time—which included a cabin on the property to live in.

It would come as a shock to Ian's parents, no doubt, but if they could see her for themselves, they would discover a daughter vastly altered from the one they bade farewell to back in spring.

"They've my blessing," Ian said. "Especially since they don't mean to rush into things. Next summer maybe, aye?"

"That's the last I heard on the matter," Seona said, seeing Ian narrow his gaze as Matthew spun his sister in the steps of the dance, mirrored with varying degrees of success and laughter by the other couples, including Lem and Maggie.

"I wonder . . . ," he said.

"Whether your parents might come for Catriona's wedding?" she finished.

He leaned back to look at her and grinned. "Ye thought of it too? I'll ask them when I write. But I was thinking . . . with Ned in Deerfield, all of us here, I find myself hoping my parents might consider quitting Boston altogether, moving a little nearer."

"Like Albany? If I mind aright all that distance we came, that's smack in between Shiloh and Deerfield."

"Near enough," Ian said with a wink. "I'll make the suggestion."

The idea of Ian's parents living closer added another layer of joy to the day. Seona was about to spring from her chair when the music ended, thinking Hector Lacey would dive into another reel. But he set his fiddle on the stump where he had stood to play and came shuffling over to their place at the table.

While Goodenough glowered at the man's grizzled beard scraggling to his waist, he pulled off an old knit cap, revealing a head as round and bald as a pumpkin, and made them a surprisingly graceful bow.

"You aren't done fiddling, are you, Mr. Lacey?" Seona asked. "I'd like at least one dance on my wedding day."

"No, ma'am." Lacey bobbed his head again. "Just taking a break so I could give you'uns this." The old man dug into a trouser pocket, rooted around, and pulled out a folded scrap of leather Seona instantly recognized. "Found this in the yard when I went back to rescue my things, after all the hullabaloo got past. Reckon it for your'n—and what's in it."

Seona let Ian accept the folded leather, which he opened to reveal a scattering of tiny gold nuggets and a few flakes, still encrusted with earth. The gold they had meant to ransom Gabriel and Catriona—dropped and trampled underfoot, Ian had told her when she had finally thought to ask whether Aram Crane had taken the gold Cecily Reynold sent.

"Thank ye, Hector," Ian said, smile sobered by the memories of that perilous day.

"That's all I found, down on my knees in the weeds and mud. Would've missed it altogether had the sun not popped out long enough to cast a shine. Might be there's more."

Ian stood to shake the man's hand. "I meant to go back before the snows come down so far, and maybe I will. But I appreciate ye bringing me this."

Hector Lacey grinned, his wiry beard parting to bare a set of startling teeth, large and brown as a horse's. As the man grabbed a biscuit off the table and went back to his fiddle, Goodenough was heard to mutter, "Maybe best he keep them whiskers . . ."

Ian tucked the gold into his coat pocket and slanted her a grin. “Ready to dance?”

Seona stood and took his proffered hand. “What will you do with the gold?”

“Put it with the rest,” he told her as Hector Lacey drew his bow across the fiddle strings, warming to another tune. “Come spring when these beeches are budding again, we’ll build a house with it.”

“Spring,” she said and stopped in her tracks at the edge of the assembled dancers. “Beech Spring!”

Ian turned back, head tilted in question. “What’s that?”

“I been thinking on it. This place—*our* place—needs a name. Like Mountain Laurel. I’d like it to have a name.”

“*Beech Spring*, did ye say?” Ian said as they took their positions among the dancers, grinning at Lem and Matthew, who had switched partners for another spin around the cabin-yard. And at Gabriel and Mandy, standing up together, ready to dance. Or try to.

Still grinning, Ian looked at her, contentment warming the blue of his eyes. “Aye. I like it.”

45

They had gathered in Malcolm's cabin to wait. Naomi with her never-idle hands turned to mending. Ally with his big frame folded up, perched on a block chair by the bed where his grandfather lay, too tired to read his Bible. Ian seated at the table, doing the reading that morning, from the book of Jude. It was another one of those autumn days that dawns chill but clear, holding the sun-drenched memory of summer, if not its warmth.

A fire blazed in the cooking hearth, yet the cabin door stood partly open. Joseph Tames-His-Horse filled that space, leaning against the doorframe while he waited for his bride to return from walking with her daughter and grandchildren, over by the lake. Saying goodbye.

The horses were saddled and waiting. Joseph and Lily would leave for Grand River once Catriona returned with Matthew, bidding his family farewell. There was still the hunting to do. Lily would spend those months in Grand River with Joseph's Mohawk kin while he and Matthew came and went, though from the way the man's gaze was fixed toward the lake, Ian predicted a shorter hunt than in years past.

Nip and Tuck came to the door to peer inside, looking for Ally, usually out with the cattle by this hour. But Ally was watching his grandfather's still face. Now and then Malcolm would open an eye, see his grandson there, and the two would share a grin. Tuck poked his nose into the cabin and whined.

Joseph kneed the collie gently back and said a word in Mohawk. *"Satien."*

The collie sat and quieted himself, save for a sheepishly thumping tail.

"'But ye, beloved, building up yourselves on your most holy faith,'" Ian read, "'praying in the Holy Ghost, keep yourselves in the love of God, looking for the mercy of our Lord Jesus Christ unto eternal life. . . .'"

He paused to clear his throat. Life eternal had found him on earth, as had the Almighty's mercy and love, even with the pain this day would bring. Especially to Seona.

"I've never seen Mama this happy," she had admitted that first morning they awoke together, husband and wife, languid and secluded as night lifted and dawn began to gray, revealing them to each other through shutters left open an inch. There had been frost that night—Ian had smelled it—but they had been warm, snuggled under quilts, beneath the covers all their limbs entangled.

"And ye're happy for her?" He had kissed her brow, knowing the question unnecessary but thinking she needed to say the words.

"I am. I rarely thought what it must have been like for Mama, going without this kind of love so many years. God be thanked I didn't have to."

"God be thanked," he had agreed with a grin that made her squirm with laughter in his arms, and there had been no more talk of anyone's love but their own.

No more talk at all for a spell.

"'Now unto him that is able to keep you from falling, and to present you faultless before the presence of his glory with exceeding joy, to the only wise God our Saviour, be glory and majesty, dominion and power, both now and for ever. Amen.'"

Having reached the end of Jude's book, Ian raised his head and took the measure of his listeners. Ally and Malcolm shared another smile; Malcolm closed his eyes.

"Keep us from falling, amen," Naomi murmured, not looking up from her stitching.

Joseph gave no sign he saw Lily and Seona returning.

Ian dove back in. "'The Revelation of Jesus Christ, which God gave unto him, to shew unto his servants things which must shortly come to—'"

"Mister Ian?" Malcolm's voice softly rasped. "'Tis enough. I'm ready to be done."

That snapped Naomi's head up. "Daddy? You ain't done yet. You still got Revelation to go; then you'll have read that whole Bible."

"Mister Ian can read the rest to me later," Malcolm said. "Or Jesus will Himself."

Ally stood, his large frame a contrast to the wasting one in the bed. "Granddaddy?"

Malcolm looked at his grandson. "Will ye do a thing for me, Ally?"

"Yes, sir, I will," Ally said.

"Go fetch Lily and Seona. I'd say goodbye to Lily . . . afore I sleep."

With an uncertain glance at Ian, Ally went out of the cabin, collies rising to meet him, tails swiping. Ian was dimly aware of Joseph stepping away from the door too.

Naomi set aside her mending and crossed to the bed, brow creased. "What you mean by *sleep*, Daddy?"

Ian felt alarm prickle through him when Malcolm hesitated. "I'm just verra tired," he said at last. "Joseph and Lily need to be on their way."

Ian closed the Bible and started to rise, thinking he would go out and meet his own bride returning, until Malcolm said, "Would ye bide, Mister Ian?" He raised a knotted hand to take Naomi's in his grasp. "Leave us a moment, *mo nighean*? I've things to say to Mister Ian, while we wait for the lasses to come."

Ian rose and took a seat on Ally's vacated chair as Naomi left her mending and went out. Knowing she wouldn't go far, he rested his forearms on his knees, studying the old man's beloved face as he spoke of things long past.

"I've had time for thinking, these days. Thinking back o'er my life, afore ye came riding into it on your bonny red horse—and after," said the man who had served his uncle, and old Duncan Cameron before him, nigh the whole of his long life. "I dinna like to think what might have befallen me and my kin had ye no' stayed at Mountain Laurel, even married Miss Judith to hold ye to that choice, though I ken more heartache flowed from it. But so did grace. Many's the time I've thanked the Lord Jesus for the work He's done in ye." The old man paused, breathed. "Where would we be had ye no' allowed that work? Where would we be wi'out ye?"

"Malcolm . . ." Ian took the old man's hand between his own. "It's I who should be thanking ye. For giving us the shelter of your heart, your wisdom. For being the father, the *man*, I long one day to be—a man after God's own heart. Where would any of us be without *ye*?"

Though it must have hurt, Malcolm's knotted fingers gripped his firm.

"And thank ye, for Judith's sake," Ian added. "For the comfort ye gave her before I was man enough to even try."

Malcolm's smile held his memories of Judith Cameron, gentle as the soul she had been. "I will speak wi' her again in a garden . . . the garden of our Lord."

"Soon, d'ye think?" The words half choked him to say.

Malcolm closed his eyes, brow furrowed, as if inquiring of a soul making ready to depart. Finally his head moved across the pillow. "Like as no' I'll rise again from this bed, but if I dinna . . ." Still holding his hand, he fixed Ian with a gaze full of promise. "Then I will walk wi' ye again in glory, too, Ian Cameron. With ye and all our kindred."

Her mama's new name was Roussard, the surname Joseph Tames-His-Horse claimed from a grandfather met but once before the man, a fur trader, went back to his home in France.

"Lily Roussard." Seona was still murmuring it to herself a week after the wedding, a day that had been filled with all manner of delights. Perfect but for knowing her mama and Joseph would soon be leaving for Grand River.

That day had dawned. They were headed back around the lake, Gabriel and Mandy dawdling behind, trying to skim a stone across the water's surface like their daddy could do, each determined to succeed first. Observing their efforts, Seona thought it could be some while before that contest was decided.

Lily paused to watch Gabriel's stone plop into the lake with barely a ripple. Her mama wore a simple braid for the journey, her feet clad in moccasins beaded in a flower design, a gift from Willa MacGregor. They were wrapped in shawls presently, for it was cool over by the lake, but a new wool cloak and hood waited for her mama, back at the cabins.

"Still surprises me to hear it," she said of her name.

"I'll miss you, Mama."

"I know, girl-baby." Lily took her hand as a breeze stirred strands of hair across her sculpted cheekbone. "Otherwise . . . are ye glad now we didn't stay in Boston?"

Seona couldn't help grinning. "You know I am," she said, minding something Ian said on their wedding night, alone in their cabin.

I cannot promise ye no evil will ever touch us again, that there will never be disappointments or losses. But I promise ye I'll fight to defend ye with all that I am and have, and what I cannot prevent I'll walk through with ye, reminding ye always of God's good plans for us.

The truest vow a man could make. One she had made her own self, to him.

"If I've learned anything this past year," she added, holding to her mama's hand, "it's that this life is the only chance we get to walk by faith, trusting the Almighty."

"Aye," Lily said. "We're always wanting to see what's coming down the road, when what we need is deeper trust in Him for the grace to meet it."

Behind them the children squealed. They turned to see the pair, stone skimming abandoned, hunkered over something at the water's edge that had caught their interest.

"Come on, you two!" Seona called, knowing Joseph waited, that Matthew, journeying west with his uncle and new auntie, would arrive any moment.

They couldn't put off the inevitable.

"It's going to be a long winter, but after . . . ," Lily began, a new note in her voice—eagerness or some deeper joy—then both yelped in surprise as Nip and Tuck rushed past their knees to meet Mandy and Gabriel as they came running.

"Lily . . . Seona!"

They turned to see Ally trotting toward them across the harvested field. He stopped and waved them in, waiting until they reached him, his broad face troubled. "Y'all need to come on. Granddaddy wants to say goodbye."

"All right, Ally, we were coming." Lily spoke calmly enough, but Seona caught her faint frown.

Matthew and Catriona were riding up the track when they reached the cabins, leading a string of packhorses. Naomi and Joseph were in the yard.

"Mister Ian in there," Naomi said. "But Daddy wants you two now. I'll mind the babies. Go on in."

Seona felt unease descend. It deepened when she stepped into the cabin doorway and heard Malcolm's reedy voice: ". . . then I will walk wi' ye again in glory, too, Ian Cameron. With ye and all our kindred."

Ian sat on a block chair by the bed, holding Malcolm's hand. He straightened and stood, giving place to Lily. Malcolm sat up a little higher. With a swift breath of relief, Seona decided he didn't look like passing right that minute. Just on the near edge of sleep. Ian's face lit up as she tucked herself against his side, but she saw he had been crying.

"It's all right," he said, an arm coming around her. He kissed the top of her head and briefly her lips when she raised her face. Then Malcolm was talking to her mama and they quieted to listen.

"Mister Ian's been reading to me, and we've talked a wee while. I'm gi' out for the present but wanted to see ye afore ye go awa' west to Joseph's people, to lay my hand upon ye as my daughter. For that's what ye've been to me, Tsigalili."

Never had Seona heard Malcolm call her mama by that name. It startled tears from her mama's eyes that ran down her cheeks. Lily didn't speak a word, but her love filled that cabin, warmed by the hearth fire as Malcolm rested his hand on her bowed head.

"The Lord Almighty bless and keep ye, Lily Roussard, as ye step into this new life He's given ye," Malcolm said, voice husky with fatigue and emotion. "May He gi' ye and Joseph safe journey, then a long and fruitful life together. May He gi' ye blessings in proportion to all the years ye've waited in hope to see them."

It seemed to Seona that these weren't the parting words of those who expected to see one another again. At least on this earth. Ian's arm tightened around her as Lily drew a shaking breath and asked, "Malcolm? Should I not go with Joseph? Should I stay?"

Malcolm wasn't quick to answer, but when he did so, his words were certain. "Ye've found a husband to care for ye and love ye, but he has other kin dependin' on him, aye? 'Tis as it should be. Go wi' him."

Lily wiped at her tears, then sat up straighter, a light returning to her features. "What I meant was, go with him for now."

"Mama?" Seona asked.

Lily turned to her. "I was about to tell ye, girl-baby, when Ally's dogs came rushing up. Joseph and I have been talking over something these past days, praying about it. We discussed it with Neil and Willa this morning. It's decided. We'll be back in spring."

Seona felt her sorrow lift to hover over her heart, uncertain now of its place. "For a visit?"

There would be that to look forward to, through the long winter.

Lily's smile was as radiant as on their wedding day. "More than that. Joseph needs to speak to his kin, but come spring, summer at latest, he and I plan to return to you here, build ourselves a cabin at the north end of the lake—if that's agreeable to ye, Ian?"

Some of her own joy was breaking over Ian's face now. "Ye'd be more than welcome."

Seona felt suddenly like a little girl, wanting to jump up and down where she stood. How fitting, her mama and Joseph living on that spot between his sister's farm and theirs, where he had stepped from the trees and turned her mama's mourning into dancing.

"Joseph's willing?" she asked, hardly daring to believe it.

Her mama didn't answer, for Joseph had come in, Ally and Naomi behind him, and spoke for himself. "Among the *Kanien'kehá:ka*, a man goes to live with his wife's clan. It is right and good that I do this."

They all crowded into the cabin then, even the collies, and for once Naomi didn't shoo them back out. Catriona and Matthew stood with hands clasped. Gabriel and Mandy dashed through crowding legs. Ian scooped up Gabriel. Seona held Mandy.

Malcolm looked up from his bed, around which they gravitated, his gaze passing around their circle, pausing at each face. Brown and amber, copper and white.

"I may yet live to see ye all together like this again," he said, "but even so . . . Ian, would ye hand me that Bible?"

"I thought you were too tired for reading, Daddy," Naomi said as Ian reached back for the Bible left on the table behind him.

"Never mind tired," Malcolm said, eyelids drooping like a little boy fighting a nap. "Find the Psalms for me?" he asked Ian, who opened the Bible near its center and placed it on Malcolm's lap. He turned crinkling pages, upon which fell the window's light. "Thank God He left me eyes sharp enough to see this tiny print. . . . Here we go. I wanted these verses before me to be sure I dinna misspeak them. Get them down into *your* hearts, children. Take them wi' ye, ye who go. Hold them fast, ye who stay.

"'The Lord is my shepherd; I shall not want. He maketh me to lie down in green pastures: he leadeth me beside the still waters. He restoreth my soul . . .'"

Ian pressed close to Seona's side, the arm not cradling Gabriel enveloping her. She held Mandy in both arms and leaned into him as the words flowed over her like those still waters of which they spoke.

"'He leadeth me in the paths of righteousness for his name's sake. Yea, though I walk through the valley of the shadow of death, I will fear no evil: for thou art with me; thy rod and thy staff they comfort me. Thou preparest a table before me in the presence of mine enemies: thou anointest my head with oil; my cup runneth over. Surely goodness and mercy shall follow me all the days of my life: and I will dwell in the house of the Lord for ever.'"

Seona saw not a dry eye in that cabin as Malcolm came to the end of the psalm.

Naomi sniffled as she took the Bible from her daddy's hands. "Time for sleep," she said, unnecessarily, for Malcolm's eyes had already closed, his breathing deepened.

They all filed out of the cabin—Lily last of all, holding Malcolm's hand briefly while he slept—Seona wondering if Malcolm would see tomorrow's sunrise.

With a heart both raw and soaring, she held her mama close outside in the cabin-yard and kissed her one last time. *For now . . .* She embraced Joseph as her daddy. She watched as Catriona and Matthew parted with many a tender promise. Then those who remained stood in the yard while the three rode away toward the lake and the ridge to the north, Joseph taking the mountain route he knew best, though he was free now as any man to pass through Shiloh.

When the riders rounded the lake and the trees hid the last packhorse from sight, they put the children down to run again. Ian wrapped his arms around her from behind and asked, "Are ye all right, Seona?"

As had Malcolm on his bed, she paused before answering, testing the lines that moored her soul . . . and knew she could release her mama and Malcolm both, if need be. A firmer line had her anchored. *Hope.* Not in the home they were making with its green pastures and still waters. Not in the promise of her mama's return. Not in her children or even Ian, given to be her husband, her heart.

Her hope was anchored in the One who had restored her soul. Whose mercy and grace had followed her all the days of her life, whether she had had the eyes to see it or not—and would go on doing so, until she went to dwell in His house forever.

Ally had gone off to his beloved cattle, Nip and Tuck at his heels.

Naomi was back inside the cabin where Malcolm slept, no doubt seeing to vittling the rest of them.

Catriona chased after her nephew and niece. Seona heard their laughter.

She turned in Ian's arms to drink in his handsome face, his mouth with its corners curved on the verge of smiling, eyes like the sky with the smoke from their cabin chimneys cutting across it. Waiting for her answer to his question.

Then, because she knew he liked it when she did such things, she put her hands to his cheeks, rough in need of shaving, pulled his head down to hers, and kissed that mouth, full and sweet. Letting that be her answer.

A Note from the Author

After authoring seven historical novels set during the eighteenth century, I decided to set myself a new challenge—making my eighth novel a sequel to *two* of my previous books, instead of one. *Shiloh* blends the story worlds of *Mountain Laurel*, this book's prequel, and my 2013 debut, *Burning Sky* (in which the primary story of Neil, Willa, and Joseph Tames-His-Horse is told). While I'm very pleased with how these story worlds merged and completed each other, I confess that the writing of *Shiloh* turned out to be a challenge indeed and a lesson in crowd control. As much as I would have relished letting more of Shiloh's denizens romp across the pages and tell their stories twelve years out from the ending of *Burning Sky*, much care and attention was given to ensuring this story's focus remained on Seona and Ian, while at the same time delivering on my long-standing promise to give readers more of Joseph Tames-His-Horse's story.

My gratitude goes to my long-suffering and hardworking editors on the Kindred duology, Jan Stob (who also acquired these books for Tyndale House) and Sarah Rische, for that care and attention. Their efforts to corral a sprawling cast of secondary and minor characters who, each by turn, tried to steal scenes, chapters, and sometimes whole subplots, cannot not be overstated.

Readers may or may not know that *Mountain Laurel* is the first historical novel I ever wrote. *Burning Sky* was the second, though it was published first. By the time I had finished writing *Burning Sky*, I'd discovered the connection between those two books through the characters of Joseph Tames-His-Horse and Lily, Seona's mother. I knew they were destined to meet and quietly fall in love in the shadow of Ian and Seona's drama. But how to forge this connection between them and find a plausible reason for a large contingent of my *Mountain Laurel* crew to wind up in the Adirondack foothills remained a mystery until I began researching what was happening in New York in the last decade of the eighteenth century. Enter Judge William Cooper, founder of Cooperstown, New York, and—thrillingly for me—the father of James Fenimore Cooper, who would grow up to write *The Last of the Mohicans*, the inspiration behind more than half my novels.

Alan Taylor's Pulitzer Prize–winning book, *William Cooper's Town: Power and Persuasion on the Frontier of the Early American Republic*, is an engaging exploration of a man born from humble Quaker origins who rose to the status of merchant, frontier land speculator, landlord, politician, and the inspiration for the character Judge Marmaduke Temple in his son's novel *The Pioneers*—as the town his father founded at the foot of Otsego Lake would become a model for James's storied village, Templeton. In the pages of *William Cooper's Town*, I met a man, still rough around the edges (and a hopelessly atrocious speller), who could be wildly generous in attracting other men to settle on the New York frontier. This book provided such richly layered detail about Cooper's life and doings that I had no doubt the man—by now become a congressman—might well have been traveling that Pennsylvania road at the time I placed him there during a late spring thunderstorm in 1796, ready to cross paths with Ian Cameron, himself on the move and needing to resettle.

One last note on the Coopers: contrary to my presentation of young James Cooper in these pages, he did not adopt his mother's maiden name of Fenimore as his middle name until he was an adult. Readers will, I hope, excuse my bestowing it upon him as a child, for the benefit of those unfamiliar with the family connection. I simply couldn't resist giving the author of *The Last of the Mohicans* a small but blatant shout-out.

It is December of 2020 as I write this author's note. Even as I spent much of this year looking backward, immersed in the past, 2020 changed the way I think about my future, here on earth and eternally. After all we have experienced nationally and globally, my earthly future seems at present more uncertain than I ever thought it could. Given the year in which most of this story was written, it's no surprise *Shiloh* turned out to have much to do with our need for choosing what, or who, will anchor our souls in the midst of life's uncertainties. To use another metaphor that frequents these pages, in what sort of soil, and by what streams of water, will we sink our roots for nourishment?

Seona and Ian made this choice in a world that cries out for justice, but one in which all efforts to achieve justice can be only partially successful. Their anchor was their hope in the Kingdom that Jesus promised before His ascension, when He also said we would join Him in it. A Kingdom where wholeness, justice, joy, and peace surround and overflow all who dwell therein. That promise inspires us to engage in the works God has prepared for us to do across the span of our earthly days. I have no better words to tell you how to keep yourself anchored in that hope during these difficult days than what Malcolm said to Seona: "Read [God's] Word for yourself, every page of it. Then read it again. Learn who He is. Who He says *ye* are. That's how ye learn to trust Him, to love Him." All other sources of hope will promise to satisfy, anchor, or deliver, but they will fail.

In addition to editors Jan and Sarah, I want to give a shout-out to the rest of the fabulous Tyndale team it has been my pleasure and privilege to work with on the Kindred duology: Madeline Daniels, Andrea Garcia, Andrea Martin, Libby Dykstra (designer of both gorgeous covers), Erin Smith, and Aimee Alker. Your professionalism, kindness, talent, and grace have made the long-awaited publication of Ian and Seona's story a dream come true, and you have *all* been a dream to work with. Thank you!

Last but never least, Wendy Lawton . . . I'm so thankful you're still with me on this journey, most especially that you never gave up on these books that brought us together. Thank you for holding them in your heart all these years and giving them that one last chance to fly.

One final note: A key character from Mountain Laurel didn't appear in the pages of *Shiloh*—Thomas Ross. What in the world has he been up to, aside from that brief visit with the Boston Camerons that Seona related in one of her letters to Ian? I intend to answer that, and a few other questions readers might have about certain Kindred characters, in a follow-up novella called *The Journey of Runs-Far*. A December 2021 release is planned. To keep abreast of this and other book news, visit my website at loribenton.com, and while you're there, sign up for my newsletter.

Until then, I wish you happy reading!

Lori Benton

About the Author

Lori Benton was raised in Maryland, with generations-deep roots in southern Virginia and the Appalachian frontier. Her historical novels transport readers to the eighteenth century, where she expertly brings to life the colonial and early federal periods of American history. Her books have received the Christy Award and the Inspy Award and have been honored as finalists for the ECPA Book of the Year. Lori is most at home surrounded by mountains, currently those of the Pacific Northwest, where, when she isn't writing, she's likely to be found in wild places behind a camera.

Discussion Questions

1. Though second chances at love abound in *Shiloh*, they don't come without patience and effort. Ian and Seona rekindle their romance through an exchange of letters, but barriers still exist between them that cause misunderstandings and resurrect old hurts. What are those barriers? How do Ian and Seona overcome them?

2. While still in Boston, Seona observes that "Family was like the sea . . . full of hidden currents and undertows." Ian and his brother, Ned, are divided by a lifetime of entrenched patterns of behavior and thinking toward each other. What are these patterns? How do you think they fell into them? What heals old hurts and finally helps them see one another more clearly?

3. Ian struggles with the choice between possible futures and the weight of all the lives he feels responsible for, yet John Reynold encourages him with these words: "God will make the way for you . . . Be ready to be surprised by His goodness." In what ways does this promise manifest in Ian's journey from North Carolina to Boston, then to New York? Do you live expecting God's goodness? How would your perspective on your future change if you did?

4. As Seona heads westward to begin her new life, she fears how she and Gabriel will be received in Shiloh and wonders whether she should hide the truth about who and what she was. How do these fears hold her back? Which characters challenge her fears, and what advice does each give?

5. Mentioned in one of Seona's letters, the Gaelic word *dùthchas* (a sense of belonging to a place and the people who lived there before you) is a legacy Ian desires to create for his children on their farm along Black Kettle Creek. Is he successful in making a start? What threatens his efforts to create such a legacy? Have you experienced this type of connection to a place?

6. Ian sees in his new neighbors the MacGregors an example of what he longs for with Seona and their children—family both by blood and by choice. Name the characters who choose to be linked with Ian. Why does each make this choice? Though Ian is an imperfect man who doesn't always get things right the first time, what do others see in him to desire this connection?

7. New starts can come as a relief. They can also be frightening. Seona finds the reality of starting over in Shiloh—with all its possibilities and unknowns—unexpectedly paralyzing. Why do you think this is so? How does Lily view the idea of a new start in Shiloh? How does Catriona view it? Malcolm? Naomi? Ally?

8. Lily lives a guarded inner life, but Seona and Ian both wonder if her mother desires more from life than circumstances have granted her. Were you as surprised by the quiet blossoming of Lily and Joseph's romance as Seona was? Looking back, what clues to its development were present that Seona was too distracted to notice?

9. Many characters in *Shiloh* must learn to navigate life as free persons after years of slavery—in Malcolm's case, nearly an entire lifespan. We are privy to Seona's internal struggles with freedom, but what about Lily, Malcolm, Naomi, and Ally?

What opportunities does freedom grant each of these characters? How do they embrace them? What are their challenges? Do they overcome them?

10. In the story's opening pages, John Reynold implies that the gold found on his land was almost more trouble than it was worth, foreshadowing the difficulties the gold would cause Ian, Seona, and those connected to them. Do you think the gold caused more trouble than good? Who do you think was at fault for the fear and insecurity that came of it?

11. Matthew MacGregor wants revenge against Aram Crane for the crimes he committed. When he tries to take it, he is nearly killed. How might the story have unfolded differently had Matthew not attacked Crane? Were you as surprised by Ian's offer of grace to Crane as Matthew was?

12. Though Judith's death occurs early in the story, her tender spirit casts a long shadow, as do her dying words, "Grace. It *is* enough." What does Ian initially think they meant? What do they come to mean to him?

CONNECT WITH LORI BENTON ONLINE

at loribenton.com

OR FOLLOW HER ON

 facebook.com/AuthorLoriBenton

 @LLB26

 Lori Benton

Thank you

By purchasing this book from Tyndale, you have helped us meet the spiritual and physical needs of people all around the world.

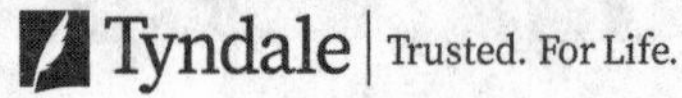